T0149343

Melodies of Love

Yuri Kholodov

authorHOUSE®

"…In Yuri Kholodov's short stories the special system of literary thinking of the musician is distinguishable… the more get a grasp, the more sensation that before you the pieces of music written by letters on a musical staff … Describing life as music, the author deduces his heroes – people with strange and inconsistent destinies – for limits rigidly ranked world of art. Deduces in life where the most valuable appear to hear «live music – singing of birds, a rustle of grasses, water murmur …»

«Difficult music of characters»
"Day", Kiev.

"…The prose collection breathes solidness and nostalgia – the ideal combination for a respectable magazine… There is nothing deliberate or contrived in these stories. It is as if the author chops off, piece by piece from himself, every story – childhood with his granny, musical lessons, loving experience of youth, the first wounded duck, and, of course, music: music which sounds in every story – sometimes by relief, sometimes just by a hardly seen shade… The confession of each hero in narrative "Requiem" is bright, serene, and heartfelt as well as all of Kholodov's prose…"

"Literary Symphony"

"Book Review", Moscow.

"…The favorite hero of Yuri Kholodov the same that of E.T.A. Hoffmann (too who is masterful united in one person talents of the musician and the writer) - the artist capable on the basis of bored impressions of the everyday validity to create the own world - fine and surprising. And the conflict, in general, the same - loneliness of the artist, inability to come into contact to this most ordinary validity and people, its occupying, - to find long-awaited harmony between dream and a reality…"

"The Butterfly in Shop"
NG - Ex Libris, St-Petersburg.

"…Special refinement, chamber elegancy, and psychological profundity of his performance style, as reviewers note, are reflected in his literary compositions which show his inspired emotionality, romantic excitement, and soft humor. The music of his literature works affects our feelings and brings us esthetical delight."

Zinaida Raskina-Pasternak, official of culture
St-Petersburg - Savannah, GA.

"...His prose is wonderful because reading even the saddest pages brings joy. These pages are transparent and sweet as "cheerful, gray water" – epithets of Alexander Dovzhenko – of springs nourishing the river Dnepr, as love of the lyrical hero of Kholodov's stories..."

Vladimir Lobas, author of novels "Taxi from Hell" ("Yellow Kings"), "Dostoyevsky"
New York.

"...It's rarely one can meet in rather "casual" sending so high level of prose. This is a real artistic psychological writing..."

Mikhail Epshtein, professor of Emory (USA) and Durham (England) Universities, member of Russian Pen club and Academy of modern Russian
Atlanta, Georgia.

"...Such components as precisely built rhythm of a narration, a leitmotif the sounding theme of each character, and complex polyphony of the whole, which have been so successfully introduced by the author from habitual world of music, are inherent to all his literary creativity in a great measure... Amazingly, with what surprising ease the author reincarnates and leads life of the different his personages – the unfortunates growing old woman, ridiculous writer-loser, and even the cat that has run away from bothered owners..."

"To live by own life"
Alexei Pasooev, literature and theater critic
St-Petersburg.

"...Devoted the main part of his life to elite chamber genre and brought up on the classic examples of the string quartet art – one of the absolute peaks of world musical culture, Yuri Kholodov remains in his literary creativity the supporter of classical style. He believes that the advantages and spiritual values of the previous centuries should be preserved and multiplied in contemporary art, often penetrated with commerce or ideology. "Vestigia semper adora" (Latin) – "Always be in awe of traces of the past…"

"Personal Truth" of Yuri Kholodov",

Literary Criticism. Za-Za Verlag, Germany.

AuthorHouse™
1663 Liberty Drive
Bloomington, IN 47403
www.authorhouse.com
Phone: 1 (800) 839-8640

Published by AuthorHouse 03/04/2016

ISBN: 978-1-5049-8271-9 (sc)
ISBN: 978-1-5049-8273-3 (hc)
ISBN: 978-1-5049-8272-6 (e)

Library of Congress Control Number: 2016903678

Print information available on the last page.

CONTENTS

PREFACE TO AN AMERICAN EDITION

I've decided to publish this book of stories to appear in English hoping to spark an American reader's interest in the life and character of my former compatriots, particularly the Russian and the Ukrainian people, both of which are often considered these days from an exclusively political angle. Having lived in Eastern Ukraine for the greater part of my life, I can assure you that no ethnic conflict between these two people has ever existed. Neither I nor any of my associates ever made distinctions between them, often not even bothering to learn which of the two nationalities was listed in anyone's official papers. I think that as much was true not only of the music community I was in, but also of the majority of scientists and cultural workers, to say nothing of the technical intelligentsia or the populace irrespective of language or locale. At the same time, as it has been widely acknowledged, anti-Semitism in the Ukraine was manifest on the official government level and fairly mundane among the average citizenry subordinate to the regime.

I realize that the reception of some of my pieces in translation may pose considerable challenges due to their local color and their peculiarly Slavic mentality more akin to the European one, and that certain portions of the American audience might be therefore unable to truly understand or appreciate them. I hope that those American readers not put off by the seemingly bizarre judgments or the possible flaws in translation, will obtain a more immediate and accurate view of the daily life, character and temperament of my fellow countrymen than they would get by consulting historical and ethnographic accounts. I have sought to render faithfully and to the best of my ability certain ideals that determine the spiritual and moral basis of my compatriots' existence.

Yuri Kholodov, 2016

"PERSONAL TRUTH" OF YURI KHOLODOV

Prose written by Yuri Kholodov is most interesting because it is created by a first-class musician who is aware of all the subtleties of his performing art. He was the laureate at the International Competition and the State Prize in the name of Taras Shevchenko. He also won a prestigious award known as the People's Artist of Ukraine. His literary art is uniquely connected with the personality of the author and reflects his outlook on life and music. His prose is merged with his perception of life, and his work manifests his "personal truth" without which, according to Ivan Turgenev, "everything in art is negligible".

The worldview perspective the writer maintains was formed and highly influenced by a mystical communication with nature as well as from features of national Ukrainian life. His painting style developed by emerging metaphysical and soulful excitement at the sight of seductive beauty of Ukrainian landscapes. His childhood was spent in a quiet provincial backwater town of forest-steppe zone of Ukraine, in Poltava, in blessed region where the Ukrainian writer Gogol once lived. There he learned to absorb and work with bright, ever-preserved impressions of charming and in a way, ancient Ukrainian landscapes. As a teenager, Yuri wandered alone just before dawn to hear the sounds of triumphant life, multiplying by the voices of birds singing to celebrate the new day, which was a blissful experience to him that influenced his art. As a young man, he became interested in hunting which took him into spectacular woodland groves, lakes and meadows where the corncrake creaked out its song and quails called asking to join them in the celebration of the day and life itself! They called out… "Drink - sing - go, drink - sing - go!" Yuri saw them in the Kiev region when he attended a special school for music at the insistence of his powerful grandmother who was once a church choir singer. She had her back up, refused to hear any objections, and demanded Yuri to study music at this special metropolitan school.

This life-experience was reflected in his early works that were filled with romantic overtones of the world and life itself: "A Country Etude", "An August Tune", "Variations on an old theme", "One Summer in Hydropark", "Dimka's love". A captivating freshness blows from these pages. These works cannot be read without warm and pleasant feelings, and the very nature of his images causes his romantic heroes to possess a regal beauty. The pathetic "convict" Trophim was the host of an island lodge that gave shelter to wounded and lost souls. Another character, old man Vsevolod, was a craftsman and a connoisseur of folk songs who became a hermit and gave up on creating his own righteous laws. The author's rich imagination allowed his characters to come "from the wind that rustled in feathered grassy steppes and carried a free and pure spirit in itself". It was a rural matron Nastya Arhipovna with an amazing degree of humility who resigned herself to her ungainly appearance, and she held her life with few expectations. Another character was a young man with a mysterious passion for witchy, rustic beauty. The other one, a sufferer Grisha the Small, fancied the intricacies of fishing and caused envy and admiration from the inhabitants of the coastal community. It seems the author lives with his heroes within a mutual and dual life. He is a passionate fisherman and hunter himself, and possesses the life values of a hunter and a fisherman and their typical commitment to noble ideals and justice.

When a person is in a romantic mood, he is incapable of being false or cruel. The author departs from his hunting passions, from "the dark ancestral spirits within the confines of his soul". With bitter resentment he recollects "the last ecstatic cry of a snipe racing on sun beams on a clear August morning, a ruby drops on the delicate plumage of long-nosed lumps, still warm, or a beautiful wounded hawk whose look is full of horror and surprise".

The time for conservatory rehearsals arrives, and music takes possession of the young romantic man. He has become familiar with the composer's intentions. How he can penetrate and pass the subtle shades of creative thought of the great dissemblers whose only recourse is within the souls of the listeners? Now they become his teachers, institutions and mentors. He seeks to penetrate deeper into the musical narrative in order to extract hints that transmit the thoughts of their creators. Often he reads a promise of something special in musical compositions, something inscrutable, some insane delight, embarrassing him, forcing to perceive the world through his artistic sense. Under the influence of communication with the great composer's legacy, his sense of beauty continues to form. The world of images of outstanding musicians enriches his own artistic world. All this gives rise to the musical fabric of his prose with its special musical rhythm that captivates the reader. A "looped back" plot of his "Elegy" or "Da capo" in the first edition (*Da Capo is a musical term in Italian, meaning from the beginning (literally from the head), is a composer directive to repeat the prior music*) tells about love and creative work. These amazing soulful events excite agitation, dramatics and torment. Imbued with dramatism, the story of love and life is so different in outlook "physic" and "lyric" – "StoryCorps" (*an American non-profit project whose mission is to record, preserve and share the stories of Americans from all backgrounds and beliefs*). "The Sixth Sense", according to the author, has been inspirational to bring forth a vague delight and a special scenic state of mind that can suddenly cause a departure from normal life and cause the perceiver to live quivering and full of love within the sounds of a musical instrument. These autobiographical stories provide the reader a unique opportunity to trace the genesis of the artist's personality.

The first stories by Yuri Kholodov about musicians reveal their quarrelsome dispositions with harsh reality of egoistic absurdity. They often clash with life's collisions, and they cannot overcome them. These are the heroes of autobiographical stories including "A Chance Encounter", "Romanov", "Kirusha", stories about the unsuccessful fate of his colleagues – "Strange people", "Inessa". The motive behind creating a rift replete within external conditions of the interior existence of various people who are gifted with creative energy and acute sensitiveness is fairly obvious. It appears many times in the works of such masters as E.T.A. Hoffman (as well as the author, musician and writer), Ivan Bunin, and Vladimir Nabokov. The reality surrounding the heroes destroys their dream, their faith in goodness, and bright ideals.

As Yuri matures and begins to reach a high level of competence as an artist, he expands his circle of communication and begins to develop an ironic tone within his writings. The author combines a high transcendence of his soul and the ordinary everyday life which he finds both mystical and beautiful, and never does he show mediocrity or, in any way, vulgarity. The combination of "the sublime and the mundane, the ideal and the real", in the thought of Boris Pasternak, is "like major and minor in music", harmoniously for the writer. Stories including "This string quartet", "Quiet Music", "A Conductor", "Paris, Paris...", "It's okay!" attract by comic touches when the author describes the characters and situations in life generated by customs and orders (ways and behaviors) of their environment. However, this "misanthropy" manifests an intimacy with his heroic characters, and his ironic tone is perceived by the reader with a smile of recognition. Yuri gives his characters a gentle humor, which is easy for him because he is endowed with a sense of proportion and balance. He avoids rigid satire, but at the same time, his penetrating gaze covers the range of actual human relationships and this ability manifests the truth about the times and the people living within these times. His commitment to reality does not allow him to enter a discussion of the socio-political events that occur or to show a "mental asceticism" leading to avoiding the issues that normally affect modern people.

Yuri has a great ability to create a special inner world in his heroes. He is especially focused on immigrants in some of his books that he wrote after he moved to the U.S. to be with his wife who worked in an American University, and where he continued his performing activities. They stand before us as life-like portraits, and the author does this in a very skillful manner. He creates various characters, like cheery Roy in "The End of July in Salt Lake City" who adapts himself to his new life keeping his independent personality. Author also creates a very humorous family of immigrants for the story "Fine Rosemary". They perceive "delicate psyche" of wealthy and educated American inhabitants first with fear and distrust, and then with a humorous undertone. "Requiem" is a story about elderly residents compelled to live in homes for the poor. These characters remain in our memory because of the enduring depth and humanity of their experiences. This book was written with deep emotion as Yuri shared with the characters vivid memories of arduous life as an adult living in Soviet times. The heroines of the story "In the backyard" draw attention to the experience of starting a new life. The author transcends the primitive pastoral life he once knew, and his stories now involve the acute social problems of our time particularly in America. The next story "Look here!" provokes deep sympathy from the reader. The story's about a successful businessman and city guide who is constantly burdened with worries about his "foster children". He is warmly caressed by tourists from Odessa, and Yuri gives these characters a special earthy Odessa's humor which captures the reader's heart.

Within Yuri's stories, there is always a subtext, which is invariably captured by the shrewd reader. He deals with the difficulty of hereditary intelligentsia, who doesn't understand the requirements of business, and Yuri imbues these characters with excellent craftsmanship and has them penetrate into the minds of the readers, and he does this competently in the story "A castle for a business diva". This hidden mockery of numerous tourism fanciers who, as noted by IvanTurgenev once in his letters "From abroad", "are not able to travel with use and sense, and as a prisoner in "Dead Souls" satisfied with the remark that in Vesyegonsk prison is cleaner, and Tsarevokokshaisk prison is much cleaner, in the same way our tourists can only say that the city of Frankfurt is bigger than Nuremberg, and Berlin is even much bigger". The same thing we find in the story of "The Restless", although the heroine is sympathetic to the author and he participates willingly in her most difficult and ascetic life. This also is pernicious influence of money power and amenities to the artist transforming him in the pursuit of the benefits into a craftsman, and then leading him to a gradual degradation of his personality, in the story "Strange people". In the story "One Summer in Hydropark" Yuri creates an allusion to the prolonged, dysfunctional illness that plagues Ukraine. In this story a talented professional of fishing craft is stricken by destroying internal ailment. Other stories are also poignant. In the story "A Goner" Yuri creates a documentary dedicated to the memory of his father who experienced the madness and starvation in the Nazi death camps and then the tragedy of forced immigration. His father somehow survived. Even in his old age when his memory lapses often occur, he still remembers the loss of human dignity which became trampled. He remains within a mental trauma that is apparently incurable, yet his insanity is a final refuge for a fading soul.

Devoting most of his life to elite chamber genre and brought up on classic examples of the quartet art - one of the absolute peaks of world music, Yuri Kholodov will always remain within his literary creativity, which vaguely can be defined as a classical style. He believes that dignity and spiritual values of the previous centuries should be preserved in contemporary art. He is aware, however, that the modern art is often penetrated with commerce or ideology. "Vestigia semper adora" (Latin) – "Always be in awe of traces of the past".

Yuri's prose is based on human principles of spirituality. This is contrasted against the lack of spirituality within our cruel world. But the redeeming grace that stays with those who have eyes to see is the overwhelming beauty that can be found if one is looking for it ("The Artist", "Where the Light ", "Houses and People"). This creativity is the driving force that artists like Yuri strive to attain in order to seek perfection in their writing and in their works of art.

Y. Danilova,

Za-Za, Verlag, Germany.

ELEGY

The long white room is completely empty. Light curtains are barely swaying on the tall windows; the mosaic of the marble floor is lightly reflected in the large mirrors. And, as if from nowhere – the quiet tinkle of a harpsichord. She is standing and waiting for something, barefoot, dressed in a long nightshirt. There are fear and curiosity in this expectation. Then the cold hugs her knees and crawls up scratching her back. She runs to the window, and there are the hot sun and trees in bloom.

Every time when this dream came again, her temperature rose. She had a possibility not to go to school where evil teachers shamed her in front of the entire class for an unlearned lesson, for an unsolved task or for the inability to find something out there in the blue-green stains of a huge, full-board map. Only in the fifth grade, when she started to wear glasses, a noisy school life began to get the outlines of a clear reality, to enter her mind, not having become more attractive because of that. Her memory stored each harsh word spoken to her, every moment of humiliation. The reaction to that resentment, which accumulated and didn't let her live in peace, was an awakened desire to rise up and become better than the others. She was pushed to that by natural, but not yet conscious vanity, without which it is so difficult to stay afloat in life.

Then still in the fifth grade, she discovered a secret, which made it easier to be a sentenced prisoner of schooling period. Her memory had become an excellent assistant to that. The texts were completely memorized on the third reading almost word for word, and she didn't have to delve into the meaning of the written words. By the seventh grade she is the top student in her class and the teacher uses her as an example to motivate the other students, but she remembers everything and doesn't forgive, she strays away from diligent students, makes a friendship only with spoiled and hopelessly backward girls. Besides, they know much of what agitates her and bring her closer to real life. On the other hand, communicating with them, she often feels as though she herself is fashioned from an entirely different matter, she may have been born destined for another life, the sublime spirit of which filled many novels she read. More and more often, having locked in her room for a long time, she examines herself in the wardrobe mirror looking for hidden signs of an aristocratic breed. To her great displeasure, her reflection reminds her of a green pod - dark cuttings of hands, her neck is rather short and the breast is boyish. She wanted to be transformed quickly and have her life turn into a colorful mosaic made of dazzling sequin of days. How much she wanted to see all her life now, to look at it from the other end, right now, when she could fix, tint or swap something – to bring it to perfection and fill it with special meaning...

But let's go back to the beginning, to the leisurely flow of dull everyday life, when it was still only a vague longing, annoying teachers, horribly shrilling girls at the recesses and those wonderful dreams, after which it was possible to be ill so sweetly, stay in bed for hours stargazing. And there were the novels of Balzac which were the first books she ever read.

In that period, her mother worked hard and didn't pay much attention to her upbringing. Her father also was home rarely. Only her nurse Olga always stayed with her, illiterate, brought by her father from a remote village. She never had children, and all her unspent tenderness was given to her Yulka, who, in fact, was nursed by her from the cradle. The nurse enjoyed her pleasures with her, endured her and forgave her all her whims. And Yulka seemed to be rooted to her repaying love with love, but she also was jealous of her love for father and mother. In any case, she tried in every way to establish herself in her full right to own the nurse.

Summer came, and she was allowed to walk alone sometimes not far from the house. A stone pavement, warmed by the sun, abruptly ran up. In the middle of the pavement, between the tufts of grass, a brook was babbling. If you walked along it up the hill, it soon became quiet, and then completely hid in the rocks. The curved street suddenly turned into the wide asphalt rivers between large and heavy houses of the alien world, incomprehensible and hostile to her, the entrance to which without the adults was forbidden. There, on the very edge of it, as if having escaped from the heavy stone embrace, St. Andrew's Church ran up the steep steps and soared over the precipice in its cheerful blue dress with pointed faceted domes. When Olga took her to the holiday services in secret from her parents, the discordant choir and the whispers of the prayers prevented her from listening to another detached music sounding in the tingle of the censer and in jitter of the candle lights. The mysterious chill of the marble floor began to wade through the rag laid by Olya to protect her knees and was aimed straight at her heart, which was why it sank, cringed and suddenly shot like a firecracker, and in a moment it became empty and scaring within her. She frantically clung to Olya's shoulder, and she, having broken off her praying, fearfully grabbed her hand and pulled her to the door, and she refused and whispered that it was not scary at all.

But more than that, she enjoyed lurking in a sunny hot day somewhere in the thickets above the cliff and getting drunk from the heated infusion of herbs and flowers mingling with the frightening smell of dampness rising of the ravine. She also liked to watch the sparkling river far below or, waiting for a large dragonfly to sit on her hand, to bring it gently to her eyes, until it starts to turn into a fabulous monster. Having come out onto the balcony, Olya will call her to come home and out of mischief she will not respond, and the nurse will have to come down from the fourth floor, cross the street and climb the steep slope up to the hill. Then Olya will grumble a lot and after their reconciliation they will sit down to read something, or rather, she will read, and Olya will sit next to her wearing her washed off kitchen apron, having put her small soft hands upon her knees and looking into the book from time to time to observe if there are any pictures. Then she will say in a thoughtful way with a kind smile, "When I retire, I will learn how to read."

Modest flowers of childhood quietly withered, but adolescent years didn't bring a long-awaited prosperity. Yulka was still a green pod and kept a place in the shade. Infrequently she visited dance parties where guys came from a neighboring school. She always sat in a corner and watched with envy how cute yet backward girls were chosen like hot cakes, how mellow they were, how funny and easy they communicated with each other. When one of the boys suddenly noticed her in the corner, she experienced a strange feeling of unease and met the inviting boy with refusal. A childish chaste idea, that every touch is intimate and possesses a special secret sense of anticipation or the promise of something, still lived in her. Rejected boys dismissively shrugged their shoulders and never looked in her direction again.

Once one of them was more persistent, he cheekily insisted, as though she herself was "making eyes" at him, and now he was ashamed in front of the other guys. In that verbal skirmish, they were both looking for a convenient way out, but soon they were quite confused. Then he forcibly pulled her into the circle of dancers. Like a nestling thrown from the roof, she experienced an instantaneous fear and then the joy of liberation and flight, and while the boy was quite unprepossessing, she was grateful for his determination. After that incident she became less unsociable and communicated more with her peers, but the side of life that opened for her, not adult yet, but a completely different life, where she sought, was not so generous and no longer behaved like those colorful depictions of her favorite novelists, which seemed to be able to guess her thoughts and desires so accurately. What if, she thought, everything would go round that dull and familiar circle, boring and not interesting, like her parents' life was? And why couldn't her mother, who was attractive even at thirty-eight, pass her traits to her? Maybe she was born due to an accident, as the late shoots are being born and die, she noticed, in the deep shadow, without blossoming into flowers, without giving fruit.

Desire to escape this shadow became the stronger, the more tightly the wall of indifference and neglect of those, who attracted her and seemed to be interesting, rose around her. In some ways, of course, she was to blame herself, often not forgiving their verbiage, that playful carelessness with which they tried to get her to light flirting. After each failed attempt to rendezvous, trying to understand its causes, many times she would play those little scenes, understood the details, recalled every gesture and every dropped word. It was not comforting, but the thoughts that arose in the course of that game, often carried her so far and fascinated her so much, amazed her by the quirkiness of their branches, that the return to the event, which gave rise to them, was not so painful. Having done with the analysis, she determined the place of her next hero, attached to him a label that was meant as a keepsake - sometimes it was a couple of sentences, but more often it may have been several pages of notes - still row and hot-cast. She accumulated a whole folder of them, and she started to dream about how to collect those cards in one deck and, having shuffled them thoroughly, to lay out one large solitaire, to force her new heroes to live their lives as noble and intelligent people that were entirely invented by her. Everybody will be absorbed by her novel.

Soon the plans of future chapters began to appear in a separate folder, as well as sections and schematic designs of whole episodes, and in each of them, she imagined herself in the lead role. The paucity of real life was compensated by her fertile imagination. At certain moments, a feeling of superiority over others became so strong that it seemed wild to her that it couldn't be noticed, that it was possible to remain indifferent to it. It surprised, resented and baffled. She wrote in that period, "Mankind has long been in conflict with nature, it does not live by its laws. So it takes revenge on us producing crowds of physical and moral cripples. How could I live among them?"

But now school was left behind. By that time, her parents changed their apartment, and St. Andrew's descent, where they had previously lived, that amazing, not city-like street draining into a flood of old Podol and, like an umbilical cord, connecting her with her childhood, with a sleepy protracted adolescence, all this somehow sunk into the depths of consciousness, replaced by a gushing stream of new experiences. The institute's life was not like years in girls' school, leisurely in their flow. It swept her up and carried her away by whirling her to meet different people new for her. In the center of each of these whirls was HE or SHE daring to play adult life, with its virtues and vices. Some people, at the same time, tried to be themselves. Others behaved deliberately which was ridiculous.

Caught up by this movement, she stopped for a while to think about herself. Only sometimes, having seen her reflection accidentally, she would suddenly smile – she was not so ugly, she could play not worse. She rejoiced in noticeable changes. Still not a princess, but not Cinderella. Of course, her neck is a bit short, and the waist could be thinner, but the hips are quite elegant, and her breasts promise to be feminine. Her finely defined lips had swollen and purchased sensuality. She liked her eyes in the past, but lately an increasing myopia made her look more mysterious, with a magical mysterious shimmer somewhere in the depths. Not so long ago she was oppressed by constant doubts about the necessity of her existence, but lately she celebrated the increased attention she was receiving. She gained self-confidence and ceased to be a spectator. Bonding with one kind of people, she quickly lost interest in them and easily escaped to the other while unwittingly leaving behind her invisible traces of destruction, as a coastal wave blurs sand fortresses and castles...

They called themselves "The Dunhill Corporation" which was a combination of Western-style nicknames Dun and Hill invented by them. They both dreamed of getting an after-school arts education, but at the time of their entering, the public policy pendulum had swung back in the direction of greater oppression of Jewish offspring, resulting in a dire situation wherein Dun who was from a hereditary, matrilineal family of physicians where his grandmother was a member of several European academies, had to graduate from the Polytechnic, and after that he had to learn the boring methods of welding in his father's department of the Paton Institute. Hill, whose father was not the last in the management of trade and communications in their city, didn't want to use his preferences due to the abrupt solidarity of the youth and entered the Graphic printing which had always had a shortage. A ripe protest against the injustice of the hostile society, to which, as they believed due to their naïve stupidity, belonged their parents, who were proud of titles and awards earned, as they often liked to repeat, by their honest work, was just a pretext for their rapprochement. A real friendship that precious sense of platonic love, allotted to everybody to the extent of his emotional needs arose later, when the craving for the literary preoccupation became all-consuming.

They tried to write something together, discovering the phenomenon of the interpenetration of thoughts, as if embedding in a single tone, and in the moments of inspiration sounding almost in unison. They often spent entire days in that creative bout. At night, Hill had drunken dreams, and in the morning, those dreams spewed out onto the surface of his consciousness a patchwork of whirling faces, of elusive scraps of phrases and bizarre movements of thought not yet wrapped into words. He hurried to his friend and, after the traditional, instead of greeting, "what's smart?', he wrenched out on the table all that he could remember and record, then he ruthlessly threw it all away into a basket a minute later. They both marveled at how quickly the colors fade in the daylight and how poorly formed thoughts roll up in pathetic curls toasted by the funny jokes of Dun.

Dun didn't prepare anything in advance. He was fond of improvisation. Being quickly incorporated into the work, he picked up the exact words and leveled the thought. Hill tried to keep up bypassing the blockages that he piled up himself the night before. Overcoming them, he often woke up at night, jumped up and grabbed a pencil. Then they both were entered this alluring world of the creative jungle where it is easy to get lost. Dun often burst forward, easily smashing his way. But then something broke his thought, and he fell silent listening to something within himself. And then Hill pulled forward, he took revenge - after two or three attempts he made a coup. Maybe at that point Dun was simply waiting for his lagging friend who excelled not only in strength and growth, but also in the ability to stay on top always, to be witty and easy to talk, to remain artistic and charming in all circumstances.

All that didn't have much value in that period of their creative bouts when they both understood each other perfectly, and in the moments of special inspiration almost physically felt themselves as one intelligent entity. Differences manifested later in life and in their leisure hours. Each of them was the leader of a circle of peers. But if Dun was not required to use excessive force for this, Hill often went beyond what was permitted to remain in sight. Taking into account his small body height, he was not so much frail and could always stand up for himself in a fight, but he never dared, for example, to invite a tall beauty into their company, as Dun did on the first bet, followed by Robert and Bob. Those ample-bodied Amazons quickly settled down into their circle and became friends. At parties, they tried to stay a little away, chatting about all sorts of women's trifles yet not forgetting to motherly watch their clever boys, a riot of imagination of which at any moment could find the most unexpected forms. Hill stood out particularly in that respect, and when there was a lot of booze, he often became completely unmanageable. But on the runway to unconsciousness and emptiness, he sometimes managed to play with Dun an impromptu vaudeville involving in it all the people present.

And yet, no matter how well and how smoothly they played, no matter what success they had, he always felt his inferiority, he always believed that even the most empty of those busty fools saw him just as a fun jester. Why I had been born, he thought, as a small Jew into this barbaric country where such thoroughbred mares are bred. But as it happens that way, why shouldn't I make a row and hell around for my own consolation. And he boldly swore, inventively behaved outrageously around inciting others to this, provoked and preheated.

Dun readily supported his friend in all such endeavors. A small detente was necessary for both of them.

When they didn't have money to spend on booze, they brought something from home to the commission – some of his academic grandmother's antiques or when it was Hill's turn, dragged hidden on a rainy day family silver to buy-in.

In the art of getting drunk to the point of oblivion Dun gave primacy to Hill, rightly believing that drunkenness in Russia has always been a very simple, safe and comforting form of expression of protest against the injustice of life. He himself preferred to relax using his strong fists. His faultless lasso who was sensitive to the changes in his mood, often sought and found a reason for that and, anticipating the first blow, almost always provided him with an easy success in the fight. In case of failure, she stood up for him to the very end, covering the retreat with her own breasts and, if necessary, removed her wounded knight who had lost power, but fledged the spirit, from the battlefield.

Once after an early crumbled party, Hill accepted the invitation of a classmate who lived almost next door. They had a family celebration there. The festive table still held some remains of virginity and it smelled quite at home, but there was no vodka - a few unfinished bottles of dry wine and a decanter with compote. Nowhere to go wild – he thought. Closer to him, as pies in a hot oven, rosy red-haired girls were huddling in their colorful costumes, which couldn't host their lush bodies. Their bare arms were constantly moving, carefully translating into sign language the meaning of words poorly distinguishable in the din and clatter of dishes. Their halters launched from the shoulders and exposed wet bushy armpits shamelessly appealed to his sensibility. There was something sweet and cloy in this abundance of full-breasted hot bodies, a kind of overkill. His gaze traced the table as if it was a butcher's showcase, as if he was searching for munchies, holding a half-finished glass.

Almost at the end of the table, like an olive in a tomato salad, Yulka was sitting and waiting for her favorite strudel. She was familiar with Rayka, who was a heroine of the day, from childhood. They lived in the same house and, although she didn't have much sympathy for her, Yulka could not resist the temptation to enjoy a masterpiece of her mother's culinary skills once again. According to tradition, such feasts crowned each family holiday. The solemn moment approached, and Yulka was all aglow in anticipation.

There are your munchies, thought Hill picking her out from the table in his mind to get a better look. He began to make some signs to get her attention, but she wasn't wearing her glasses and saw nothing further her plate. Finally, the strudel, like a baby wrapped in a towel, lay on a wide dish, and Hill noticed her childlike sigh of relief.

Oh, you're my silly, oh, you're my sweetie - he immediately cheered up – that's a plot for you.

Holding that thought, he pulled from a stool adhering to his sweaty ass, which was not so easily, walked around the desk and, having leaned towards Yulka's ear, whispered, "Let's go out and have a smoke."

A tender corner of her mouth opened slightly. A thick curly hair strand slung on her chest, touched his cheek. They went out onto a wide balcony, in the midst of which, wearily leaned against the wall, an old cracked cupboard stood, which kept a useless household trash. It was quite cozy and dark behind it. The light from the balcony door and indoor voices melted dissolving in warm depths of the night. Rare soft lights of a narrow river of Andreevsky descent shone beneath gleaming with a spill of quieting Podol. And in the right corner of that night splendor, illuminated by searchlights, St. Andrew's Church triumphed.

Hill opened a pack of *Dunhill* stashed for such cases and handed it to her. Seeing how awkwardly she took a cigarette and how shyly she pulled at her cigarette, he decided to hold a session on a shortened program, offering her to engage in a little erotic walk with him to interesting places and attractions. His naughty hands started to perform habitual movements, but then he felt a mild resistance. He tried again to push, but the girl laughed, saying that for a start it wouldn't hurt to come up with at least a small entry. He lied something hastily, afraid of losing the pace, and she jokingly commented and complemented why all his hasty chatter lost its sense. Finally, they both cooled off, and it became clear that it would not succeed to go back and play the scene differently. The girl was not so stupid, she managed to wriggle out, and if he wanted to achieve something from her, it was necessary to withhold himself and spend some time to prepare. Thinking about him, she, in her turn, didn't quite understand why she had not let herself soak within those little caressing bubbles of heated desire that filled her every move with pleasant heaviness.

Someone came up to the balcony door and dropped a cigarette. Breaking a gleaming trace, it reached into the depth, like a falling star, and scattered sparks on a dark street. Hill took aim and threw his, but it went out and didn't reach the ground. Yulka remembered the resent times when, walking up this road to school, she took cigarette butts, that reminded her of swollen little corpses, out of the water with the stick, treated her trickle naively believing that there would always be funny splattering in her life. She suddenly wanted Hill to leave, to come back to the table and save her from unexpectedly arisen irritation, but not only with him, but also with herself. When he finally felt it, he was gone. She was standing there for a long time, fearing that he would come back, and didn't dare to pass by abating feast to the front door.

Their first meetings were painted with his growing desire to overcome her resistance, but all the moves invented by him, all his thin, delicately built strategy, instead of the usual tactics of the onslaught, did not give the result. Easily, at a glance, they began to understand each other, found common ground even in the most difficult issues, but as soon as the conversation turned intimate, she immediately transposed herself to the rough joking tone artistically copying the soft tone of sarcastic Dun. Hill introduced them, and it was his second mistake. Near her, Dun as if was overgrown with soft spikes of wit. He loved to talk with her, he liked the way she listened and felt the intonation. Perhaps, it was because he never showed his male interest to her, attracting more of her attention to him. Since then, whenever Hill with his new tricks carefully drove her into a corner, he suddenly felt as if he was naked before the altar and began to realize that all that was in vain, that everything had been defined at their first meeting, that he missed something in her from the beginning, having not felt the responsibility of the moment.

Prior to that, he had already had a few easy victories – just stupid chicks who allowed doing everything with them that gave rise to his drunken fantasy. All that has evolved from his darkest depths, and the ancestral traditions of sophisticated debauchery, not otherwise, had their way in him. Each time, having got sober, he felt for some time as if he had returned from a dirty barn wherein he renounced that he would never return, but after a short time he already replayed in his memory all that indecent, found it attractive and even creative.

Finally, he promised to satisfy her curiosity and to introduce to her the people whom he used to spend his leisure time with. She was late to the appointed time, and when they came, all who gathered in that day, had already relaxed to the desired condition.

"Yuliana," he introduced her. "I beg you to love and cherish her. She's a rare creature, an endangered person, not adapted to local conditions."

In the corner, lounging in low chairs and right on the carpet, big beautiful girls were finishing their second or third bottle of *Tsinandali*. Cigarette smoke, like a lazy cloud, was sprawling in the dim light of a bronze lamp. Some crumpled candy wrappers and cigarette butts, tumbled out of the crowded ashtrays, lay on a low table. Men's half of the company was located separately at a high round table with vodka, half-eaten sandwiches and a jar of homemade pickled tomatoes.

Dun nodded pleasantly, "mommies" studied her in silence, what a rare bird she was. Prior to that, Hill had always come alone. He was obscure.

Overcoming her embarrassment, she went to the big table and without waiting for an invitation poured vodka into a glass. She drank it slowly without wincing. Then she shook her hand in a jar and took out a tomato.

"Wow!" approvingly exhaled people around the big table. Dun gave her a clean handkerchief. Having wiped her hand, she tossed it into a dirty plate and only had time to think "it seems, I've chosen the right tone", as once she swam in the pulsating sounds of voices. Her legs seemed to be filled with heaviness, they began to shake. In order not to fall, she got down on the carpet. The girl who was beside, put her shoulder to Yulka and eagerly stared at her with a curious gaze.

"Are you really some of the rare?" she asked sensually opening the soft pinkness of her lips.

"I'm a Gypsy," Yulka joked.

"Then tell fortunes," the girl extended her hand.

The words were born within themselves, as if someone else wove them into a thin sound script. It was pleasure to smooth her big plumpish hand in search of lost lines. The girl was purring quite like a cat and seemed not listening to her.

While this was happening, Dun-Hill were cranking out funny millstones of well histrionic vaudeville where all the people sitting around the big table gradually were drawn. A light friendly sparring, gaining momentum, gradually turned into a real fight, into a farceur battle in which everyone got a measure of pleasure as well as injuries. Together, they soon drove the rest of the people into a corner, and then, when the game began to lose its subtlety, Dun rolled away and became a kind of outsider kept to him. And Hill, deprived of support, still continued to bite, kick, stomp, and stab, losing any sense of proportion and causing the rest of those present to respond to him with gross rudeness.

"Kitten, Hill is chinning again. I'm leaving," said a "mommy" who was sitting in the corner of the room and keeping close track on her boy so he wouldn't get more than the others got. She hid a non-opened bottle into her woven bag and swam to the door. Bob with the annoyed smile of a dog who just intended to take a crap in the middle of the carpet, trailed out the door behind her.

When Yulka finally came to herself, vaudeville had faded significantly. Hill, having fallen drunk into his own floundering, was splashing mud around it, but it became boring. They all left one by one in order to avoid his obsessive sticky behavior.

"We'll walk you over," Dun whispered as she began looking for her handbag.

"I'm fine," said Hill and followed her into the hallway.

All the way, he held her in dimly lit places of the street convincing her that he intended to clean himself from the inside finally, and she could help him to do it, that they were both so smart and should be together. He really believed at that moment that things could be very different with her. But she quickly pulled him into the light experiencing the growing hostility and simultaneously feeling sorry for him...

They'll remain close to each other in the strange intimacy of two passengers who had passed a dangerous turn in life. Soon he will publish his first story and begin to write screen plays. Then he will graduate from Directing Courses in Moscow and will be awarded with "The Golden Pen". Inviting her to a restaurant to celebrate his next ascent, he will wait for her praise and, catching the right moment, once he will ask, why, finally, she will not become his lover. And she, biting his rush, will convince him that it will add nothing to their relationship, quite on the contrary, it would shift to the existing balance in the direction of denial, and that she wouldn't really want to. She will elude from him like a frightened squid releasing a cloud of ink, and he, having stuck in it, for some reason, will decide for himself whether it is possible, so to say, "to tip the balance" and what it might mean for him specifically. Then again, the "denial", the denial of what? Words will distract, will draw off and he, losing confidence, will depart again until next time.

Like every woman, she kept her treasured door, where he was so eager to enter, ajar - simple and natural desire to have more proof of own appeal. She even unwittingly fueled his interest in her. But once, during one of their confidential conversations, they touched specifics of the creative process and unexpectedly discovered that they both, and quite often, were prone to hypochondria. She complained that she didn't know how to overcome it. He, in his turn, forgetting about the rule never to be disclosed to a woman thoroughly, inadvertently shared his experiences.

"Huh, it's very simple," he said. "You just have to take a bottle of vodka and a new woman. The bottle always works well, and the woman - each of them, has her own antics. And that's the most interesting."

"Is that all?" she asked while noticing that to her mind "a new woman – her own antics".

"Well, no. This process takes time. In the morning you're already quite bad, and you start treatment. You should do exercises, drink vodka, and then a steam room. Again, a little vodka and some exercises again. Now a conversation with a sidekick friend would be good. Complain to him that you are a bad and horrible person, you need to repent. And it's all in fun, and you like it incredibly. Then you take out bins, wash them for a long time in the yard when all the women are sympathetically and appreciatively watching you. Then again, a steam room, and exercises again. And this way, gradually, on the fourth or fifth day, you see, you has already written two or three pages."

"And you like it incredibly," noticed she for herself again.

"Well, and what if you can't write after all this?" She felt somewhere inside her the door lock clicked.

"Then I'll try the method of Dostoevsky. If there is a jam on the paper, it's always easier to slip under the dictation. And then everything that didn't work out may be discarded."

She tried on the notes she postponed for herself, and immediately felt itchy all over her body, as if from the touch of someone else's, not quite clean linen. This is definitely not for me, she thought to herself.

Now, when men desiring to take communion near her altar were as common as blackberries, and when all her peers had long passed their defensive positions and didn't hesitate already to discuss different women's issues between them, she was still a virgin. Every time, when the next bidder was standing on his knees near her doorstep, she immediately found in him a bunch of inconsistencies to her literary ideals that were still alive, and after talking to Hill she, above all, became sensitive to the faint smell of sewage from carefully concealed cesspools within each of them. Gradually it turned into an obsession, into a dangerously growing ghost of frigidity evidenced by the fact that she parted with them easily, without compunction, not forgetting to leave a memorable impression from each of them for her future novel, the idea of which never left her. Letters, notes, amateur photographers and quite professional poems were stored in separate folders. Each time, complementing this folder, she swore to herself that this was the last time, that she would never torture anyone else, but when somebody knocked her door again, a certain sense of escapement occurred, and she quietly asked herself, "Who's there?"

The former Merchants' Hall in those years still retained the unique acoustic properties that attracted the best performers. Visiting philharmonic concerts for some people was included in their daily life, became prestigious, for others, who always believed in the viability of cultural traditions, it was natural and necessary. Parterre tickets were bought up a year in advance, and a wide balcony, stretched along the perimeter of the Philharmonic Hall, could not accommodate everyone. Students fought for tickets and broke through police cordons. During the summer, Natan Rakhlin used to take his orchestra out onto the open stage at Central Park where everyone could contemplate for free that brilliant fat man who knew how to turn the orchestra into an awakened volcano with magical gestures of his short-fingered hands.

At the first, she tried not to miss any of the Philharmonic concert, in the same way as in previous times she read through all the rows of books that had been collected by her mother in the old bookcase that stood in the hallway. But then, having begun to get tired of the abundance of sounds, she discovered the quiet charm of the quartet evenings, not so crowded and not noisy at all, which were perceived by her, with appropriate programs, not even as concerts, but rather as spirit séances, at which, if you concentrated and did not look at the players on stage, you could sometimes feel yourself in the heart of the sounding sphere, like once in childhood at the divine worship in the St. Andrew's Church, and feel somewhere close by or even within yourself, as if there was the blissful presence of the creator. If someone close to her began to rustle with candy wrapper or dropped a cloak-room ticket on the floor, she shuddered and opened her eyes. But even when something mysterious disappeared, the musicians on stage, in her view, were not just playing, they were engaged in a secret conversation, the meaning of which was gradually picked up by her. This meaning didn't match its verbal interpretation proposed by the printed announces. Sometimes music sounding on stage seemed to her an exquisite love game. Having trusted one of the voices, she gave herself to its will, and if the musicians were worthy of each other, she didn't notice how soon she began to transpose from one to another, overflowing with sensual delight into tears. After such concerts she once wrote,

"A rare aesthetic pleasure, not devoid of sensuality. Do any others experience something like that? In some moments, it seemed I gave myself to all four of them."

The last sentence was deleted, and then written below, "What nonsense!.. How to put into words that movement of feelings and thoughts?.. And that was so good there (within)."

The first time when at St. Andrew's Church there was allowed conducting chamber concerts, she came there one of the first, sat in the mostly unlit place and, having plunged into the cool silence that protected her from the noise of urban votes, as if again having turned into a little girl listening to Olya's story wherein people bringing their sins to the church. After the penitential prayers, they hide them somewhere in a corner, and they are there for a long time until the chief angel comes and clears everything with fire. She then listened to her story and saw how the great fire of the gilded iconostasis brightly flashed and ominously flared. She shuddered from the leisurely shuffling steps behind. Could it be the angel-cleaner? Has he come for her? She wanted very much to have her own, at least the smallest sin to always keep it with her and protect from others. Now, when the sweet fruit of her imagination turned ripe in her womb, she thought sadly that perhaps, she would never be able to deliver.

Concerts had not yielded the expected joy. Whether the repertoire was improper, or the style of performance was not fitted to floating and sprawling acoustics of the hall. At times it seemed that crippled sounds, having broken against the stone church walls, were rushing in search of salvational exit, facing each other, breaking harmonic melodiousness.

She visited those concerts less and less, and if she did come, she often couldn't wait until the end...

On that warm May evening, attracted by the program, she went there to listen to a local quartet. They had just replaced one of the musicians, and it promised to be interesting. Contrary to expectations, the surprise didn't happen. While three of them in a fairly coherent sled pulled diligently to the culmination, she immediately felt that the taken pace was too rapid, and the cart might soon collapse. She imagined, as if a brand new foal galloped alongside them bucking and running forward, looking around in surprise. But then he caught the movement, the sound became deeper and far more penetrating. She even put on her glasses to see him better - his beautiful baby's face was distorted by a tense grimace. It seemed that he did a hard, backbreaking work. Poor boy, she thought to herself, who makes you suffer so much? And then she remembered her bitter experience learning to play the piano and the last phrase that her teacher Clara Avnerovna said to her mother, "Stop torturing the child!"

When bowing, he smiled with relief and joy as if he was allowed, finally, to play with his toys. No, she could not leave just like that. It was curious to see what was inside him. She came and thanked him for a good concert.

"Not true," he said simply. "Tell me the truth."

"Well, to be honest," she said in a lowered tone in her voice that was audible only to him, "all the bones ache as after riding in a cart on cobblestones."

"It's my entire fault," he was confused. "I was lost completely. This was my first concert."

"Not so bad. Sometimes you kept up and sounded just great."

"Are you also a musician?"

"I love quartet madly."

"It's interesting," he mused.

They exchanged some more unimportant phrases, but the meaning of their words already conceded the magic of glances, facial expressions and gestures.

"If you're not in a hurry..." she gently touched the string that was stretched between them. It subtly echoed inside him.

"I'll see you home..."

The city was already sparkling with the diamonds of evening lights, having endued in a soft velvet dress, but the park lights had not been switched on yet. On coming down the St. Vladimir's Hill and walking past the brightly lit windows of Philharmonic Hall, from where there were heard sounds of the orchestra muffled by heavy curtains, they turned into dark alleys.

Tersely and hardly choosing his words, he talked about himself trying to go faster all the time, but she restrained him, as if by accident touching his arm, and only occasionally suggested a word that he was struggling with in order to express himself. He seemed nervous and warily started and stopped his sentences and it began to agitate her.

My dear little animal, she thought to herself. Why don't we live in an age of palaces and ancestral homes? You would have been my page now or a boy for playing games.

She listened to his confession, that diverse set of pages, which were snatched from memory at random and dotted with children's scrawls, and she couldn't understand why she was so irresistibly attracted to him in a way that grew stronger every minute. After all, he didn't fit the image of her hero. What if, the thought flashed in her mind, the Fate itself throws this imperfection to me, this supple and adorable nubbin, which you could sculpt something from. What a romantic!

They came to her house. The street was empty, and the thick crowns of lime trees quenched the light of the lanterns. She gently took his hand.

"Here we are..." She didn't let him go on purpose. She heard him shaking, she felt how those nervous willies were transferred to her.

"Will you have more concerts?" It's time to stop, she ordered herself feeling how irresistibly rising tide of desire swept all the obstacles within...

How responsible and how unique is the moment of the first rapprochement. How our memory cherishes its every nuance. And how easy it is to destroy it with only one insensitive gesture or a wrong word.

After a few minutes, they ran in different corners. She, barely holding back tears, when the elevator transported her to the sixth floor. He, confused and depressed, when wandered to his Podol. Something scared him when she put pressure on him. Something hurt her in his words...

For almost a week they suffered alone. He felt that his life had come to its dismal end. She didn't know how to fill that suddenly formed and all-consuming emptiness. Again, she had a dream of a white room. As though she wandered in its cold light while listened to the pulsating sounds of a harpsichord falling on marble. She looked into the high mirrors, reflecting nothing, and thought that if she decided to touch herself, she would feel nothing. Ding-ding - a note stuck like a fly in a web.

Suddenly she saw him. He was all clear too, as if made of crystal. And inside him she could see her reflection, a lot of her own reflections and even a whole white hall with high mirrors, a church, and a stream between smooth stones cold to the touch. He dipped his hand into the icy water and splashed the cold water on her chest...

When she awoke, she thought she was dying. Her heart discouraged a disorderly tap, her breathing, like a wet lump, was stuck in her throat. Probably, they started washing in the house, and Olya forgot to close the bathroom door. She ran to the window and, having opened it, plunged into a refreshing stream of cold morning air.

Downstairs, on the opposite side of the street, someone in a blue roll-neck alone was hovering at a lamppost. It was impossible to distinguish his face. She tried to find her glasses, but they got lost somewhere. She went to the window again, looked more intensely and could now distinguish something dark and oblong beside him, very similar to a violin case. Wearing just a bathrobe, she popped to the staircase and, without waiting for an elevator, ran down slapping loudly on high steps. Just outside the front door, she caught her breath. Has she imagined that? She carefully looked outside, but nobody was near the lamppost. She jumped onto the sidewalk and saw someone with a case over his shoulder who had just turned the corner. She managed to scream. Having frozen in mid-stride, he turned around and approached her with a slow gait of a wounded man. She wanted to go out to meet him and could not.

As a continuation of my dream, she thought. Now he'll enter the sunbeam and dissolve. The deathly paleness of his face just reinforces that impression.

He sank to his knees before her, picked her jumped off thong and began to pull it awkwardly over her foot.

"Get up, get up," she whispered, leaning toward him.

"I have to, I was going to tell you," he said in a hoarse voice timidly slipping with his haggard look down the soft swell of her slightly opened breast.

"Stand up. There are windows all around."

"I was thinking so much. I wrote poems and so..." He took a crumpled school notebook from his pocket.

"Later on, later," she pushed him to the door.

Some people were already descending by the elevator, blatantly breaking the silence with their coarse voices, and they ran up the steep steps wincing at gunpoint of peepholes, tightly holding hands, as if they were afraid to lose each other again.

At the very top, where it would seem that no one could prevent their small triumph, they sat down on a wide clean windowsill... An oil painting was not quite dried out and now, when they got up, some of the paint peeled away and hung from them in dabs of blue-green flaps in the most inappropriate places.

She found sweatpants for him to wear in her wardrobe. Then she stuffed her terry robe deep under the couch where it lay till the general cleaning occurred. When Olya took it from there, she pondered for a long time what it could mean. After that, it served them for a long time as it warmed the balcony door.

Her father, a continually busy government official, was suspicious of musicians considering their profession to be worthless, but knowing the nature of his unbalanced daughter, he did not contradict her, but asked to show Ilya to her mother. Yulka hesitated for a long time knowing how her mother had changed recently. She picked the right time and was offended by neglect and indifference with which she met her chosen one.

"What have you found for yourself?" her mother asked sarcastically. "He listens, that's right, but he hasn't learned to speak yet."

Her mother really changed a great deal. The reason for that was a deep hypertensive crisis which had happened to her a few months before that and left in her mind the fear of being close to death. Then diabetes was added to that, and her psoriasis, which had been dozed within until then, suddenly scattered bright markings around her still beautiful and slender body. Lively and sociable, a fine companion, she who always gathered around her many fans, appreciating in them, first of all, their breed, now cut all her old ties, left the editorial board and, having been registered as a freelance translator, worked only out of her home. Accustomed to being in the spotlight, she unwittingly sucked now all her close people into the circle of her experiences, forced them to live through her fears, often repeating that all the women in her family died from heart disease at a young age, and that if she would not die soon from a heart attack and live for some time, then a developed diabetes would necessarily cause her to go blind and develop gangrene of the feet. She absorbed all kinds of drugs and was waiting for a permanent compassion to herself from her family members keeping them in a continuous state of tension by her complaints and fear for her life.

"Click, and you're not rushing, you're not going. You're just hanging back in fear along your own life absorbing the cold emptiness with your back." (From the folder named "Characters")

The first years of their married life, which had been lived in the same apartment with their parents, were marked by constant scandals arising often on trifles. Working in an academic institution and being engulfed up to her ears in scientific research, Yulka just could not stand the tense nervousness that reigned in the house. Her mother, having been knocked out of the usual rut of life, seemed to be specially searching for motives to start a quarrel, to draw attention to herself once again. She deliberately went to those sensual strains, behind which, according to her script, a turbulent reconciliation had to follow. Her daughter ceased to understand her soon, and the process of alienation steadily led to the realization that they just couldn't exist together. Her mother often went into hysterics turning into heart attacks. Her father greatly feared these scenes, Olya usually huddled in a corner, and only Ilya, who suffered from those scandals no less than others, was somehow able to reduce their intensity and, if he got involved not too late, the dust settled by itself.

The first time Ilya left to tour with the quartet, Yulka suffered terribly, she just tied herself up in knots - everything dropped from her hands. Having heard from him, she hastened to answer, but everything she was trying to write to him, seemed corny, whiny and banal. She tore the letter apart and began again, searching and not finding the appropriate words. Desperate, she took a post card and just scribbled few agonizing lines.

"It's raining here... In fact, all people are ugly and miserable. Come back quickly, until they drive me crazy."

Gradually she got used to his frequent trips, and after they changed their apartment and were freed from gravity of constant maternal presence, she even began to find a special meaning in her solitude - it returned her to a fantasy world, the world of fictional characters that had patiently waited for their incarnation on the pages of her future novel. It seemed that reality was forked in her mind. In one half, she lived alone with her fantasies and dreams. In another half, there remained her father, Olya and her mother who learned now how to control herself and, gradually wilting, started to express a belated interest to her, compensating up for lost time with regard to her upbringing with cautious worldly advices. Her beloved Ilya, meeting with whom after his long absences gained special acuteness and freshness, even though he was as a connecting link between these two worlds, often gave her considerable grief. It seemed he was resistant to good manners, and she just, for the time being, had to hide him from others as she knew that he could at the most inopportune moment manifest any *faux pas*, out of embarrassment or something else – she could never understand. He loved to spend the summer in the countryside and forced her to wander with him on the river to the point of exhaustion as he searched for some special fishing places, and he felt quite comfortable there, while she suffered and experienced considerable anguish, but when in the evening he generously bestowed on her the tender caresses of his big warm hands, she forgave him everything.

Now, when the dissertation work had been completed, and Ilya was again very far away from her, the idea of an unwritten novel reminded itself. It seemed she had only to sit down and the chapters would begin to form themselves. Once she came from the institute, pulled out a folder with title "Characters" and, having let loose one of her heroes into an imaginary scene, tried to play with him a little skit. But the actor was helpless and couldn't play the role. She tried another one, and another – everything was not serious, just childish attempts. It was not the time, she thought, she had not yet tried the big stage, where real masters played, from whom she could learn something, to peep something. Ilya was not a person she could explain this to. Come what may - decided she for herself...

Life became more cheerful. Within the thin networks of her charm, she easily kept those who had seemed interesting. Passionately surrendering to every new hobby, she even lost control for some time. But as soon as the next of her chosen ones opened up, she immediately broke into his secret possession, gutted it eagerly penetrating his muddy bottom and shook, checking for its strength, his vital foundations, and, when having been sated, she soon lost interest in the game. Then she often asked herself, "How can I?" Some people felt the danger of those intrusions raising doubts about the legitimacy of their life values, while others resented for a long time, someone drew a joke trying to maintain friendly relations. It was always interesting with her, she seemed to be surrounded by an aura of spirituality. She attracted to herself.

They were all very different and mostly mature people who had already achieved some success in various spheres of activity. But something, in her understanding, prevented each of them from seeing life through her eyes. Some of them seemed to have been blinded by the radiance of their own greatness, while others surprised her with their extreme cynicism, and the others who awakened in her no less interest, measured themselves with a vainglorious desire to quickly go ahead of others and habitually drove to a maximum simplification of all their contacts with reality.

She often remembered later that once she had met one of them at a concert. He spoke only of scientific problems, complained that he was going through a losing streak and was stuck up to his ears in a prospectless experiment, for which he had already spent a few precious years and a lot of governmental money, that it could happen that he would soon lose his department. Some rumors reached him.

Having been tuned to another wave, she listened inattentively and tried to divert the conversation from a painful theme for him, but he could not think about anything else, kept talking about the scarcity of the technical equipment, the dishonesty of the employees who could not conduct a clean experiment and manipulated the data, and that no one could be trusted. In general, the man painted his life just in gray and black colors.

The second bell rang, and he followed her upstairs while not stopping to talk. It was as if he was talking to himself. Before entering the hall, she stopped at the large mirror and could not help but smile – what a beauty!

"There are many other interesting things in life," she interrupted him. "You have to just don't turn a blind eye and don't limp."

A live spark of desire flashed deep within his inflamed almond eyes. Squinting in the blinding light of sconces, he timidly touched her elbow inviting her to enter the hall. Imagining how those who sat in the aisle as they walked by would grabble them with their eyes, she wanted to mute the bright light emphasizing his untidiness and the wrinkles in his suite, she wanted to smooth out and hide somewhere the rolled ends of his tie.

In the middle of Beethoven sonata, he leaned toward her and whispered with a suddenly changed voice, "God, if I could play like that, I would now be saved." He smelled of simple soap and even dampness, the way it smelled once out of the ravine. She looked closely and saw his greasy tie and his neck overgrown with gray swirls and thought with regret that he would never rise again.

When they met again a few years later, nothing seemed to have changed. He talked again about global issues in science that they had accumulated lots of experimental material that could not be processed and linked together, that his department had nothing to work with, they had no the required instruments and lacked the most basic medicines. He wore shoes with a cracked top, a baggy jacket and that strange, low crowned straw hat with a hatband, torn from one side and faded from the time, which was casually patched together with laboratory tape. She felt nothing but a pity for him.

Another of her choice, who was forced to support for years "the philosophical thought of the country" perverted by Soviet ideology, was too smart to maintain the illusion about himself, and once he jokingly warned that he had long ago turned into a cancerous tumor metastases of which germinated into everything he touched in life. Therefore, he was running away from his wife and children. Women were like a drug for him - the simpler the easier.

Communicating with him, she could often come up to the very origins of the birth of thought and, following its development with admiration, watch the way he was able to give it the most unexpected and intricate form. He never ceased to be amazed by the fact that she didn't meet his established ideas about the possibilities of female intelligence. They stayed close to each other until his departure from life when, making up for lost time after suffering a heart attack shortly before, he died suddenly right in the bed of his next idolatress. One of his graduate students had to go to his wife to bring a ritual suit and to lie something to her. However, he deliberately went to such an end.

One of her favorite men treated women with great care and, although he wasn't a confirmed bachelor, all his attempts to start a family remained fruitless. In each of his new romances, he developed the same scenario. A week passed and he found that his new darling had so many flaws it led him to despair, and in such a state of mind, he could not write his funny stories. After another fiasco he came to Yulka (he called her this name as Olga did) with his complaints, ate her dumplings or borsch, listened to her advices and comforts, then, having stuffed a cigarette with cotton wool and taken in a few puffs, he took on his former complacency. He immediately processed an anecdote or a good joke, which he had heard somewhere, and turned into a fable easily picking melodious rhyme, laughed with childish contagious laugh enjoying each successful combination of words.

She was pleased to be included in this process. Stifling his immoderate enthusiasm, she quite accurately noted this or that place of his new creation where, in her opinion, the bar of good taste did not rise to the proper level. Having irascible and stubborn nature, he couldn't recognize it immediately and began to argue quickly increasing the tone of his voice, and by the end of the skirmish he refused to mince his words and peppered his speech with obscene words as naturally and easy as previously he played with poetic rhymes. She paid him back in kind and didn't cede. Their disputed were usually interrupted on the stairwell where each of them was in a hurry to stick something nasty instead of saying goodbye and to have the last word. In a day or two, he usually called her, as though nothing had happened, read the updated version and, having been approved, joyously burst of laughter.

After several unsuccessful attempts to get married, he calmed down and bought himself a small dog that didn't distract him from his work, didn't require special attention and gave him the feeling that he had a living soul in the house...

After she got married, Yuliana visited crowded parties less frequently. Of course, it was because of Ilya. All her efforts to fill in the gaps in his education were not very effective. Naive and wildish, even if he barged into general conversation, then he quickly got into his own "verbal snares" from where he extricated himself with great difficulty. At the table, when the toast traditionally passed from one person to another, she never heard him speak two intelligible words. Even on their infrequent family gatherings he hided behind her as though he was a child or hung around in the kitchen where he warmed, sliced or served something only to remain in the shadow and to attract less attention. It always remained a mystery to her. She knew that if she could whip up the dark pit of his mind, there suddenly splashed subtle and elegant judgments about things, interest to which he never seemed to show. She could sometimes find a solution to some difficult questions there, often the only correct and simple one. But it was not easy to whip up. Even talking with her, he barely cracked a word, and it seemed strange to her that he changed completely when they visited her mother. Ilya was always attentive to her, jocular, completely at ease, and she responded to him with warmth and affection. Why, thought offended Yuliana, why can't he do this with me, with everyone? He withdrew into himself, limited his life to only music but still walked in any weather to the river, to which, that was not funny, she began to become seriously jealous of him, as, indeed, to her own mother. As a consequence, there were short quarrels between them, during which she even allowed herself to have little tantrums quite deliberately dosing them, just to get more proofs of his devotion and love. Sometimes, however, a sad thought came to her mind, which was that for Ilya, as for a weak man, that river, and she herself and their house were a reliable shell in which he hid from life frightening him, and that, perhaps, many people lived like he did. She herself often needed such protection. But life suddenly flashed in front of her with a new face and an uncontrollable desire to look beyond its sharp edge won that fight.

The living heroes of her unwritten novel surrounded her everywhere, and the more they seemed to match her conception, the longer the next craze went on. And the more painful was awakening. Records of that time, written in the "Characters" folder, increasingly begin to look like a laboratory journal: backgrounds, previous moments, comparing of characters, related thoughts, virtues and vices, roots of incompatibility and so on. Fleeing from depression normally following that, she pulled Ilya to a concert, a performance or an exhibition. Often they visited the familiar artists, right in the studio. They were always pleased to communicate, showed them their new works, made strong tea or treated them with wine reserved for such cases.

That's where the real kindergarten was, enviously thought Yuliana, that are those who never suffer, who know how to enjoy life within the smallest things, who manage to keep the necessary share of naïveté, perhaps helping them in their work and providing a quiet confidence in the correctness of their choice.

In those workshops, a special atmosphere always prevailed, and even simple tea had some unique taste. But even when there happened a miracle of birth of the next masterpiece, she never had a desire to venture forth her favorite game to one of the masters of brush and cutter. She already had her own Ilya who was cut from the same cloth as they were.

Work on the conceived novel continued to be postponed. And although she was quite accustomed to the big stage of life, life gave her not less questions.

"What is the destination of each of us? Does all this diversity exist only to diversify our life somehow, to embellish and finally distract? Distract from what?"

She was involved in serious scientific work, which took up a lot of her time and effort. Once in the system, she quietly transformed herself into a mechanism, a part of this system. Why did she choose chemistry? Not to argue with her mother who wished to give her daughter a normal profession. She attended lectures at the Institute without a serious interest, as once she attended school without interest. She learned lessons frivolously, easily discarding all unnecessary on the second day after a final test or an exam. However, she liked chemistry - this lively and beautiful science of interactions of such disparate elements, their mutual support or incompatibilities of the most unexpected positions in various combinations and connections, and if you look closely, obeying the same laws set by someone governing the existence of united and eternal harmony. Weren't there conceived the same laws of harmony for the human community? But why, then, no one living creature, called a man, corresponds to the law of Supreme Harmony? In contrast, the more complex and intricate an exemplar is, the more inconsistencies and deviations you'll find in it. But maybe within these deviations one can find the meaning and the dynamics of mankind's development?

Her interest in chemistry was caused also by the fact that an extraordinary teacher taught that subject. There are talented people who can turn even the most dry and academic subject into a real art. He was a short man of inconspicuous appearance and he had a congenital disorder of the hands, but all was forgiven when he began to speak. When he went to Israel it became a big scandal, she was one of the first persons in the crowd who saw him off. By that time, she had already graduated from college and suddenly had time to experience the bitter taste of scientific romanticism, which he grafted to his students with such pathos.

Her walk-off to biochemistry, as to a field with richer opportunities, was accompanied by familiar problems. She lacked basic chemicals and modern appliances. In the departments of the Institute, which was new to her and where she began to work after her Ph.D. defense, they mainly conducted applied researches - for the needs of medicine and agriculture. Scantiness of the obtained results was complemented by the skill to beautifully arrange them in scientific articles, a certain amount of which was to appear in each annual report. Many researches followed the path of repetition of the experiments already described in foreign literature, adjusting their often-questionable results to the ideas obtained there.

Yuliana tried to work clean, but what it was worth for her! Bumping from time to time into the negligence of her colleagues, she came to despair and questioned all the work they had done. Till late night she rechecked laboratory notebooks, searched for the reasons of digital scatters, sometimes she repeated experiences. She just tied up in this quagmire. Ilya often forced her to leave the Institute, but at home, and even in her bed, she couldn't stop thinking and talking about those issues. He diligently attended and even tried to suggest something, but then quickly drooped.

"Why would he need it? Why would she herself need it?" she thought to herself in a wearily way while listening and feeling his tender caresses.

A new round of the life spiral spun and spun. Having been started, as once in her school years, with the darkness, with wandering alone along confusing mazes and obstructions of endlessly emerging problems, it gradually emerged from this state and became drawn in perspective. Step by step, she learned how to get out of these difficulties, she sought and developed her own approaches and gained experience. Her excessive sensibility gave way to balanced pragmatism. The time had come, and her scientific articles with its logical completeness and language became recognized as the best in the Institute, everyone gladly cooperated with her and invited her to be an author. She was considered to be a leading expert in her field now, she had a high "citation index" and began to gain prominence within international scientific circles.

Doctor... Professor... But was that the fame she once dreamed of? Hill had lived for a long time in New York, he published his novel. When he left, he called Dun to go with him, but he was already seriously ill and grimly joked, "Does it matter what worms eat you?" He lived for another six months. Medicines, sent by Hill, didn't help. What an injustice!

The hourglass of life. You never know how much time is left, and you keep postponing and putting things off until later, may be the most important things that should be done, for which you had been called into this life.

Now she wasn't looking for new heroes. Those who were gathered in her folders could be enough to carry out her plan. It was only necessary to release the time to focus on it, to capture the appropriate attitude. Summer holidays were nearing, her working plans were not bothering, Ilya went to his regular tour. And again, she decided – she gave herself a week break, returned home early and sat down at the table. By the end of the fifth day, the first chapter was completed. When she reread the written chapter in a few days, she felt deep disappointment, though, it seemed there was still the thought, logical consistency and balanced shape. Yet there was no sensation of life. It looked like a scientific article – an introduction, an outline of the main ideas, the results and a final discussion - a good scheme. Hill was probably right when he said that any perfection must have its flaw, and virtue and vice are always somewhere nearby, and you only need to skillfully dispense this proportion to achieve this goal. Hill was the first who understood her when he was not clowning around, didn't get drunk and didn't pretend to be a jester. Maybe it was he, who was able to give her a clue now.

That evening she sat at the table for a long time leafing through old records and wandering the back streets of her past life, as if she was saying goodbye to it. She wanted to return to something and remembered something with regret.

Will her dream, which lived within her all these years, ever come true or will it wither away being drowned in the monotony of everyday life? And will she ever dare again to sit down and play this great game with her heroes?

***

Once she had a dream. In that dream, she saw a strange street that was paved with large and smooth slab, which looked like a gravestone. Smoothly curving, it led to somewhere. Flat thick-lipped shanks of trumpets hidden in the ground were glistening in the middle of the pavement with their dull copper. It was gloomy and clammy around. Neither a tree, nor a blade of grass, nor a flowerpot in the window. They were actually not windows, but cave eye-pits in the castle walls. Low over her head there was knotty plexus of heavy arches and frightening sinks of granite niches on the sides. Faceless figures, wrapped in dark cloaks, were moving silently along the pavement that ran down the slope where it was far too dark. Occasionally, one of them stopped and sat down at the thick-lipped copper shank. Heat rose in the air in thin streams, and it stirred around their clothes. Looking inside, you could see a live fire deep down, which were burning logs. Some deeper niches in the walls of granite pavement were lit up a bit. Everyone wore a cloak, yet their heads were not covered, they seemed to be bent in supplication or perhaps they were praying to someone invisible and menacing. Suddenly someone, who was draped in a gray hood, dutifully went into the street and, having stood there for a while next to a live fire, joined the crowd that was crawling into the darkness. First, second, third.

She is looking for a sacred door, behind which her white room is hidden, where are high mirrors, light curtains, and harpsichord sounds, but everywhere are only cold granite walls and impersonal faces that have cooled down long ago...

She woke up. Ilya was moaning in his sleep. Perhaps, she thought, he suffered from nightmares also. The day before she quarreled with Hill on the phone again. Since he started taking psychotropic drugs, he became unbearable.

Her aching back and leg were hurting her causing her immense pain and predicting rain. Suddenly she thought with sadness that soon, very soon she would have a lot of free time. She remembered Olga, how she was going to learn how to read and write, when she "retired". Again, as it had been often recently, an intoxicating thought twirled within her mind, whether she should try again, suddenly it would work – she didn't have much time left.

Ilya moaned in his sleep. She wanted to wake him up, but decided against it. Recently dreams had become more interesting for them then life itself.

That night he dreamed of a big dog. As if they were alone with her in a small room. She's running from corner to corner while turning everything upside down - wants to play. The dog belongs to their friends, but she is not a collinear, not Rushka, whom they have buried in a forest glade near the cottage. This is a completely different dog, too sweet and large. She runs up and pokes her stupid face into his hands. He needs to feed her, thinks Ilya and finds a cup of non-squeezed cottage cheese (Rushka always loved it), then he finds some boiled new potatoes (he was just going to cook them on the eve, that's why he dreamt of it). But the dog disappears. He seeks her out among things that are scattered everywhere. How could she hide, thinks he, so big, in a small room?

Then someone knocks on the door – Yuliana is on the glass veranda. He shouts to her that she shouldn't open the door – the dog can escape. She can't hear him, turns away, and he also looks in that direction.

"Hurry up, they're waiting for us," says the one standing next to her and shakes her hair curl with a usual affectionate gesture, which people usually make talking with the kids.

"Where are you going?" Ilya screams. A blush, erupted on her cheek, burns him. "Where are you?"

She strokes his arm.

"What did you dream of?"

"Well, all sorts of nightmares. Such nightmares predict rain," he says listening to the alarming rattle in his chest.

Yuliana hardly climbs out of the bed, pulls on her robe and goes to the kitchen to put the kettle. The cups, unwashed from the evening, are shifted to the side of the table and in the middle of it there is a stack of pages scribbled by Ilyusha's uneven handwriting.

"What is it?" she asks in amazement, hardly examining the first words.

"Light curtains are barely swaying on the tall windows; the mosaic of the marble floor is lightly reflected in the large mirrors. And, as if from nowhere – the quiet tinkle of a harpsichord. She is standing and waiting for something, barefoot, dressed in a long nightshirt. There are fear and curiosity in this expectation..."

Her eyes are getting dark and filled with moisture. In a string of exciting events, her life goes in front of her. Her fresh breath is becoming more tangible. The music of familiar voices is becoming more distinct. But here it is snapped, and then – blank pages. As if waiting for her touch... And outside the window – the alluring smile of a sunny morning, the autumn leaves that are falling from a magnolia tree, a white azalea bush in late bloom and cardinal-birds on its branches dressed in their ceremonial plumage. As though they are on fire.

Kiev - Savannah, Georgia.

"STORYCORPS"*

*"Love your fairy tale, the fairy tale of your life.
Everyone's life is a fairy tale
Told to the world just once."
V. Rozanov "The Transient", 1914*

I can't imagine how I've managed to tell an awkward joke. I didn't think that you would take the offer to participate in this project, "StoryCorps", so seriously. A silly row snatched from life as much as several days. And how many more are left? It seems that during many years of living together, we learned to feel the slightest changes in each other's mood, barely catching the incipient thoughts. But it turned out...

Now I understand that it's for yourself and for me you are leaving a mark on the blank wall between oblivion and life, so that later, after hundreds, perhaps thousands of years, when we are to be born again, on having read these words, we would again be able to recognize and find each other.

"I was born in Ukraine (city of Kharkov) in December of 1937, the year that went down in history as the year of mass repressions in the Soviet Union. My earliest memories relate to 1941. When the war began, my parents were mobilized, father as a reservist, mother as a civilian employee, and we were evacuated from Kharkov with the base hospital in boxcars where we were constantly short of breath, I gasped, and I've been remembering this for my whole life. It seemed to me for a long time that people die only from lack of air, to die is to choke. I was only about four..."

31

Much later you found out that your father, a peasant's son Daniel, who had lost the whole family in the years of famine, was not your blood kin. That your mother Lyudmila, a blue-eyed beauty, married early not for love, but rather from a desire to annoy the neighbors' girls, who were ready to fall into the arms of young Lev, who had just returned from abroad where he had trained as a chemical engineer. Lev turned out to be jealous; he made her suffer and always played ugly scenes with his southern temperament. When he had been taken away in 1937 on the charge of spying for Germany, she was not afraid to go to Moscow, to stand in a long line to a terrible room trying to prove that Lev couldn't be a spy, that he was just a crazy and an idiot. The chief smiled at her and promised to investigate.

In that difficult year, Maxyuta, Lev's work colleague and a chemist as well, came to her almost every day trying to support her, to help somehow. She favored him. Once, on one of the holidays, they sat up late and he stayed until morning. They began living openly. Three of them: she reared little cub Vilka - Valentin.

Lev came unexpectedly when they were not waiting for him. Wearing a rumpled jacket and boots without laces, with the eyes of a hunted animal. Lyudmila said to Maxyuta, "Go away. He needs me. I can't leave him now." And after three months, you were born. The gestational age showed that they both could be the cause of your birth.

Lev soon came around again and began to show his fangs. Maxyuta walked in circles somewhere nearby. Life with constant scandals turned into a living hell. Finally, your mother escaped from both of them with two children to quiet and safe Daniel whom she soon got used to and even loved. She eloped with Olga, the youngest of three sisters from the dispossessed family, which had moved to the city to survive somehow. Olga was not just a nanny to her children, but more than that, such an uncomplicated source of soul warmth, to which she didn't admit anyone later on. Mother was even jealous...

Mother Ludmila, 1932   Parents: Daniel and Ludmila, 1946

Ludmila, her husband Lev, and son Valentin, 1935

"From that time, I remember the episode when everybody shot out of the boxcars by someone's order, and it became easier to breathe. People fell in the scratchy grass, and German planes swept above us with a deafening roar. And someone's scream sounded, "Woman - a white shawl!" This was my favorite Olya, who covered me – she wanted to save me from bullets. I also remember Siberia. Novosibirsk, Kotelnich. A lot of snow and a bitter feeling of loneliness and fear, when I was left alone in a huge room with lots of iron beds with side rails, where I once poked my head and cried for a long time desperately trying to pull it back. I also remember a lot of bloody bandages, sheets, linen cloths and just bloody rags endlessly being washed by my Olya.

In 1944, we returned to Kharkov, and for the first time I saw a piece of fluffy white bread - a real miracle that struck my fancy. Someone fed me with incredibly delicious sweet cakes, I ate them until I got sick, I started vomiting and my Olya prayed, asked God not to leave me. In the same 1944, we arrived to Kiev, my father got an apartment in a ministerial house on Andreevsky descent, and I went to first grade.

Our house was located just opposite the St. Andrew's Church where we often went with Olga. We used to stay there on our knees for a long time (I remember feeling cold on the glazed tiles), listened to the sermon in the Old Slavonic language, of which neither I nor Olga understood and prayed not knowing for what. For the church holidays Olya dressed me up in a Ukrainian costume, put on a wreath with beautiful ribbons, and I participated in the processions around the church with gonfalons and singing, and then, on coming home, we broke our fast with "blessed gifts from Bulky village" that my Olya received from relatives. Home-made sausages, "kovbyk", fresh bacon, blood sausages with buckwheat. At Easter, we added colored eggs and small sugar-topped Easter cakes baked by Olya in tins left from canned food and sprinkled with colored millet. At Christmas, we always had "kutia" made of wheat, honey and nuts, "uzvar" with wondrous dried fruits from the same Bulky village, and at the Savior feast - apples and a variety of all sorts of other sweets.

"We used to go to St.Andrew Church together with nanny Olya", 1946

Nanny Olya – Olga Borovik, 1950

St.Andrew Church (arch.B.Rastrelli) in Kiev where the childhood of the protagonist had passed

In that post-war period, my parents were busy at their works from morning till night, and my only friend and tutor was Olga. She also drove me to school and back. In the first grade, I often took cold, missed lessons, and generally, I didn't imagine what I had to do there. Coming after another illness, I couldn't understand what those "new" letters were and where the "old" ones gone. I used to sit at home for weeks. I loved to hear Olya's stories about God, about sins, that there were devils in the world, and about how brave our soldiers were, how bad Nazis were and how good Stalin was, who had saved us from those terrible Krauts with rifles and bayonets. I remember, in my seven years, I was inspired by those stories (I remember physically that tightness in my chest), and they took the form of lines written on pieces of paper by my clumsy hand.

When our heroes shed their blood,
When the Nazis threatened them with guns,
Great Stalin came to us to help.
He highlighted our path with good...

Olya never got mad at me or cursed, she spoiled me and required nothing in return. I got so close with her that when my parents sent me to the children's sanatorium in summer and then came to visit, probably, I was the only child who didn't rush to meet own parents. I cried, asking them to take me home to Olya. After their departure, I became seriously ill with malaria. I stayed in a sick-room for a long time, talked deliriously, called Olga. They brought me a book from the library; I didn't read a single word from it. I still remember its name – "Eupaty Kolovrat". That strange name disturbed my imagination. Horned heads of real devils flared near the lamp hanging directly overhead, with blue and pink neon flames. I already knew from Olya that all people are sinners, and it seemed to me that strange Eupaty Kolovrat was hiding behind the cover of the book, perhaps the uppermost of the devils, and if I only opened it, he would immediately jump out and shout, "Here you are!" I was trying to remember my "sins" in fear.

The teacher didn't like me; she often abused me and called my parents. "What kind of a wild child you have," she said. "She never listens to what she's told; somewhere up in the clouds and silent all the time." I distinctly remember that until the fourth grade, I didn't understand what it meant to be engaged, then not to just sit there with a book and dream about something, but to dive into the text, to learn something, even to remember by heart. Once we were asked to memorize the oath of Stalin from the history book for the fourth grade, saying that we should repeat every line four times to do this. Each paragraph began with the words, "Passing from us, you commanded..." and ended with, "And we vow to you, Comrade Lenin, that we'll honorably fulfill thy precepts." I remember, it was enough for me to repeat them twice, and the next day, to everyone's surprise, I read it "with the expression" at the blackboard almost without hesitation, got a good mark (B grade) for the first time in my life (previously I got only C's and D's).

Then it seemed like another life began. New subjects and new teachers appeared in the fifth grade. I realized that there was an external world available to communicate with. We were taken to the Museums of Russian and Western Art where many lectures were organized, we learned to analyze the paintings of different artists from different eras. Our school invited well-known artists - singers, reciters, musicians.

In the early 50's, our detours to the church with Olga ceased. It was closed. It ceased to be functional."

After living in the village, a great city, in which Olga had got familiar with two quarters next to the house, frightened her. She always thought that something might have happen to you. Until the seventh grade, like a hen, she brought you to school and took you from it. When you forbade her to do it, saying that all students in your class laughed, she followed your trail for a long time hiding behind trees and at the end of the lessons happened to be round the corner as if incidentally. She lost her head at all when you started to run to the movies, to a rink or to a gym with the girls. And she blamed your mother in everything that she had not kept the caul, in which you had been born.

"Olya, where are my new pants?" rummaging in the closet, you screamed to the kitchen.

"Well, you forgot them at your *kiskitball.*"

She refused to take money for her work, but your mother insisted – it's necessary, to be formal. Olga kept them in a beaded handbag, in a chest under the sheets, along with an amulet and a holy picture, the size of a matchbox, which had been brought from the village. She never knew how much she had and never spent them – she saved them "for death".

"By the ninth grade, I became a successful student and our English teacher's pet. Back in the days, she worked in Paris. She had some connections in the Ministry for Foreign Affairs from there. Some people brought to her literature that was not allowed then. We read James Joyce's "Ulysses" and Nabokov's "Lolita" with her, looked through the reproductions of Russian and foreign artists from the archives of the UNESCO, which were unknown to our people."

The closeness of the teacher and her favorite student remained after finishing school. You often came to her for advice. When the weather permitted, you walked together in the park that was situated in front of her house across the street, along which a tram ran. In the winter, you spent hours at her cluttered apartment where the reproductions of great masters were plastered on chests, once fashionable in Ukraine, on boxes of books and lids of boxes with linen. Even the trash cans were covered with cartons painted with fragments of paintings by Miró, Kandinsky, Malevich colored with pencils. Withered, small, completely gray-haired, she buried herself in an armchair like in a cocoon. Lively curiosity shone in her eyes half-closed with eyelids and understanding everything.

With catlike softness, carefully avoiding the angles, her elder sister entered with a tea tray. At once, the large room became cramped.

"Thank you, Lyolya, my dear," she said softly to her. "What could I do without you..."

And she complained that she could read only detective stories by that time. She turned over a page and immediately forgot what was on the previous one.

I apologize in advance that I break the flow of the narrative. Suddenly I wanted to jump on the bandwagon and go at least a couple of stops along that life.

Post-war childhood, 1946

I think, in that place, where our début was planned, they deliberately detained my birth for a week to have the same constellation as yours - Sagittarius. They wanted to help us, so that it could be easier to forgive one another in this long, but so short life.

We were both born in the same hospital. Me - in November, you - after me, thirteen days later. But we were able to meet only twenty years later.

I'm still twelve in 1950. I live in the Conservatory hostel for the whole year – my uncle, a ministry official, didn't want me to live with him until my mother changed her room in Poltava to at least something in the capital. He called somewhere to settle that. I was assigned to share a room with two students. One of them was a balalaika player, another – a singer. He was also a photographer. I still keep some of his pictures. The hostel had stove heating. In a tiny room, there was a narrow gap between the wall and the stove. A wooden couch is barely squeezed in that gap. In winter, because of the heat from the stove, I dream of burning houses every night. But it's still summer, there are no classes, it's still freedom, and a fabulous city seems to be the capital of the world after provincial Poltava.

The left bank of the Dnieper has not yet been built over. The high right bank is shining with the golden domes of *Pechersk Lavra*. On the right, if you look from the river side – the colored lights of *The Green Theatre*. Plank seats, bats, and midges. But what a magic is that big screen! Above the hill is *The Toad*, a round dance floor surrounded by a high fence. Some petty punks are always hanging around there. More serious people gather at the Philharmonic in the billiard hall – to gamble and settle important matters. Every evening there are concerts at the Philharmonic. A few times, I managed to climb in through the window. Getting by on pies, it was nice to dinner with my aunt on Pechersk once a week, in the weekend. I have never eaten such *borscht* anywhere. After the duty visit, having finally waited for the evening, you can go by the tram down to Kreschatik, where near already finished gingerbread skyscrapers, having cooled the internal heat with two glasses of lemonade, take the most convenient bench and, like a hunter in ambush, wait for an evening flight, or rather a promenade. Many ample-bodied girls come to show themselves, dressed up in dresses mostly altered from their moms'. Every second one seems to me beautiful. Breathtaking. Flocks those are thicker but smaller – still just young girls. They make eyes, glancing from side to side – in a hope that someone would treat them with an ice-cream or, at any rate, invite to the movies –there are some summer cinemas near – "Komsomolets of Ukraine", "Vladimirskaya Gorka". The girls who are more hussy and bolder, when it gets dark, go to the parks over the Dnieper splitting off into pairs, sit on the benches like moths and tremblingly wait for their choices in the wrong light of infrequent lamps. Dark alleys know how to keep secrets.

Then we didn't know anything about each other. That first meeting at a concert of Vlach's quartet hadn't yet happened. Perhaps a foreigner, I thought then. Her delicate oval face had a tinge of something otherworldly, some kind of spirituality in a mysterious look of her myopic eyes. Dark skin. Wave of curly hair cascading over her shoulder at het little breast. And, as an unexpected contrast, slightly opened, as if for a kiss, childishly swollen lips outlined with love. Our seats were close, but you seemed so distant to me, inaccessible, like a butterfly of rare beauty, hidden in a transparent cocoon woven from thin strands of sounds. After the concert, you asked me the time. I pulled out my big watch without strap and suddenly noticed that the hand on the dial moved in the opposite direction. I thought, perhaps broken. In excitement, because you spoke to me, my breath was taken away. I said something like, "Nearly eight by mine."

You even clapped your hands.

"Turned out well!"

And suddenly you approached, as if you wanted to get a better look, I remember it well, you said very quietly, just for me, "So, we'll meet again..."

"Our seats were close, but you seemed so distant
to me, inaccessible...", 1959

And after about ten years...

Do you remember how our future character and the author of "The Yellow Kings"* celebrated in "Cuckoo" taking the Lomonosov Prize for his screenplay for the film "A Portrait of a Surgeon" about Arutyunov? He ordered a carafe of vodka for the dinner, excoriated a sluggish waiter (he had such a need!). After drinking, he began to teach us how to live. He bragged that he could penetrate into the most inaccessible office, that he thought over every word and calculated each answer preparing for a breakthrough, built a strategy and tactics of each break. It seemed you were elated with him, and I didn't know how to fit into the conversation and felt almost superfluous at the table.

41

"I never back down," every minute he grew in his own eyes. "In order to carry my point, I'll go the whole hog!"

Then something broke in his voice. He scowled. Drunken tears in his eyes. Clutching a fork, like a dagger, he turned to you sharply.

"What's in him that I don't have? Why not me, but him?"

We had been together for two years, but you never told me that he was in love with you. At that moment I knew that I should come to you for help, but the words that passed through my mind were kind of shameful, not appropriate to the moment, like the one that it was not our choice, not here but somewhere out there, we had just been prompted, pushed, we didn't know that such thing happen. I thought he would laugh and swear. What am I compared to him? He's already a *maitre*, a master of the pen, a prize winner, he can afford going to restaurants. And suddenly I imagined: the next moment he would get up, pay the bill and take you away...

Now I know that often, just out of curiosity, you loved to play a dangerous game. But then I thought, you were with him, and, as if apologizing, made me even more confused, "He (he – that's me), he also tries to write."

Then my surprise contender mounted his favorite hobbyhorse. His tone became didactic again, "If you want to learn something – not a day without a line. Every morning - three hours at the desk. Then – a warm-up, for example, take out the trash bins. Ponder the behavior of your character... Six months later, you'll be able to show something."

Having smashed me completely, he took you by the hand.

"Let's go! Tell me about your polymers. We'll start a new screenplay."

You joked, "First, you should learn how to play violin."

And suddenly you became serious, "You're asking, why not you... He plays. It's always alive. It never bores."

"My mother, a philologist by training, believed that a young person needed to have a technical profession for life, to feel a complete human being. Liberal arts students were not held in high esteem at that time. I graduated with honors from the Department of Chemistry, began working in a chemical laboratory and wrote a Ph.D. thesis in 1963. Passing minimum requirements exam for a Ph.D. degree, I was fascinated by philosophy. I read with interest not only Mach and Avenarius, but also Kant, Schopenhauer, Nietzsche, Russian thinkers and philosophers. I was impressed by each Kant's categorical

imperative from "The Critique of Practical Reason": "Act so that the maxims of your will do not affect the interests of other people." I tried to follow this principle. Unfortunately, in our time, time of business and corporate interests, it's already obsolete. It's been replaced by healthy pragmatism.

At that time, the "Knowledge" Society actively functioned involving young scientists in their work. Pretty soon, I was summoned to the Regional Committee of the Komsomol (we were automatically Komsomol members from 14-15 years) and offered to prepare a lecture on the subject of "Religion is the opium of the people". At first, I thought it was very funny. Intellectuals were very critical of the supreme leadership then. We had already witnessed Khrushchev's speech at the Twentieth Party Congress of the cult of personality and the atrocities of Stalin (1956), in the early 60s there was a short-term so-called Khrushchev thaw of 1962-1963, the underground press widespread – we read the underground and forbidden works by Pasternak, Solzhenitsyn, which were never published in the Soviet Union. But the repressions didn't stop. Ideological explosions took place in the Writers' Union, all sorts of condemnations "from the name of the people" of those objectionable to the authorities, such as "haven't read, but condemn!" After Khrushchev's dethronement (1964) the hounding of intelligent people continued - Solzhenitsyn, Rostropovich. Of course, we understood the barbaric nature of our totalitarian regime, but it was dangerous to talk about it out loud.

Naturally, I protested against the proposal to give this lecture. This, so to say, is not my specialty. But a responsible comrade from the Regional Committee of the Komsomol made it plain that some people were aware of my past. Like going to church I had to understand, it was incompatible with the title of a Soviet scientist. And, together with that, I was handed a thick catalog of possible topics of anti-religious lectures, and he graciously allowed me to choose at my own discretion. In the course of further negotiations, it seemed to me that those cute boys, who smiled so friendly, just performed some orders from above. In fact, they cared little for what and for whom I would read. As a result, I chose a six-hour course for the University of Culture – "Structure and origin of the Old Testament and the New Testament texts and scientific criticism of the Bible", and demanded a year to prepare. I was given an exemplar of the Bible with the corresponding seals (For Official Use Only). The Bible was banned in the Soviet Union then.

To tell the truth, I was very interested to learn more about the history of the origins of Christianity, the origin of the texts of the Old and New Testaments, and during a year, I used to run to the academic libraries in my spare time, finding all sorts of sources there. Fortunately, it's not so easy to wipe off the research papers from the face of the earth, and I learned a lot of interesting things about the archaeological findings, historical events that shed light on the stories of the Scripture, about the sacred books of other religions, the Quran, the Rigveda, filled dozens of notebooks with my close handwriting.

Finally, when my lectures were held before the solid audience of the Regional Committee of the Party, a very solid man said, "Listen, girl, you are, of course, sleight of mouth, but it's no use to anyone. We'll leave for you only "The Scientific criticism of the Bible", and you'll give it all over the place for believers and young people, debunking the biblical miracles."

I began to celebrate life after that. I was included in the teams, which traveled to different regions of Ukraine. I told about the history of the rise of Christianity, of the Qumran discoveries, of the composition of the Old and New Testament books. I told them, which of the Old Testament stories could be natural events in the country of the pharaohs. At first, my students looked rather grimly, but by the end of the lecture the audience usually got merry, and someone would obviously come up to me and say, "Danilivno (reference by patronymic is frequent among the people), it would be so great if you were a god mamma for my kid – we would get drunk so nicely!" Or, "If we could sit sometimes at the table and talk about all these things. Oh, that could be great!" However, there were several cases in Transcarpathian region when I didn't see any reaction of the audience. As it turned out later, the lecture took place in the Hungarian village. My students didn't care what language I spoke, they knew neither Russian nor Ukrainian. The main thing was that the event was held, a report from the local authorities to the Party organs was fine.

After the lectures, all our team used to be taken to a local restaurant where we were treated with a sumptuous dinner ("Everything is fresh, right from the farmstead") with an incredible amount of vodka. And because of the Komsomol habit to be a close-knit family, I was forced to drink on par ("Well, Danilivno, we cannot help but to toast for our fine youth! Well, another one for our next meetings!"). It was impossible to refuse, so I pretty damaged my liver.

Of course, it was hard to maintain such a lifestyle for a long time. Fortunately, I was coming out of the Komsomol age, and I was not going to become the Party member and gradually was able to minimize my educational (as we had been instructed, it should be propagandistic as well) activity, still remaining a Chairman of the Youth Commission and a member of the Scientific Council on atheism in the regional organization of the "Knowledge" Society for a long time. The public activity was required to obtain good characteristics of the so-called Triangle (a director, a party secretary, a chairman of a trade union) to travel abroad with the reports for international conferences, symposia and congresses."

At that time, I lived like a snowbird. Traveling in tours all the time. Our friend, the poet and satirist Pavlusha (Glazovoy), as we affectionately called him, wrote a humoresque about this, called "Ivan with a suitcase". He was a frequent guest in our home, and probably the only one to whom I was never jealous in that time. Many of your circles of acquaintances - artists, poets, musicians and just occasionally met talented specimens of the human race were ready in their souls, I believed, to lay down at your feet on the first call. We quarreled, for a long time, and sometimes it seemed to everyone that invisible threads, which bound us together, were not so strong, they could break, but every time as if someone invisible, who was wiser, brought us back to one another.

After your lecturing trips your damaged liver increasingly reminded of itself. Doctors advised to go to Truskavets, to the "Crystal Palace" resort closed for ordinary mortals. Then you went to that resort almost every year. Those were for me the months of anxiety, painful fantasies built on omissions in your excited stories about the fabulous feeling of novelty when you got into the environment of the "servants of the people", who were confident in themselves, but willing to open up to you to feel free - yes, they said, we run in the same harness. Each time, all this brings me back to the memories of those few, but so bad moments of life when it seemed that you were ready to give up our ship, which was losing control, and speed off to the unknown horizons... I guess this is typical for beautiful women.

And suddenly, trouble came; it seemed, from nowhere. It was 1977. Time of the Brezhnev's stagnation.

"*I wrote my next doctoral thesis to achieve the higher academic degree and was waiting for an approval from the Highest Attestation Commission in Moscow where it was under an additional review. At the same time, I had to go to an International symposium. I had already got a characteristic from the administration of the Institute, including the mandatory wording that I was "politically literate, morally stable and ideologically mature". And then ... one of my friends met by chance (a party boss from the Academy of Sciences) asked, "What had you done that the City Party Committee made a closed decision on you?"*

I was at a loss. I went to the Chief of the First (secret) department, and he, having locked the door, showed me the decision of the City Committee marked "Confidential" and signed by the First Secretary of the City Party Committee with a personal record that I remembered all my life, "She's arrogant, contempt to people, puts personal interests above public ones, as well as gives unhealthy anti-Soviet judgments including the ones of pro-Zionist kind. But the administration gives her good characteristics".

I was shocked. I had expected nothing like that. I felt diminished and crushed. Of course, that put an end to my career, and not only to this. But why?! I had never been a member of the Party or an active fighter for the rights and liberties. I was the most ordinary person. I loved and valued human communication, loved my job, loved listening to music, going to exhibitions, to artists' studios, reading new books, chatting with friends. Of course, I didn't believe in the light ideals of communism and other propaganda fables, with which we were fed, and hardly anyone around me believed in them. I always knew that there were those who pretended, those who were ready to lend themselves to dishonesty for the sake of earthly blessings, and yet I didn't know who and for what had made such a personal record. After all, those who had signed it didn't know me.

"Judgments of pro-Zionist kind!" Oh, that ever troublesome Jewish trail!"

"And suddenly trouble came; it seemed, from nowhere"
(art. T.Gavrilenko, 1977)

I know you faced with the "Jewish question" for the first time somewhere in the beginning of the tenth graduating grade. It was 1953 when, preparing for the issuance of certificates of maturity, the school authorities announced the "right" names of several classmates: Tanka Petrovskaya turned to Tauba Srulevna, Rayka - to Rachel Meylahovna and Zinka Grach was Zelda Avrumovna actually. You told me that you were surprised. Some schoolgirls were mysteriously smiling, as if saying, of course, we understand, they just wanted to hide their nationality, others laughed openly: now we know who you really are - Srulevnas, Mordkovnas. You have no business to steal our ancestral names...

Later, several other female students, including you, changed their surnames. Instead of the usual, like mother's, you began to carry your father's name – Donka's (as you used to call him), which didn't make you happy: the surname was so long and unusual, and it sounded like a Polish one...

Gradually some of the details became clear: the first husband of your mother (who regularly appeared in Kiev and kidnapped his son Valentine, wherefore your mother fainted and fell into a swoon not knowing what happened to the boy) turned out to be a real Jew by nationality.

Once, it was in the tenth grade, he came to your school, called you from the classroom and asked bluntly, "Do you know who your father is?" And answering to your puzzled look (because you had always known that your father was "Donka" with whom you had lived since birth), he suddenly said, angrily, "Your mother is a whore, and you are a daughter of Maxyuta. Or maybe she said that you were my daughter?!"

You heard a threat in his voice, but next to you, on the garden bench, a very handsome man was sitting, and the only thing you really wanted was that at least someone of your classmates would see him. You had no other thoughts. By that time, schoolgirls had been friends with the "boarding's" - boys from the English boarding school. Absolutely no one was interested in you - you were still a long-legged, long-armed, skinny teenager. A neighbor of your classmate, whom you sometimes went to after school, once said with embarrassment, "I would have invited you to the company, but when my friend saw you, he laughed, "What a green pod she is!"

So, it appeared you had another weird unknown father. And this secret multiplied your inner sense of exclusivity, which had already made its way in the depths of your consciousness, as it was evidenced by persistent introspections in your notebook, which I read much later.

"What if handsome Lev is my biological father? And then, this ancient alien blood really flows in me.

I remembered how someone once asked me at school, "What is your nationality?" - "I'm Ukrainian," I replied without hesitation and heard in response, "Um, you don't look like her!" It seemed like a mockery, didn't it?

My memory preserved several more intent long looks aimed at me, from which I felt uncomfortable. Perhaps something that they were looking for slipped into my myopic, sometimes sad and interrogative eyes. I even remember how once my mother, blowing off steam, yelled at me, as the accusation, "You've got a Semitic complexion!"

One day, I asked one of the Azerbaijani emigrants by the name of Ali-Zadeh, who came to America through the Jewish channels, "How do you know that you are a Jew?"

"What do you mean by "how"?" she laughed. "From grandfathers, from grandmothers..."

Where are you, those grandfathers, grandmothers – Davids, Sauls, Solomons? Explain to me, finally, what you know about me and what

I should do in this world. Or I was called, as Faulkner's character, to smell and see the shadows of my blood belonging to another tribe, to hear an echo of the ancient vibrations of its strict ceremonies, and to feel the depravity and illegality of my unity with my surroundings, the inner ban to live by their rules? Of course, it's good for Oksana Bayul – a pretty Olympic champion with the appearance of a rural simpleton, with whitish straight hair, who says with a clear Ukrainian accent looking like a novice, "I have Jews among my ancestors, so you may say I'm also a Jewish. But I love all of you, I love my Ukraine, I love America, which gave me an opportunity to become what I am now."

All these thoughts flashed through my head like a muddy stream. Maybe this was my main "sin" before the Soviet power? But no, there were some more.

I remembered how I had overheard the story of my father as a child, about his working visit to Moscow for approval of the budget of Ukraine (he worked as the Head of Department Agriculture financing in the Ministry of Finance). He said that Stalin was a tyrant, his reactions were unpredictable, and it was difficult to communicate with him.

I had already known that my mother's first husband, who once struck my childish imagination so much, had received higher engineering education in Germany and was imprisoned on false treason charges in 1937 as a German spy. Therefore, when Stalin died, and all of our ninth-graders were crying, I gazed at everyone's "grief" with an inner smile.

My friend, the artist (he was a Jew and his family suffered from Stalin's repressions) was jailed for that when he learned about the death of the "leader and teacher", he said aloud, "Well, that's good, one bastard down!" He was released only in 1956 for the absence of the event of a crime. Probably, I had commented somehow that emotional outburst.

My institute's thesis supervisor was leaving to Israel in 1971. He called me and asked to see him off after asking whether I was afraid to do it because he was a known defender of the rights of conscientious objectors. It didn't enter my head that I couldn't accompany a man, who was a scientist, who taught me a lot in terms of professional discipline and whom I respected. I remember how I walked with him, it was quite a procession of people unfamiliar to me, cameras clicked, and we were infinitely shot.

My great friend, the poet and satirist Pavlo Glazovoy, as I remember, told me on the phone about his visit to the Central Committee of Communist Party on call, "He teaches me how to write poetry, stews my brain, and I ask: and where are your volumes, so you're teaching me? Show me what you wrote. Where are your writings?" Of course, I laughed along with him. I was familiar with incompetent interference of any kind of the Party ideologues in different areas of our lives.

I leave open the possibility of other similar comments from my side. As I learned later, our phone had been constantly tapped."

While you were searching for the reasons of the trouble, that fell upon you, in the roots of your foggy origin, I wanted to believe that things would come right somehow, I comforted you, as best I could, distracted saying that all that was nonsense, there was no need to panic. "Well, what can they do to you? The times are not the same, they will understand." But I had a terrible sinking feeling inside me. I was afraid to admit that I really wanted to become invisible, like a rabbit, who noticed a flock of vultures above him, to hide my head in the grass.

Anything could happen!

I remembered how in the Conservatory, by the order from above, a talented musician had been expelled ignominiously from the fourth year, because he was a Baptist. How they made a "cleansing" of the faculty: Golfeld went to Minsk, Pecker and Staroselsky – to Novosibirsk. I then asked my teacher, who was just appointed to the position of the rector of the Conservatory, by whose hands all these activities were carried out, "What's happening here?" He popularly explained, "That's the way it should be!"

Why? I didn't think too much about it. I lived then, like many musicians, artists, and poets - each in their own isolated world.

"I lived then like many musicians, artists, and poets– each in their own isolated world" (art.L.Feigin, 1978)

The concert of Ukrainian State Lysenko Quartet in St.Andrew Church (A.Bazhenov, B.Skvortzov, L.Krasnoschek, Y.Kholodov), 1972

"Well enough, finally! It's necessary to pull myself together. What do they incriminate me? Isn't it a usual reaction of a normal person? Why should I care for some persons from the City Committee of Party?! Does it really matter what they think of me? And then it became clear, very distinctly - the main reason for my suffering was that in general, by our laws, with this wording you couldn't be a Doctor of Science and that meant the State Commission for Academic Degrees and Titles in Moscow wouldn't approve my doctoral thesis, in which I had put so many thoughts, efforts and energy, and I wouldn't be able to continue to work in this field. And all that was INJUSTICE!

I tried to leave all my doubts. Despite the open wound in my chest, which bothered me each time, particularly on waking, an attractive young woman looked at me from the mirror, the suffering expression on her face gave her, as I thought, an especial finesse. I decided not to give up and to begin discussing the situation with my friends, the poets, who had permanent curators from the Propaganda Department of the Party Central Committee, and sometimes we met outside of work. In front of me appeared a true picture of the relationship at the highest levels. "Why do you worry so much?" one of them said to me. "We still don't have that paper. When it comes to us, we'll throw it into a bin. And if you want to go to their main ideological authority (Head of Propaganda Department in the City Party Committee), tell her that you'll go to Moscow with a complaint to the Central Committee of Communist Party of Soviet Union. She will shake like a leaf, because most of all, she cares about her chair and they are not in a very good relationship with Moscow."

This way, I learned that the "masters of our destinies", the City Committee and the Central Committee of Party, didn't get along because of their inner ambitious discord, that the decision was made by a certain time according to the instructions for the ideological testing, that there was also a procedural violation, because the Directorate was to confirm the report from the KGB, which they didn't, and that a serious struggle for power boiled within the Institute.

My conversation with the Head of the Department of Propaganda of the City Committee looked like a bargain. Of course, I was very worried. I said that there were no any anti-Soviet and pro-Zionist propaganda from my side, that my doctorate, over which I had been working for about ten years, was sent to the State Commission for Academic Degrees and Titles for approval and I would hardly be approved with this characteristic, that I had to go to Japan with a scientific report, about which there was no question now. Next, I took the advice of my friends, having referred to the planned visit to Moscow, to the Central Committee of Party to discuss this situation, because I had nothing more to lose.

The result was not long in coming. I heard from my conversation partner something like, "Oh, you're such a beautiful woman, and you came to visit me without hair-do. Make it immediately. What do you need now? I promise that your thesis will be approved soon, unless, of course, it's worth it. But as for the Congress, I can't let you go this year, because the decision has been issued, and it can't be cancelled. But a year later, I promise that the very first invitation from abroad to any scientific forum that comes on your personal name will be realized, and you will go with a report."

Everything happened like that "under the watchful governing eye of the Party".

Interestingly, that those few, who were privy to the story, sympathized me internally, though they didn't express it out loud. Perhaps they were aware that under the current system none of them had immunity from any turn of events. I remember, for example, how my boss, the Head of the Department of the Institute of Biochemistry, seeing my deplorable state, organized an expedition to search for the vegetable sources of insect molting hormones - ecdysteroides, with which I was working then, and how he was worried when I used to stop the car at different dives to drink a glass of red wine, which probably helped me, and how he came up with various excuses to shield me from that habit. It was very touching. Sometimes I purposely found reasons to stop, to feel that at least someone cared about my condition.

Of course, we are all hostages of political events in the country, and they can't pass over the fate of each of us. My efforts and my supply of energy, like those of many of my colleagues, have been directed not to fight for the rights and freedoms of the individual, not to political activity (maybe it's bad, but it used to be that way), but for learning and, if possible, development of specific laws in science and in life. To each his own...

"Happy End".
Portret of Professor Y.Kholodova
(art. R.Bagautdinov, 1988)

"Happy End".
People's Artist of Ukraine
Y.Kholodov, 1986

And finally, "Happy end". I've got subordinates, and then some graduate students - a total of 10, including 3 foreigners, I became the Head of a Department with 23 employees, a Scientific Editor and, for a short time before leaving to America by the contract, the Chief Editor of a well-known Biochemical Journal. I also obtained a chair of Bioorganic Chemistry in Agrarian University, wrote a textbook for the students of Agricultural Universities in Ukrainian language, organized and led the Research and Innovation Center "Natural Bioregulators" where we developed and produced biologically active drugs, became a full professor, actively participated in International Symposia, lectured and worked abroad by the invitation of foreign scientists, was a member of various Scientific Councils, published three monographs, more than two hundred scientific articles, got more than a dozen of inventor's certificates, etc.

At the end of 1993, I moved to the United States by the contract. I received a Green Card there as an "outstanding professor and researcher" and plunged into a completely new life for me, with all its advantages and disadvantages.

But that's another story.

When people ask me, who played the most important role in my development and had the greatest influence on my formation, I always answer, "Of course, this is my Olya, to whom I was very attached, and I couldn't imagine my existence without her up to 14-15 years, because I had always been protected by her love from all my children's sorrows and troubles. It's also my school English teacher, who introduced me to the masterpieces of world art and taught me how to understand them. Finally, it's my doctoral thesis advisor at the Institute of Physiology of the Academy of Science, in the department of which I worked, being a Ph.D.- candidate of chemical sciences by that time. It was a brilliant school at that time - they organized scientific and educational seminars in English at their department, we were visited by foreign scientists, we traveled abroad giving lectures or doing professional internships. Our chef, who enjoyed a rare charisma, was not only a renowned scientist in his field, but a great educator of scientific personnel. I remember how, instead of scolding me for some incorrect actions or behavior, he told me, "Think. Think!" And it exposed much more than getting it in the neck. He instilled in me the desire to acquire knowledge, ability to deeply analyze any situation; I certainly acquired many things from him, such as efficiency, perseverance, ability to conduct discussions and self-control in a variety of circumstances."

School English teacher – Eugenia
Sukhova-Goldental, 1952

Science Adviser – Professor Platon
Kostyuk, 1969

When our stay in this world comes to its logical conclusion, we falter, often become indifferent to the environment, we don't know how to find comfort and support. For many people, religion becomes a quiet bay where we think we can hide from ourselves. You, I think, are deprived of this consolation. The confirmation of this is the last harsh words of your confession.

"Of course, I don't believe in life after death. I understand that it's easier to live and die with this faith. Unfortunately, it's not provided by human nature. I don't deny that the idea of some kind of transpersonal primacy, especially in the sphere of unexplained, generated by our consciousness, may lead a person to the obedience of Church, especially if he needs consolation, living in our cruel world. But the dogmas of faith, such as the resurrection, the ascension and other miracles, I think, are perceived to be very conditional in our time.

I'm not impressed by the current Church boom in Russia, which is forced by the authorities – following the example of the Russian rulers, more and more people are turning to religion, and this is a good way to distract them from pressing economic and social problems. From the mouths of party officials, most of whom used to be die-hard communists persecuting believers and declaring religion as "the opium of the people", we now hear phrases of other kind, which they declare with the same conviction, "I am a true Orthodox Christian, and I believe in God." Russian leaders publicly sanctify themselves and kiss the icons, accumulating wealth, with little concern for others, for keeping the commandments. It has become fashionable to recollect God. If the Communist Party was a kind of fetish during the Soviet era, and it was glorified by any means, now the divine rhetoric often dominates in a society.

I think that the fostering of humanistic ideals and moral values, as well as education, are the problems of secular power. And the state should first deal with it on behalf of teachers, scientists, and culture and art public figures. Church as an institution has a centuries-old tradition, for a true believer, and not only for him, with its hymns, celebrations, rituals, moral establishment and educated clergy, it will long remain an unshakable part of our diverse world."

Yet who, choosing from millions of babies being born on earth, turns them into our idols? Leonardo da Vinci. Caruso. Richter. Jasha

Heifetz. I remember when Rostropovich gave a demonstration lesson at the Conservatory. A student asked something like, how to overcome the technical difficulty in some of the compositions, and received the answer, "It's so simple. Give your hands freedom."

Who taught us that, no matter what happens in life, each time we should return to the sacred altar of love?

When I'm in a hurry to show you the heroes of my stories, these children conceived by the mysterious movement of the soul, not yet bathed, casually dressed up in clothes made of the templates, eagerly waiting and hoping for a blessing, I often stumble upon such a rejection, such an outburst of indignation that I regret why I didn't burry them still in the womb. When you, not yet feeling any sympathy for them, are trying to direct their thoughts and actions in some logical direction, and I'm collecting their remains after the explosion in a mystical fog, we suddenly begin to realize how little each of us knows about the other, as if we meet for the first time. At these moments, it feels like we get to know each other again. We gain the opportunity to see something that is stored somewhere deep in the mind of each and previously was not available, not only to outsiders, but also to ourselves.

And then, it seems to me that this is the mystery and uniqueness of life given to us by someone.

Savannah, Georgia.

NOSTALGY

A long time ago, in a former life in Leningrad, Vera Nikolaevna, the official host at Bolshoi Philharmonic Hall, made a casual slip-up on stage while announcing one of the upcoming numbers. "Diubiuk. Little B-iu-rd," she stammered, the syllables in the composer's name somehow spilling over into the piece's title. The two words suddenly came back to Dina as she was grooming herself in the morning, their half-forgotten sound clinging dully, relentlessly to her mind. With rising annoyance she inspected herself in the mirror: the saggy and, as the janitor woman from their Leningrad courtyard would say, "wrinkle-ridden," neck; the skin on her legs full of age spots and tiny scars and grown paper-thin from years of steroid cream treatments; the eyes dull and withdrawn, the increasingly beak-like nose, and as for the hands – well, their fingers seemed more like gout-stricken chicken feet! God, she thought, look what I turned into. The echo of "Little B-iu-rd... Little B-iu-rd" kept knocking against her temple. She smoothed down a shock of stiff grey hair, then began rummaging through her closet – what should she put on? One had to look decent after all, just in case someone would drop by.

The entire month before Lyova's death, she lived with the sense of permanent strain: ambulance calls, doctors, hospitals – it always felt as though she'd missed or overlooked something important. The constant fear for his life was mixed in with the guilt about her occasional lack of patience. There were times when everything about him aggravated her so much that she almost wished to break loose and run off somewhere – so much so that she became rude and short-tempered, checking herself only upon realizing the full extent of his humiliation. Afterwards, she tried not to think about it.

Clearly, life had once again brought her to that line in the sand that could never be crossed without losing your bearings and becoming unsettled, unmoored. It seemed she was fated to pay twice the price for those long-gone years after the war, years of unclouded happiness with a beloved husband in a beloved city. Genrich too spent much of these recent years in hospitals – he'd suffered two strokes and survived two clinical deaths. She stayed by his bedside for months, fearful of losing him, struggling to sustain him as best she could. Still, she couldn't hold on to him in the end. And when it was all over, she somehow found Lyova drifting back into her life. He wasted no time either, declaring he always loved her and stayed true to her, promising to never leave her side now that they'd been reunited by the common fate – he had buried his own wife just a month before. He wanted her to come to America with him, asked not to worry about a thing – he and Pernella had already taken care of the paperwork. All that fine talk – but not a word of his many illnesses…of, say, the fact that after his ten years abroad, having been kicked out during the sweeping wave of expulsions, he'd now come back nearly deaf...Or that he was also living with a hole in his stomach from an intestinal cancer surgery… And that's just the half of it… But why dwell on it now, anyway?

"Come with me, darling," he pleaded. "You'll find peace there, nothing will remind you of the past." Drop by drop, day by day, he kept pouring hope into her. "Just think – a new life in a great, free country…"

And all of this, in his advanced years… and barely speaking his new language… What a fool she was to believe him! As though one could simply squeeze one's life out like a sponge and start over without looking back.

Now that she was alone, she found herself revisiting the past more and more often, reliving the life that seemed to have flown by all too fast. She noticed how some events faded and blurred while others, on the contrary, took on new shades and combined into scenes as though in a play, so finally it was hard to tell if all of it really happened, or came from a dream, or wove its way in from books – especially since reading had long been her favorite pastime.

Here, for instance, is Genrich at his white piano, starting the day with a – is it Beethoven? – while she is making breakfast. The neighbors know: the sound of music means Genrich is up and about. And here is she, alone by the piano, inside the orchestra. Alone? Well, why not? After all, back then, after the war, it was quite easy to enter the conservatory and graduate with a degree. So much for the Americans, always bragging about their education... In fact, she could have even become a soloist if not for the war. Yes, she could see herself entering the stage, wearing a stunning dress with a long train. The hall would grow silent with anticipation. All you hear is the murmur: "Here comes our Queen!" Her, the Queen! Then, flowers fall upon the stage...

At times it seemed that if one could only put it all together, trace it all the way back as it were and follow it through from the beginning, then a whole new significance or purpose might suddenly beckon from the depths of her hitherto-unillumined life.

Of childhood years, all but little remained in her memory. Inside a living room with six large windows there was a piano, a huge square table and a mahogany bed – "Dinka's bed", the one she was born in. Her grandmother was dead but the grandfather, a country doctor, was still practicing, and her mother was dead set on having him deliver the baby. Six years later she brought her daughter there once again for the summer. There was also an aunt with her three children living in the house – she'd returned from abroad and owned a hat store in Mogilev, called "Paris Fashions."

Grandfather was quite strict with the children, but then they were really a handful. Mishka, the most rambunctious of the bunch, was usually the one to get into trouble. Yet he just kept on making mischief, pulling one prank after another. For instance, he'd sneak into a closet where barrels with condiments were kept under grandfather's newly-starched doctor's gown hanging on a string, and he'd either get the gown all dirty on purpose or stuff a pickle into its pocket. Or, while no one was looking, he would coax the others into the room they'd been forbidden to enter – the one where grandfather received his patients – and once there he'd clap on the white cap and placed a wooden tube on everyone's belly to listen to their breath. Or else he'd get to the cupboard with silverware for Passover, climb up it like a tomcat and steal Danishes from the big pan covered with a towel. He'd eat them right there too – that's why cupboard doors were always sticky with jam.

Fridays always spelled trouble for the children. They had to get up early in the morning and carry their potties to be emptied in the far corner of the courtyard, next to the latrine wildly overgrown with burdock. Dinka asked once, "Grandpa, how come there is all that huge, prickly burdock there?" "And what did you think should grow there, roses?" he replied gravely. "Nothing but burdock can grow out of your urine since all of you little rascals are stubborn and lazy and uninterested in either reading or music." Then old Nastya, who came every Friday for a spring clean, would check if they washed their pots and drag them into the bath annex next to the closet. Having washed everyone in a wooden trough and tossed them into bed so they wouldn't get in the way, she stripped nearly naked to wash the painted wooden floor and scrub the kitchen tables with a large knife – first the table for cutting meat, then another for fish and yet another for milk and dough. No one was to get up till the aunt came back from the market, her basket brimming with food, and began to prepare holiday dinner. They would scamper by her feet like puppies as she pulled a wide pan with hot cakes out of the oven. Each would get one if grandfather was not watching. He was a real stickler for rules, that's for sure.

Come Passover, all the curtains in the house had to be changed. Old ones were stuffed into bags and put out on the porch. Fresh table cloth was placed on the table and silverware taken out of the cupboard. When grandfather was in the mood, he would sit at the piano and demand that everyone sing while he played. In which case there was no use arguing, one had to just pull out all the stops and hope for the best.

That house often comes back to her in a dream, its high wooden porch all blackened by rain, the heavy courtyard gates still bearing the brass plate on the door that read "Dr. Vainstein". It seems to be winter out in the street, and she is clinging to the windowsill to peer inside. She can see the table – it's been moved right next to the tile oven. Down there on the left where the warmest spot is, and Mishka is snuggling against it, his back against the heat. Her mother, father, and Aunt Elena are all sitting at the table. Grandfather is reciting a prayer before his meal – only the edge of his wide black beard can be seen. She wants to be there with them; she calls, knocks on the frosted window, but they don't seem to hear her...

Grandfather would die quite soon, and the beautiful back-from-Paris aunt, oddly enough, fell for the common blacksmith, survived the war and returned to Mogilev after the evacuation to live there quietly for the rest of her days.

As for her second grandfather – the one from the paternal line – she barely remembered him at all. A few times in early childhood she stayed at his house while her parents left for Kislovodsk. All she knew from her mother was that he was a commoner who made his fortune floating timber. He built a synagogue in town, paid for entirely from his own pocket. At its opening, he threw a gold coin into each corner. He was also a bit of a skirt-chaser. All his wives came from the same family; he survived three of them and ended up marrying the youngest when he was ninety. When he went to visit his son in Leningrad for the occasion, the first thing he asked was "So where is your bath?" After steaming himself, he drank a bottle of vodka and went out shopping for a green blouse for his new wife...

After their morning walk, which of late had gone no further than the seesaw in the middle of the courtyard, they would sit down and read. Dina read some of the latest books she received in the mail. Lyova, with his habit of a lecturer in foreign affairs, read newspapers. Unfortunately, he read the key parts aloud, which came as a distraction as it kept her from fully immersing herself in the music of words.

Ah, the words. Now she would happily listen to even some idle chatter. If only someone would call! They probably didn't know how frightened she felt to be left here all alone.

Yet it wasn't too long ago that she threw big dinner parties at her place. There were often as many as twenty people crammed in her six-floor apartment – Russians as well as Americans. Someone would play a guitar. She always planned the reception well in advance and prepared very seriously: composed the menu herself, chose a separate sauce for each dish, used her own recipe for the salads, tried to pick something new for desert. She wanted to surprise, to delight. She'd stay on her feet all night, now serving one plate, now carrying back another. "Oh no, thank you, I'll do it myself." Constantly worrying about something: are the blintzes not getting burnt, the meat not getting too dry in the oven? Barely managing, with her broken English, to steer the conversation in the direction everyone could follow. And feeling quite awkward and maybe even ashamed when Lyova, with his air of a speaker climbing a podium, would get up from the table to deliver his customary toast.

"Dear friends, may I have your attention please." Well, at least *he* wasn't groping for words. "I'd like to drink to the prosperity of our great America, the country that gave all of us another chance in life."

"*Bravo*, Lyova, *Bravo*!"

"I am so glad that Dina and I are now Americans, and am truly proud of our adopted country!"

He seemed to be calling on everyone to witness his new-found loyalty. Gosh, she thought, this whole exile thing must have really broken him down. She felt sorry for him, looked for justifications.

"Excuse me everyone, excuse me...Just a few more words if I may... I'd like to make another toast now – two in one, eh?.. To you, Dinochka, you who've brought light into my life, you who've been sent to me from above and whom I've loved desperately all these years. Every day I wish to marry you all over again; you are so beautiful and caring and full of joy. May you stay as you are for many years to come, an inexhaustible source of vitality and goodness!"

"*Vivat! Lekhaim!*"

It was as if he was undressing her in front of everyone, trying to show her off. And to be sure, once the guests left, this clumsy display of affection was habitually followed up by a sequel of sorts. He would kneel before her and kiss her hands while she, taking some perverse joy in his humiliation, let the scene drag on before finally locking herself up in her room. Afterwards she would always berate herself for making him suffer and became pointedly attentive, even obliging. Still, she knew she could never overcome the resistance that rose inside her each time she as much as imagined him lying next to her in the same bed.

On the telephone desk, next to the photograph in a black frame, a postcard:

"Dear Lyovushka! Congratulations on this glorious anniversary – the age of wisdom and peace. Our own golden years are still filled with the sound of life's music, and you too should cherish every minute God granted us on this Earth. I will do everything in my power to ensure your health and happiness..."

Just words, yet again. Words, more words.

The reprisals came fast on the heels of Kirov's murder. Kadatsky, the chairman of the *Lensovet*, was the first in their building to be taken away. After that, someone would disappear nearly every night. Of their entire apartment line only Dr. Chernov's family was left. Her father, the admiral of Baltic Fleet division, was arrested "without the right of correspondence" in Kronshtadt, where he'd been stationed and where she and her mother would often visit. One of his friends phoned within a few days: "Raya, take the kids right now and run as far away as possible." She grabbed what little she could and ran to the Vitebsk

Railway Station. In Mogilev, where they'd often accompanied her father ("Look, Mendel's son is here!") the first person they ran into was the chief of the NKVD police. He pretended not to have recognized them. By the time they reached their relatives her mother was so shook up, she could barely utter a word for the fear he would denounce them and they'd all be arrested. She lived with this fear for years to come, hiding from everyone, afraid to even look for a job.

Dinka eventually graduated from trade school and made up her mind to go back to Leningrad and apply to a university, even though she hadn't yet decided which. Her mother cried and tried to talk her out of it, but all her pleas were in vain. She could only stand there and watch her daughter pack.

"Go to Aunt Rachel then, she should be able to take you in."

Earlier, during famine, they used to take Rachel's children to the dacha in Kronshtadt where Dina's father could give them his naval officer's rations.

It was in the middle of the night when, having walked across half the city, Dinka finally rang the bell. Rachel, pale as a sheet, didn't open the door right away.

"Dinka?! What are you doing here?" There was a catch in her voice.

"I…I was just hoping you'd let me stay with you for a while…"

Rachel's' dull eyes grew bloodshot, glaring from under her grey, sleep-disheveled mane as she made to bar the door with her hand.

"Just look at what they've come up with! Don't you realize the danger it puts us in? You know my children are communists – the true kind! And you are enemies of the people, all of you … Go and look elsewhere before someone sees you."

She sat down on top of her suitcase, straining for the voices behind the door that had just slammed shut, as if wondering if they would reopen it and invite her in. Finally she recalled the address of her father's brother. Once again she had to cross the city by foot. It was nearly morning by the time she got there. The minute she knocked, all of them rushed out into the hallway: uncle Volodya, his wife, the old grandmother. Everyone seemed quite alarmed.

"What happened to you, Dinulya?"

"Well, I came to study in the university. I know Mom told me to never come here but see, aunt Rachel wouldn't take me in. She said I was the enemy of the people."

Her uncle put his arms around her shoulders:

"Never mind, sweetheart, we'll figure something out."

She had never seen a man cry before.

Later in the morning, haunted by her mother's plea that she must never pop up at her uncle's, she slipped out and went to look up her cousin Asya at the Pedagogy Institute dorm. They boiled tea in a huge teapot, munched on pretzels, strolled through the city till nighttime, trying to catch up. There was so much to tell. Her uncle, a professor at the Institute of Chemistry and Technology, helped her to enroll, asking only that she never tell anyone they were related. And then two weeks later he got arrested along with his entire family, and she never found out if it happened because of that one nighttime visit.

Their student life – a life full of excitement despite all the hardship – was cut off abruptly by the war. They were given army papers and sent to a mobile field hospital on the Leningrad front.

"Go easy on them, will you," the head officer said to Nikifor, top sergeant in charge of stationing their medical platoon of first-and-second year female students. "They are just rookies."

And indeed the mere sight of them nearly brought Nikifor to tears.

"Women...My dear girls...Sweet little chicks..." He shook his grey head. "Just think what this Hitler bastard has done. What am I supposed to do with you?" He looked Dinka over. "There ain't going to be no uniform that fits you. I mean, look at you, you got no legs on you to speak of."

Finally he brought some tarpaulin boots for them. The closest he could find to her size 33 was size 40. He also gave her a pair of footcloths and showed how to wrap them around her feet. Immediately she got bad blisters.

In the morning he called everyone in for the pep talk.

"The fascist German beast has attacked us without warning." You could tell from his voice he'd rehearsed this. "But we are no cowards, are we?"

"No, we are cow*girls*!" Dinka teetered.

"We are all of us going to... de*feat* this scum and... de*grade* our red banner into that evil Hydra's heart!"

The girls kept snickering, eager to needle him.

"Hey, where do we find this Hydra?"

"Why, Berlin, where else."

"No way, we'll never get that far in these boots."

"Hey, do I get sick leave when I m feeling delicate?" someone asked,

"Cut it out, now! I may not be the best-educated fellow but I ain't no fool either: I know feeling delicate means the dog's in heat. Ain't my fault you females are being drafted – it's the German's. But you're still too young and better keep in mind that every fellow down here, he's just passing by. So you should all keep faith for our Victory...If we ain't finished with this Hydra till winter, well...We just got a delivery of them underpants, so you can make them into...what do you call it... that thing for your bosoms... You know what I mean, women don't wear those things in our village."

There was little fun to be had after that. The wounded came by truckloads, heaped together like wooden logs. There was a shortage of bandages, so they soaked used ones in lizol and dry them afterwards. They were on their feet 24/7. They'd get so exhausted, they'd fall asleep while walking. Often they could hardly tell day from night. Yet they never complained and tried to be supportive of one another.

Once, already in winter, she climbed down to the river to get some water. The ice hole was all frozen and she had a hard time breaking the surface, so she jumped on the ice, only to see it collapse under her weight. She screamed, called for help. She was rescued by the soldiers who pulled her out and carried her to the hospital. They rubbed her body with alcohol and gave lots of hot tea to recover, but before nighttime she was burning up. Soon she was sent away to the rear with pyelocaliectasis. There she got patched up and soon ended up back at the transfer point. They caught at her report:

"Did you say you were a chemist? Some trainloads of supplies have just arrived, you'll be inspecting them."

So she wielded a probe to pierce holes in bagfuls of groats, took samples, made kashas to fatten those poor soldiers recovering from illnesses and wounds. They seemed to always hang around competing for her attention.

Then it was transfer point once again. Everyone was waiting for the opening of the Eastern Front.

"Can you speak German?"

"Yes, I can."

Of course she was lying shamelessly. All she could remember was a few words from high school and a dozen or so from the university.

She got assigned to the Seventh Unit of the *Politotdel*, the Political Department. "Work among the population and enemy troops," read the task description. It was only at that point that she finally realized what she'd gotten herself into. It was only a matter of time before they checked her record and found out she was the daughter of the 'Enemy of the People.' If the truth came out, she might well be looking at a court-marshal. Fortunately luck was on her side, she must have somehow slipped through the cracks. She managed to enroll in a special program in *Komsomolsk-na-Amure* and soon graduated as a lieutenant, proudly swapping her sergeant stripes for officer's shoulder boards and tarps for boxcalf boots. And yet, despite it all, the fear gnawing at her like an impacted splinter remained with her for the rest of the war.

Out of all she'd gone through during those years, the flight to Pyongyang stands out the most. It was just her and a few Red Army soldiers on their *Douglass* plane. Everyone was given a parachute and received basic instructions – which strap to yank and on which count. The soldiers were swearing like troopers: "Forget it, if this one gets blown over to the Japs, no way in hell we're going to find her." She figured it was just banter, but seconds after they pushed her out the door she blacked out, coming to only on the ground, her body being dragged along the fallow earth till one of the guys hurried to her rescue. A cloud of black smoke was rising across the forest, not too far away.

She kept the chute as a souvenir. The material turned out to be fine silk. Later her mother would put it to use by cutting it into pieces and sewing white aprons for girls to wear in school.

Another memorable episode involved her trip to Pyongyang to deliver some papers. A Korean man was waiting for her at the airport with a car. He spoke some Russian. The ride was long. There were women sitting by the side of the road, right on the ground, selling strawberries and some fruit. Frequently the driver stopped to buy some berries for her and sighed wistfully as he watched her eat. Finally they reached the city.

"Wait *shortah* time, *shortah* time," he says, gets out of the car and disappears into some nondescript building down the street. She is waiting and waiting; half an hour passes, then an hour. No trace of him. What on Earth could have happened, she wonders. Finally some Russian patrolmen came over.

"Hey, where's the driver?"

"See that door? He went in there."

"Figures," they laugh. "It's a brothel."

And that's when he shows up, looking all perked up.

"You waited *shortah* time? Now we drive *fastah*."

Those things come naturally to them, she muses. A man may be out walking with his wife and kids and he'll simply excuse himself whenever he has to. Easy, just like going to the restroom.

Khabarovsk, the end of the war. Everyone is out in the street, kissing and crying, laughing and firing their guns like crazy. It is a miracle they didn't shoot each other.

At the train station there was a regular crush – everyone was scrambling to leave. Even with a ticket you couldn't elbow your way to the car, and with a suitcase and a parachute bag she simply didn't stand a chance. She threw a desperate glance at one of the soldiers, pleading for help. He seized her in his hands and lifted her like a baby above people's heads. "Make way for a lieutenant," he yelled, wedging through the crowd.

In the car's narrow passage, suitcases and handbags were piled up to the windows. A coronel locked himself in the first compartment with some broad – he was drunk and kept threatening everyone with a gun. The only seat left was the one next to the bathroom. She stayed there for the entire ten-day ordeal.

Moscow was no different either. The railway station was like a roiled anthill. She dropped her things next to some babushka sitting on the floor with a child.

"Could you keep an eye on these? I just need to get to the ticket window."

"Where do you need to go?"

"Leningrad."

The woman shook her head. "Forget it. No way they'll let you through. People have been waiting in line for three days already. They'll crush you before you get to the window."

Dinka had dark circles under her eyes. She must have looked like she was about to sink down onto the floor and fall asleep right there and then. The woman handed her a pillow.

"Here, stuff this under your coat and make it bulge out."

She did so and went over the window to inquire.

"Is this the line for Leningrad?"

Those in the back of the line began to grumble.

"See, some people have fought and others fooled around. Get a load of the belly on that hussy!"

One of the men came to her defense. "Give the wench a break, you don't want her going into labor in here."

She just stood there, waiting silently, when it suddenly occurred to her: what would happen if she really were pregnant? She'd be probably crying her eyes out by now. Before she knew it, tears were indeed streaming down her face.

"Come on, folks, let her through already."

She could silently congratulate herself after walking away minutes later with a ticket in her hand. "Way to go, Dinka, that was quite a performance. Guess you are a born actress after all."

For the first time in years, the fear of being found out – of being denounced as the daughter of the Enemy of the People – had finally receded to give way to new hopes. Her beloved city seemed to be opening its arms to her. Live, just live, she could hear it whispering. Even with the January frost outside, there was a riot of springtime birdsongs in her heart – a bold, exuberant melody. Everything seemed so simple and natural that she felt she could accomplish anything. She'd get some gig to last her till summer, then reenroll in the university and try her hand at either theatre or film, assuming she got admitted into either program.

She went over her wardrobe, examining those dresses she'd brought along – why not flaunt them? But something told her to wait. She put them aside and donned her uniform and military coat once again. Still, she couldn't resist ditching officer's boots for the high-heeled shoes that made her instantly taller.

She saw some plain-looking billboards by the Philharmonic and thought, why not go in and ask.

"You are here to see Ponomaryov?" inquired the secretary at the reception.

"Hi, how are you. Actually, I was just wondering if you might have a job for me."

"What sort of job?"

"Pretty much anything."

"Are you a musician?"

"I guess you could say I am in the field. I was learning to play piano before the war."

"Just a minute, let me ask." The secretary opened the door behind her. "Afanasy Vasil'yevich! You've got some help coming our way."

"Well, well. Top lieutenant. Tell me about your skills."

"I know how to use a handgun, an automatic…"

"Fighting as such is not what we do here. Fortunately, I might add. Can you play any instrument?"

"Only a little…But I am a quick learner! And I'd accept any position."

He glanced at her shoes, smiled.

"Tell you what. Why don't you check with the concert bureau one floor up, see if they have something for you."

There were no plates on any of the doors on that floor. She asked someone. "You need Pismalter's office. That door over there." Pismalter? What kind of name… He must be pulling her leg. Actors! But she entered anyway.

"I am looking for comrade Piss… Piss…" It was on the tip of her tongue.

"…serman?" someone prompted from behind a line of desks.

"Yes, comrade Pisserman. I was just referred to him regarding employment."

A tiny woman in the corner lifted her head and squinted at her through her thick glasses.

"It seems you got the wrong door, young man. We are not the recruitment office but a cultural establishment devoted exclusively to music."

Thanks to Dinka's ability the nickname eventually stuck: Pismalter became Pisserman. And although the poor woman was the best music editor who knew every single note of nearly every score by heart, she'd since become the butt of everyone's jokes. Which wasn't entirely surprising as she herself was partly to blame. After all, this was someone who, during a pause in the rehearsal of Mravinsky, would climb on stage and poke her finger into the score: "Listen, Zhenya, the orchestra is playing well but you have really screwed up this part."

So Dinka achieved what she wanted. For a week she worked as a "stamp pigeon," placing stamps on concert tickets. Then she became a secretary in the control room. She had to call the musicians, telling them when and where they were scheduled to perform. She was earning as much as forty rubles a month, plus food stamps. Life was clearly turning into one continuous feast.

They gave lots of concerts everywhere, their music group always in demand. They performed in clubs, factories, plants, for workers during breaks. People craved art after having been deprived of it for too long. Several times she had to fill in for an announcer, preparing for each occasion as though she was a lead actor: memorizing her lines for flawless delivery, ransacking her suitcase for the finest dress, even working on her own style of movement on stage. She wanted that irresistibly charming look.

And she did get noticed. The Philharmonic's male employees began to frequent the control room, displaying clear signs of attention. Whenever she was allowed to actually organize concerts, many of the performers were eager to participate. She considered each of her admirers without committing to any, as though trying on gloves.

With Genrich it was mostly just running into each other in the hallway. Once, when she happened to come by the Rehearsal Hall, she caught a glimpse of him at the piano. He was big and solid looking, with the fine-shaped head of a thoroughbred race horse. "He is playing really well for an administrator!" she thought. "Well, he is probably out of my league anyway." Then, as she detected his initial signs of attention, she began to hope: "And what if it's serious?" But Genrich was tentative, circling her while keeping his distance. And she was not about to make the first move either for the fear of making him think she was easy. Meanwhile spring was already around the corner. "At this rate one may as well just grow old," she kept reproaching herself. And just then the Omsk chorus happened to arrive for a concert tour. The director, a rather handsome fellow, made a play for her. After once of the performances he invited her to a restaurant. This was courtship Siberian style – a 25 ruble tip to a cabbie, then dinner with Champaign and music, the works. Right on the spot he announced he wanted to marry her. She was flattered: no one proposed to her before. She said she needed time to think, kept imagining herself as a bride, all glamour and grace in a pink chiffon dress and white high-heeled shoes.

The next morning at work she told her friends: she is getting married and is leaving for Omsk in a week. This caused quite a stir. She was called into the Philharmonic's director's office.

"My dear Dina, could you please tell me what this is about? What do you even find in this chump?"

"Look, Afanasy Vasil'evich, you are married, Flaks and Mendelssohn and the others are married. And as for the younger ones, they are all airheads looking for fun."

"Well now, Dinka." He looked flustered. "I mean, this sort of language, coming from you…And just as we were thinking of placing you with our finest group. You know, you could easily make either head administrator or announcer…"

"Thanks but no thanks, I've already made up my mind."

"But what about Genrich? I do notice things, you know…And he is divorced, by the way."

"But I already promised…" She dropped her eyes."Do you realize I am no spring chicken? I am already twenty five, you know."

"So this is serious, huh?"

How odd that now she can't even remember the name of the man who once nearly altered the course of her life and her entire destiny. He arrived in a week, as promised, a huge bouquet of roses in his hand. There was a taxi waiting by the entrance.

"You haven't forgotten your passport, have you?"

She rummaged through her purse. Where could it be? She used to always carry it with her. They went back to her apartment and ransacked the place, all to no avail. He was trying to calm her down.

"Never mind, just call me once you get a new one and I'll fly right over."

He gave her his number. The following Genrich called her into his office.

"We are looking into forming a group for the summer trip to Kislovodsk. Is this something you could be interested in? It would give me a chance to see you in action during a tour."

"But I am about to get married. I am just waiting for…"

"Hasn't he left by now?" He casually handed her her passport. "You can't be too careful about such things, you know."

Dinka's jaw nearly dropped. Who could have seen *this* one coming! Finally it all clicked. But what a sweet surprise!"

"Yes, of course… It would be nice if you saw me in action… I mean, in a concert tour."

He blushed like a boy.

Taciturn and shy, not to mention eleven years Dinka's senior, Genrich turned out to be quite inexperienced when it came to expressing his feelings. At the beginning, consumed by curiosity, she tried repeatedly to break through the barely-opened door of his soul, only to encounter his light-yet-stubborn resistance. This fed into her growing doubt: would she be able to keep him? She became possessive, trying to spend each free minute with him while imagining all sorts of hidden threats each time his name was mentioned in quiet tones in the hallway.

One thing was clear: they had to seize the day. She spoke with the *Evropeiskaya* restaurant about letting them pay with food stamps for dinner meals. The food was nothing special but the service and the ambiance were a cut above the rest. On weekends she dragged him to *Nevsky*. They ate pastries at *Norse* and bought freshly-baked crème buns. Sometimes he took her to *Astoria* where they always served his favorite – cod fried Polish style – and which also had extra space for dancing. What a splendid couple they made! He, slender as a tree; she, flitting next to him like a butterfly. Everyone threw them admiring glances.

He proposed in May. She'd been holding her breath, waiting for this moment. She burst into tears, threw her arms around his neck.

"I can't. You know what I am, the Enemy of the People. I wouldn't want to get you in trouble."

He drew her toward him in an embrace that seemed to tell her he'd never let her go.

"This makes two of us. My father's been branded a "bourgeois," just because he used to keep a pharmacy on *Nevsky*. So we'll go down together if it comes to it…But for now I wouldn't worry about it."

The wedding was private, with only the closest friends and relatives for guests. Dinka tried her hand at baking, treating them to a pie that would soon become her specialty.

For three years he kept her close even as she began, vaguely, to crave new things. Each summer the Philharmonic performers and theater actors headed south for gigs in hastily-formed groups. The money wasn't great but when the concert tour was over they could usually find some spot to relax and carouse around. Having overheard their artistic director talking of putting together a group, she set out to persuade Genrich.

"You yourself wanted to see me in those big tours. So there is a bunch of artists going to Odessa and Kislovodsk with the 'Night of Musical Comedy.' Nikolai Yanet will be there, Ardi from *Tovstonogovsky* will be there. And then you could come and join us in Kislovodsk, it'll be our vacation."

He tried to talk her out of it. There were always all sorts of issues with these groups. Someone gets sick, someone hasn't yet found a pair. She kept at it, brushing away his excuses, cajoling. "Please, Genriysha, do this for me."

Finally he had to give in. He knew that once she set her sights on something she'd always get her way.

There were huge fliers and show-bills all over the city. 'Leningrad *Artistes*,' 'Perikolla,' 'Nikolai Yanet.' Their morning concert on *Deribasovskaya* was sold out. During the performance, however, Dinka noticed that her appearances drew an odd response from the Odessa crowd. Each number was met by thin applause and even a few jeers. She tried listening closely to what was happening on stage. The young tenor filling in for Yanet, who had fallen sick, could barely be heard in his duet with Perikolla. She for her part was singing fairly well but was a clumsy sort, a woman with mustache and hair in a bun who for some reason recoiled from her partner whenever he was about to embrace her. As it turned out, the two were having an affair but had just broken up earlier that morning. And then there was Ardi, pummeling away at the piano in an apparent attempt to impersonate an entire orchestra, and the two erstwhile ballerinas, Irka and Kalmykova, who were dancing up a storm, whirling their skirts and wildly kicking up their legs. With all this going on it was small wonder that only Lebedev's stand-up comedy bits drew a response. Indeed, you could never go wrong with humor in Odessa.

After the concert Kozak, the chief administrator, came tumbling in and ran right up to her.

"Zaven wants to see you tomorrow morning. Be there at nine, sharp."

Zaven Tarumov, the Director of the Philharmonic, spoke with her in a stern manner of a teacher lecturing a misbehaving student.

"I am sorry but concerts like these won't fly here. This is Odessa, you know. We've already taken down the show-bills and you can get paid at the Bursar's. By noon you should be all packed and waiting downstairs. We are sending you back today."

"But… what is this? What are we supposed to do now? The plan was, ten concerts here, then on to Kislovodsk. Ardi has already sent his wife there."

"Too bad for him. Nothing I can do."

"But my husband and I have also made plans…Genrich…

"Ah, so Genrich is your husband?" He threw her a quizzical look. Couldn't he dump this stuff… somewhere closer to home?" He picked up the phone. "Genrich? Listen, what is this sorry excuse for a team you've sent us? Yes…Yes, I see… Damn right you dropped the ball. You want me to let them stick around? Well, even if I do, you are not getting off this easily. And you are not afraid to leave your wife all alone?... Well, all right then…But remember, I am only doing it for you."

He summoned Kozak.

"Dima, can you help us sort this thing out? Genrich is asking if we could put them up somewhere till Kislovodsk. Why don't you look into Izmail. Can you expedite their papers?"

"I'll try, but no promises."

Seems like a close call, she thought. Still, when she got back she told everyone to start packing – they were being sent back to Leningrad. This had everyone up in arms. They immediately ganged up on her, yelling that it was all her fault, that she should have stuck up for them, should have raised hell. She shot back with whatever barbs she could summon.

Dima was back by five, carrying their papers, steamboat tickets and some of the rescued playbills. He'd managed to set up two concerts for them in Izmail, he said, after which they were on their own. As he was boarding a bus after dropping them off at the pier, he turned to look back at her.

"You know, sister, you gave me one hell of a headache with this thing. Next time try to take care of everything yourself. You've got to keep it tight in our line of work."

Many times after that, whenever he was dispatched to pick up their troupe at either the airport or the railway station, he would always greet her first among the entire bunch. "There she is. You got it going on, girl!" "Just trying to keep it tight," she'd shoot back.

There were still four hours left till the boat's departure. They had to wait there with their bags packed and languish in sweltering heat. She decided to take a leisurely stroll down the quay. You had to keep your distance to show them who is calling the shots. Plus, it gave her the chance to admire that white motorboat by the far end of the landing, a real beauty next to the retched old tug by its side. She spotted a sailor scrubbing the deck.

"You know who's in charge of this boat?"

"The Commander-in-Chief of the Fleet."

She figured chances were low but it was still worth a shot. Getting past the guard wasn't easy; she had to nearly push her way into the cabin.

"How can I help you?" The Commander put down his paper and wiped the sweat off his brow.

"There are some musicians over by the pier, all huddling on their suitcases and stewing in this heat. They are supposed to be back on stage tomorrow but must wait five hours for the boat to Izmail. They are all well-known, celebrated artists, by the way."

He was staring silently, as if she were a manikin in a store window. She guessed right away that there was no counting on Genrich this time; she had to go it alone. She knew what would work on any man: a subtle gesture here, a coy glance there. But something about this man's smoldering gaze told her he was half-hers already.

"I mean, just think of it. The heat. The famous artists, all packed and ready to go. The public performance tomorrow. And you've got your boat here standing idly by."

"Hmm... This surely isn't right. How long did you say you were planning on staying in Izmail?"

"Ten days."

"Then we just might be able to solve this." He flipped through the calendar, calculating. – "Well, let's see. Unless something comes up during the week, the boat is all yours. There is plenty of room, so all of you can stay. And I assure you our cook could give any restaurant chef a run for his money."

"Wow." She was nearly dumbfounded. "I don't even know how to thank you." Immediately she regretted it: what if he wanted something then and there? May be she had taken it a bit too far after all. But no, her misgivings proved unfounded: he turned out to be a real gentleman who knew how to handle himself.

"Just let me know if you have another concert in Odessa. I promise you I'll come."

In the end he wished her luck and even asked one of his men to drive her back to the pier. It felt terrific to be able to drop casually after stepping out of the car a few minutes later: "All right, everyone pick up your things, we are getting on that white boat."

She got busy immediately upon their arrival in Izmail – distributed show-bills throughout the city, spent half a day on the phone trying to set up more concerts. Things got rolling; they even got a few spots in nearby villages. She was selling tickets, Ardi doubled as a checker to make sure no one sauntered in from the street. Nearly every night, no matter how later they got back, he played his accordion while they danced after dinner.

They performed pretty much everywhere, even at the customs office where they were offered a tour of a contraband goods store after the show. Before they could clean the place out she warned that first she was spending some of their shared earnings on gifts for Tarymov and Dima. Just let them try and protest, she thought. But everyone took it in stride, apparently sensing her resolve.

Ah, the memories. You want so much to linger here or there but time keeps pressing on, your memory suffers lapses, events shift back or forth in time, names get all confused. You feel as though you were jumping from one block of ice on to another, terrified of falling into the cold, dark water below...

Another trip comes to mind. The program was billed as 'A Night of Ballet,' but some vocal and instrumental items were included as well. She was trying to get Misha Koric to join them: an aristocrat and a pedant, he was also an accomplished piano accompanist for ballet dancers. At first he tried to brush her aside.

"Ple-e-e-ase. Why would I want to do that?"

"Look, it's such a beautiful place. There is a bus tour from Sochi to Erevan. When are you going to get another chance?"

"But I hate sightseeing. I'd rather go stay at my *dacha*."

Somehow she managed to talk him into it.

So there he was in his white suit, sitting in the front of the bus. Behind him a thicket of ballerinas' legs rose up like a bunch of sticks – they'd plopped their feet on the back of the seats as soon as they got on the bus, presumably to keep the muscles fresh for the evening show. They were barely out of the city when thick clouds of road dust burst in through a hole in the rusty bottom of the bus. You couldn't open the windows either, they turned out to have been nailed shut. Everyone got loud and indignant but in the end they had no choice but to keep moving. Misha did not drop a word for most of the ride, he just kept sighing and fanning himself with a handkerchief. Then he suddenly let loose.

"Fucking hell. Some tour, huh?"

It turned out the hotel was fully booked, so they had to stay right at the theater. The staff brought in some beds and mattresses. Each morning the girls went out for some exercise and insisted that she join them.

"Come work out with us, you've got to keep in shape while you're still young."

A guard would often come by. He'd sit on the floor by the entrance and watch, shaking his head in disapproval.

"Listen," he would say to her. "They are all so scary-looking, just like sticks, nothing upstairs, nothing downstairs. And you, you've got e-e-e-verything about you. So what do you need their...this... thing for? Why ruin your life? You put them in a, what do you call it, a *fly*, no Armenian man will look. So you don't come here. Let them kick up their legs. You'd think the evening is enough – but no, they must do this in the morning too. Makes me sick just looking at them."

Now those remote days came to her as part of some eternal holiday. They were always on the move, always in the thick of things. She could still summon it all: the flicker of scenery in the windows of buses and trains, their scrim of images dashing by like stage sets. That tingle of excitement before her turn on stage. And every trip, a race where ultimate prize awaits her at the finish line: Genrich waiting at the station, a bouquet of flowers in his hand, solid and strong and always a bit bashful, like a schoolboy on his first date. And those enchanting White Nights...And the pleasure she took at gradually awakening his senses. How easily she could let herself go back then.

After Genrich was gone Lyova, trying to persuade her to go away with him and sensing her resistance, talked mostly of the uncanny resemblance of their fates, of how together it would be easier to cope with the loss of mates, of how change of scene would help her heal. As for him, he would be there for her no matter what – a true, devoted and unselfish friend. But just a few months later, after one of their parties wound down and the guests had left, he suddenly launched into a desperate romantic scene. Throwing himself at her feet and, pressing his grey head against her knees, he kept mumbling something about his need of a woman's touch. The poor wretch nearly drove her to tears, and, finally wresting herself free of his prickly embrace, she ran away and locked herself in the bedroom. She could hear him totter about the room, pace around by her door as he begged her to let him in. Suddenly she found herself gasping for breath, overcome by a fear more terrible than the one she felt during her parachute jump. For half a night she tossed and turned, and when she finally fell asleep out of sheer exhaustion, she dreamed of spring on the Neva. She was running toward the shore, hopping about like a sparrow, fearful of falling into the dark freezing water. Suddenly she saw Genrich. He is standing by his white piano, wearing his military coat, his hands livid from cold, his legs nearly knee-deep in water. "I am here, Genriysha," she cries. "Take me with you!" And that's when she woke up. Gray dawn was already breaking outside. She strained for the sounds from the living room, but everything seemed quiet. She stepped out into the kitchen, washed the dishes, careful to not make any noise, and tiptoed toward Lyova's room to take a peek inside. He was sleeping with his boots still on. She contemplated the sight for a minute. Under the shock of hair on his temple, a black mole resembling a giant wood-louse. A hooked, sharply protruding nose. Between the sunken cheeks, the gurgling cavern of the mouth. In a glass of water on the night table a pair of pink dentures flashed its predatory grin. Next to it, an array of medicine bottles, including an open vial of sleeping pills. Out of some obscure impulse she snatched it and, clutching it in her hand, went back into the kitchen. There she poured herself a glass of wine to soothe her nerves. Mechanically, as though not knowing what else to do, began to water the flowers…

Lyova woke up because of the burning in his stomach. Having fumbled in vain for his bottle of water on the night table, he headed for the kitchen. The door to Dina's bedroom was half-open. He peered inside. The bed in disarray, the pillow on the floor, the small body in an odd, contorted position. He entered cautiously.

"Dinulya."

He touched her hand. It was quite cold.

"Dina, are you asleep?" His throat felt dry. "Come on, Dina, wake up!"

79

He dashed to the phone and called an ambulance. He was so shaken, he could barely pronounce his address...

She was in a coma for two days. The doctors said the prognosis was grim: even if she regained consciousness, her speech, awareness, movement...well, there were no guarantees. Lyova wouldn't leave her bedside, feeling lost, devastated by the prospect of living without her. But the very next day she suddenly came to and whispered, motioning weakly with her hand.

"They are all lying, you know."

"Who?! What?!" He rushed towards her.

"The priests...They are all lying...There is nothing there...It's cold and dark, that's all."

"Oh, thank God, Dinochka, thank God," he muttered, kissing her hands.

Following the attempt something seemed to have shifted in her outlook. The figure of Genrich, for so long the erstwhile guardian of the tottering fortress of her soul, had finally receded to assume its rightful place among the rest of her significant others. She began to pay more attention to her health, visited doctors and followed their regiments. Her life, while far from exciting, was quietly following its course. Yet there were still days when something seemed to push, or rather, irresistibly pull her downward. Deep down at her core she could feel some feral, fluid force beginning to stir as though in recompense for that chaste life to which she'd felt unfairly condemned. At such times she was overcome by some strange feeling, a mix of desire, loathing and fear. She was haunted by a recurring dream: she is in bed with a stranger, his caress so passionate and tender, while Lyova is standing nearby and quaking all over like a trapped mouse. She would wake up feeling irritable, looking to find fault with and humiliate him or else threatening to leave for good and go stay with her relatives in Germany. She would end up going out and browsing her favorite boutique shops where she could console herself by trying on fancy outfits.

Lyova got used to this pretty soon. He waited for her patiently, bought flowers, got down on his knees and recited well-rehearsed speeches, careful not to lay it too thick lest he scare her off once more and ruin everything – he knew she would never fall for that sort of thing.

She responded by acting doubly considerate toward him: making all sorts of new dishes in the kitchen, washing and ironed his clothes, trying to make up to him and own up to her fault. So he could finally relax, take it easy and even enjoy life. He would pour over the papers for hours, sprawled in his cozy chair and drifting from time to time into a light, pleasant sleep.

Whenever she opened her scrapbook, each picture instantly invoked a whole page of her life. Here's Nikolai Cherkasov, the first of their artists to visit India. He went on to write stories about this mysterious country and to read them on stage. Once she managed to talk him into going on a trip with her: Tartu, Tallinn, Pyarnu. Before they left, his wife Nina turned to her with a request.

"Would you please keep an eye on him? You shouldn't cut him too much slack. He likes to blow off steam after a concert."

Tartu. Winter. After a concert at the city university they were offered a cab ride.

"No, no, thank you. We'd rather walk, the hotel really isn't that far."

They barely began walking when they saw a horse-drawn carriage riding toward them. The coachman was wearing a top hat and an embroidered wadded jacket. Cherkasov waved him down.

"Are you free?"

He handed her the flowers and flipped open the carriage top. They sat next to each other, like a bride and a groom.

"So, how much is this going to cost me, my dear fellow?"

The old man shrugged as if unsure.

"Whatever you are willing to spare...All I need is some oats for my horse. These days they mostly travel by taxi. Not like in the old days... My father was a coachman, and so were my grandfather and grand-grandfather. And me, I am the last one in all of Estonia."

"And tell me, my dear man, what do you pay for a bag of oats?"

"Oh, that's expensive! Anywhere from twenty..."

"Then here's thirty. Why don't you buy your filly a bag of oats."

The man tipped his top hat and cracked his whip.

"Then she is ready to drive you around town all night."

In Pyarnu they had another little adventure. The small hotel had only one spare single room. Cherkasov found it funny.

"So we'll stay in a single. I am not the dangerous type."

The folding bed was set up, the sheets brought in. He called his wife.

"Ninochka, Dina and I are staying in the same room. Nothing... Oh no, she is a good girl. Too bad she wouldn't let me drink though."

Somewhere down the road he had managed to grab hold of a green bottle of liquor. She found it and hid it while he was taking a shower, burying it deep under the mattress. For nearly half the night he patiently reasoned with her, explaining eloquently why she should give it back: because she should never interfere with a well-established course of events; because as an artist she was bound to appreciate the importance of the final touch after a well-spent day; because an unopened bottle would only play into any woman's fears – his wife would only suspect he had abandoned one vice to embrace another. And so on.

Dinka kept breaking into titters. Curled up in bed with a blanket pulled over her head, she had to struggle to fall asleep. Woken up by some noise in the middle of the night, she suddenly found herself imagining his slender fingers slipping under the blanket and sliding over her hips and breasts while groping for that divine vessel under the mattress. Now she was scared: "Come on Dinka, get a grip, you are losing your mind." She took out the bottle and put it gingerly on the floor, pushing it some distance away from the bed.

Many of the others in her album she couldn't even remember. The names got erased like those on tombstones, flushed from memory without a trace. But those she held most dear, those she loved and admired, remained alive inside her.

Here's the picture Shulzhenko gave to Genrich. Her autograph underneath: "That's how I looked when we first met."

Here's the young Pauls – "love's sad fount," as someone famously called him.

Vertinsky, already after his return. She used to be the host for many of his shows. "Listen, could you please explain something to me. I just don't get it. They keep deducing some loan fee from my wages. What is this loan fee?" "Well, they are taking it not just from you, but from each of us. It's like you are temporarily giving them some money for the welfare of the state." "But what if I don't want to?"

Maksim Shostakovich, at his debut concert. Dmitri Dmitrievich was sitting in front row. He was so anxious, he looked like he was about to faint. They had to be constantly fetching him some water.

Lyudochka Zykina. She still calls sometimes. "Dinulya, you know I've always been crazy about that unforgettable soup of yours. When are you coming over to visit? You could stay with me at my dacha, just like old times." When on a concert tour with her, Dina used always bring a cooking pan, a frying pan and a hotplate. She still keeps the concert dress she got from her – a gift from the Japan tour. She also brought shoes that turned out to be two sizes big. A month before Genrich died, she sent him a parcel for the New Year – caviar and a pair of woolen socks she'd knit for him.

His brainchild, the Leningrad Concert Hall, quickly became popular, attracting lots of big names. There were performances by Retsepter, Victor Pikaizen, Mark Reizen, Utyosov, Piekha and Seryozha Yursky; debuts by Lena Obraztsova, Zhvanetsky, Kartsev and Ilchenko; concerts by the Moscow Conservatory graduates; season subscription events for young audiences. Lots of artists dreamed of appearing on his stage. Some of them got shot down while others became objects of his relentless pursuit.

She took a letter out of a yellowed envelope.

"…I honestly don't know what to tell you regarding the possible dates for a concert in your Hall. Things have been so hectic and my schedule once again so packed that I simply lack the power, not to mention the know-how, to change anything. Here is a brief outline of my plans.

February 3RD – 10TH: concerts in Lvov;

10TH – 14TH: rehearsals for the symphony orchestra concert in Moscow I am conducting;

15TH – 22ND: rehearsals for the opening performance of Ernst Mayer's new violin concerto;

From February 25TH through March 15TH I am going to be in GDR. Immediately upon return I am beginning to rehearse with the National Orchestra as a conductor for the March 21ST concert;

23RD and 24TH: recording with Igor;

On the 25th, leaving for France and Italy till either the 15th or the 16th of April;

On April 19TH, beginning rehearsals with the Moscow Philharmonic Orchestra for the trial run of the US tour programs. The preliminaries are to be performed in Ryazan somewhere in the end of the month – 5- 6 rehearsals followed by 3 concerts. I am not including my season subscription engagements in Moscow and Leningrad since I am not even sure I'll be able to keep them. Most likely some of the programs will have to be pushed back to the next season – which unfortunately will *not be any easier since the England – the US tour alone should keep me busy from early October through late December. And then there's the Conservatory! At this rate one could easily lose one's wits.*

Nevertheless, I intend to stick to my promise, and the only time I can possibly think of is the beginning of May. I'll be glad if this works for you.

I should be In Moscow on the 2ⁿᵈ of February. If possible please call me in the evening (I am leaving again on the 3ʳᵈ) so we could discuss this further...

Hugs to you and best regards to your wife.
Sincerely yours,
David Oistrakh."

Dmitri Dmitrievich's handwriting is angular, growing more illegible over the years. The album still contains a few of his letters as year after year Genrich used to open the season with the maestro's concert.

July, 1967. "*...Sorry about the long delay in answering your letter. To be fair, it's not entirely my fault: I've been sick, out of Moscow, etc. Assuming things are fine with me, I'll be sure to come for the season opening; it would be a great honor and a very happy occasion indeed. In the meantime am sending my best regards. Yours, D. Shostakovich."*

August, 1968. "*...Thank you for your letter and an invitation for the September nineteenth concert. I'll certainly try to make it, assuming nothing urgent intervenes..."*

September, 1973. "*...Unfortunately my heath has taken a turn for the worse. I am having real trouble walking; getting up and sitting down is also extremely difficult. And my mental state really alarms me, especially when I find myself in a crowded place. Please accept my apologies..."*

August, 1974. "*...Thank you for your invitation to attend the season opening. Due to my chronic illness I have been largely confined to my apartment, so I am in no shape to travel. Many thanks once again, and please extend my heartfelt gratitude to all of the artists taking part in the concert. I shake your hand firmly and am sending my best wishes..."*

It wasn't long after that Genrich too got his notice from beyond – his first stroke. "Guess we are in for the coda," he'd quip ruefully. She begged him to slow down, even to consider a career change. He promised to think about it. But the minute things seemed to improve he was back in the saddle. And who knows, maybe if he took her advice he wouldn't go on to live another ten years, years filled with those magic, unforgettable encounters on stage to which, as to an altar, every one of his guests always brought their very best...

For a whole month now she's had pains in her legs and an unbearable sharp ache in her back that does not abate even at night. The old wound on her leg has opened once again – it had to be wrapped in bandages right up to her knee. They've been giving her something in spinal injections – supposedly the last resort. She is like a little bird in a cage, hopping from one perch onto the next – bed, bathroom, couch, bed. Poor Dinka, what have you turned into. If only she could spread her wings once more, could break out of what had long ceased to resemble a life and simply dash away – somewhere far, far away... But where? Not Paris, not Hawaii... *Peter*! Yes, back to Peter... To breathe that keen morning air by the river, to stroll down Nevsky, scanning the crowd for the faces of dear ones the way you sift through the sand when looking for amber beads...

What an insane idea though.

She should try to make herself something to eat, to boil some soup may be. Or do the laundry – the curtains are all dusty...

Then: the shrieking of an ambulance siren... The screeching of brakes... The slamming of doors...The interminable hallways with their white walls... At each turn someone is holding up her head. "Let me go!" she screams. "I can't take this pain any more. Lyova, where are you?!" "Calm down, Ma-am, it's all right. Everything is going to be alright. Just calm down...She needs some morphine ...morphine, yes... The double dose..."

An intensive care unit. Dina's got tubes and electrode wires all over her body. There's the IV line, the heart-lung machine. In the next room, the doctors have reached a consensus: due to considerable brain damage recovery is practically impossible. Besides, they have the patient's Living Will, signed about a year earlier. The statement is unambiguous: if pronounced to be in persistent vegetative state, it is the patient's wish that she be taken off life support.

No more than a handful of people – only the closest friends – have gathered in the hospital room. Someone has brought a violin. Incongruously, we all feel as if she is about to sit up in bed and start talking to everyone...After all, this has already happened to her once.

"We are right here with you, Dinulya. Come on, sweetheart, you can fight this thing."

"That's right, we'll show them yet!"

"Look, she is dancing!"

"She's squeezing my hand."

"She is crying..."

...In the middle of the room some guests have gathered by the empty table. I look around: not one familiar face. Still, it somehow feels as though she were around. She could easily be in the kitchen, arguing with someone while making patties. On the frying pan they begin to crumble, the stuffing is about to get burnt.

"Retsepter?... Of course, his *Monoteater* version of Hamlet was pure genius. But he raised the bar too high, after that in the theater he could reach quite the same level. And it tells, too – throughout his book he keeps constantly reverting to his earlier hero. What's that? You disagree?... I can't hear you! Ah... Yes, that's true, but I am not into that sort of thing. Now Seryozha Yursky on the other hand – he is really a cut above... You know, I've been meaning to call him and congratulate on something – I just can't seem to remember on what...But you've gotten awfully quiet. You don't agree?...Yes, I remember... But it is no use to be arguing with me on that score. Seryozha is phenomenally gifted. Marvelous, just marvelous. Anyway, listen, can you feel this rhythm? This is Genrich playing his piano. I need some light in here, could you turn up the lights? You are not letting me see him. I see the curtain is going up...My turn. Quick, composer, title. 'Diubiuk. Little B-iu-rd.' *Little B-iu-rd...* But what are those voices out in the hall? I can still hear them..."

Dina lived another week. On August tenth, without regaining consciousness, she died.

Savannah, Georgia.

WHERE THE LIGHT...

Having come down from the high hills, covered with slender forests almost impassable because of brambles and fern, the road, framed with flowering grasses (yarrow, mint, poppies), merges imperceptibly into a narrow street passing small manicured fields interspersed with meadows where old apple trees grow to revitalize the landscape. The severe medieval appears before you: the buildings that have two floors, the windows looking like loopholes and hidden from prying eyes, the high wooden shutters that were blackened by time, the tiled roofs which necked downward and were covered with moss in places. Just below there is a round plaza with a simple fountain, a post office, a shop, a hotel with 8 beds – the second floor, an entrance from the yard, with heavy oak gates which closed the whole gap and were fettered like an old fortresses. On the ground floor, there is a restaurant and hostess's rooms. It is neither a city, nor a village.

The tower clock repeats each hour twice with a two minutes delay, so even if you're in a hurry – you won't be late. Here is a Roman Catholic Church looking like the large wreckage of a sunken ship that has grown into the ground, which once used to be the seabed, like a great gray hulk. It's always closed, but illuminated from below until eleven in the evening by two spotlights. Their light goes out, and immediately, as soon as your eyes adjust to the darkness, you start to guess some movement near it, the rustling of wings, as if the spirits of ancestors have become alive and flocked to the old church from all over. Next to the church, as a contrast to it, there is someone's homestead built in a contemporary style. You can often hear the sounds of violin and piano from there.

Several years ago, at a distance from it, a new church was built – the Church of the Holy Transfiguration, which bordered a convent courtyard. The murals inside the new church are almost completed - a pure, soft coloring and mature style. To the left of the entrance there are some bells under a small canopy. On the right side, there is a door to the women's monastery – a former landlord's possession. Through a broad, squat hall with numerous large and small icons, illuminated by hundreds of candles, which was fitted once, 60 years ago, for church services, you walk in a spacious courtyard with two rows of lime trees that were pruned to have the similarity of candles, but lately formed a head of young green leaves. There are two or three parked cars between them. In the shade, there are a few chairs and a table. Here you can rest. Novices will offer you tea or coffee. The door to the monastery is always open. Everyone can look into it. Look closely at the faces of the nuns passing by. They are friendly, accustomed to visiting guests. And if they haven't received blessing from Mother Olga's for "obedience" and they're not in a hurry to go into the kitchen or to the garden to pick fruits and vegetables, they will come over to meet the visitors for a while and ask polite questions like the place you come and what is currently happening in the world. They are simple, open, friendly and ready to compassion.

If you got to this place by accident, stay for a little while, adjust your ears using a tuning fork of living "in simplicity", and you'll hear how the long forgotten childhood fluids emerge from the depths of your consciousness: the strawberry smell of a parent day holiday, the tar smell of fir branches when you run away from the camp passing through the checkpoint counselor as you run to meet your family.

More than half a century ago in this small Burgundian village, within the quiet sanctuary of Catholic France a few women decided to organize a Russian monastery. They were nuns forced to leave their homeland (Mother Evdokia (Courtin), Mother Blandina (Obolensky), Mother Theodosia (Solomyansky) and another female Greek worshipper who recently joined them), sisters not by blood but in spirit who where enthusiastic about the idea of a Russian religious revival. They dreamed of a monasticism open to the world and modern culture, going to the people with love and compassion.

The big neglected house was gifted to them by a law professor whose name was Boris El'yashevich. The gift demanded enormous effort to turn it into a monastic cloister. There was no money to do the repairs, and the sisters worked hard in the field and in the garden to somehow survive. There were moments it seemed they wouldn't bear it, but Mother Evdokia who was the first abbot of the monastery, was able to arrange things so that soon their asceticism was widely known and when this occurred, pilgrims and wanderers tailed to the convent, some of them just out of curiosity, but the most were broken by life, those who felt uncomfortable in this world and looked for support and protection within Orthodoxy.

The novices, who arrived from afar, were taught Russian and surrounded with attention and care. The newcomers didn't always easily join the life of the monastery. Brought up in different cultural traditions, often with difficult temperaments, still prisoners of worldly passions, with the desire to establish themselves, sometimes to impose their will – Mother Evdokia took within her heart all of them, she could forgive and taught them how to be humble. She became a mother to many of them. The villagers remember her with love. They remember how she arranged a Christmas tree in the house, how she with her sisters prepared gifts for the village children.

After her death, one of the founders of the convent, Mother Theodosia, who possessed an overbearing temperament and realized it, didn't want to be elevated to the status of the head of the convent for a long time, she considered herself unworthy of her predecessor. She sought for liberation of her spirit in constant prayers, grueling fasting, heavy and simple labor. Often, after all-night vigils she slept in her chair. In the winter time, she used to get up long before matins and, having cut wood, she put it next to each cell (as they still heated with wood). Always caring for others, she was strict on herself. When she felt upcoming weakness, she was very adamant in her decision to retire because she was afraid her senility would become a burden to all...

Mother Olga is now the abbess here. She took care of the convent before the death of Mother Theodosia. Even before, under her order, she nearly ran the monastery and was not afraid to take responsibility when solving urgent problems. Educated, soft-hearted by nature, always tactful, able to support and help overcome the difficult path to a new life. She gives the women in the monastery the freedom to express themselves, looks for undiscovered talents believing that the Creator gives the part of Himself to everyone at birth. "Whomever you meet on your way," she likes to say, "come with love. He was sent to you by God and is the image of God. Learn to see and love Christ in each of them."

After the morning service, you are invited to drink tea with jam made from the fruit from their own garden. On their table there are cheese, butter, fresh French bread and honey from their Holy Father's hives.

"Does everyone have enough?" asks novice Svetlana when she passes the tables. "There is a plum pie left after yesterday's dinner. We must save it. Who would like some?"

Don't balk. It's very tasty.

Nuns have their tea in the bigger refectory. They have dinner there as well, but after the liturgy they are all together at the table - sisters, pilgrims and visitors. They serve wine with dinner on holy day.

Father Athanasius is cheeked and giggly, he's not yet thirty. If he stuck a beard and mustache on his face and put a bag with gifts on his shoulders, he would be the best person to go to the children at Christmas. After the meal, he used to go to the monastery courtyard, bless everyone, carefully pick the right words for each person and ask for how long they would be visiting and where they came from.

"Oh! You are from Ukraine! I studied there at the Theological Seminary of the Kiev Pechersk Lavra and then served in the Carpathians in a convent. The abode was high in the mountains. It was a wonderful place. Clean cold streams, great spaces, silence. The grace of God... But also those simple notorious aunts." He laughs. "They all know from birth what should be and should not be, what right and what wrong is. It was so difficult with them. Simplicity, it is, in fact, also different. Sometimes, I felt myself a recluse in the convent. It's different here. We are like a family, and we work, worry and take holidays together. Together we share our shelter and earthly food. Many sisters, who had great trials in their lives, have found solace and protection in the monastery. We delight in helping them regain their selves... The souls of people will always remain a mystery and the miracle of miracles. Nobody knows where they come from and where they go after our demise. It is very hard to save this fragile divine vessel within this earthly world. Having tempted vanity and pride, in the rush of doing, we often take the wrong steps and lose landmarks..."

There is something in the words of the priest that attracts you. This soft voice of pure spirit and this celebration of life within his eyes. It makes you feel like you're endearing his charms, yet you still resist.

"Father, but what about those rulers who rob and kill people, who are greedy, cruel and merciless, who frequently make the sign of the cross before the altar?"

"We try to help everyone who wants to be on the way to cleanse, strengthen awakened faith in their souls."

"Now in fact, it has become fashionable to be a believer after decades of prohibitions and persecutions. Whether their faith is true? Are they ready to follow the commandments, or at least repent of their deeds?"

"Let us be patient. The path to Faith is not easy, and everyone is entitled to choose his or her own way."

"But our life is but a brief moment of consciousness, beyond which is the incomprehensibility of eternity, and all earthly roads lead to the same end!"

"We are called to bring light to the people and the goodness in this world, and if within the last hour our hearts are filled with love, we will take it not in fear, but in goodness."

"I would like to meet with you, out there on the passage."

Forgiving your *faux pas*, he smiles.

"All is in the hands of our Lord."

Having made the sign of cross over us, he passes amidst the huddled small groups of parishioners and leave the cloister. There, across the road at the far end of the garden, in a former garage of Mother Olga with Michael's help who is an irreplaceable jack of all trades within the monastery, he built a cozy reclusory. He installed a stove for heating in the winter, planted tiny flowers in the courtyard, as he had done at home, in a Romanian village near the Ukrainian border, where he was treated kindly and had grown up in the church under the supervision of five sisters. Here in the monastery everybody liked Athanasius because of his pleasant, soft voice, soft melodious pauses at the end of each prayer, giving mood to the singers, for his smile, which had probably thrived in its infancy and never condescended from his lips.

The Church of the Holy Transfiguration is light inside. There are fresh paintings on the walls. Disembodied faces of the saints are like thin, transparent vessels, each of which, if you look closely, is filled with light. In the dome, above all, the Almighty, the archangels are beneath, below - the prophets, and in the triangular sails - four Evangelists.

Yaroslav, dressed in his working clothes smeared with paint, with a graying head, which had not been cut for a long time, brings you to the scaffolding at the side wall.

"There will be two more holidays here: "The Resurrection" and "The Descent of the Holy Spirit". Down below – "The Communion of the Apostles". In the dome - holidays in detail. In the heart – "The Holy Transfiguration". In the forechurch, which is separated only with poles, you can see a picture of the various events in the Old Testament, the first day, the second and the third day, the creation of animals and man, as well as God's resting. Ibid is the expulsion from paradise, Ilya ascending on the chariot, and Moses receiving the Tablets of the Covenant."

His voice is low, smooth, without nuances, but his look under his heavy, inflamed eyelids is tenacious, all-absorbing, it seems as if he zeroes in to a model standing in front of him.

"On the plate is Virgin Mary. Sometimes she is with the infant, like in St. Sophia in Kiev, sometimes she is standing or sitting on a throne. Here, when we enter the temple, she is covered with iconostasis a little. To make her visible, I just made her a baby from above."

Having felt some uneasiness in his last sentence, he looks around, but the church is empty by this moment.

"Somehow the nuns are not very zealous in their prayer."

Fatigue and cautious slowness are in his every movement.

"Is it hard to be alone?"

"Mother Colomba is returning today. She helps me sometimes. She's a former violinist. Ten years in the monastery. I love it when she regents during the service. The voices sound so clean and smooth..."

"It was very difficult when we painted the dome. It's not possible to put the scaffolding any closer. I had to lie on the table and outline the lineaments with a long bamboo stick with a piece of coal tied to the end of it. It is not easy after a stroke. My hand was getting numb, sweat burned my eyes. Now I see where I could fix it, but it's hard to move this big chandelier again..."

"Tell us a little about yourself."

"I am an architect by training, but in the 60s and early 70s architecture was very boring, everybody built boxes. Therefore, I became a painter, worked in television, doing projects, sketches of background scenery. Then I became a member of the Artists' Union, not to be considered a social parasite. My wife worked there also. We scratched along somehow. I have loved icons since my youth, I didn't paint them, just admired, but then my financial worries seemed to increase. I started taking orders. Sometimes they came from individuals, sometimes from the church. In Vilnius, for example, I painted icons. In the 79th, before the Olympics in Moscow, the government allowed to repair the temples. In a church near Moscow we washed oil painting, very mediocre, maybe, 19th century. We decided to make new paintings in the closed altar. In caved places, we imitated the fragments of an older painting, photographed them and sent the photos to the Ministry of Culture in order to get permission to do the reconstruction of these fragments. But later on, the icon painter who received a blessing from the patriarch to work there and whom I helped, fell down the stairs, and I had to finish it alone."

"I taught for two years at the school of icon painting at the Academy, I painted with my students Semyonovsky temple. They ask me, "How?" "You may do it this way, but you also may do it that way." I could not say that it was necessary to paint only this way, and not otherwise. This is a special case, teaching. I like to work alone mostly..."

"It was good until 1992. We built new churches and opened old ones. Then there was inflation. Nobody paid money. It became impossible to live... I was offered a job in the south of France. And later my wife joined me, so I was happy... Nice temple, of Ivan of Athos... With my assistants we also painted two churches in Israel..."

"I have a good story to tell about the Cathedral of Christ the Savior in Moscow. They had reconstructed the upstairs in 19th century style and first floor of the Cathedral was new. If you know, the temple was built on a small hill. It was destroyed by the Bolsheviks, and they leveled the hill in this place, they wanted to build the Palace of Congresses or Soviets with a giant statue of Lenin stretched up to the clouds. It turned out that there were floaters there and the land would not keep it. They dumped a huge amount of concrete and iron piles, but then the war began. Metal was taken to be melted down, and this huge foundation remained. After the war they made a pool in the location. Evaporation from it began to harm nearby museums, and the mayor of Moscow supported the idea of rebuilding the temple. Because the hill was destroyed, but the structure had to be raised to the previous level, this foundation formed a huge emptiness. They partially were used for the lower church, which previously didn't exist. I painted three altars in it in 2003. Now there are so many painters that probably they forgot about me."

"Are there your icons, besides these magnificent murals?"

"Nor in this church, not in the old one. I came to think of that painting icons on request is like committing a sin. This is not a painting. This is, if you want, a special reflection of the soul. The strength of their impact, I think, is derived from how the painter cleanses before God. Go to the old church. All those icons, small icons were painted by these nuns. They are rather primitive in both color and pattern, but most of them are priceless... I don't paint icons currently... Now Mother Colomba came to help me, and we are still talking..."

Mother Elizabeth is in a white wimple, she's surrounded by tourists and visitors. We hear German and French language. Two deep wrinkles surround her young, inquisitive eyes that shine on her pale face. A child of the White emigration, a direct descendant of the ducal family, derived from the Empress Josephine, King of Bavaria, Russian Czar Nicholas I - we have a particular interest in her. Her demeanor is free and uninhibited but, at the same time, somewhat detached - she took it from her mother. And the tone of her voice, and unexpected bursts of her throaty laughter. As a gift of God, she keeps her mother's love in her heart, remembers all the stories about distant, mysterious Russia, captured within her memory as funny pictures of festive balls drawn by her childhood imagination, where the noble maidens, who had been brought up in severity, lost their heads in the arms of the brilliant cadets. And the other ones – scary stories not intended for children: their escape, how she narrowly escaped death threatened from the Bolsheviks at first, then from the Whites, then from their own people. How she said sadly, "God will judge them."

Leaning on her staff, Mother Elizabeth leads you into the monastery garden.

"Have you come from Florida? This is very far from here to fly by airplane. Do you like it there? It's nice to live near the sea, the air must be totally different. Only there are those... big waves... I lived in North Carolina for a few years, in Asheville. It's so hot there in the summer, but you can escape the heat by going to the mountains... This tree stands dangerously, totally tilted downward… I must say Misha." She spreads her family albums on a bare wooden table, gently turns the pages worn out by time. "This is the 21st year, when my mother and father left Russia. Here is their wedding in Rome. Have you been to Rome?... This is my father and grandmother in San Remo, and this is of a castle in Bavaria, which once was an old Benedictine monastery founded in the year 999. During Napoleon's time the monks were expelled, and it became a private possession..."

"The Russian branch of the Dukes of Lichtenberg started from the grandson of Empress Josephine of France, Maximilian, who took Grand Duchess Maria Nikolaevna for his wife, the daughter of Nicholas I, who consented to their marriage with the condition that Maximilian would serve Russia. All Russians in our family origin from there. I'm the last scion in this genus. Now, when I became quite old, I find it pleasant and sad to return to the past sometimes..."

"Here's a nice picture: Tsar Nicholas II, near him are my grandfather George and his brother Nicholay in a hussar uniform. In the 1917 in Russia he lost everything, he moved to Bavaria to live in our patrimony - the King of Bavaria's gift to Josephine's son, Eugene de Beauharnais who was the father of Maximilian. Immediately the emigrants began to visit him. There was a lot of space. They lived there for a long time."

"Grandpa gave them money and helped to move to France, to America. At the time, everyone hoped that Russia would rise again... Here are Nikita and Daniel Volkonsky, Wrangell, Repnin, mother and son Golitsyns. This is General Krasnov and his charming wife. He signed this photograph... "A good horse is under me, the Lord is above me." He loved to play hockey on the lake, and in the evening he came to our living room and read his memories, after which his mother fell into a depression. Do you see how awful he looks? She imagined the Bolsheviks throughout, all the time she lived in fear that someone would come and do something terrible. That fear was killing her..."

"Where did this fear come from? It's a long story... In the 18th she was still in Moscow, she wanted to participate in those events. She persuaded her uncle to take her into the organization "Glavsakhar", which had the purpose to recruit the volunteers and send them south to fight the peasants who had plundered the sugar factories. In fact, they secretly helped cadets and junkers under the guise of the Red Army to move to the White Army. Then they listed them as killed in battles. She was assigned as a nurse, though she knew little in this. She evinced the tendency to adventurism when she was still at the Institute for Noble Maidens. She told that she "cheated a little", by forging the signature of her mother, which allowed her to gain authorizations for Sunday Weekends. Then it was handy. Often she subscribed the trips instead of the political commissar, Kurochkin, who was deputed to supervise them. Soon they began to suspect them. She was arrested several times, and once she was nearly shot."

"They lived for a time on the train, and at one of the stops somewhere near Kursk, they went to a restaurant for breakfast - her mother, two cousins and her uncle. Someone ran into the restaurant and warned that people from the KGB had come and started to arrest everybody. They came back and were immediately arrested. Her uncle tried to explain something, asked them to let him to call to Moscow, but no one listened. They all were put in front of the car to be shot."

Her mother tried to be brave, she began telling them what a mistake they were making, that it was a misunderstanding. She feared they would see how her knees were trembling. She just talked and talked without ceasing. She didn't understand herself, where her words came from. She thought if she stopped talking, they all would be shot immediately. The KGB people wanted to blindfold them, but her mother refused. Their senior officer counted three times the command words… "One… two…", but she continued to urge them not to do so, that it was their mistake, and then they would regret… And suddenly they were released. They were held under arrest for three days, they sent her to a car to diagnose patients to determine what happened with them – they just checked. "Spanish flu" was in vogue then…

In the summer of the same year (her mother was already married), returning from their last business trip, they came under fire twice. In Bryansk, they were taken from the train at the station and her husband was arrested, they searched for Prince Chavchavadze, but her mother had forged the documents and changed their last name to Chichinadze, and it saved him. They realized that at the station in Moscow, they would be waited for. Just before the stop they succeed to jump out of the train.

They managed to escape from Moscow. There was a long, dangerous journey to their side. Mother tied her head with a scarf, trying not to show her beautiful, manicured hands. Yet, unfortunately, they carried two suitcases with them. It also betrayed them. There were just deserters in the boxcar - drunk, wild faces. They looked at them with suspicion, hostility. Somewhere in the field their train stopped. Everyone ran to the engineer to know the reason. They took advantage of it and threw out the suitcases.

Their flight was probably not immediately noticed. The cars were not lighted. Her husband ran to the village and when it got dark, he returned with a cart. They hid in the hayloft for several days, then the peasants helped them move closer to the south until they joined a string of carts that was going for salt. They stopped at a roadside inn – further on was the front line. Inside the inn there were many Red Army soldiers returning to the army. All of them were half drunk. The host looked like a robber, with a black patch over one of his eyes. It was a shame, she said, knowing they could be killed the three miles from their people, but there was no way out, and she decided to be open with their host, she gave him all the money she had, which was a tidy sum, and asked for help. He promised to forward them to the other side of the river that flowed nearby. There was the White Army there. They didn't sleep all night listening to the many-voiced beastly snoring of people lying side by side on the floor. Early in the morning, the host touched her shoulder – it was time. Trying not to graze anyone, they went into the yard and followed him to the river where they saw a boat. When they were on the other side, she told us, she wanted to sing and shout for joy. Her mother said to a rider, a Cossack, who came to them, "How happy we are to be on this side!" But their misfortunes did not end. They were arrested and taken to the headquarter for questioning.

The senior officer was Prince Golitsyn. From the beginning he seemed to be hostile towards them. The documents were false - mom had made them herself on the letterheads that they traded from the Red Army soldier for some cavalry jacket on the last day before leaving, - their last names, for fear of being disclosed, were modified. Besides, she noted that near the headquarter several soldiers were hanging around, with whom (she immediately recognized them) they rode in the same car. Probably they played the two sides at the same time. One said to the prince that he knew them, that her mother was a Commissioner who tortured white officers. She felt it was highly insulting that he could believe them. The further, the scarier. They were sent with two Cossacks on a cart to the main headquarter - where they were sure they would understand who they were. On the road in one village they arrested a man, they decided that he was a Jew. They stripped him to his underwear and drove him in front of them barefoot along a freshly mown rye field. He asked, "Please, don't shoot, don't kill me. I am not a Bolshevik, not a communist. Please don't shoot." She saw, when he fell, as his blood was running over his white shirt. "And you will be next," said the one that was riding behind. Probably Golitsyn allowed them: if they run - shoot.

About thirty officers were in the main headquarter, all of them were Cossacks. Her mother's husband was released after fifteen minutes, but they tortured her and interrogated her until midnight, everyone was waiting for her to tell something. One captain was particularly angry and sassy. She asked to call to Kiev to speak with Prince Chavchavadze, and he shouted, "We have no time to mess with you. There are two witnesses that have stated that you tormented white officers. At five in the morning we march off, and in half an hour you will be hanged in our backyard." It's a terrible feeling, she said, when you're not trusted. It wouldn't hurt so much to die from the hands of the Bolsheviks, but from our own people...

In the third hour of the night, when she lost all hope, the door opened and a tall general that wore a Circassian coat came in. He asked, "What's happened here? What are you doing with that girl?" "She's a spy." He took her to his room and asked who she was. Suddenly he remembered, "I used to meet your mom at dance class." This was the first time somebody talked to her so warmly. She burst into tears. The general reassured her, "Please, understand," he said, "whom this army was created of. Russian names don't specify anything for them. Cossacks are embittered and hardened, they saw how the Bolsheviks raped their wives, now they are ready to kill anyone who came from there, they don't believe anyone. General Brusilov's son died this way. No one knows what other sacrifices await us. May the Lord save you in this madness." He ordered the soldier, who was going on holiday, to guard them all the way to Kharkov, where the relatives of her husband lived, his mother and a younger brother...

Her husband immediately enlisted in the army, and within two weeks, they were sent to Yalta. The White Army retreated. It was October, and on December 18 (she learned about it much later from a nurse) he died of typhus fever in hospital...

"In Yalta, they lived through a year, which was hungry yet calm. My mother was pregnant. She did what many people did during this time, she sold her newest stockings in the bazaar, bought some anchovy, which is a small fish, dried the fish on threads upon the roof near the chimney. Friends of the family supported them as they could. My future father was among the people who helped support her. When the Reds broke through Perekop, he helped them to leave the country on an Italian merchant steamship. She told me how the officers at the port, who knew that they were leaving Russia forever, cried like children as they released their unsaddled horses... For a few days they slept in the hold, right on the floor, where the ship carried a supply of coal. The worst of all was the situation with water, and some ladies were horrified when she collected it drop by drop from the pipes in order to dilute canned milk for two months Irene. My father found them later in a small village near Trieste and made her an offer of marriage..."

Mother Elizabeth interrupted her story and carefully tucked the precipitated picture into the slots of the page.

"From these horrors that she endured, Mom was sick a long time afterwards. She was tormented by nightmares, was afraid of people. A good doctor from Switzerland said that he could cure her. Under hypnosis, he forced her to go through all this once again. She screamed terribly calling out for help... But then all things passed..."

"Here is our castle in Bavaria. Such a long corridor, and at the very end – do you see? – is a large, stuffed bear. Grandpa loved hunting. On both sides of the corridor, within the former cells, there are children's rooms. One of the rooms has been arranged as a chapel, a home church... This is our famous English governess. Such people no longer exists. She spoke fluent Russian, French and German. There are many forests around the castle, where we used to walk with her every day. It was a real spring. Everything melted slowly, snowdrops began to appear... This is a daughter of Grand Duchess Xenia who died later in London. These are our husky dogs lying at my mom's lap, they're like kittens. So wonderful. We called them Altai and Ural, wild, they used to flee and steal chickens from the neighbors... And this is Irina Yusupova, the wife of Felix Yusupov, the man who killed Rasputin. He was in Paris then..."

She paused, as if listening to a distant voice, adjusted her thick horn-rimmed glasses.

"You know, when the war with Germany started in 1914, the Bavarian king offered that my grandfather and his brother would remain in the castle, but he, as my mother told us later, said it was his duty to return and fight for the Russian land. The steward was left alone in the castle, and when in 1919 the Duke returned, everything was in place as it was on the day of departure. Only all copper pans had disappeared from the kitchen – they took them to be smelted in order to make cannons. It was so amazing – he fought against the Germans, came back after many years - and everything was intact. The people in the village loved my Grandpa. He organized a school for children, gave people felt boots in the winter, put the fur-tree in the castle on Christmas, prepared gifts for all the children."

"After the revolution, the estate was flooded with immigrants. Many lingered there for a long time. Soon it became impossible to keep the eighty-room castle. Everything was lost in Russia, they ran out of money, and they had nothing to pay their mortgages with. The estate passed to a new owner, and all of us fell on hard times. My poor grandfather soon fell ill, the doctors found he had brain cancer. He suffered so much. They made a surgery and that was the end... It was known so little about this..."

"Somehow we had to live on... My father, who obtained an incomplete education as a military engineer, and my mother with a certificate of graduation from the Institute for Noble Maidens could not have a job in Germany. It was impossible to imagine that the Duke, whom everyone knew, would clean boots and have his wife wash floors. Perhaps, like many other white officers, he had to become a driver. Marquis Albitsky helped them. He invited his cousin to Canada. My father went there alone at first and began to give ski lessons there. In the summer, his disciples came to Bavaria, and my mother drove them around Europe and showed all the best places. She was strict with them and didn't allow them to put their feet on table and talk loudly..."

"In 1939, we were living in Bavaria when war was declared. American friends helped us go to New York through Norway... My younger brother entered Harvard University. My sister Irene and myself, after we had served in the Navy, wanted to learn too, but we had no money... Here is our brother... What sad eyes... When he became seriously sick, I prayed a lot for his salvation, but that was desired by God... He was so bright, brilliant, he never complained. He died so peacefully... I loved him very much and I painfully suffered this loss."

"And it came to pass: I was painting a cross on his grave, when a monk ran over and told me that the abbess came from France and she wanted to see me. She told me about the Russian monastery in Bussy, how much work was there and how they needed the help of young hands. I thought, "I'm leading an empty life here... maybe this is a message from God." I prayed and even imagined somehow that my brother blessed me. I decided at once and began to gather my belongings..."

"The sisters took me as one of their own. We prayed a lot and worked in the field like simple peasants work. I never knew how nice it could be. We even had a tractor. Sister Juliana, our first soprano, worked with the cows. She got up at four o'clock in the morning. When she milked the cows, she always sang. When she died, her cows cried for her. Yes, it's true. And I had to learn how to milk. It worked out very well... I was very fond of those cows. They are so melancholic..."

"The man in this picture with the big mustache, is our Cossack, a colonel, a remarkable personality. He had suffered from frostbitten feet, but he chopped wood and walked to the fields with the goats. Everyone in the village was so amused when he spoke to these goats, "Left! Right!" he taught them how to walk. All were amused. In 1975 Solzhenitsyn came over and met him. He could remember everything that took place there, in Russia... He died quietly and well. His face was like a child's..."

The bells are ringing for vespers. The last page of the album is turned, and Mother Elizabeth rushes to finish her long-running story.

"Our nuns are mostly well educated. Mother Anastasia, for example, was a professor of linguistics, she knows many Asian languages. Mother Olga, mother Nektaria, mother Eugenia, mother Silvana - they all have their writings, translations. I remember how mother Mary who was the right hand to our Mother Superior, translated the liturgical texts, I and sister Xenia typed them and sent to all parishes in England, America and Canada. The type-writer was not redeemed yet, and when it came time to pay, we had no money. But on that day, when they were coming to take it away, somebody sent by mail an amount necessary. It was a sign of God's blessing for us to continue our work. Mother Olga once said, "Every day we live within a miracle!" Yes. It's true. Have you noticed? Everyone is smiling here. Our Mother Superior is a very wise woman who allows each nun to display her talent. This, I think, helps them forget their former misery... When I came here, I knew very little about life. Now, when my parents are gone, I have begun to understand why my mother, who experienced so many troubles, always mentioned Russia in her prayers and asked the Lord to help her people to keep their faith and love for their land. This craving for all Russian is from my mother. Our monastery, though the believers gathered here from different parts of the earth, for me is especially the tenement of the Russian soul, a torn island of great Russia."

Matushka - this kind word perfectly suits Seraphima. Talking with her, you feel a special sense of spiritual comfort. Radiant and childishly trusting, she is always ready to oblige. Having made the cross sign and picked up her robe, she sits behind the wheel of her "Peugeot" and, with the blessing and at the request of abbess Olga, drives you to see the beautiful basilica of Mary Magdalene, from which she takes a descent to the narrow medieval street where almost behind every door is a small salon: sculpture, painting – everything is bright and original. In the evening you are already together at the concert at Abbaye de Pontigny, between Auxerre and Troyes, where maestro Jean Belliar fascinates you with his execution of Josquin Despres's motet. But she wants to show you another completely different, holy place - a spring, which is not far from the monastery in the forest.

"On the next day it will be quite simple. Absolutely. It will be good to go there after dinner, just as soon as I am free. Each of us will take at least two bottles. It may not be hard. We'll need to walk a little there. I think it's possible."

Have you noticed? She literally translates her words from English. She studied Russian a little at the University, then at the courses, after that she spent four years in Russia.

The car stops near the lake. Then – along the trail. The rows of slender trees are at the left, and at the right is a solid wall of dense, trimmed shrubbery, tightly twisted with barbed blackberries. Mother Seraphima waits while you enjoy the ripe berries.

"There was a cross over there, it was so significant, but every time we put it, the cross was dug from there... Why is this place holy? Once, the people told, a blind boy of eight or nine walked through the woods, and an angel appeared near him. He asked, "What's the matter with you?" "I want to see." "Why do you want to see?" "I want to see God." Angel said, "You will see God"... I don't know how it happened, but then, somehow in a simple way, his blindness was immediately gone, and the boy saw everything clearly. In my opinion, the angel was still there when it happened. And then, when he was gone, a spring started to flow at that place. Maybe I'm wrong in something when telling. I think it was like that."

Scottish by birth, she lived in England, raised her three sons with her husband. They were always together, loved to travel, to discover other countries, to meet new people. She said that all their life they were taught to fear Russians, that's why her desire to visit Russia just enhanced. She knew about it only from books. The Russian soul irresistibly attracted her, literary heroes of the novels she read were oddly overgrown with flesh and displaced the vivid images of real life.

She was 54 when her husband died. She was lost at once and sought for solace at the Russian monastery, but, having been accustomed to an active life, to the frequent change of impressions, she missed a lit at the first time. The Abbess, Mother Theodosia, was strict, she recalls, she didn't let them even go out from the monastery gates to buy bananas. She found support only in her prayers and in the letters of young priest Oleg, whom she met and with whom she became friends before entering the monastery at their friends who had visited him in Russia, and then invited him to their place. A new era was coming. He proposed her to visit their village parish, he told her that the real spirit of Orthodoxy still lived in Russian province, but in that time she had just arrived to the monastery. Father Oleg wrote her often, and mother Theodosia read those letters – nothing can be kept secret in a monastery. And suddenly, it was so amazing, she let her go for a month. Her dream came true.

It was as though the pages of the novels, read by her, became alive. The manor house of count Tatishchev, the creation of the Italian masters, was in the middle of the field, and the poor peasant's houses were around. The village people were trusting, open and simple - like a family. It seemed to her, as if she had known them all her life. But the temple - it was so painful to see – was almost in ruins. Father Oleg tried to repair it as he could, but the door was difficult to close. Inside were the damp walls, a few old women and many old wooden icons. Faces of the saints seemed to have appealed to her, "Save!"

She prayed a lot then, she says, thought about how to help them. She wrote to England, to her friends to raise money. Already in her first visit there, she and Father Oleg decided to build a new temple in Semibratovo, six kilometers from the village, there were more believers there. It was time to go back, and he asked her to come again, to live longer.

"It was sad to leave them. We had become so close. Not only the parishioners, but also all the villagers." She laughs quietly. "They are quite different. It is surprisingly easy with them... As an example, Father Oleg told me that there lived a wonderful old man, he had suffered much for his faith, sat in the camps. Do you want to hear his sermon?.. In a remote village, a very simple one, where the peasants were completely without education, there was a lot of talks about the end of the world, the second coming. Rumors appeared, that Christ would soon visit this village. One old woman said that she had had a vision that Christ would come to her soon. During the whole week she was baking pies, cleaning the house and waiting. A neighbor came to her and asked, "Help. My cow gives birth to a calf. I can't cope alone." "Go away," she said, "God will visit me soon. Get out." Another neighbor came to her, an old woman, very sick. She asked, "Help me a little in the garden." "Go away," she said. "I'm waiting for God." And three times like this. Then again, she had a vision in her dream that Christ had passed by. She cried, "I've been waiting for you, I baked cakes and cleaned the entire house. I've been waiting you so!" "And three times I came to you!"... And it must be understood. A wonderful sermon."

At Mother Seraphima's home everything is like there, in Russia. The towels embroidered with roosters near the icons, dolls, painted ladles. She gladly accepts and settles all Russians who come to the monastery, with the blessing of Mother Superior. The smallest room is hers, it should be like a monastic cell. There are some trees in the courtyard: some plum trees, some apple trees. They're very old, their crooked trunks are damaged by bark beetles, just trash left, but each of them has two or three green branches still giving fruit.

After the evening service, she sets the table in the garden. Buttered bread, salted red fish, shrimps, nuts, a bottle of white wine – "it is good for your health to take a little before night sleep, in moderation, of course." She hustles, runs to the kitchen to check if anything was forgotten. Her neighbor's dog can't calm down, he tries to break through a chain-link fence.

"He barks at me. He doesn't like that I wear black all the time."

On saying her prayer, she invites us.

"Help yourself. Sorry that it's so modestly. I haven't prepared. At least, here are a few... Help yourself with fish. We should eat all shrimps... cookies, those, which are more ugly, I cooked myself."

She began to remember again.

"When I came back from Russia, I wanted to go there again so much. Mother Olga agreed saying that without it I would never be able to arrange my life. But I never thought that I would live there for four years. It was winter, the month of March, frost was on all the trees. So beautiful. I often walked to Semibratovo, six kilometers by feet. There we began to build a new temple. Then the putsch happened in August. I thought I would just perish with all the people. For three days, we didn't know what would happen. I was not afraid for myself. I was sorry for our Father, our parishioners and the children. I used to listen to a small radio, I brought it with me, and I didn't understand what was happening.

They tried to reassure me, saying, don't worry so much, the trouble has not come yet. In those days, I even felt superfluous... I had come there to teach them how to live, and then realized that I had to learn from them. Their great patience and humility... The first time after the putsch was the hardest. All products disappeared from the stores. We got up at three o'clock at night, lined up for bread, but I think, in the big cities it was worse. In the village, they knew how to live from the ground, because they had always been poor. They all had their land, and no one starved..."

"My English friends, who, in a sense, wanted to help us, collected so much money that we were able to build a small temple in the heart of the village, and then the great temple, and around that there could be like a spiritual center, "The Orphanage" - a school for orphaned children. We tried to introduce them to the spirit of Orthodoxy. The school still exists and works well, and I hope it will continue, even though Father Oleg no longer serves in the church, and the new one, who is young, alas, and drinks alcohol, doesn't come to school. I've been there two months ago and made good friends with a priest from a neighboring parish. I asked him to try to do something. They may appoint the second priest from the Diocese. I don't want to harm this poor young priest, because he is sick, but it may not be so, when so many people are in need of care and custody. Recently I've learned that almost all ancient icons were stolen from the rural parish where Father Oleg doesn't serve anymore. This is a tragedy, but I don't think that someone, with whom we were so close, could do that. Absolutely. I want to believe in these people. I hope our Lord will not leave them..."

Saying good-bye, Mother Seraphima wishes us *bon voyage*.

"I'll pray for you."

In the soft evening light, which wipes the traces of daily worries from her face, she will be remembered as a bright face from the icon, written in a childish manner, but with love and naive faith in miracle.

The spotlights extinguished on the square in Bussy, the stars twinkled in the high sky, their living reflection became brighter - peaceful light of lamps near the icons. In a moment, you might think that a miracle happened: time had stopped and reversed, your soul is in infancy, and as if the mother's voice over the cradle creates her prayer, "Lord, guide and save."

***

Probably, one day you'll want to come back here to experience again the enveloping warmth of this shelter where time flows slowly, where you will be greeted with a warm smile and, without asking, they will understand you all at once, forgive and calm you, where those, who are cheated by fate, feel so easy and lovely, those who need support and soul warmth and for whom it is so terrible sometimes to live in this cruel soulless world.

Monastery of the Intercession of the Most Holy
Mother of God, Bussy-en-Othe, France.

SUMMER IN HYDROPARK

"Hydropark station, the next station is Levoberezhnaya. Accelerate, please, debarking and boarding."

Already on the platform in the cool breath of the nearby river, you can catch the sharp tinge of heated spices and smoke. Near to the exit of the subway you get caught in the toils of hawkers in tight narrow rows. Sun-dried and dried fish, shrimp and crayfish, *vatrooshkas* and bagels, homemade cakes, 'angel wings', and other sweets, and fruit, fruit... you can easily loose count. Behind the vendors are former lockers that have been turned into painted cafes serving hot snacks, chicken on a spit, many types of draft beer, coffee, and ice cream. Further down the line is a real binge - pasties, kebabs, music from the restaurants, often the music is live.

Right from the bridge on the opposite shore of the Venetian channel there is a paid beach sparkling with cleanliness. Several rockers gleaming with their wet black armor offer a ride on their diabolical beetles flying over the water. The charge is fair if you don't convert it to the scale of what the average person makes for either wages or pensions. Just somewhere in the middle of that for a 10-minute fun.

No, I am not going there. I'm staying on this side with the fishermen which are close to my spirit, as someone angrily quipped, with the remains of the drunken working class. Do you want to join us? Please sit down, don't hesitate, and just lay a newspaper where it's cleaner. Just watch out for any bone or a piece of a broken bottle that may get stuck in your ass. And for the fact that you didn't disdain, they would definitely pour you something "for acquaintance", but there's really your business to listen or not, or just to look at the water. The river is alive here, alive and free, and the fish comes to this side, because they all feed it here and feed themselves too making it easier to survive.

They are different. Some are lazy and clumsy, they like to rest in the shade, having thrown a porridge bait and listening to the sound of a bell at the end of the whip. Everybody has got 2 to 3 angling rods and his permanent, legal place on the bank. Others swarm around with light rods picking up small fry. Those are mainly come-and-go people or small children. Their various cheerful floats aimlessly dance in the small gaps between the steel strings of the spinning reels going far into the depth, stumbling and pushing each other. Whenever a bell rings on a string touched by someone, which is their fault, a lazy swear arises gently out of the bushes.

Of course, there are some professionals in this community. And this is a striking scene when they skillfully shoot their large sliding floats into the middle of the strait and there, among the floating bodies, drifting boats and racing boats, they catch a subtle bite, and after that they successfully reel in the fish through all imaginable and unimaginable obstacles. They are, I tell you, the real masters.

And here one of them is coming down to the river, one can say, he is an uncrowned king. Simple-minded by sight, an average person, but he's got a sharp tongue and an inescapable sneer in his eyes. Somebody is moving in the bushes, somebody who is not asleep yet.

"Vitek! Come to us," they call to him.

Today he hasn't brought his kids, so he can relax. Behind him Pasha the Half-Loaf hurries up along the bridge (he's almost late), he's paunchy from the front and flat from the rear side (maybe that's why they call him "Half-Loaf"), sleek as if taken from a skewer, and covered with black hair curls sticking together from head to toe. He always tries to be closer to Vitya and imitates his every move. Now his rod is not worse, and he can throw the float almost to the other side, and he takes amphipods* from the same heap, but that's all worthless as teats on a boar. When he takes anything – he surprises himself. In short, a loser. People laugh at him, play out, and he doesn't take offense, he accustomed to it and he even plays along with them. At any moment they pour him some vodka and give him some fish. He knows they need him to behave in this way, they use him as a whipping boy, but not out of malice, but just to relax, they treat him as though he was part of the family...

Well, of course, it's not enough. They are whipping round, and Pasha is going to the left bank to the "Tramp" shop - the cheapest vodka is there, people say, they make it themselves. Vitek cheered. With jokes and rhymes, he reached for amphipods. Then he dumped a whole bunch of shells onto a tarp, and the small children with their rods immediately pounced to disassemble a live heap. They know he won't shoo them away. His fans are coming to him one by one. There is something to see. He accurately puts a float in just the right place, gracefully cuts down and slowly reels in dropping the end almost to the water, perhaps too slowly.

"Come on! Come on!" pinch him the spectators.

"Pull faster, or it will be gone!"

And he stops twisting at all and winks slyly turning to me.

"What do you think about when you are on a woman?"

"Well..."

"Right. To make it last longer. And do you know what woman is the best?"

"Double," someone suggests from the crowd.

"The one who is silent," enlightens him. "And if you hadn't taught her in 20 years, you would never teach her. Do you get it? Fishing, for those who understand, is the same sex, only with a plus sign. There is an old man under a bush. Why does he creep here? It is not moving down there, but something is tapping here," he poked his own chest. "Look how he's reeling in a squirt, relishing, an old lecher. And those! They've thrown their rods all along the bank - there is nowhere to insert one. Rusty brains... Well, he takes twenty pounds of fish food with him and he feels no difference if there is a fish on the hook or a tin can. A bunch of gobbledygook... Hey, grandpa!"

The old man turns around and pricks up his ears.

"Well, have you screwed a fish?"

He raises a cage, and it boils with thin silver sequins.

"Oh, you have a harem!"

"Why are you asking?"

"Well done, I say!" Vitek bawls and turns back toward me. "Have you seen? Just put such old men under every bush, and they will hassle the river in one month. Bark beetles!"

***

That was a magic, motherly generous river.

I remember how, before sunrise, I raced past the sleeping lockers, kvass tanks and overturned garbage bins to its shores in order to be the first to enter the water, still untouched, and lowering a goose float into its smoked mirror, anxiously waited for a miracle. The sun rose, and a fish cage was filled with silver. But then the owner of shooting that was almost on the beach came there, and crystal silence was shattered. A padlock thundered, a metal door creaked, and a speaker, hoarse from the past night, began to whine from there. Beachgoers were lazily sprawling on free coaches, filling the shore, and the entire fleet of rental rowboats came from Rusanovka. And when they started to dump water from the dam and a strong current was lunging onto the shore, it became impossible to fish.

Then Grisha the Small appeared. Without going into the water, he threw his simple tackle and began to withdraw such fish right under our feet that we had not even dreamed of. Each time, having thrown the bait, I enviously watched this performance, and when one day, having thrown some steamed peas on the roll and tied his bag, he was about to leave, I could not help asking, what, in fact, was the secret to his success. Grisha smiled childishly and, having taken a piece of fishing paste* from his pocket, he handed it to me. Of course, it was special, not like the paste we have used. But that was not all. He began to share generously with me the intricacies of manufacturing of his fishing gear and the special nuances of the technology of taking fish. We talked until the evening then, and a day later I was standing next to him enjoying the novelty of my sensations. It seemed to me, that I fed the fish right out of my hand, so it was easy to imagine how she plays with the gentle carefully plucking laterally, how she tries to knock it off the hook or slowly drags it away from the pack forgetting about the danger or trying to be ahead of others.

While we called our type of fishing "rolling", in fact the tackle was more consistent with a rod without a float equipped with a small plummet and a rather short leash running from a spring hook slightly higher than the line and allowing the bait to play at the very bottom. A wire reel and not a very rough rod made it easy to run out a big fish. All the complexity of this type of fishing was in the instant slicing down, and, at first, it always went wrong. The relationship, we can say, was one-sided, that is, I methodically fed the fragrant Grisha's fishing paste to utterly insolent in their impunity choals crowding almost at my feet.

"Use your imagination, penetrate, penetrate," prompted Grisha gently reeling in the next ide to the sand. But no matter how hard I tried, the underwater playing field of my imagination, apparently, was hardly consistent with reality. That was obviously one nuance, imperceptible for prying eyes, that distinguishes a good player from the total number, that special flair "penetrating imagination". Later on it came naturally and everything worked out. Only our good goof Pasha, having become a loser by that time, who could clearly imagine just an opened bottle, didn't master our method. He went from me to Grisha depending on who was more fortunate, and constantly put his heavy sinker into the water trying to have it sink deeper. Having run out of steam, he soon dozed off on the warm concrete slabs but he woke up every time when one of us would catch a good fish. Then he took his rod and started fishing again.

One evening, it was going to rain. Fish took badly, and then it was completely cut off. Grisha, having left his rod, was sitting at the water's edge and thoughtfully rolling his fishing paste in a ball between his fingers by force of habit. Suddenly he asked quietly, "Do you feel anything?"

"No," I answered. "I'm just suppressed before the storm."

He shook his head and, having carefully propped himself up, became to stare intensely into the water near the bridge supports. I also looked in that direction and suddenly saw the water was shining from under the thin ripple created by running wind.

"What is there?"

Grisha didn't answer. Having grabbed the bag, he shook everything out onto the sand and began to tear the fishing paste frantically into large pieces throwing it into the water. Always unruffled and calm, he was changing right before my very eyes. He nervously wiped his sweaty baldhead with a cloth, clutched his fishing rod and cast it on the ground again.

"Why are you tearing around?" I could not resist asking him.

"Have you seen that?" He opened his hands wide. "He's big like this!"

"So stay here and catch him."

He looked at me in bewilderment.

"It's not like playing in a sandbox," and after pausing he added more calmly, "You have to think, it's necessary to think here."

Having picked the spilled peas up from the sand, he threw them into the water, quickly got his gear together and hurried to the subway station without even saying goodbye. At first I was a little offended that he hadn't taken me into account, but looking after him, at his frail figure of an orphanage teenager, I suddenly realized that he was no longer young, and in that opportunity to express him in extraordinary way, there probably was a special meaning for him.

Having determined not to be a hindrance to him until then, I deliberately finished catching fish before his arrival and, having sat down next to Pasha, who had incidentally overslept by that time, watched silently. Grisha failed to invite us as he usually did to stand and fish near him. He was withdrawn and silent. Diligently plying at the bridge with his coarse tackle, only in the evening he, having fed the fish all his fishing paste and having made a track of slightly welded peas along the river down to the slough, he suddenly became excited, assuring us that the meeting was about to take place, that there are some special signs noticeable only to him. We agreed and supported him friendly, but he felt that we were insincere in our support, became silent and withdrawn again.

Yet he existed not only in Grisha's imagination, that handsome wild carp, the last of the once large shoals that survived after years of battles with an army of fishermen, the memory of which still remained in his thick lips with the wreckage of rusted hooks. He was justly the host of the Venetian channel and had not been flirting with fishermen for a long time. Lonely sated existence without his own kind weighed heavily upon him, and above all, it became noisy in his native slough. And in a memorable for us pre-thunderstorm evening, he perhaps for the last time was walking around his possessions to go forever to some unfamiliar, but deep and quiet places.

Hardly moving his fins, he swam along the shore avoiding familiar traps and stopped right under the bridge being attracted by the sweet and new to him smell of the bait generously scattered on the river bottom. Small shoals of roaches bustling near its large lumps parted in fear at his approach, and he, having carefully taken not the biggest of the bait pieces, tossed it up, checking whether an insidious leash stretched behind it. Then, after waiting a little longer, the fish grabbed it stronger and came back to the stream quietly going to a deep place. He held it in his mouth for a long time, savoring. And the next evening, when the fast water rolled its gold peas into the maelstrom, the familiar smell powerfully led him to the bridge.

The first few days he didn't play with the bait that was floating like a heavy plum on a short leash. He waited until a small fry knocked it off the hook and then he picked up the scented pieces. Because of everyday walks, he gained momentum again, and the former tendency to funny and dangerous game quietly woke up in him. Now, coming to the bait closer, he smashed it on the bottom rocks with a powerful jet ejected from his mouth. The next time he gently flattened it with his lips and mischievously struck the line with his tail, sometimes leaving a silvery scale on the hook, as large as a penny, as though he was paying for the meal.

Grisha was despaired. In extreme nervous tension he lost himself and made blunders one after another. As the days passed, the fish persistently avoided an open meeting. Utterly exhausted, Grisha hesitated for a long time to defraud, and even after that, when he decided everything, he didn't say us anything.

It was a tricky and treacherous course. A lump of fragrant fishing paste was playing on a short leash, but under it, on the longer one, hiding a snake's sting in bottom stones, there was another hook, completely naked. Having been accidentally stung, it firmly entered the pectoral fin, and after it there entered another one, that had been on a short leash. From a sharp sweep it lashed the eyes, scraping cheeks. Having been taken on two hooks at once, the wild carp powerfully moved towards the slough, while carrying little Grisha behind him.

"Pick it up! Pick it up!" he shouted hoarsely to the fishermen standing on the shore while barely keeping up with the fish, and those guys quickly took their fish food out clearing the way for him. The fish led him deeper and deeper, pulling what was left of the fishing line from the reel. Grisha was already up to his chest in water, barely holding fish's pressure, and he would have probably gone under the water struggling to a finish. But suddenly the fish stopped, turned around and... swam against the tide toward the bridge; he was lunging into the stream, as if he wanted to feel again the excitement of the real struggle.

The fight was just beginning, but a crowd of fans had already gathered on the shore and ran to the bridge. Some people advised something and offered their help, but Grisha was aware of only tinnitus and jitters in his rapidly weakening hands. Their forces were unequal, and the wild carp, having felt that, was ready to finish the fight with a spectacular coup when a sharp upper fin easily cuts the thickest line. But in the first attempt a soft pull anticipated his spurt knocking down from a stream and pulling to one side. A new maneuver – and a new and anticipatory pull reduced a distance between them. Soundlessly moving his thin lips, Grisha persuaded the fish gently raising him from the bottom and provoking a new somersault. He still did not believe in success. And when, finally, the fish's golden side flashed by its wide mirror on the rocky shoal, the crowd on the shore hooted in surprise.

Perhaps, the wild carp himself was surprised, having seen thin baby feet first, and then him personally, such a small man and not scary at all. The loud noise and the movement of the crowd on the bank gave the fish strength, and he, throwing stones, turned himself with his own tail, having completed his maneuver. Already free, he looked at little Grisha with his round eye, as if remembering, when suddenly the crowd on the shore swayed, and immediately a dozen hands seized him and threw him ashore, and enthusiastic "Hurrah!" resounded from the bridge. Someone popped him a steelyard pushing it right into his face, someone tried to measure the fish, and children grabbed the tail and poked their fingers into his eyes. He was still making a stand in an attempt to break through the stockade of feet to the river. The fish frantically pulled his thick lips into the water, but he was thrown back again, scraping his sides, plastering his eyes, mouth and gills with mud.

Grisha stood knee-deep in the water and whispered looking in confusion at the raging people, "I wish you'd leave."

"You bugger!" a man shouted pounding the carp's head with a stone. "Did you want freedom?"

Wincing his broad tail, he soon calmed down covered with dirty mucus. And then, Grisha the Little came ashore, picked him up, carefully washed and carried him to the bridge not looking at the crowd.

"Oh, boy! You're the king," the crowd cheered.

"The king, the king," echoed from the bridge.

"The King!" screaming kids ran after him.

After that he seemed to be cracked, and maybe the disease had been lurking somewhere inside, waiting for an opportunity to express itself. All the same, he came to the river, moved close to us, but his "penetrating imagination" was left somewhere inside, reinforcing the growing sense of fear. That fear echoed with trembling in his weakening hands and squeaked in his joints growing numb. Later he came without his fishing gear, sat down quietly close to one of the fishermen and stared at the water for hours. And every time when a fish, having flashed its silver side, escaped from the hook, hope arose in his quivering bowels, "Maybe it is not the end? Maybe it will come by?"

***

Pasha emerged from the bushes with a superior air as he pulled off his wet shirt on the move. The coast brethren stirred moving to him. Vitek also came out of the water and called taking off his boots, "Come on and clean the fish that will be a fairing for your wife."

"Let them pour me something first," shifting from foot to foot, Pasha shows his toothless grin.

"Well, you are a smart ass! Do you think we won't leave something for you?"

"I know you. Not for the first time."

They pour vodka for him, and the glass goes around in a circle. Someone crosses himself, "Forgive me, Lord", someone sighs "Who would drink it if it were not for grief", and someone drinks silently to wet his whistle, not to care a wit about anything. Vitek takes the last.

"Well, guys, to be able still." And he looks towards the shore, where in the shade of curve trees, in a faded windbreaker, having thrown onto his sharp shoulders, Grisha sits with a fixed waxen face. Among the coastal debris he resembles a throw-away doll which someone stuck a piece of gray beard as a joke. Only his fading, but still childlike eyes say that there is still the warmth of life within him. On seeing Pasha cutting open the bellies of the fish, trembling in his hands, with his cobbler's knife, he feels his painful gut squeezing from inside, and he hardly takes a look toward the river where he sometimes sees a magical glimpse of its inner light.

Kiev.

STRANGE PEOPLE

Not every musician is able to turn notes into living sounds. It is even more difficult for a composer to seek their successful combinations in waste dumps formed by the centuries. But how this game of imagination is exciting!

Kim, though he didn't study at the composition faculty, gave all his free time to a new hobby, as he gave it to poetry once in his youth and to the art of mixing paints later. A dozen of pale still life pictures painted on cardboard packaging scraps has been stored under the bed in his hostel as a memory of the time when it seemed that his Pegasus was about to spread its wings. Now everything is repeating itself. These little black-tailed demons on the musical staff, sitting like birds on the wires, seemed alive to him. Having picked up the violin, it was possible to get them to sing, scream, and moan.

He was the best violinist on the course, handsome; girls liked Kim, but all their attempts to get his attention were fruitless. He used to hide somewhere in a cubbyhole on the top floor staring at his music book and humming something to himself or wandering across the Dnieper steeper one fine day and looking for a quiet corner in dense thickets where he wouldn't hear the noise of the city, where only birds' voices were heard and the sounds of music that he had inside of him. There was talk once that it didn't work out between him and a student singer, but soon all was quiet. He was of no interest to them anymore. They decided – the boy was just kind of nutty. They filed him away in storage like a museum piece with the warning sign "Don't touch!"

On that day, Kim routinely got into the corner after the bell rang, took a thick music book half-filled with writing and was ready to enter the beckoning realm of the mirror-world, but the teacher of music history was late, and it was too noisy in the classroom. The students were chatting, munching sandwiches, someone sat down at the piano to improvise. Having opened the notebook, he mentally played the variants of a violin concerto scribbled by him the day before, fingered them as a bunch of keys to the cherished doors, but none seemed to fit. The lid of the piano slammed shut. Some chairs creaked. He heard a soft female voice calling to order:

"...the teacher is sick, and I was asked to replace him."

It seems she's a student too, Kim thought. This face has already flashed before his eyes somewhere. A pale, thin-lipped face with big sad eyes.

"If someone is determined to leave - I don't hold you. But it's possible I'll have to conduct your exam."

The students didn't calm down. Iya went to the piano and tapped the note "A" several times, as solo pianists usually do on stage tuning the orchestra. Well, are you kidding, he thought imagining himself in her place. When their eyes met, he nodded encouragingly – be brave! But he switched off at the same moment. A theme appeared as if from nowhere, a simple non-intrusive melody – that's what he was looking for the solo violin. It makes sense to oppose a piano part to it and to give each instrument in a concert its role instead of boredom of well sung voices, to break the academic form. It is not clear what may come off. But how tempting it is!

Having coped with anxiety, Iya felt that she was listened to. She spoke about the composer as if she had heard about him for the first time only yesterday. She invited all who were interested to discover his special world together. Her story, free from moss-covered piles of routine terms and words, so unlike the boring lectures of their old teacher sluggishly fulfilling his duty, caught the interest of all the students so soon that later they tried not to miss any of her lectures. But only Kim, having been huddled in a corner, often looked at her blankly. He was somewhere far away, not with them. Bar by bar, note by note, faster and faster he picked up the sounds, which seemed to be dropped by someone, into the piano score. His imagination drew light reflections on the wet pavement, then a girl playing hopscotch. Each hop gave birth to a new sound. An easy passage swept them up and away.

When his big curly head bent over the table, it sometimes seemed to Iya that there were just two of them in the room. Something trembled

117

inside her, like leaves tremble from falling drops, and it became insulting that he didn't hear her.

Sometimes communication between people appears as if from nowhere. It seems you don't think about it, but as soon as you become a little closer - here it is, you're tied, bound.

Kim was last to take the exam. He was hoping to slip somehow. When Iya sat at the piano and played several themes, he realized: she purposely picked out the rarest ones that didn't sound familiar. He tried to guess, but never came close.

"What have you been doing all this time?" she tried to be severe.

He didn't know how to answer her. Composed? Wrote? Eavesdropped? Should he say that her voice was as a background shade to him, or a backlit, or something else...

"So what were you composing?"

"Concerto for Violin..."

"It's interesting to look at. I heard you're a good violinist. I would not want to spoil your diploma... I don't even know what to do... Although it's against the rules, I'll give you one more attempt. Prepare yourself. Three days later, on Tuesday, I'll be at 61st classroom at ten o'clock in the morning... Don't forget the music and instrument. I'll keep your mark book."

What nonsense is to keep in mind this jumble of fifty random music patches! He put them together this way and that for three days, in order to remember better. Some of them clung to each other easily as if span from one ball. Others needed to add a note or two to stick together. He even liked this invented game. One day he'll write in the humorous genre of potpourri, for a ballet scene, for example.

On Tuesday, on the stroke of ten, having taken his music and instrument, he knocked on the door to the classroom. Iya was waiting, sitting at the piano. A long narrow skirt, a black turtleneck. An ill-disguised glee in her eyes.

He gave her a piano score. She slowly turned page after page. It seemed she purposely held a pause. As if she was waiting for something. He took the instrument and stood behind her.

"Let's try to play?"

Accidentally he touched her shoulder. She flinched, but didn't move away. An unwelcome blush flared on her cheek. Her excitement passed to Kim. Iya touched the lower case keys - smooth chords were like stone slabs polished by centuries. Entry of the violin was a play of passages' semitones flushing to a theme soaring in upper case. Its wings become transparent with every takeoff. It is much closer to perfection. Suddenly a sharp dissonant syncopation at the piano permeates the theme, then another, and the third. The gaps between them become shorter, speeding up the tempo. This is not a child's play anymore. Ups and downs. Fall again. Chasing. Hounding. Clatter of hooves or boots. Unrelated chords are like boulders, like rock slides burying everything beneath them.

Iya stopped, closed the lid of the piano.

"It's horrible!"

"But we haven't finished yet. There's a hint of the enlightenment at the end."

"Not that it matters."

She avoided eye contact, as if anxious to cut herself off. But the next moment she managed to restrain herself.

"Of course, in harmonic terms, this is quite interesting, but I think everything here is too straightforward. After all, it's music, not life."

And suddenly she confessed:

"I've been waiting for something different... At least, music must inspire hope."

Without saying goodbye, she quickly walked to the door.

"Well, by the way..." she gave him the mark book. "I wrote everything there."

The feeling of disappointment came over him. He didn't understand why Iya hadn't played until the end, where, according to his plan, the saving door to his private intimate world closed for others finally opened. He came to the window. Downstairs on the sidewalk, a hopscotch course crookedly drawn with chalk was covered with pools after the May rain. A green ball rolled along the pavement straight under the truck's wheels.

He was taken to the Conservatory doctorate program as a performing graduate and to the violin class as an assistant. It was pleasant to go to the dean's office in a new role, take a register, and give a smile to a secretary. But somehow it didn't work out with newly enrolled students. The left hand of one student was locked, another one bowed badly. He often didn't know how to help them. He had not thought about how to overcome this kind of problems before – it came by itself. It was easier with seniors. He told them how to control themselves on stage, to learn to listen to themselves as if from the outside, how to link, to pack into a single movement phrase by phrase, to count dynamics, the ability of the instrument and, what seemed to him the most important, to learn the art of creating an illusion of the first reading. He even planned to go through his Concerto with one of the most advanced. Yet, he thought, Iya was too categorical in her assessment. Now he could argue with her. He even looked for her in the log, in the list of teachers – she was not listed anywhere. It seemed she didn't naturalize.

Soon Kim stopped thinking about it. A new life, which replaced student's freedom, was gathering pace. In addition to working in the classroom, he prepared a solo concert, played in the Conservatory trio, began to compose a sonata for violin solo. On Sundays, he tried to catch up on sleep; sometimes he allowed himself a drink.

He'd got more free time at the end of May. He played a solo concert in the Small Hall, finished the sonata. His students didn't take much effort too. He adjusted himself. He didn't spread himself too thin. He learned not to get bogged down in details; he smoothed things over, caught-up a little to make his students pass the exams decently.

Spring in Kiev is a great time. Birds have not enjoyed singing yet; dust-free leaves are on the trees. On Sunday he climbed the Montmartre of Kiev to admire how masters of pencil deftly punched still pale faces of female tourists who had wandered here by chance - standard shapes of eyes, usual variants of noses and lips. The same way as a musician on stage, having a set of mature techniques, he can easily fool the audience remaining on the sidelines. Not everyone hears it.

It is overcrowded down the descent. The tables are almost touching each other on both sides of the narrow sidewalk. Piles of *matrioshka* dolls, jewelry-boxes, women's trinkets, wood carving, military awards. There is the jam ahead. Someone was hooked.

"Low price! Low price! Aren't you a foreigner? Look how it polished, how varnish is laid. It's a good price. The following will be worse and more expensive... Are you buying not for yourself? There are cheaper ones. The motive is traditional - Russian fairy tales... That's cheesy? I see you are well versed in the art. Here you are, for the connoisseur, two magnificent works of our local artists. Exclusive. Not for sale. Samples. But you may order... Are you leaving today? Don't look at the price – it's for foreigners... If you take two, I'll sell it for half-price..."

Having passed St. Andrew's Church closed for repairs, he came to a crossroads, then – across the square with Bogdan dancing horseback, along a broad sunlit street. It was fun because of a strange premonition that something was going to happen. Something similar had happened in the moments of creativity, when it seemed that a hand directed him like a child caught in a labyrinth of sounds. We need only to listen and trust, obey this movement of the soul.

After passing the Opera House, he went down the boulevard. He visited the Transcarpathian wine shop. He drank two glasses. His hearing sharpened. As if someone prompted him: "Hurry up!" At the corner near the crosswalk, he met Iya. She walked up from the opposite direction with a heavy shopping bag. She smiled.

"Kim?" she got her breath back. "I didn't expect to meet you."

"How interesting, I have just thought about you," he lied.

"Look here, I bought everything. Enough for my kids for the whole week."

"Do you have many of them?"

"Six. Five girls and a boy."

He was surprised: "Dear me, when did she manage?" He asked: "All yours?"

"Mine now... People go somewhere. And dump them out. Bonya stuck to me himself... And you thought that..." she laughed.

Getting drunk quickly, he seemed immersed in a pink mist."

"I'll take you home."

"We're close." She carefully took his arm. "It seems you were my student only yesterday. Are you writing something?"

"A little bit. I've just finished a sonata for violin solo, a few romance songs."

Their steps didn't get in rhythm. Their bodies touched each other inadvertently.

"Do you remember, Kim," she suddenly switched to first name terms, "how we played together in the classroom a year ago? I talked some stupid things."

"Yes, really, you were right. I don't experiment like this anymore. But now I sometimes think that everything that I write has been invented by someone long ago. I just eavesdrop. I catch the moment. As if someone from outside pushes, directs me. This feeling has been haunting me since the very morning."

Iya tried to keep pace with him.

"I guess we musicians are all dreamers. I've just thought now, if I had gone away from the market a minute before, we would not have met."

"Maybe it's true that we are just someone's fun, someone's toys? Today that someone chose two suitable ones, tuned, set in a tone... Are you laughing? It's easy to check."

"How?"

He sang a few notes of his last romance song. Iya picked up and finished the melodic line. It turned out quite different, even better than his one. It would be nice to remember, he thought, but said aloud:

"Look how amazing, every note is identical."

They walked past the Botanical Garden. A pack of stray mongrels threw themselves in front of their feet from under the fence. They squealed, jumped, and poked their wet noses to their hands.

"They're celebrating today," Iya said pulling a large parcel of meat scraps out of the bag.

Dogs, trying to squeeze closer, pushed, climbed on top of each other.

"See, they're not biting. They know I don't like it."

It was strange to see her standing on her knees in front of them. The whole gang followed them to the very Tolstoy Street.

"I live here. Thank you for helping." She took his bag.

""The Queen of Spades" is at the Opera tonight," he said hesitantly. He wanted to be with her for a little more time.

She hurried, as if scared of something. Her large eyes shone with sadness.

"I have to finish an article for a magazine."

They stood facing each other for a moment. Kim got lost waiting for clues, but the voices inside were silent. Suddenly she invited:

"Come on, I'll make you tea. Just don't be scared. I've got a kindergarten there."

We went to the entrance with off-painted walls, climbed to the second floor. The door upholstered with leatherette opened with a meowing creak. At the threshold, they were met by a dull grunt of an old shaggy dog.

"It's Bonya. He followed me all last fall. In winter, my neighbors whipped him away from the entrance hall. I had to pick up."

The room they entered was probably prepared to maintenance: a table, a sofa, and a piano were covered with sheets. Soft back and legs of the chairs were torn with claws. Meowing, hissing, jumping from above, cats ran to rub against their feet. Iya sat down and petted each one.

"Rhea, Martha, Mimi - all of them were street girls. Only Faina lived in a house, at the neighbors the floor above. When they were leaving for Israel, they asked to look after her... This is Pa. She never yawls, but look how she walks!"

Having noted that Kim doesn't show any interest in her pets, she took him to a small bedroom, which was empty except a narrow bed covered with a bright plaid blanket, a nightstand table and hanging shelves with books and prompt scores. A non-covered typewriter was standing on the only chair. A scattered pile of sheets was on the floor.

"Sit right on the bed. I'll bring it here."

She's gone. In a minute, Mimi's head popped in a wide gap of the door that wasn't completely closed. Shoo! He could not stand cats since childhood, their heart-rending yawls of passion under his window in the early spring, their hidden treachery. He remembered as in a hungry year the most brazen of the local aboriginals had got into the habit to climb through the window to their room every night, and if he didn't have time to whack the cat with his shoe, it pulled down the lid of the pan laying on the table and tried to pull out a tidbit.

Kim came to the window, pushed the easy opening casements wide. The air, densely saturated with the smell of lilacs, was shaken with a dull sound of St. Vladimir Cathedral's bells ring. Iya was humming something in the kitchen, clanking with the dishes. The theme was familiar, but he couldn't remember. Waiting began to bear him down. A tram drove along the street. One. Another. Someone seemed to touch a thin string. Ding. Ding. He turned around – those were cups on a tray. She has already managed to change clothes – a tight skirt, a familiar black turtleneck. She placed the tray on a window sill.

"One more thing... You aren't in a hurry, are you? My article is almost ready, and I would be interested to hear your opinion. The topic is close to you - the role of small musical forms in shaping the style."

She wants to arrange another exam, he thought. He sat on the edge of the bed, tried to focus. He somehow started to shiver from the tea he had drunk. Swirls of words, like birds, flew past his consciousness.

"Kim!" she suddenly called. "Aren't you interested at all?"

He woke up.

"Strange. I hear you and don't understand anything. You're very close but your voice is as quiet so far as the Amati violin, which had not been taken up for a long time. Do such things happen to you?"

"You're probably sick," she put her hand to his forehead. "Right, you're burning up."

"My temples are pounding."

She was happy:

"It's a good reason not to let you go. I know a lot of home remedies from my mother. In the morning, it will be vanished as if by magic. Go to bed."

Kim was embarrassed. He didn't expect such thing from her.

"There's only one bed here."

"That's fine. I'm small. Somehow we'll fit together," she looked at him with love. "I feel so sad at night sometimes..."

There was a thunderstorm at night. With the first thunder Bonya burst into the bedroom, crawled under the bed.

"He's scared... don't shoo him away... he'll leave later. They, like us, have phobias. So am I, used to come back home and imagine suddenly: I open the door, and they're crawling on the floor, torturous, with broken legs... I thought, I would cure them, give him harborage at my friends... I would have gone somewhere for a couple of days, but I can't. It's not possible to place them at my neighbors - they are unfriendly people. I can't drive them back to the same street. And I got used to them... I guess someone has to be responsible for all the living things close to us, to balance human callousness..."

She remembered how once, in the village, where her mother placed her on vacation every summer, boys brought her to tears with their games. They used to dig a hole in the sand on the bank of the river and herd fry into it. Then they pulled her to watch them die there in muddy water. Or they caught grasshoppers and beetles in matchboxes, arranged the execution: broke their legs, torn wings, burnt them in a fire. She remembered how once an adult man performed a trick for them: he caught a gopher, took off its skin and set the animal free. It fled away, all sticky, in drops of blood, rushed over the ground in search of a trampled hole, accompanied by the wild enthusiasm of the kids. After that, she could not hear about the rest in the village.

"This is not serious," Kim tried to speak softly. It seemed Bonya was listening and sighing under the bed. "It must be changed somehow... I know there is a beautiful vivarium in Bogomolets Institute of Physiology. Animals are fed and kept clean."

"And conduct "acute" experiments: cut and torture them, dig almost into their souls. I've heard about it."

"Think about yourself."

"Be silent for a while," she clung to him tightly. Pawed his curls, as gentle as child's, with her slender fingers. "Give me some time."

She wanted not to think, to throw everything out of her head and experience the joy of ups and downs once again. Mad. Mindless...

A grumbling thunderstorm slipped somewhere to the Dnieper steeper. Lilacs were fragrant. Violins were sighing sweet, flutes were singing in the music of lulling eavesdropper...

A month later, Kim signed a contract. Mexico City. Conservatory. An orchestra. Possibility of solo performances. He tried to persuade Iya to formalize their relations - an excellent opportunity to change the life. She asked him to wait until she could arrange everything. He'd gone. Called her every day. Then less and less. Rarely.

Six months later, a violinist from Moscow sat in the orchestra as his companion. She rented an apartment next door. They began to go to the rehearsals together - the numbers of their cars were not similar (in huge Mexico City, it depends on the car number, in what day of the week its owner is not allowed to leave the garage). Sometimes he began to invite her to his place to relax in their free time. He kept her out of kitchen. He cooked himself. He grilled cheese, baked fish in foil, invented various salads. They drank wine and talked late into the night. Six months later, she moved in with him.

In a crazy whirlwind of days, he was no longer given to his favorite hobby. Another mirror world opened to him now - two or three shot glasses of a strong drink easily removed constant stress, made him calm.

They lived together for ten years. When she died suddenly (perished in three weeks of sarcoma of the lymph nodes), Kim's been learning to live alone again for a long time. On rare free days, he went out of town to the foothills. He ordered a fresh trout and a bottle of vodka at a roadside restaurant. Then he went to the valley down a steep slope, to a small lake, and there he sat on the shore in silence till night trying not to think about anything.

A Mexican neighbor came to clean the apartment once a week. Sometimes, if he was not too drunk, she stayed with him until morning.

For many years, a huge smoggy city hadn't become home. Not once he was about to go to Kiev, where he had been always drawn to, but he kept putting it off. He was afraid to be disappointed. And once...

Cafes and shops jostle each other. Pink dummies are frozen up in the show-windows barely covering their senseless curves. Pale waitresses are bustling around the tables standing right on the sidewalks. Jostling in underground walkways is like at the marketplace. Everybody is buying or selling something.

The city seemed strange to him. The "intimate" places which used to be his favorite once where you could be alone and feel free from everything were trampled or completely disappeared. But even those that were still intact, seemed to have lost their magic power. After a week he counted hours before returning.

On the last day before leaving, he went to the Conservatory where he shuffled among students, visited the administrative arm. There was another secretary. He couldn't immediately remember what he wanted to ask. A phone number.

"Iya. She taught us the history of music... What year was it..."

"Last name?"

"I don't remember ... or rather, we didn't even know. She stayed with us just for half of a course."

"I'm new here," she looked at him as if he was a patient.

He went to a bathroom, took out a flat bottle, which he always carried with him now, made a little sip. He recalled that his fellow musicians asked him to bring souvenirs from Ukraine. He climbed up the Andreevsky descent on foot - barely caught his breath. Everybody has already wound up there. Pictures were taken from the walls, stacked in boxes and loaded on trucks. Not choosing anything, he bought several jewelry-boxes. Someone called him:

"Maestro, c'mere!"

On the steps leading to the church porch, with an unfinished bottle of beer in his hand, an artist was sitting, of which someone could judge by his unshaved gray stubble. A cast iron figure of a violinist stood nearby. Small horns stuck out of his forehead, under a tangled shag of curly hair.

"Do you like it?"

"A good job." He lifted the cast to take a closer look. It seemed that he had already seen it somewhere. Then something opened inside. Long forgotten, living.

"God Himself sent you. It's almost night, but I'm still dry... In the morning, I wouldn't give it even for three hundred bucks ... Take it for a hundred, until I changed my mind."

He wrapped it in a newspaper, tied with a cord.

Kim drank another little bit and took the violinist under his arm. Again, like many years ago, he was as though pushed somewhere. He didn't resist and surrendered an invisible guide without an excitement this time, mostly out of curiosity...

He saw a very strange poster on the bulletin board at the Golden Gate: ""Collegiums". Monthly International Scientific Magazine on the Art Scene." The evening was dedicated to the memory of Marina Tsvetaeva. Number 90 was printed on a thin handbill sheet in the color of a pink lipstick and below there was the explanation of it, a quote: "You could not withdraw your moving lips..." Another quote on the handbill confirmed that the event actually was going to be "scientific and artistic", that was Mandelstam quote: "These worlds tempt us with stirring grapes".

A narrow hall of the House of Actor, which was in the former synagogue, was occupied mostly by little white old women. They hadn't yet taken their seats and huddled in the doorway waiting for the delayed arranger and host of the evening. Big and burly, he carefully made his way to the stage, as if he was afraid to hurt any of them; he bowed and shook their little hands. Once a month they trekked out to this cultural event out of their mossy holes, powdered, dressed up. Two of them were already on the scene at the piano representing their first joint opus - a tiny collection of romance songs (which had been given out to everybody at the entrance). The words drowned in the confusion of sounds:

Fascinating, cool day in May.
Windows are open in a sunlit living room.
A glass of wine and white lilacs...

Throwing devoted views to their idol, they're looking for compassion and understanding in his eyes. After all, their hearts still, as before, "hungry for love", but "again, deception and magnificent dreams", and again, "desires without an aim and unfulfilled dreams". And he's already representing the next couple, Zhitomir guests: "Ave Maria" - works by Bach, Schubert, Cassini.

Probably, thought Kim, the one who composed a program was drunk, and for him Maria is the same as Marina, as like as two peas. In addition, the singer caught a cold on the road and all the time lowered the high notes not to fall off. God, where am I?! He frantically groped an almost emptied bottle in his pocket. He dropped the handbill to have a reason to bend and swallowed. He relaxed at once.

"My name is Marina," announced the host, inviting a slender reader on stage, a touching embodiment of feminine weakness. Skillfully using the technique of sudden voice breaking, from enthusiastically ringing high notes to a whisper and sighs, she kept the audience on the edge of their seats for some time. But many of the listeners were cloth eared, and Kim, at first trying to hold a sluggishly unwinding thread, soon ceased to listen to the rustling of illegible words and, fighting the urge to sleep, tiredly contemplated how thin hands of the nervous actress fluttered a light colored shawl.

It was stifling. His neighbor to the right was already asleep. People began to drop away from the back rows. But the actress suddenly wrung her hands, screamed and dropped the shawl to her feet. Someone carried flowers to the scene. It will be finished not in a long time, he thought. An old lady sitting next to him suddenly woke up and began to sing softly: "I'm a sick and old clown, and in the glow of my crown a glimpse is burning down... Shit! Couldn't they make the passage wider?" Clinging, stepping on toes of sitting people, she crept to the door. The others followed her.

Someone else read poems by Marina in Ukrainian, but for Kim, who perceived poetry as a supplement to music, they seemed as a heavy dense flow hardly making its way among the stones.

Already going out of the hall, he saw Iya. Somewhere in his subconscious a feeling was ripping all the time that it should have happened. She was sitting alone in the back row. Her cheeks were sharpened, wrinkles appeared under her eyes and a carelessly whipped mop of her hair had silver streaks. Only the former sadness and surprise were in her eyes.

"I'm here by accident," as if she tried to find an excuse. "I was told that they would read poetry by Tsvetaeva in Ukrainian translation."

He kissed her hand.

"Good to see you... Will you attend me? I'm afraid to walk alone at night."

So simple. As if they parted only yesterday. For a moment, years disappeared in a narrow memory lapse...

He led her gently by the arm. They barely spoke. They were afraid to damage a suddenly revived sense of intimacy with some careless word. The Opera House was left on the left, and then they passed St. Vladimir's Cathedral and the Botanical Garden. Is it possible, he thought, that she's still alone? Maybe, he should drop everything and try to bring that time back?

They stopped at the entrance.

"Will you invite me for tea?"

"I have not cleaned the room... Pa is sick... Come back tomorrow. I'll cook something... Do you like a gooseberry jam?"

"Tomorrow..."

He remembered his childhood. High bushes, twice as high as he was, thickly studded with pink berries with green streaks. The whole alley. Large pointy spikes were hidden in the garlands of small fruits poured with sweet amber. Kim handed her the violinist.

"Take it. Keep it at your place till my arrival."

A grey dawn. Five in the morning. A taxi driver turned out to be talkative. All the way, he complained about how difficult it was to live. At the airport, a flight delay due to technical reasons. He didn't have enough time to transfer. He went to a snack bar and ordered a glass of brandy. He wanted to call Iya. While he was looking for a piece of paper with her phone number shoved somewhere, he changed his mind. She will understand everything anyway.

Farewell, beloved city.

Kiev - Savannah, Georgia.

ENJOY!

Playing the largest instrument in an orchestra, in the real world Ian was timid; he tried to avoid sensitive issues, but not knowing how to get around them, quietly suffered comforting himself with the thought that everything happening to him had been predestined. It was three months since his wife left him. His pleas and prayers didn't help.

"Scrape your double-bass," she screamed packing her suitcases. "I'm fed up with this potpourri. Ten years are lost – with your temper, there is neither pleasure nor money."

He didn't earn much money, in fact – a miserable provincial orchestra, a few students, some occasional gigs. As for the pleasure - she was right, as well. He was timid in the bed games, and if he had the desire to stay longer on a sensuous wave – he immediately saw himself as if from the outside and got ashamed.

On hearing about their divorce, his colleagues, out of curiosity, asked when meeting him, "How are you? How are you?" And he answered, as usual, with a smile, "I'm fine!"

He would rather come back to his *communalka** now, where, as it now seemed to him, it was always comfortable, even though it was impudent sometimes, but if something happened, you could go directly to a neighbor without hesitation, to his very soul, deep to his bones, in tears.

Somehow, the summer heat fell upon suddenly. A built-in air conditioner in the window hummed without rest. The cooling fan in his old Chevy was broken. The season was over, weddings were rarely held. He had to move somewhere to the North. He chose a last-minute trip to Alaska on the Internet, with a Russian group, and in a week, in the early morning, he was already looking for them at LaGuardia airport.

It wasn't hard – they huddled at one of the exits obstructing the flow of passengers. Pale faces, still blurry from lack of sleep. In the center, with papers in his hand, perhaps, a guide. One man was already taking photos. He saw Ian and came to him.

"Leo. Nice to meet you," he poked the camera lens almost in his face.

A voice in the crowd drilled, "David, David, who else are we waiting for? David, check the list. We'll be late."

"Fred, calm down, don't be nervous," David put on his glasses. "Emilia has not come yet... Oh, yeah, we're meeting her at the transfer airport. Well, we may cast off."

The crowd began to stir and crawl.

"Lev, isn't it hard for you?"

"Clara, baby, I'll take everything," he humped a large bag.

Lion-haired, iron-gray handsome Lev looked like a boy beside his wife.

"What a stout woman! Not a woman – an alive double-bass," thought Ian giving way to the crowd. Elderly couples, some single aunties in traveling dresses, no makeup - quite wilted. It's all for the best, he decided, without any worries.

Redheaded Emilia is slender and taut, an English princess to a hair. Dressed not *en famille*: a light dress, shoulders are covered with an airplane blanket. Probably, she was cold all the way through. She couldn't forgive David that he had noticed her not immediately and made her worry. He apologized, jokingly admitted a special sympathy to her, and this theme was then played out by everybody with great enthusiasm. Ian praised her ability to look younger than her years, but her hands – you'll never hide your hands, and her neck was wrapped in a wide scarf, for elegance.

A puppet bus with a trailer for luggage was waiting for them at the Anchorage airport. Clara hardly sat on the front two seats.

"Will they drive us in this drip pan?"

Grandpa Tsypa and Grandma Avi were pushing their grandson Yasha, "Take the front seats. In our travel voucher..."

Fred stood in the doorway, "What's your number?"

"No numbers here."

"I've got number thirty, for example, but there are not even twenty. Shall I go in the trailer or take a taxi?"

"I get carsick when sitting at the back. Tsypa is disabled," cinched Grandma.

Fred retreated, "That's why we couldn't build communism!"

"All right, sit down at last. We'll get it all sorted out in the morning."

Lev, having thrown his suitcase in a trailer, was making notes in a notebook. Leo captured their loading on video, commenting, "First steps of our travel... Enthusiastic faces... A jolly bus from children's set..."

Lev asked, "In what genre are you directing?"

""Obvious – inconceivable", if the material permits."

"A good choice. I feel we'll have a chance to be surprised."

They sat down at last. David counted everybody. Sixteen. Closely packed as in a cartridge clip. At the edge of exploding.

"I hasten to clarify. I'm not responsible for transport. My responsibility is to provide you with a hearty breakfast and to conduct sightseeing tours to the extent of funds allocated for this. Now we're tired, but I urge everyone from the first minutes to get into the characters of the pioneers of this beautiful land, still little populated fortunately, with pristine untouched nature, not defiled with a stinking breath of our big cities."

Someone still grumbled, but sluggishly. "They'll repine and calm down," thought David. "It's always easy to work with the Russians."

"To the hotel now. By eight in the morning – be downstairs with your suitcases. We're going to Denali Park. It's a long journey – we'll have time to get acquainted."

David is more than seventy, but you wouldn't call him an old man. Strong, short-haired, quiet, unsmiling eyes, round fleshy ears, a flattened nose, like a boxer's. In Moscow, he headed the department at the Institute of Crystallography, worked for the military.

They stopped at a modest hotel's signboard at a completely deserted street where several buildings could be seen in perspective. Someone asked, "Where could we eat?"

"The town looks like a big village. See for yourself. And, like in any village, I think, everything is closed. But there are coffee and tea in the rooms. I'll feed you tomorrow. We'll drive the whole day then, so be patient and save some food for dinner. They promise a hotel somewhere close to Denali Park. It's quite a wasteland there. We'll drive to the supermarket on the way... I would advise to shut windows in the rooms. The nights are short here."

Having loaded suitcases, they took time to perch on the seats. As there defined a majority of Brighton and Brooklyn habitants, they quickly found a reasonable solution to the distribution of seats - in size and weight, so the bus wouldn't roll and heel. They also took into account the age. Having heard about this, Emilia first went to the very end. On the road, from time to time, she drew David's attention to herself, and their playful intimate sparring warmed everybody up and refreshed impression of landscapes suffering from monotony.

Before leaving the town, they stood at the monument to Cook, walked through a completely deserted square, reminiscent of freshly built scenery for the play. Some chiseled pendant lights with yellow and blue balls of flowers irrigated from the inside in some clever way, a pile of granite blocks left untouched - a monumental work of nature, framed by blooming mosaic. And not a soul around.

Someone said with a sigh, "I want to live here."

"It is quite realistic," objected David. "No winter, summer is cool. It's possible to buy a house for a ridiculous price."

"Just talks," said Leo. "How can you manage without Russian shops, without Brighton boiling like a pot of laundry?"

"Our Salt Lake City is not worse," Fred turned the phrase. "Our air and fishing. No salmon? But what carps! My wife will cook this fish so good – you'll lick your fingers. I invite everybody!"

David arranged a roll call in the bus, "Everybody should introduce himself. Lev?"

"A journalist."

"Fred?"

"A former electronic engineer."

"Leo?"

"An engineer in the past."

"A physician with forty years of experience."

"A teacher."

"Once..."

"In the past..."

"Just a woman... was and remain," Emilia threw a challenge.

No one objected. Fred could not resist answering, "I would like a little more detail."

His wife pulled him down, "Will you clam up?"

David paused.

"Let's return to our topic."

He knew how to inspire. The events of a century ago, like a cleaned ancient mural, came to life and, having filled with interesting details, turned into a real detective story. When the attention of tourists, weary of shaking, flattened, twisted, packed like sardines in a tin, with a heaviness in the stomach after eating one pound corn pancakes for breakfast, weakened, and even Leo ceased to jump up and stick his lens into a narrow upper slit of the window veiled with dusty ruffles, David allowed himself a break, relaxed...

They couldn't find their hotel at once. Five or six barrack buildings in a wasteland. But it was pretty well inside – America, anyhow. Fred showed concern, came to everyone and asked if they knew where they should switch on heating in the rooms, he was also ready to help with boiling water – he had prepared everything.

Ian threw his suitcase and went out to warm up. It was damp after the rain, fresh. Other people went out too, crowded together talking loudly among themselves, still deafened by traffic noise. There was nowhere to go; only the wasteland was around. A grassy swamp came close to the hotel buildings. A disturbed female moose wandered through it toward the thicket.

"Have you managed to take a video?" asked David who had appeared in the doorway of his room. "Tomorrow we may not see them in the park. As luck would have it. I specifically ordered the eight-hour excursion. I'll torment you a little bit. But then the life on a ship will seem like paradise."

A rain, that had started again, chased away all of them.

The driver asked to fasten their seat belts and arm themselves with patience - it was, he said, not a zoo, but, nevertheless, promised that someone would appear on the road, it never happened when they saw nothing... They slowly rose from pass to pass. Spruce forests were replaced by tundra softly tinted with delicate tones of flowering herbs, the valleys of rocky rivers opened to them, they were framed by snowy peaks punching thinning clouds and going far into perspective. By and by, the clouds were left below. The road was shining because of wet clay from the last rain. Having stopped, they clung to a steep rockslide, giving way to oncoming vehicles on serpentine turns; it seemed they hung directly over the abyss. Ian's hand involuntarily grabbed the seatbelt.

They finally went down to a river in the valley. Worn out passengers dumped out on the shore. There was a wide stone bench near the scope. On that bench were two pairs of deer antlers that decorated, probably, more than one hundred men's heads in family albums. They peered into the scope by turns, looking for some animals at the distant slopes.

"We're hanging around here for two and a half hours, and no animals."

"I warned you," David found excuses. "As luck would have it."

They started to worry the driver with questions. He assured, "We'll see... Chances? A grizzly is 27 percent, a wolf or a moose – some more, a deer – that's for sure."

Leo raced with his camera at the ready, pursuing a fleeing gopher.

"Grizzly! Grizzly!" people shouted after him.

"Leo, come back! Don't leave us!"

Again, they crawled to a pass. A new valley opened behind it. A thin forest. A river glistened far below. Some sunbeams broke through the clouds, poured fresh paint. They noticed some movement at the water. The bus stopped.

"There, look there!" a hunting passion erupted with a bang. "Over there, on the shore."

Well, finally! The people cheered.

Having stopped for a minute, no more, as if demonstrating the ease and the dignity with which he could wear the antlers, the deer disappeared into the bushes.

"Worked off," noticed Leo.

The driver started the engine and declared, "I've got a radio message: they saw a grizzly ahead. When we come, try not to make noise."

There can be no jokes. Everyone is at the ready. Granny Avi was agitated, "Grizzly! Is that the one that was in a glass case at the airport? Do you remember? What paws! Yasha," she turned to her grandson. "Isn't it dangerous for our bus?"

"Don't worry, Grandma, everything is figured out in advance."

An overcoming "shuttle" was standing in the middle of the bridge over a stream with his engine cut off. But where is the promised surprise?

"Over there!"

They jumped up from their seats, glued to the windows.

Having crossed the stream with his lazy gait, a bear trudged from tussock to tussock, from bush to bush, sniffing something in the air. Cute, very homey. He stopped, turned his back digging his nose into the ground. He sat down. He scratched behind his ear with the hind leg. Come on! Come on!

Someone couldn't resist,

"Hey! Teddy! Show your eyes!"

He shook himself, became quite round - about to take off.

"Oh, dear! You made my day. What an actor!"

Ian unfastened a safety belt, looked over the heads into the window muddy from dust, but saw nothing there. Only Grandma Avi and Emilia remained in place - over the seat behind him. He nodded to Emilia sympathetically, as if saying, the show is not for everyone. In return - a strange, fixed stare, as if in a void. Like a cat, when it sees a mouse. And suddenly she blinked. More ... Nervous tic, he thought and turned away, but it stuck in his head: wouldn't that be a sign?

Their exaltation gradually subsided, and when some animals, that had been late to the exit, began to appear almost at the road on the way back, their hunting fervor had died down, fatigue took its toll. Only Leo, having moved closer to the driver and refreshed him from a flat bottle, was wrapped up in work, he finished the last shots of the "Denali Park" series.

"Here is an elk coming out for an evening stroll... a wolf running a sprint race... we're passing the most dangerous serpentine... Chinese kids... everyone's asleep..."

David promised to deliver them to the hotel in three hours. Everything will be closed there, unfortunately, but he will buy something on the way. Realizing that his team was not in a position to accept new information, he didn't load them entertaining with anecdotes and offering others to join. Ian could also recall something funny from the former tour life, but the orchestral habit to lie low, keep a low profile... Let, he thought, the others...

But the voices began to weaken, pieces of words drowned in the engine roar, glances faded, someone even snorted. David sat down next to Yasha and stretched his stiff legs.

"How long will I last?" he thought. "A year? Two? Roll on the day when we cruise on a steamship. There they'll disperse, he'll be able to relax, go to a steam room."

They stopped at a gas station. David went to the owner to check if it was possible, as he had promised, to provide his team with dry rations. He came back with a big box.

"He's got just sweet rolls and eggs in his freezer. Each of you will get an egg, a bun and yoghurt." He began to dispense food. "There is one broken – I'll take it myself. An extra roll appeared from somewhere. We may compete for it."

Hearty poured with sugar glaze, it thawed, stuck to his hands. Fred threw a trial balloon, "I agree to take the bun. I'll give my egg... balls..."

"To good hands," said Lev.

"Still we need to check what he's giving. Who will have *a Geschäft* from this," joined Leo.

They all came to life.

"David, we advise you to think. Not to get a bad bargain with this bun. You'll open a cafe named "Greetings from Alaska" on Brighton, and your wife will make the same ones."

"There is another suggestion: to name that cafe "The Bun of David"."

"Great idea!"

"You will not need to suffer in such buses."

"The Jewish head!"

"What do you think? As we say in Odessa: such heads don't grow on trees."

Imperceptibly they switched to jokes. The bus was like a pan on the fire, it boiled, burst, sprinkled with laughter. Even Grandpa Tsypa remembered something about a brothel. Only Yasha didn't participate in the general merriment, he called his girlfriend, "The elderly are going mad already. I don't know how they withstand this load."

At the hotel, all of them were scattered to different buildings, so in the morning they delayed the departure to the ship, and when they got there, "Princess" chained to a dock - a magnificent creation of human hands - was already taking into its pure womb a seemingly endless ant stream of passengers, eager to surrender quickly into caring hands of the well-trained team. Ian had never seen such a huge ship before.

"Here it is, the Ark of Paradise! Here is Communism promised to us!"

"Welcome aboard. We are very happy. Sir, your cabin is E-218, Deck "Emerald". Sir, the elevator is in front of you."

Suitcases had not been brought yet. A bed beckoned him with its pristine purity. But first, he had to throw something into his beak. He rummaged in the bag, took out his sweatpants. Got the David's bun. To trash it? Well, no, he was not brought up like that. He stuffed it in a freezer – it will come in handy.

Two bar-rooms were open at the fourteenth (Deck "Lido"). Young fairies at the entrance sprayed a fragrant gel on his hands, gave him silverware wrapped in a linen napkin on a warmed platter. Forward! Now, just not to miss. Everything dazzled. Meat in every way, seafood, some convoluted capriccios made from vegetables, fruit, omelets, pies, cakes. Oh! And the desserts!

My God! Why so soon? And so much... The dish is heaped high already. Stop! How to do without a salad to meat? Six kinds of sauces. Which one to use? You can't just stick a finger to each of them to try where all could see? Cherubs in uniforms of cooks are nodding approvingly, cheering him: come on, they say, don't be shy; you are not a guest – a host.

Shrimps, crowning the pyramid, moved, one of them slid to the floor. Ian pressed it with his leg and looked around. David, in his constant waistcoat, with an expression of polite indifference to what was happening around, stood nearby. A slice of a watermelon coyly pinked on his dish.

"Tomorrow we're meeting at the dock at eight. We'll walk in the city for an hour. Don't order excursions. They will be cheaper ashore."

The second shrimp, having dipped into sauce, crawled to the edge of the plate. He held it with his thumb. He felt a bit awkward. Oh, those enduring Soviet complexes - always in a hurry, afraid not to be in time.

"There is an excellent steam room. I recommend."

Having wished bon appetite, David got out of a hungry crowd, carrying his watermelon to the open deck where the rows of straddled deck chairs around the pool were still empty. Feeling relieved, Ian glanced at the already half-empty tray with pieces of Napoleon cake. Well, excuse me! He squeezed between two Japs and threw a few smaller pieces to the plate. Now it's fine. He hurried to a free table by the window.

I envy gourmets who keep in check the inherent nature of our passion for the rapid saturation. The ability only to heat your desires knowing how illusory are pleasures of the flesh, how they are quickly replaced by disappointment – is a special style. Of course, there is an excuse: another school, a difficult childhood, and hungry student years. But still...

Only half of the pyramid on a large plate, where everything was mixed up, had been pulled down, but he felt the resentment growing inside him. Two old Italians standing nearby nodded to him sympathetically - slender as cypresses, real aristocrats. On the table, there were a bottle of red wine, a couple of shrimp, sushi. Perhaps they were artists – they are able to see the perspective, to <u>proportion</u> everything.

Ian pulled a plate with Napoleon cake to himself, but didn't start to eat. His stomach was seething. He wrapped it in a napkin – he couldn't know what was waiting for him on the beach in Vancouver, Seattle. He rushed to the elevator. Leo ran towards him with his camera at the ready.

"Where do they tank up?"

He's sparkling, full of creative impulse.

"Sir, the door is in front of you."

"Do you want to see what I have shot?"

"Excuse me!"

He would be happy just to run up. He raced down the hall... What does it matter? All rooms are odd. It's a usual thing - he loses control at the right time. Finally! He took antidepressant in hope to stop the impact of the physical disorder on state of mind.

Have you heard in Russia anything about depression, not the best invention of American life? It wasn't up to it. Here, half of America reposes only on drugs – they try new ones, select, change the dose balancing between a state of trance and hysterical fun. Ian tried not to follow them, but there is a special occasion – because not every day you're in a cruise.

He went to roam the ship. All are pounded, everybody's looking for something. Russian language can be heard here and there. Where to hide? He felt so sleepy. It was possible he had mixed up some pills. Some musicians from Odessa ran a simple quartet repertoire for American parties on a high semi-circular stage in the center. Aside, down below - a white grand piano, large armchairs. He drowned in one of them. Glass elevators in colored lights glided up and down, up and down...

He woke - the musicians had already collected their instruments, and Pat introduced herself at the piano - fragile, like a little girl. She took off her gloves; the dark wings of her hands touched the keys. She sang barely audible, almost whispering, as if playing with herself.

Here is a spring where he will come in the evening to freshen himself up. Something still swayed and nervously shook within and completely subsided suddenly. Released. Sounds of the grand piano easily fluttered, improvisations were born of themselves. Oh, dear, insidious little Pat! Where are my young years?

The chaotic movement of passengers behind his back had found a meaningful direction toward the wide-open doors of two restaurants, Vivaldi and Savoy, located left and right behind the scene. Grand sonny Yasha led by the hand his Granny Avi dressed up in an evening dress. Tsypa followed them, wearing a red tie and a *yamaka* instead of a usual hat. Here goes dandy Lev, in a tuxedo, in a colorful vest, beside his majestic girlfriend. Don't bustle about at their feet! Leo raced. Emily sailed by in something airy with sparkles.

A place near Emilia at the big table was free. She sat so close to him that it was possible to see a thin mesh of wrinkles under her makeup, to catch the familiar exhilarating smell of French perfume. His wife loved the same. She caught his eye, "Would you help me with an order? Preferably without cholesterol."

Ian opened the menu.

"There are so many of everything. You can get lost."

"I bravely give myself to your choice... Something stimulating."

"I don't even know. I hesitate to advise you."

"What men surround us now? No initiative."

Again, it was uncomfortable in the stomach. The very thought of food caused nausea."

"Ask David. He has more experience."

"That's right," she didn't let him go. "You're just like my husband. He came up with a phobia - fear of any movement. He hasn't come out of the house for three years."

The waiter, having opened his notebook, waited patiently. Jan thought he had seen him somewhere. David came to the rescue, "In cruise, in the evening, it is recommended to drink strong coffee and wine. They add a couple of hours or so of unplanned, almost free pleasures. I checked."

"How interesting," Emilia switched to him. "It turns out we talk about the odd things the whole way. Share your experience."

"It is an intimate conversation. Let's postpone it until a personal meeting."

The waiter reminded about himself, "Whale! Whale!" he pointed to the sea horizon going to pinkness of sunset.

"Where?! Where?!" exploded at the next table. People jumped up, stuck to large windows.

"A whale? Where? Where to look?"

"There. At half past five," a joker quietly took out a rubber toy and forced a pirate whistle out of its belly.

Laughter, roar, rye spilled through the hall, like a wave. Enjoy! Having hid the toy, he came back to the table.

"Are you Russian?" asked Emilia.

"From Odessa."

"That's interesting. What does it mean "at half past five"? I've heard they say so about impotents."

He smiled.

"Just for convenience of indicating the direction, the ship's bow is always on twelve by the clock hand. Consequently... Have you chosen something?"

"Veal in a white wine sauce. Well done. "Sea Fantasy" salad. We'll talk later about a dessert. Will Ian help me?" she jokingly patted his knee.

Her hand stayed there and it seemed even moved higher a little provoking a counter-movement against his will. He noticed how Leo, sitting just opposite, reached for the camera. Have they decided to play him up? It became even insulting. He stood up, apologized, citing discomfort, went back to the white piano. But Pat had already gone. The concert at the theater ended, the yawning audience resolved in their cabins, and those who hadn't lost hope of success still tried to recoup at the casino.

The deck was cool and windy. Several pairs, sparsely scattered on deck chairs, were cooing softly, having covered themselves with blankets. He'd been standing for a long time, watched how a wave was arising behind and thought: everything is not easy, to live together or alone...

Having crashed on the edge of the sea, a sunny yolk became to burn. Suddenly, as if cherubs started to sing in the rhythm of samba. The door opened behind him. Inside, in the dim light, the chairs were placed in a wide amphitheater. The musicians were to the right of the bar. He and she. A *duduk* moaned in her sensual lips. Her partner, a keyboardist, keeping the rhythm, played along. Several viewers had settled closer to the center where a couple was dancing in the flood-lit circle. No longer young, but what a graceful movement, what a thrilling ripple of motion of love passion hidden in the dance. He threw back his graying tangled mane and glided around her with feline grace.

Ian came closer repeating his every move in his mind. What a pleasure! To touch, hold for a moment, then let go. Swirl her by this way and that. And she, captivated, is already burning with sacrificial rapture, firing.

God, where is he blowing to?

The musicians changed the rhythm. Two other couples came into the circle. As if gray paint was splashed onto an almost finished canvas. Gouty old men wearing tuxedos and their female partners shaking their drooping asses were missing a beat and pulling at each other.

"Ah, there you are! Cozy place," Emilia had managed to change the outfit. "Did you want to escape? I won't let you go now. Today you're my partner. Let's go a little bit crazy... Shall we dance?"

"I don't know how to dance."

"Never mind. Look at these - almost ruins," she pulled him into the circle. "Why are you like a stone? Relax. It's so nice to feel free occasionally... Are you married?"

"Kind of divorced."

"You see, I thought so," she laughed. "You probably never allowed anything like this with your wife?" she rolled over like a wave. "The main thing, forget your complexes. Let's cross the barrier of conventions. It's so easy. I learned a lot from the Parisians."

"I just don't know what to tell you."

"Don't say. Listen to me..."

Firmly holding his hand, Emilia took him to the far end of the hall, pushed into a deep armchair.

"Close your eyes. Up we go..."

A crude smell of alcohol mingled with the delicate fragrance of her perfume.

Skagway is a miserly town even by local standards. Eight hundred residents. A street of centenarian freshly painted two-stored wooden houses looked like a totem lying on the bank and beckoned with its underwear – a sparkling cleanness of the jewelry stores' windows. Women were excited, and David held pause waiting for laggards to begin. Those who had gone forward couldn't stand, dived into an open door of the first store. In a minute they popped out - diamonds in their eyes. Come on, *Davidik*, don't keep us in suspense!

Accustomed to discipline. Remember? Everybody - to the meeting! After the break – don't run out. We'll vote.

David keeps everyone waiting, cunning – a little more and they'll scatter in all directions. And there - out, free until the evening.

"There is a museum in your schedule. There, across the street, in an opposite house where there are no windows. Watch an hour movie about the victims and heroes of "Gold Rush". In any case, I remind you: we're sailing off at four."

…The lesson is over. The clock is ticking. Past the museum – to the radiant royal gates.

That's where the Klondike is! That's where gold mine! How can you stand? They offer you the best goods at the most affordable price. Only for you and only today the owner is giving a great discount. That's because you seemed so nice to him. Emilia is one of the first.

"Where is your accent from? Ah, from Ukraine? My grandfather was born in Berdichev. My grandmother traded fish on Privoz... The fish here - what can I say? – is even better than in Odessa. Do you like this stone? It suits the color of your eyes... Why not in silver? The mafia is here too. Understand this - then no one will buy it in gold. They keep the price... if for you, take the entire set. Twenty percent discount. I'm giving it at a sacrifice."

David warned: don't hurry.

"I have to think about it some more."

Losing interest in her, the owner catches the other's hand, "Are you from San Francisco? A luxury town! My grandfather... Today only we have a big discount... You have good taste."

Ian awoke only about midday and immediately remembered the night adventure. Although he felt more like a victim than a partner, this event in his mind had become particularly acute, requiring continuation. Lazily stretching his arms, he gave free rein to his imagination, but a shadow of doubt snuffed out his creative impulse: wasn't all that had happened to them, just a euphoria of the first day on the boat and wouldn't it become a subject of discussion, like in a *communalka*, between neighbors. That prospect frightened him.

He went to a bar-room, carefully chose what he would eat. He looked into the art gallery, which hosted an auction. There were just few art lovers, and those that had come, if you looked closely, increasingly loaded up with champagne. Two or three serious hobby players. The leading master stoked their interest, "This masterpiece is available for purchase at half price today... Any suggestions? Gentleman on the left. One... Lady on the right... Left... Right..."

Pictures followed one another. From glass to glass paints on the canvases became fresher and brighter. Here is nice scenery: a narrow quiet river, a cracked overturned boat on a sandy beach. It's ours, decided he, and no mistake. He remembered a stormy night on the Desna River, a heady scent of new-mown hay, a cheerful dropping on the tent's canvas and a quiet beautiful morning after the rain, as a gift of fate. He also remembered some details: a wet bathing suit thrown in the grass, the taste of fried bacon on the knitting needle. He couldn't believe it had happened to him...

Another glass... He rose heavily. A light pitching in the feet. Probably they have already sailed. They thanked him, gave him handouts and prints.

Enjoy! Enjoy!

"If you haven't chosen something for yourself, come the day after tomorrow. We'll be glad to help."

How nice, he thought, this hospitality, though faceless, but it's convenient and easy. Not that we have – think a hundred times before you take someone's disposal. You never know what and how much it will cost you.

Enjoy! Enjoy!

He went to the Savoy for supper. Alone. A cozy half-light. Corrugated ceiling decoration in chocolate tones. Like in a chocolate candy box. Fluttering sounds of Mozart's serenade and boys in blue jackets gliding between the tables.

"Is this place near you vacant?"

Dear me - Emilia. He has just thought about her.

"Have you decided to cloister yourself? What have you ordered?"

"Crabs."

"How do you guess my desires?" she took the menu. "What beer will we drink? Beck? Budweiser?"

"I haven't yet..."

"This one is soft..."

"But ..."

"This is my treat. May I afford?" she caught his sight. "See, we are already watched," she waved her hand welcoming someone.

The familiar Italians at the next table poured from the second bottle.

He ordered a second portion for some purpose. For a long time, he was picking something in a pile of claws and legs. She didn't leave, chatted about all sorts of trivia, noticeably fading.

"Be an American, finally!" something pushed him from inside. "Everything is at hand here: a swimming pool, a Jacuzzi, a sauna – at option, a massage room, a gym, and any food - anything you want. Sex? - Emilia is in front of you, probably ready by now. Everything is so simple."

And it blurted out, "Well, come what may! Enjoy! Enjoy!"

"Don't you want to give me another dance lesson?"

"With pleasure," she blossomed again.

"I'll be a diligent student."

"Sure!"

In Juneau, where they docked the next morning, Ian celebrated his victory. He got up early, before breakfast, went to the gym, spun a cycle, ran the track, past a bored girl offering a massage (not all at once!), and went to the pool. He only hoped to resist!

Proud of himself, he was wandering around the city. Alone. He walked into a little Russian church - three wooden benches, several icons, like a rural hut, only with a dome. The hostess at the gates was selling souvenirs. He fiddled, chose a postcard.

"How much?" he asked in Russian.

She just nodded politely, "Please, please."

It was about dinner time. A remitting wave of tourists from three liners standing at berth rolled toward him along the sunny street, filling the stores' niches. He saw Emilia in one of them – she was trying on some furs in front of the mirror. "Well, it's for a dessert, is not the time," he thought and passed by.

There were still three hours before supper. He needed some time to snack, just quite a bit. He ran into Emilia at the bar-room doors. Wearing a bathrobe, with a turban on her head.

"Tonight, after supper," he reminded her. "We're switching the roles: I'm a teacher, you are - in the fifth..." he estimated her with a glance, "...in the third grade."

"You'd rather say in the third rate..." she looked askance. "I can even be a goat..."

"What's wrong with her?" he thought. "Such things happened with his wife. You're telling her a compliment, and she..."

"I'm sorry. It seems yesterday..." she frowned, "it was too much, like in a card game, blackjack, you know."

"...See you tomorrow, then?"

"We're over!"

"I don't understand."

"Look, musician," irritation in her voice. "You're an intellectual, and pretend to be deaf. I repeat: not interested. It seems all the men are the same. You wait something from them; you hope, but as a result - nothing, no subtlety, no taste..."

Laughter behind his back. Russian language.

"Ciao, Bambino! You're free," Emilia curtsied. "You may go back to a common table."

"What a bitch," he was rightly outraged. "Grabbed me, as a blanket on a plane. But how she raged all night long!" But he didn't say it aloud.

Ketchikan is the last stop on a cruise. The same stores again - jewelry and souvenirs. David didn't leave them all day. Museum of totems - Indian traditional art objects. The largest, who were not fit inside, stick out like phalluses between the trees all around. A local attraction is "House of a prostitute", since those times. A sturdy bed, a collection of bed-pans and urinals instead of toilets non-existing in those times.

Ian tried to stay close to Emilia, but she didn't notice him. Not a word, no mention whatever, as if they were not familiar.

Six days of the cruise passed like a single string. In the morning, before landing in Vancouver, he went to the bar-room early. David was already there. He was finishing his green tea. A huge suitcase was standing nearby. What does he carry in it, Ian thought, a diving set, a parachute?

"Now - to the plane. They called me at night, asked me to join a bus tour around Western Canada. Something happened there with the guide. There are more than forty people in the group. It will not be easy."

"How do you survive?"

"I'm used to. I can't imagine another life for myself. All the time, as in a kaleidoscope, moving somewhere, changing places and people. It distracts from sad thoughts. Later, however, you scroll it in the memory and see - everything repeats."

"Places?"

"And people, too," his look is alert and calm. "Don't worry. Two days in Vancouver and Seattle you'll be served by the local Russian-speaking office. If you have any problems, I gave Lev all the phone numbers." He rose heavily. "I hope we'll meet again." He went to the door with a slightly rolling gait of a small grizzly.

After passing customs, they lost Emilia. Someone joked, "She departed with David."

They went to look for her. It turned out she hadn't attached a colored tag to the suitcase.

A bus was the same, only in a different color. Lev congratulated everybody, "Happy return to our native *communalka*."

The driver, who was also the owner of the company, asked for attention, "All this day and tomorrow morning I'm with you. Time is running out. Now we're leaving things at the hotel and at once - to the ferry to Victoria. We'll return only in the evening. I hope everyone had time for breakfast?"

Fred interrupted, "For information. Who didn't have time - I can share. For such cases, I have the bun of David in store."

"Let's listen!"

"In today's schedule you have The Butchart Gardens. Tickets cost thirty dollars."

"Here's our Russian service!"

"The Gardens were in the trip purchase terms!!"

"Okay, I'll call New York to clarify it."

"David! David! Why have you left us?"

On both sides of the road, right, then left - miserable dwellings of Indians, surrounded by heaps of rubbish.

"Here you may see the fruit of the influence of our civilization at the way of life of these people though primitive once, but not without a certain sense," commented their new guide. "Receiving a lot of money from the state, a thousand dollars a month per family member, they no longer work, they have taken the worst from us: drunkenness, drugs. Few people, who have migrated to the city, are engaged in small industries: jewelry, wood carving... Why so filthy? They must pay for garbage collection."

How old is he, wondered Ian, thirty, thirty-five? Twice younger than David, but his voice is already tired, an ill-concealed irritation. Probably, they were not at the time.

They came to The Gardens. He gave out the tickets, appointed the meeting in an hour. Someone tried to argue, but he was already gone.

Crowds of people are inside. The air is hot as mulled wine, it's impossible to breathe. They're wading through the flower jungle, stick to drinkers with icy water. He poured water on his head. How's Grandma Avi? It became more spacious - a Japanese garden, an Italian, garden of roses. He sat in a gazebo. Now it would be nice to get back to the ship... Another drinker...

Emilia was the last to come to the bus, with a white lotus in her hair, hiding from the sun behind a transparent plastic umbrella taken from a large basket at the entrance to the park. But everybody had become accustomed to these her obliquities. She passed by without even looking at him.

"What money they scoop up!" Grandpa Tsypa didn't calm down, wiping the inside of the hat with a handkerchief. "Look how many new buses arrived. Thirty from each person. And the flowers... anyone notice? Half of them are already faded."

Lev supported him hiding a smile, "They should change them to paper ones. No one will notice in this heat."

Victoria, British Columbia. It's cool in the green park near the Parliament building. There is still time to walk along the waterfront of a cozy bay. The Indians spread their crafts on the steps. An old man in a broad brim black hat is jingling, from time to time hitting the big bottle hidden somewhere inside a small *pianola* naked to the strings. A tin is nailed to its cover, "Only one penny!" A student with a violin echoes him a little further. Sounds sink; dissolve in the noise of seaplane motors. Brightly painted like children's toys, trough-like ferryboats are busily scurrying between the white yachts...

In the past two days, nothing happened of that kind of things that you, being familiar with the traditions of Russian hangover, are ready to add to a composition. A sightseeing tour of Vancouver, the city where, in the words of the guide, every Canadian wants to live. Then they had time to run to the nearest stores to buy something to eat. The bus was driven up to the door at twelve o'clock. The narrow-eyed driver from somewhere in the East, didn't speak Russian, and English was not his native either. The suitcases didn't fit; they had to ship part of them in the back seat. The luggage racks were cut off, the microphone triggered a high-pitched feedback and turned off all the time, the hot air was driven through a wide opening in the ceiling. There was more than thirty degrees overboard. It was even more in the cabin. No one listened to what the accompanying girl was reading from crib sheet, trying to overpower the roar of the engine.

"It's not a bus – it's a gas chamber," protested Fred.

"A kind of genocide," supported him Grandma Avi.

Having interrupted reading, the girl leaned toward the driver.

"What is he saying?" moaned Emilia littered with suitcases.

"He's saying Ok!"

"What does it mean?!"

"Perhaps we should go even faster."

"Schnell! Schnell!"

The bus was spinning.

"Gentlemen! Gentlemen! Don't panic!" Lev comforted them. "Yasha has already sent message where to find us."

The road seemed to have no end. When they finally came to Seattle, the driver could not find the way to the hotel. He circled around, stopped, turned his map and shrugged his shoulders. Yasha took the lead in his hands, but the driver missed not once since then, because he had not enough time to translate the given commands.

A sullen lady administrator, offended by someone, warned:

"Hot water is at a restaurant two blocks from here."

Ian didn't find soap in his room - wait, I'll get it. It was clear by the tone – he may not wait. He took the soap stashed from the previous hotel. Already forgotten Soviet service...

Leo went over to Clara, "I don't understand why our native Russian Bureau has decided to organize such a final for us?"

"Keep it simple. They just found something that was cheaper. I'm more afraid of today's tour. If I were alone, I would have gone straight to the airport. I'm fed up. But it's principal for Lev, he says, let them unfold until the end - and then we'll arrange them advertising... He has just sketched a newspaper article."

While they were loading their things, Fred tinkered around with the microphone. He disassembled and assembled it three times. He waved his hand.

"It's all rotten in this hearse."

The driver traveled through the city searching for a free parking. They went down somewhere to the very bottom. Granny Avi was carried from there along the steep steps almost on hands. They hunched in the cramped market rows for half an hour and began to catch up to the appointed place by one or by two.

Full blaze of the sun. It would be nice to sit somewhere. Ian found a wide step at the end of a small trailer, but the driver brought a heavy box from the fish department. "I'm sorry," he nodded sympathetically. Then he took off the lock. It smelled of coolness of the sea depths from inside. *"We were born to make a fairy tale come true..."* this phrase was throbbing in his head, having stuck there in the morning.

A familiar hearse sailed to them. The Glass Museum and a tour of the City Center were promised ahead. They tried to come to the museum from different sides to approach, but couldn't do that. And near the City Center, resembling a huge tawdry construction for children's games, everybody preferred to sit on the lawn.

"I know what to suggest you," trying to attract attention to her, said the woman charge of the cultural program to people sitting and lying on the grass like a cow herd in the afternoon.

"There is a district here, where, I heard, people live free from all laws and prohibitions. I wanted to go there myself," she unfolded a map of the city. "Do you accept my offer? It should be close. Yasha will help us."

"Haven't you forgotten? My plane is in four hours," recalled Fred.

"We'll take a taxi there."

From an obtuse angle of the oblique intersection of narrow streets with shabby little houses in the international style of the city suburbs, having climbed to the peeled base, *Vladimir Ilyich* looked at them with fear, all painted as a black man, "What have brought you here?!" It smelled like something familiar and beloved. Without saying a word, they began to sing in chorus,

And Lenin is always so young,
And youthful October's ahead.
Here it is, the Land of Liberty!

Behind the intersection, on a wasteland, a rocket was sticking out of the ground painted in red – as a symbol of unchained love. Behind the leader's back, in a dirty "diner", a sleepy girl measured ice cream into paper cups by triple prices. Two free inhabitants were lying on the sidewalk. One has floated - he did his deed not getting up.

"Come to us again. We'll organize it differently. Prepare."

"Taxi! Taxi!" Fred rushed to intercept a passing cab.

The driver, fearing a crowd on the normally deserted at this time street, pulled forward, but the red light went on at the crossroads, and Yasha managed to catch up.

"I'm not saying good-bye!" Fred shouted dragging a suitcase with a clatter along the rough pavement. "We'll meet on the Internet."

"To whom are you leaving us?" sounded after him.

Someone supported sluggishly, *"Fly on the wings of the wind..."*

It was no laughing matter. Although their guide, to relieve the impression, took them to admire gateways, yachts and dancing fish, all of them were looking forward to the final.

After talking on the phone with a driver who had to meet them at the New York airport, Lev declared, "He's in Boston. It seems we have been removed from the list of the living."

He called the office. They were surprised as well, "How could that happen that you returned?.. Wait. The bus will come in an hour and a half or two. Traffic."

They began to disperse. Only Lev and his wife stayed to wait – as a matter of the principle, and Ian stayed as well – the whole day till his train departure, and Emilia. The bus arrived in more than two hours. The driver, a nimble fellow, warned them, "To Brighton - two scheduled stops. Extra ones - for ten bucks."

Russian school. That's really nothing to argue about.

Emilia was coming out first. He unloaded her suitcase.

"What about money?"

She rummaged in her purse.

"Ian, will you pay? I'll repay you when we meet again."

Clara turned to her husband and whispered, "Lev, how do you like it?"

"An interesting detail... Clara, baby, business is business."

Savannah, Georgia.

INESSA

Looking like a gigantic spider in the dim, shifting light of the floor lamp, he was torturing a cello, small and fragile as it moaned away in his arms. There was something at once eerie and fascinating about this secret rite. The sounds, mellow and syrupy like molasses, spilled over the shabby wallpaper and dripped down onto the cool floor before pooling together in dusty corners. Sunk into the pillows of an old couch, she was following intently the bow's shadow on the wall, its raptorial outline creeping menacingly toward her. His sturdy arm, swaying like some shaggy monster in a narrow shaft of light, seemed poised to leap directly onto her couch. She kept burying her head deeper under the pillow till only a tiny chink was left, and the sounds grew as faint as the mutterings of wind in a chimney at night.

In the afternoons, when he used to pick her up at the orphanage, wet snow would be falling, and the branches of trees in the park quavered as though alive, shedding heavy lumps of snow into the mud. He too was shivering, holding her tight and nearly breaking into a run, as if suspecting someone might try to wrest her away. His big nose, purple from the cold and wet from melting snowflakes, looked fake like a clown's, and every now and then she would reach out with her tiny hand and touch it. Then he would clasp her even faster and, no longer shivering, smile myopically as though still in disbelief at his own fatherhood.

She retained only a few early memories of her mother, who was always aloof and out of sight. Besides, the little girl always felt some inexplicable guilt before her, reading in mother's eyes a kind of mute reproach to her very existence. Understanding came only with time.

Looking back, she realized her father was simply too impatient – time goes by so fast, he used to repeat to his wife – so finally, his ardent wish for a daughter thwarted by the slowness of nature, he couldn't help intervening in the leisurely course of their conjugal life.

Soon after the girl joined the household, the adults began to quarrel, practically over nothing, and after a while their regular spats could no longer remain secret, poisoning even those rare moments of peace when the entire house was filled with the sweet smells of cinnamon buns and gefilte fish.

The girl was given a new name to ensure that nothing would remind her of those postwar years in the orphanage. But seeds of bitterness had already begun to sprout inside her, and father often noticed just how frequently her eyes took on an air of cool wariness and how rarely she laughed.

Years went by, yet she still lived in an atmosphere of protracted childhood. Eager to shield her from any harmful influences, the father further tightened his hold on her, which she actually didn't mind since it allowed her, already quite distant from others, to feel relatively secure by his side.

While it still affected her to some extent, anything happening past the confines of the house generally struck her as fairly remote and dull. When father wasn't around, she would hide out in her room and read children books or dress up her dolls as fairy tale characters, sewing or gluing together some cloth and painted feathers to fashion fanciful outfits for them.

Yet she still had to attend school like everyone else. First it was regular school, then the music school where father enrolled her into a violin-playing program. Showing no particular zeal for her studies, she failed entrance exams at the Conservatory and, taking this in stride, as if it was something that hardly concerned her at all, went to work for the Opera Theater orchestra which offered stage practice for student vocalists.

Just as with her studies, she responded to work with a certain detachment, if not outright indifference. She was bored by all those never-ending rehearsals of new operas, watching young vocalists barely able to carry their parts even with piano accompaniment blank out on stage to the strident outpourings from the orchestra pit. Only the dress rehearsals brought a spark of excitement. That's when dramatic personae could finally turn into her favorite dolls. And so, while the irate conductor was having a fit seeing the carefully orchestrated mise-en-scenes flop; while the soloists in borrowed ill-fitted costumes veered forward and, blinded by the lights, nearly tumbled into the orchestra pit; and while a complete pandemonium was happening in the back – at these very moments she, oblivious to it all, was secretly rearranging their costumes in her mind, fitting and trimming them according to her fancy.

One day, having come back to her place after an evening show, she lingered by a tall cheval-glass, contemplating for quite a while her impassive face with its exotically shaped eyes. Then, a few days later, she suddenly showed up at the foyer of the Philharmonic in an unusually bold, not to say provocative, outfit. The classical lines were broken into angles, a pool of earth colors spilled down the sloping brim of the hat while on the back, sprawling from waist down and all across the hips, a huge butterfly flashed its outspread wings, their square-shape eyespots punctuated by a pair of men's cufflinks. The crowd of guests making their rounds abruptly jumbled at her sight and, seemingly mesmerized, drifted the other way after the suggestively bouncing azure wings.

While the stunt itself was but an obvious replay of her childhood antics, its import was both startling and exhilarating. Taking on this seemingly small part whose full significance she hardly grasped herself, she suddenly realized how intoxicating it felt to be at the center of attention, to find yourself catching admiring glances and hearing the jealous whispers of fashion plates behind one's back. And then, how freely she could breathe at this improvised stage, without the glare of lights and the dust of worn-down costumes! How little effort it took to succeed! Now, at last, she could bring to life all of her childhood dolls with their enigmatic smiles and whimsical clothes. Others would begin to emulate her, to follow her around in droves trying to win her favor – while she, reveling in her power, she...would remain inscrutable, elusive. And everyone around her would be humbly begging her for something, something she could scarcely pin down herself, little though it mattered for the moment.

Around that time, increasingly troubled by all the ongoing fighting in her family, she instinctively began to socialize more so as to restore inner balance. Her father, continuing to jealously guard her against any potential bad influence, attempted to control her every step. If she happened to come home late by even a few minutes, he grew insanely worried, often driving himself into a near-hysterics. The first time she found him in such a state, she panicked and, gripped by remorse, hastened to reassure him – hugged him, kissed his hands. Who knew, perhaps those caresses were not entirely innocent, the deep chords of awakening sensuality already throbbing underneath. Still, it seemed so natural to her, this desire to soothe and indulge the father she worshipped. Oddly, he subsequently grew more reserved, acting in a vague, distracted manner that irked and even wounded her. And so, changing course with a sort of childish willfulness, she began to make him suffer by putting off the moment of reconciliation, acutely aware of the way it increased her power over him, the way his big hands would grow stiff and his eyes avoid hers in embarrassment. Unperturbed, she looked for ways to play upon his weakness, this novel amusement soon becoming a habit that assumed more and more sophisticated forms. The effect of her unconscious cruelty was to make him into a Harlequin and herself, an unwilling weaver of his fool's cap. And only at times, on those increasingly rare occasions when he picked up his cello and its plaintive sounds cut straight into her heart, she would run off to her room to hide the tears suddenly welling up from what some innermost core. As she continued to mature, she began to slowly grasp the true nature of this change in their relationship. But playing on male weakness had already become a habit, a need, a meaning of her entire being. And since all those local Lotharios madly infatuated by her charms invariably paled next to her beloved father, the game was now nearing its logical conclusion.

And yet, when the two of them found themselves balancing on the edge of the inevitable, she somehow managed to summon the necessary strength and retreat. Right in a building hallway, wearing a casual cut, faux-burlap painted skirt and a sleek pin-held hairdo – both befitting her image of submission to fate – she gave herself to a classmate who wasn't even one of the top contenders and who, as it happened, was already packing his bags, preparing to emigrate. He took her roughly and hurriedly, fearful of missing his chance and leaving her with the sense of duty fulfilled. How far was this momentary intimacy from those elaborate fantasies she struggled to control each time she found herself on the verge of consummation!

But now that the final step has been taken, she, running from remorse, rushes to seal the deal with her young man by a marriage contract and flies overseas, leaving behind her native shore, her beloved dolls, her courtship of danger, her stunned and now completely rudderless father. Flies towards a wholly new, uncharted, adult life.

Their arrangement, however, never grew into true intimacy. She obediently performed her duties in bed while he, taking it all for granted, applied himself diligently nearly every night, seeing the act as not merely pleasurable but healthy – the way consuming wine or red pepper was said to be healthy. For some reason he always reeked of fried fish, and after she got pregnant she could no longer stand it. He took it fairly calmly and found a replacement in virtually no time. Soon after the baby was born they split up and she took off for a small seaside town with lots of sunshine, so much sunshine you had to wear a wide-brimmed hat and a long dress to prevent excessive freckling. Her son turned out to be sickly and weak, like a prematurely rotting tree, and as she helplessly fretted over him she began to unravel as well, scouring medical reference books for ever-new symptoms of imaginary illnesses. Her social circle now limited to her students, she observed their well-adjusted, carefree attitude with growing envy. And to make things worse, she began to have recurrent dreams about her father. A father who was sick, helpless. Typically she would see him lying on some old couch, surrounded by silent, unfamiliar women in white gowns. They were walking about quietly and not paying him the least attention, while he just looked on with his big dark eyes as though straining in vain to ask something.

Once, as she woke up and saw her son's pale face beside her, it finally hit her that she was killing not only herself but him too, that life was headed for a dead end and something had to change if she was to ever get back on track.

Shaken by the thought, she drove her son to school and, still unsure what to do, headed for the esplanade, which at this hour looked nearly deserted. As was always the case when feeling on edge, her stomach began to cramp and, thoroughly confused, she stopped in the middle of a square capping the esplanade, which branched out into several streets and a traceried arch bridge over the river. As though on someone's cue, she came to a flat, incongruously narrow building with a plain sign on the façade: "Wax Museum." She made a beeline for the door and, dropping only "Where can I wash my hands?" slunk past the ticket guy into a curtained door. He followed her with a perplexed gaze, chewing on something nonchalantly.

The narrow corridor of the museum, apparently a converted apartment, was dark and empty. She took a few groping steps and suddenly came upon a large, stylishly draped niche to her right, its halogen lit space featuring an adorable young princess in a sparkling lace-and-crinoline dress. A few smaller, less lifelike dolls were perched by her feet, while across the empty corridor, inside the enclosures as cramped as horses' stalls, an array of characters from all times and places huddled together in their dusty vests, tail coats and wigs, in chain mail suits and brocaded gowns. A sort of anxious anticipation could be read in their stupefied, wide-open eyes. Unsettled, she skittered toward the safety of the doorway at the end of the corridor. But there – yet another shock – she suddenly found herself transported to the long-forgotten orphanage of her childhood. The restroom with walls painted thickly in muddy blue contained a metal sink with a single copper tap and a soggy sliver of a soap bar in a soap box. A broken hand dryer hung to the side while two cast-iron foot stands protruded from a stall, their corrugated surface slippery with sewage water spewing from the rusty pipe between them. All that was missing was the graffiti on the walls.

Those fellow immigrants, she thought, heading back into the corridor. Always pinching pennies. Always trying to save on every goddamn thing. And as though to confirm the conjecture, a label pinned clumsily by the feet of the princess she'd admired popped into view. "Catherine the Great," it read. She laughed quietly and, after trying on the outfit in her mind in a habitual gesture, headed back toward the enclosures. Face it, she mused, there is no reviving this sort of fashion. And yet she could feel something melting inside, as though somewhere an invisible candle had been lit.

She minced past the ticket fellow, letting an oblique smile glance over his handsome face. He even stopped chewing, his gaze fastening on her as if drawn by a magnet.

From that day on, she began to haunt the quiet little pedestrian street paved with parquet stone, its line of cozy sidewalk cafes peppered with some of the town's priciest art galleries, each scrupulously maintaining its own style. She would drop in and linger by a painting or sculpture that caught her eye, always welcomed by the staff who quickly realized that her mere presence tended to draw in the crowd. Her newly-recovered poise and grace of bearing complemented the solemn majesty of the canvasses, and often it did look like that many a guest would much rather admire her than the artwork on display.

Afterwards, she would saunter into a nearby cafe, order some dessert, get a table and wait. Invariably some man sat next to her and the game would begin of its own accord, particularly if he appeared shy. Those men were really easy to play, and once again she enjoyed every bit of it.

True, some would start calling regardless asking for another date, oblivious either to her growing disinterest or to the indifference with which she yielded to their pleas, so that when they were finally lucky enough to get their foot in the door, they encountered only coldness and emptiness. At such moments she remained detached from the action, amused by the way their initial awkwardness and ardor gave way to plain old boorishness. Then she stopped answering their calls, retreating back into her shell for stretches at a time and busying herself solely with her son and her students.

The son, meanwhile, had come of age and was already living on his own, his life increasingly reminiscent of his father's. Her students, too, offered little cause for joy, but at least teaching gave her the structure and the routine she could occasionally break without the fear of going to pieces.

Somewhere down the road she got a new student, a slight, quiet girl with long blond curls and curiously shaped doll-like eyes. Already during their first session she was struck by the stolid, dutiful manner in which the novice pummeled on the keys, seemingly oblivious of criticism. The girl's silent, tentative air immediately made one wish to soothe and comfort her, to protect her from some impalpable threat. Initially both teacher and student had a hard time with the lessons, but by and by they got used to one another and bonded so well, they couldn't stay away from each other for long. Eventually it reached a point where, if one got sick, the other would inexplicably develop the same symptoms without any physical contact.

The student seemed to show little aptitude for music but tried her hardest, fearful of losing her teacher's favor. But she, the teacher, felt strangely revitalized, as if some invisible cocoon was forming within, some winged prodigy readying to be burst out. Once she even had a dream where she was very tiny and someone big was carrying her in his arms. Upon awakening she lay still with her eyes closed, trying to hold on to the shifting, elusive image that seemed to have come all the way from childhood. And afterwards, as she lay in the tub luxuriating in the currents of warmth, she could almost feel a light touch of someone's big, gentle hands.

Now, cool and refreshed, she began to prepare for her grand entrance. She got herself a casual cut dress. She bought a new hat, that key detail of her new image, the necessary touch that brought out the whole.

Immediately, she attracted attention, thanks not only to the classy outfit and the graceful body language, but to some uncanny magnetism that seemed to emanate from her wherever she went. As she strolled through the gallery, she once again experienced the same youthful rush that rolled over her at the foyer of the Philharmonic on that memorable day her mere appearance mesmerized the entire crowd.

The faces around her lit up, the still lives seemed to exude the fragrance of fresh flowers. The waiter at the café, greeting her as a regular, promptly brought her usual Cappuccino while the audience – her audience – scrambled to claim the nearest tables.

Her scene partner, however, was slow to appear, and the armchair across the table remained empty. She listened to the murmur of voices rising behind her, looking out the window with feigned equanimity.

The bartender at the empty café across the street was leisurely sipping his beer, wrapped in a similarly nonchalant air. Still no sight of her leading man. Yes, something's definitely off, she thought, reaching into her purse for a pocket mirror. An errant sunbeam slipped through an opening in a canopy of palm leaves over the window and fell on her hands. She caught it, held it for a few moments and let it fly back to the window. The bartender squinted and, putting down his mug, threw a cheerful wave. Meanwhile, spotting a potential candidate that had finally materialized in the armchair opposite hers, she quickly sized him up and, tagging him as an "understudy," concluded that the game wasn't worth the candle. Her day was going so well, she wasn't about to let it go to waste.

And yet the fun was soon over. Later in the evening she got a call from her husband who, in his usual breezy manner, announced that from now on their son was going to be living with him. The young man was obviously in need of good education, he explained; besides, they had already worked everything out. Which was precisely the part that hurt – that they had gone behind her back. She blew up and began yelling at him; he laughed and said he'd call again later, when she dropped all this nonsense and finally came to her senses.

Of course she could leave her students for a while and follow her son in hopes of salvaging their tie. But she knew that the estrangement that began sometime ago was mutual and irrevocable. In fact they never really understood one another. He just took too much after his father and got too little from her. And how far was their relationship from that exciting connection that had developed between her and her young pupil, a connection that became necessary for both and perhaps even more vital to her own lonely self.

For some time after her son had left, she lived seemingly by mere inertia. Out of habit she kept on setting the table, if only for herself alone; kept on placing fresh flowers into a vase. But soon she began to have second thoughts about her choice as even the meetings with her dedicated student – increasingly rare, if still mutually rewarding – failed to fill the vacuum in which she'd found herself. She still made dramatic appearances at the "Dating District," as she called it. But those cameos were now less dazzling, the parts she chose less challenging, and her leading men were allowed to stick around longer, even though they fulfilled her far less than the rare, if already familiar, nocturnal visits of the sensual ideal laying dormant in her unconscious.

Eventually she learned to be alone, but the dread of approaching illness began to haunt her again, and the medical manual became her desk companion. Now she scrutinized herself for the symptoms she'd found earlier in her son, and feared above all that one morning she'd wake up immobilized, her body lying there alien and still while strangers walked about touching and moving her things. She constantly carried with her a vial of sleeping pills, just in case life threw her an unwelcome surprise.

Her son married early, having failed to either complete his degree or settle on a career. Now, deprived of his father's support, he would often call asking for money. She always gave in, hoping to make it up to him and even asking him to come back to the nest, even though she could hardly picture herself sharing a roof with his wife, a complete stranger she never found likable to begin with. Anyway, since he seemed to be in no hurry to return, she took it all in stride, even though each of his regular calls still gave her all the undeniable symptoms of mental distress. Eventually she came to terms with this too. Life was being gradually drained of color, taking on increasingly dull hues, and she felt nearly ready to don her old garb of penitence, just as she did years ago, before going overseas.

One day during the Christmas season, while getting ready for the concert of an up-and-coming cellist who had inexplicably detoured off his big-city orbit to land in their sleepy small-town haven, she suddenly felt anxious and found herself thinking of her father. Now that he was no longer alive, she often wondered if things could have worked out otherwise, in some completely different way. If they didn't, she had no one but herself to blame.

The phone rang, cutting short her ruminations. It turned out to be her son making his usual duty call – inquiring about her health, daily routine, etc. She absently followed his small talk as it skipped habitually from one subject to another, answering in the same mechanical manner. Apparently sensing some guardedness in her voice, he said goodbye soon, although not before reminding her about the money.

She had to sit down for a while, trying to get her bearings, hearkening to some broken string reverberating through her soul. Finally, realizing she was going to be late, she began to look for something to wear. Suddenly the same unaccountable panic rolled over her, a panic so acute it made her hands tremble. She felt like burying herself under the pillows the way she did in childhood, trying to hide from life's senseless, terrifying cruelty. Unable to settle on anything, she carefully closed the hall closet and stepped outside, still wearing the same plain dress she had on during the meeting with her student. Already inside the cab, it occurred to her she may have forgotten something. She went back and staggered about the room, shrugging her shoulders in bewilderment...

By the time she finally found her third row seat, applause had already died down in the hall, even though he hadn't yet started playing, lost in indecision as though groping for something in front of him. As tension hung in the air, she couldn't help raising herself slightly in her seat, pulling down nervously at her dress. Just then he caught her gaze, smiled, gave a light nod and gingerly touched the strings with his bow. His strong arm embraced the instrument's tall, slender neck and slipped down the fingerboard all the way to the sound post, the instrument's deep sighs gradually giving way to low moans. A flutter ran down its wide, ember-colored sides as they clung to him obediently.

Once again they locked eyes, and she suddenly heard the drumbeat of a thousand tiny mallets bursting and cracking open the cocoon that had already hardened into a shell inside her. The winged prodigy was stretching its iridescent wings, readying for flight. She lowered her eyes and began to pray...

Backstage was crowded. The guests had already conveyed their compliments to the artist and were now mingling over drinks and sandwiches. When she finally spotted him in the throng, she was instantly startled by the restless, mercurial quality of his face. It was as though he was constantly trying on masks, borrowing so many faces from the crowd the better to dissolve in it. She tried to recover the image that riveted her minutes ago, but its features remained fuzzy and elusive. It occurred to her that the whole thing could easily be part of a dream. Just then he noticed her and came over.

"So sad your concert is over," she faltered. His hands were large and warm like her father's.

"I am glad I haven't bored you yet."

"Oh, not at all, I thought it was extraordinary."

"You are exaggerating. It's my standard program, nothing more. I got here right from the airport, and must be off soon to catch another flight. Hardly a schedule conducive to inspiration, is it?"

Some kids were milling around with playbills in their hands, waiting for autographs. He scrawled his signature without looking, his eyes fixed on hers.

"This is such a lovely town, almost like the one I live in," he chattered, cozying up to her. "Don't you just love those small towns? They are truly great for new beginnings. You know, I was just thinking. I've got five more concerts lined up...Why don't you join me on my next flight? I could really use your support. And then we could celebrate Christmas together, I promise to show you around town. So what do you say? We are almost neighbors anyways, just a five-hour drive."

He was coming on so fast, she could hardly think of a response. The offer sounded so tempting, she nearly said yes, but the habit of playing by her own rules kept her back. He drew close, and that's when the mask suddenly came off. She could see his lips twitch, his dark eyes welling with anticipation. Now, may be for the first time in her life, she had to play herself, the part she wasn't ready for.

"*Presto. Prestissimo!*" He grabbed hold of her hands. "Come on, take a chance."

"I can't. It's too sudden."

"Oh no. I see I got you all scared. How like me to rush things. I am always getting ahead of myself and end up losing. Like in golf, for instance." Suddenly his face broke into a wistful smile. "At least let me call you."

"I'll call myself."

"OK, but no later than in a week. Promise."

"I promise."

She spent the entire week feeling as if in a fog: going through her wardrobe, trying on various hats, unable to make up her mind. The weather was unusually cold, yet she was constantly feverish. Finally, on the eighth day, she darted off to see him unannounced, as if fearing one of them would change their mind. She called only from a car, already about to enter the town. He didn't recognize her voice, admitting he never actually thought she'd call. But never mind that: he'd love to see her, was looking forward to it. He gave her directions. For some reason she thought of his earlier words: "small towns are great for new beginnings." In her thick sweater and a Christmas hat she felt like a sprinter who'd gotten off to a bad running start. But having gotten this far, it was too late to stop now.

She passed the first intersection. Second. Third. The window displays in the commercial district flashed by, beckoning with holiday lights. Suddenly in one of the windows she caught a glimpse of a white manikin head capped by an irresistibly charming hat. She found a parking spot not too far down the block and entered the store. Strolled toward the large mirror at the end of a narrow aisle, picking up a few patterns that caught her eye.

But something was happening to her face. Somehow it looked absent, completely out of cinch with the delicate curve of the brim festooned with colorful ribbons, bow-knots and delicate sea foam-like veil. She went through a near dozen samples, but not a single design seemed to fit any of the parts from her repertoire. And next to her in the mirror, totally ill-timed, some pretty young face flashed a coy porcelain smile.

She drew her face right up against the mirror in an attempt to mime that alluring curve of the mouth, but saw a web of lines radiating from the corners of her mouth, and some dark spot she must have missed earlier in the morning – a confluence of freckles spilling over her face – appearing on her forehead. Her blank face with its distinctively shaped eyes still seemed completely disparate from the rest. And behind it there was emptiness, emptiness filled with nothing save already-receding outlines of barely-alive dressed-up manikins, shadows among whom she never had the time – or the chance – to make out her own.

Poor Pierrot, she whispered, setting aside the last remaining pattern and pulling on her red Pom Pom Christmas hat. Poor, pathetic Pierrot.

She got into the car and sat still for a while, listening to the heartbeats echoing through the cooling walls of her soul. Finally she turned the car around and drove back slowly down the street, its lights flickering by as dusk began to fall over the small town said to be "truly great for new beginnings…"

Kiev- Savannah, Georgia.

REQUIEM

KIEV. PECHERSK

What saves us, in the end, is that we don't get there straightaway. Imagine for a minute that Nature has decided to deprive us overnight of everything it once so generously endowed us with – health, beauty, an acuteness of senses – everything we could never truly appreciate, having taken it all for granted. Suddenly you wake up a feeble and infirm old man, or worse still, an ugly old hag. Wouldn't this be rather too much to bear? No, better keep everything as is, the old-fashioned way. Come on! Keep running! Now and then you stumble by the wayside, catch your breath and jump back into the race to pursue the leader. Then, almost unwittingly, you come to realize that the leader is gone and that those running by your side and passing you are strangers, not the old pals you've been swapping words with – they must have dropped out without you noticing. You begin to lurch to the side, slowing down to mere inertia, and finally come to a halt in bewilderment… You look back and there, in the thickening fog, there is a kind of near-oblivion – mere shimmering bits of earliest memories. You even begin to wonder – did any of it really happen? But then it occurs to you: your mother is still alive, isn't she? Your mother is your witness.

"Do you remember how they bombed Poltava and how you, seizing me in your arms, ran in the middle of the night from Dvoryanskaya Street, where we lived on the second floor of a large house, all the way to grandmother's place on Kirov Street, and how you fell and bloodied your knee and she scolded you, saying you could have gotten us both killed? In the morning – remember? – we went back to our street and saw nothing but bare walls in place of all the buildings. Here and there remnants of shattered glass glinted in basement windows, and some unfamiliar women, cursing and pushing each other, were tearing them out of window frames..."

Strange, she doesn't remember.

"Remember our vegetable garden on the bank of the Vorskla? Millet was ripening, and I had to spend whole days guarding it against rapacious sparrows – weaving nets and hanging up patches of paper everywhere to scare them away. One day I saw some fishermen with dragnets and followed them, completely rapt, waiting with baited breath for that moment when the net, chirring against the sand, slowly emerged from the water, and the weeds spilling from the sack quavered like alive, full of flapping fish. The fishers left behind only the smallest, ones that looked like silver crucians. It was a lean year, and it occurred to me that if only there was something to carry them in, you could get us all a decent dinner. Having waited till the fishermen moved on and failing to find anything appropriate for the job, I took off my trunks, tightened the string and threw in as much fish as I could. I still had to clamber over the road and dash across the impossibly wide yard, past the policlinic and into the lab you worked in, but the most embarrassing moment came when I was spotted by Zoya, the lab assistant, in whose eyes I'd always wished to appear as a grown-up. As for the fish, they turned out to be 'bitterlings,' the kind you couldn't eat..."

No, she doesn't remember.

Illnesses beset you from all sides. The circle has already closed, life is merely flowing past. You settle into a new mode – one of constrained movements, diminished needs, ebbing desires. Occasionally you bestir yourself, blow the dust off, may be even pull yourself up a bit – only to sink back and, joints creaking, lie quailing low in anticipation of comeuppance.

Could it be that the Maker has simply goofed in granting us so long a lifespan? You have more than enough time to sin and commit all sorts of blunders. It seems we'd be better off living like all earthly creatures, appreciating every moment and gathering life's nectar drop by precious drop, in a manner of bees and butterflies. True, some of us haven't been given much to gather to begin with: in the last count, out of all that earthly sweetness they manage to snatch no more than one or two drops. Take my mother's building – you'll see lots of such god-forsaken folks there. Or any of the others in the neighborhood, same five-storey, no-elevator affairs with their dingy entrances, untidy courtyards and tumbledown dumpsters that are always being combed by some poor soul...

The street, like a swollen vein, is barely able to contain the roaring current of cars pushing on from the Pechersky Bridge. The howling of sirens, the screeching of brakes at street corners, the thundering of trucks. Only as morning nears do you get a few occasional pockets of silence. By then it feels so uncanny, you quickly wake up and strain your ears for any sound. You can hear the clock tick-tocking limply in the kitchen – it's really ancient and patently slow, but mother just keeps pulling up its hands, whether out of habit or in a conscious effort to preserve this vestige of her fading life. You can hear the dry rustle of a roach scurrying through the thread box...

The yellow light from a lamppost is melting in gray dawn. There's no getting back to sleep now. Gingerly, I open the balcony door. The air is cooler and cleaner than earlier in the night, but not as fresh. The half-effaced, trampled flower-bed down below scarcely pleases the eye. The old lime trees are still in blossom, but somehow the fragrance seems gone. I catch a drift of smoke: out on the neighbor's balcony hung with jerry-built flower boxes and shielded from the street by pieces of grimy plywood, there's a naked old man. He doesn't see me, seemingly rapt in meditation. Finally he stirs and lets his cigarette butt drop down onto the pavement, then extinguishes it with a thin, dribbling stream aimed through a hole in plywood. Soon the street will come awake and, along with the rising clamor, clouds of acrid dust will come creeping in through half-closed windows. Old women, at least those who still have the strength, will shamble out into the yard where it's quieter and less dusty. Perched on broken benches, they'll gossip about their private day-to-day concerns. They have long gotten used to, have resigned to this dismal life; it's just that the building's porch steps seem to be growing steeper by the day. Our fifth floor neighbor hardly even comes down anymore, she tosses out the garbage right onto the street – the branches of the lime tree opposite our window are all littered with rags and dirty cellophane bags.

The old man is still there. He is mostly pale; only the wrinkled neck and gnarled hands are tanned. There was a time when he used to get up before dawn and hitch a ride to *Hydropark* to spend a few hours before his shift plying a fishing rod in early light. Ah, those were the days! And even now his habit of getting up early comes in handy. Some mornings he steps out with his cart and, before the janitors come out, collects his nightly loot of empty bottles. After all, you never know if you'll get another chance. When it comes to picking dumpsters, the younger ones always beat you to it...

I should probably take Mom out for a walk in the Botanic garden – she is too afraid to go out alone these days.

If you cut through the courtyards, the trolley stop is a few blocks away. She clings to my sleeve, visibly dizzy.

"Would you rather go back?" I ask.

She isn't ready to give up, though:

"When am I going to get another chance?"

An old acquaintance, a cashier woman, recognizes her:

"Is this your son visiting?"

"My son, yes. The light of my life. I've been waiting all year."

We finally reach the bench.

"I need to rest a bit."

A minute later she's already asleep, leaning against my shoulder, her mouth agape. It's Sunday, the garden is pretty crowded. You can smell smoke – there is a forest fire somewhere on the outskirts of town. It's July and it's hot out. All the girls look beautiful, sashaying around the place, and you just don't want to believe your time is really gone.

The cobweb of wispy gray hair brushes against my cheek, and that old man on the balcony keeps popping into my head. I give my shoulder a tiny stir. Mother comes awake with a start and her dry lips close, covering up the gape of the mouth. She looks at me in anguish.

"Don't go away."

No matter how many times I've heard those words, they always catch me off guard...

We stroll some more down the side alley, stopping by every bench, then sit down at a café right by the garden entrance. A tramp of about ten, one empty sleeve rolled into the pocket of his clean jacket, is working the last of his morning shift – hailing the approaching cars, staggering sideways as he drags his mangled leg. He does not hold out his hand, merely intones mildly, deferentially:

"Excuse me, any way you could help me out?"

At night the walls are alive with flashes of yellow light from the lampposts. I can hear Mother muttering in her sleep. But soon, like a pale ghost, she lifts herself over the bed, fumbles for her cane and shuffles over to the table to peer into the dim glass of the dial, worried that I might miss my flight.

"How come you're not asleep? It's still early."

Hearing my voice, she turns on the light.

"But it's two o'clock already. When do you have to get up?"

"At five. Just go back to bed. Don't worry, I won't oversleep."

I brush my teeth using only cold water – they've turned off hot water again. The toilet bowl is gurgling, the bare risers are gleaming with rust, and the pipes have been wrapped with cloth and sealed with crudely applied cement. All of this needs to be fixed, I remind myself each time I get back, but Mother balks: leave it as it is, she says, as long as it's not leaking.

"You must eat something," she is stalling, trying to make me stay a bit longer.

"Thanks, but I really should be going. I still have to catch a car ride."

Still in her nightgown, she comes out to the balcony – just to cast one last look, to throw a wave. The old man from the second floor, already dressed for his morning rounds, is finishing his last cigarette. The brakes screech, the car doors open. I toss my suitcase onto the back seat.

"I'll call you tomorrow. Bye now!" I shout.

A perfectly aimed cigarette butt lands right next to my feet.

SAVANNAH SUMMIT

After the infernal summer heat, Savannah feels like Paradise. You can finally open the windows; can step out for a stroll. The roses and oleanders are in full bloom. Just this morning the hibiscus bush in the corner of the yard blazed forth with its huge flowers. The camellias hide their already swollen buds in thick foliage – the flowers will be their Christmas gift. Spanish moss decorates the newly-bare tree branches, like scenery on a theater stage. We are still in the wings, about to make our entrance.

"You all set?" I call out to Anya. "They're already waiting for us."

Savannah Summit, a senior housing unit, is a twelve-storey building. There is a modest grove of trees in front. The flower garden in the rear – a mix of fresh and artificial flowers – is Mary's domain. There is also a flagpole by the front entrance, on top of which Jim hoists the American flag every morning. If the flag is lowered, it means someone has died. The first floor has a Community Room where residents come together to play Bingo and do crafts, and where you can buy a one-dollar lunch. The manager's office, laundry room, and several facility spaces are all there too. This is where they store the free items delivered two-three times a week from *Publix* supermarket – bread, vegetables, fruit, and pastry.

The residents are mostly poor Americans on government assistance and some immigrants from the former Soviet Union, those who came to the US already at an advanced age. Faced with the language barrier that forced them to socialize exclusively among themselves, the latter initially stuck together as a kind of tight-knit family; but gradually, due to the differences of character, upbringing and education; due also to differences in public image each had in their former life; but finally and perhaps most importantly, due to a perceived lack of mutual consideration for all the various illnesses acquired with age – due to all of this they have grown more distant and guarded toward one another. Add to this their jealous scrutiny of the good graces bestowed on each by the Americans: so-and-so got too much, another too little, someone made a bad joke, another dropped a swear word.

By the time Anyuta and I took them under our wing, this process of deterioration had already gone way too far, so we naturally wanted to find some way of slowing it down. Although, to be perfectly clear, the mending of ties was essentially my idea. Anna, more shrewd and sober-minded, had little faith in success from the start. Rather, given her long-standing interest in medicine, she must have been intrigued by the opportunity of accompanying our clients to doctors' offices, using her role as a translator to appraise the local medicos' skills and even occasionally fiddle with their prescriptions.

When we first met our protégés, there were only a few Russian speakers left in the entire place: Klara, Tamara, Feiga, and a couple – Isaac and Lyalya. There had been more – Sima and Basya, Fayina, and others. Some died, others moved to another state with a better climate and a bigger Russian community. The remaining few were all in their eighties. Klara is the oldest. At ninety, she still drives a car, goes shopping, and visits her daughters. Helps to feed one daughter's dogs and makes sure the other one locks her front door when she leaves for work.

She's been in America for thirty years and, unlike the rest, has picked up enough English to get by. This elevates her in her own eyes while also allowing for a certain sense of superiority over her compatriots. Too bad though you can't really complain about your ailments to the Americans – it's considered improper, as in you aren't supposed to impose. Just stick to chit-chat: How are you? I am fine, and that's that. Nor can count on your fellow-immigrants for empathy. Everyone's got their own troubles; everyone's got a giant chip on their shoulder.

As for Isaac, he is one of those one-woman man types. A former military man, too. Once captured by a rather difficult woman, he's been holding the fort for over fifty years already. He maintains a somewhat earthy, humorous take on life, always looking for that silver lining in the darkest cloud. His wife Lyalya, formerly a French teacher and quite a beauty, used to always get her way around the house. But now, after a stroke that paralyzed her right arm and leg and left her unable to do any chores or move around unassisted, her constant whims, no longer charming and often ending in full-fledged hysterics, have driven poor Isaac deep into the trenches, from the cover of which he occasionally ventures a few timid shots back in response to her outbursts. Still hoping to somehow remedy things, he's been taking advantage of the more peaceful moments and taking her out for walks – two-three laps around the building, carefully watching her every step lest she loses balance. He realizes, even more clearly than she does, that with his sight deteriorating daily, they now depend on each other more than ever and that if something happens to one, the other goes down as well. 'God, look at what's left of me,' she often rues, combing her hair by the mirror. She can still remember all those glam outfits she used to sew. How perfectly they emphasized her slender, perpetually girlish frame! What admiring glances they drew from the students and the young officers during their evening parties! And why can't those hospital folks understand that she couldn't possibly wear that ghastly black lace-up boot with her summer dress? Why doesn't Isaac understand? She is still a woman, after all.

Tamara. A former pilot. She too has gone through the war – like Isaac and like her deceased husband, by all accounts a really sweet man who bore uncomplainingly the heavy cross of his wife's severe schizophrenia. The doctors just threw up their hands and even advised him to have her committed, but he refused and to his last day remained her nurse, cook, and laundry man. She grew so used to it, she wouldn't touch anything even during her lucid periods, having seemingly lost even the most elementary skills. After he passed away, she suddenly found herself alone and completely helpless. Her daughter always busy at work, visits only in the evening – and not every evening at that – while the girl from the health care agency, assuming she shows up at all, forgets to give her the morning medicine she needs to maintain at least a temporary hold on reality. For years now Tamara has inhabited two separate worlds. In the first, everything around her is invariably dying and collapsing, and she herself is always doing something sinister or downright evil. The second is filled with horrors of a different kind: the roar of the air conditioner; the black-skinned girl who keeps pushing her under the shower – now scalding hot, now ice-cold; the phone calls in an unfamiliar language.

Feiga is the wise one. She just kept having children while she still could; now she is basking in their care. Everyone chips in, so there is no sacrifice involved – no one feels the least bit burdened.

They always start calling first thing in the morning:

"Hi Mom! How are you feeling today?"

"Always with their 'how'" she quips. "Somehow, that's how. All things being equal."

"Please take good care of yourself Mom, you are all we have. We all love you."

Oh, if not for this old age with its ailments! There are still so many desires, so much zest for life…

ISAAC

He was never all that keen on leaving for America to begin with. Rather, this professional soldier was simply trying to rescue his only grandson from military service. Unable to speak the language, Isaac once again found himself on the front line and, as it were, surrounded by the enemy. True, he's managed to hunker down reasonably well: here there is a TV, a VCR, an air conditioner, a dishwasher. Back in Odessa, his mother Musya wouldn't even dream of any of those things. All his mother Musya had was a Russian stove, her ten children, and her tailor husband whom she also had to help out by sewing at night…Just where have all those years gone?

On those days when Anya takes Lyalya for doctor's appointments, he often whiles away the time by pulling me along into the dark cellars of his memory.

"Just where have all those years gone? I remember how, back when I was a student at Odessa Industrial University, I used to practically live at the gym. I guess I was what you'd call fairly fit. And naturally, it came in handy during the war. When we were caught in the encirclement and had to wade our way through the forest, all hungry and frost-bitten, many of us couldn't go on and would try to sit down and rest. I had to shake them as hard as I could, sometimes almost hit them. 'Come on, get up! You're going to freeze to death!' 'I'll just sit for a bit till I catch my breath' – well, you know the drill. After a while I could no longer care, I was running out of gas myself. The short of it is, some did freeze, as simple as that; those who could summon the strength to move managed to pull through. In the end, all too many remained there – some froze in the forest, others were captured, still others perished in some other way. It was an awfully difficult time, goes without saying. When we finally broke out of encirclement around Zmeyev, some fifteen kilometers from Kharkov, the soldiers fed us and brought everyone, frostbitten and covered in rags, before the division commander. 'How many men you got left?' he asks. 'Twenty two,' I report, 'all highly qualified repairmen.' 'Very well,' he says, 'you'll be guarding the area.' 'But comrade colonel, that's impossible, we must go back to look for the remainders of our Corps.' So he did let us go eventually. Just to cut us some slack, I guess…"

"Something else came up as we were breaking out from the encirclement. We happened to wonder into some empty little hamlet, no more than a few huts. Somewhere the soldiers managed to find a chicken and, plucking it practically the moment it was dead, lit the stove in one of the huts and put on a pot to boil. So we sit there, all hungry eyes on that chicken and all, and suddenly a mortar shelling begins – I guess the Germans must have spotted the smoke or something. Now one of us, Vlasov, this clerk from the Corps headquarters who was also caught in the encirclement – well, he gets all fidgety and starts crawling down into the cellar. And just then a volley from the six-barrel 'Vanyusha' hits the hut and blows the roof right off. We drop down to the floor, but it turns out no one is killed or even wounded. One shell, though, lands in the cellar where this Vlasov fellow is hiding, and breaks his arm. That's the way things work out sometimes. And that's when I came up with a rule: the guy that tries the hardest to save his skin is always the first to go under."

"But what happened to the chicken?" I ask.

"Ah, who the hell knows? I guess the pot must have flipped over. At the time we had other things to worry about, let's put it that way. May be someone did manage to grab hold of it afterwards – not me, anyhow… Yes, something along those lines. Isn't it something though, the way the guy who tried the hardest to save his skin, that guy ended up going under. That was quite a life lesson for me, let's put it that way."

Isaac is standing over by the kitchen table, cutting veggies for the soup – gropingly, by touch. This is how he does everything these days – his entire life proceeds by touch. Still, if you keep your place in what they call apple-pie order, then you know where to find anything – any detail, any little item: in the kitchen section, for instance, you've got the pots and the jars and the canned foods supply; in the bedroom, apart from the sleep-related stuff – the medicines and the files with documents of various importance, all conspicuously labeled and color-coded. Say, Lyalya is looking for some particular piece of paper – he hands it to her right away. She needs another one – no problem, it's right here in the red file. You name it, he's got it. True, every once in a while she'd misplace things and panic, launching into shouting, tears, hysterics, etc. Listen to this *schlepper* of a soldier, that sort of thing.

"Here's another bit for you. Our signal battalion commander's just been killed. So the Corps Headquarters' Chief of Staff summons me. 'You an engineer?' 'Yes, I am.' 'Good. I am putting you in charge of the signal battalion.' 'But commander,' I tell him, 'I am a mechanical engineer specializing in repairing tanks and vehicles and things like that, I know nothing about signaling.' 'Never mind, you'll figure it out.' So here I am on the First Ukrainian front, already after we've recaptured Kiev. And it so happens that an RSB-ZIS 5 mobile radio station on a hooded truck body – along with the heater, plank beds, and boxes with equipment inside – goes missing. The really bad news is, it had all the encrypted information, ciphers and time codes: say, until such-and-such a time we transmit and receive using a given code, but later at a certain time we switch to a new code. And on top of it, it's not only the station – both the driver and the junior sergeant in command of the RSB are gone too. Naturally, it raises one hell of a ruckus. The Special Sections people call the technical adjutant, captain Govorov, onto the carpet and nearly turn him inside out: apparently he was seen earlier yelling at the driver – may be about the dirt on the truck or over something else, who knows. So they begin to grill him: what *was* the yelling about?! Then they check with combat security: was there any vehicle headed for the enemy positions? 'Nope,' they say, 'over the entire night not a gnat slipped by.' In other words, they've got no clues to go on. So they had no choice but to send us new ciphers and codes *pronto* from the Front headquarters. Just shows you what a major headache this thing became for the entire front... It was only later, after a few days or so, that it all cleared up. It turned out that while in Kiev, the driver had met his uncle, who was top sergeant in the Ministry of Internal Affairs. And this uncle said to him, 'Listen, why don't you stay here and keep the truck. No one will ask any questions. People get lost all the time; you'll just slip through the cracks'... Now, if it was just a regular vehicle, to hell with it – I'd had that happen before. But this was a radio station, mind you! As it turned out though, those guys couldn't care less: they just dumped all the documentation in the corner of some shed, tossed out the heater and began using the vehicle as a cargo truck. Unfortunately for them, there was this top lieutenant from the Special Sections – which, mind you, wasn't called SMERSH, or 'death to spies'[1] for nothing. The top lieutenant went down to Kiev and somehow sniffed things out, busting everyone – the uncle, the sergeant and the driver. They all got court-marshaled eventually. Well, something along those lines..."

"Isaac!" Lyalya cuts in. "You didn't forget to put some dill in the soup, did you?"

"No worries, Mommie, we are going strictly by the book."

"You should turn the fire down a bit."

"Will do."

A minute later he pokes his grey curly head out of the kitchen, his hands busy with a large wooden spoon.

"And then there was this other incident. The Germans just clobbered us again to the South-East of Kharkov, but as we managed to salvage the battle flag, the Corpse not only didn't get disbanded but was, on the contrary, rebuilt and even renamed. We used to be the Fifteenth Tank Corps, and now we were the Seventh Guard Corps; later we'd become the Kiev Berlin Corps and so on, according to the cities we captured. Long story short, I was one of the few surviving Technical Support officers. We looked among the remaining units and put together a team of licensed drivers, just over a hundred men, and the next thing I know I get an assignment: pick up two hundred trucks from the Gorky plant

---

[1] SMERSH, acronym for *smert' shpionam*, literally: "death to spies." (Translator's note)

and transport them to Tula. So we hook up the trucks to make sets of doubles and, with me heading the column that carries our emergency repairs team, set out for Tula, cutting around Moscow and staying overnight in some village. Upon arrival I do the count and realize that one two-truck unit is missing. We wait and wait – nothing doing. I head back with my team and retrace our route nearly all the way to Gorky. No sign of them. In a couple of days I report to the Assistant Head of the Corps Technical Support. 'Never mind,' he says, 'Once the action begins we'll write them off as lost in enemy bombardment.' Eventually it all came out – the driver happened to be passing by his collective farm and someone took him in, along with the trucks. You know, stay put and lay low, we'll get you new papers or a note if necessary, that must have been the deal. I don't know what they were thinking. Those SMERSH guys were always busy ferreting out who had relatives and contacts, and where. Long story short, they got the deserter all right... That's the way the world wags... As for the trucks, we never did get them back. But soon no one gave a damn – there were bigger things to worry about than counting those numbers..."

"In fact, let me tell you, an officer would only get hell for so-called 'non-combat' losses. I remember this one guy from our signal battalion, the commander of radiotelephone Communications Company – the "wire" company, as we called it. During a let-up we were spending the night in some peasant hut, and he was sitting at the table half-awake, cleaning his gun. At some point, he would recall, he went outside looking for drinking water, leaving back in some signal operator broad, asleep with her head down on the table. What in the world made her want to pick up the gun? Whatever the reason, she inserted the magazine, racked the slide and went back to sleep. In a minute he came back, picked up the weapon and decided to, you know, run a check of sorts: pointed it at the signaler, aiming right for the open mouth, and pulled the trigger. Follow? Now, that's the sort of thing they mean by non-combat losses. Than came the court-marshal trial. Before the entire formation they announce the sentence – several years behind bars; but then in the last moment they commute it to three months in the penal battalion, the *Shtrafbat*. They rip off his shoulder boards and take his belt and lead him away, followed by two guards, bayonets at the ready. You know that by and large the *Shtrafniks* never returned – they were thrown right into the machine gun fire. The fatality rate was often as high as nearly one hundred percent. He, incidentally, did make it back. They had this rule that if you get wounded while in *Shtrafbat* and survive, your honor's been redeemed by blood, so your awards and rank are restored... Some of the *Shtrafniki* actually gave themselves self-inflicted wounds – shot themselves in either arm or leg. The trick was to shoot through a loaf of bread, which took care of gunpowder residue."

"Isaac!" Lyalya cuts him short. "Did you already turn off the soup?"

"Sure did, Mommie. I was just about to serve it."

With the help of her cane she sidles up to the table and, upon taking careful aim, plops down in the chair.

"Oh, look at what you've done! You are going to drive me insane one of these days. Can't you see it's boiling hot?!" Aggravated, she throws down the spoon. "Now we'll have to wait till it cools down. Well, don't just stand there, do something!"

Isaac does some poking around and then moves to take cover in the bedroom.

"I'm going to listen to some radio, if you don't mind. Just to keep my mutton out of your way, so to speak..."

"Listen to this lout! Always with his sailor mouth."

Seeing that we are getting ready to leave, Lyalya besieges Anna with requests: could she check her blood pressure one more time? Draw a new list of her meds and put them all into pill boxes? Help her sort out the mail?

"By the way, Lyalya," Isaac joins us, reemerging from the bedroom. "I wanted Anyechka to take another look at that letter we got from the bank, the one with the 25 dollar offer. Remember, Anyechka, you read it to us a while ago? What were their terms, again?" He hands Anna a glossy yellow envelope. "I guess this must be it."

"No, this is your Generation One* seminar invite," Anya laughs. "They promise tips on how to manage your finances. Free refreshments and lunch."

"Really, this isn't it?" Isaac frets. "Please don't tell me I lost it again. Where the hell could it be? It's always the same story with those letters. All because you, Lyalya, keep taking them from the right stack and putting them into the left."

"Stop 'causing' me, Isaac, and start looking," she snaps back. "You must have mislaid it yourself, for all I know. Same old story indeed."

"And I am telling you," Isaac charges indignantly, "that I haven't taken it. Want me to swear an oath?"

"Oh, shut up already! You can't be talking and searching at the same time," Lyalya snarls. "Just keep looking, save the talk for later."

Isaac falls silent and resumes pulling envelopes out of various hiding spots he alone is privy to. Finally, he produces the letter. Anna begins to explain:

"If you refer someone to the bank and they open an account, you get a twenty five dollar bonus."

"What about them, do they get a bonus too?"

"Well, yes, they also get their twenty five dollars."

"Great! Then we can refer our daughter Lina and get fifty!"

Now, satisfied, they finally seem ready to let us go.

"By the way, Anyechka, I have one question for your manager. Would you please ask him how come they no longer deliver heads of cheese from the supermarket? We've been getting this really low-grade stuff instead."

"Umm...I'll be sure to mention it at some point," Anna promises diplomatically. "Meanwhile, don't forget to take your medicine at bedtime, the one for swollen feet."

"Sure, why not..." Isaac nods, genially. "It's a crapshoot anyway, if you ask me."

Today's Wednesday. The 'food supplies day.' Isaac comes lumbering in, sporting his double-knee flannel pants. He's just made a successful sortie to the 'londra,' as Feiga calls it, claiming two packs of bread, three cans of white mushrooms, and a bunch of asparagus as trophies.

"Mommie, look what I got here. Looks like a case of bolts."

He's clearly in an upbeat mood.

"Same tripe, I am sure," Lyalya drops sourly.

"Any windfall's a blessing. Now, where could we fit this in?"

"Why don't you ask Anya."

Given detailed instructions on utilizing newly-arrived and yet-untested raw materials, he diligently sorts all the items into the assigned locations and, seizing an opportune moment, resumes his account of those distant, though gloriously thrilling, times.

"There was this one time I was tasked with delivering a group of newly-repaired tanks to our new Corps commander. The tanks were still uncrewed, unmanned. This, mind you, was on the eve of the battle of Prokhorovka – hardly a minor point. Well, they somehow managed to find some soldiers, and then my team of repairmen volunteered to fight as well. Believe it or not, I got to be tank commander. By that point we'd already heard all about those new armored vehicles – the Tiger and Panther tanks and the self-propelled gun Ferdinand. The Germans had been even dropping aerial leaflets promising, in effect, that the Russians were to finally get a taste of the full fury of Führer's arms. On the accompanying image, our soldier with his puttee coming unwound was chased by a German who was stomping on that putty with his impeccably well-made boots. True, a hit by the Tiger was typically lethal – the shell would go through the T-34, our famed top World War Two tank, like knife through butter. But we also knew that if you got real close, the Tiger's shells would go over since its gun depression was fairly low, seven or eight degrees. Now, our driver and mechanic was Fedya Startsev – a soldier, not one of my repairmen. The boy had a real gift. During the battle he not only outmaneuvered the enemy tank, he was able to get right against it and ram it head-on. Boom! The Tiger's caterpillar thread comes off, and the tank begins to spin on the spot. After that it was just a matter of technique. We fire one shell under the turret, and the whole thing bursts into flames. Interestingly enough, those tanks had aviation engines on them. Take the Junkers planes – they ran on diesel fuel; but the tanks used aviation benzene and burned quite nicely as a result… So, yeah, that's the way it went down… Afterwards, our Corps Tech Support's second-in-command, Vetrov Alexandr Alexandrovich – he would later make lieutenant colonel – came down on me like a ton of bricks: what the hell did you think you were doing, running into enemy fire and losing your men? Why couldn't you just stick to maintenance? This was all part of the battle on the Kursk Bulge, I mean the entire Prokhorovka episode. Over a thousand armored vehicles from both sides were involved; Stalin would later call it the twilight of the German Army…"

"Before retaking Kiev, I remember, we initially crossed the Dnieper about one hundred fifty kilometers south of the city. The tanks were being moved at nighttime on pontoon rafts. The Germans were dropping bombs and parachute flares. Despite heavy casualties, we secured the Bukrin bend and even tried to launch an attack, though without success. And at that point the Soviet High Command came up with a deceptive maneuver: they picked a spot close to the German positions and planted the body of some captain with a half-torn Top Secret document in his map-case – an order to begin an offensive from the Bukhrin bend. There were Stalin's and Zhukov's signatures, the precise date and time of the attack, and so on. The Germans found the document and decided to crush us. So, I remember it as clearly as yesterday: it's a clear, sunny day and we, the maintenance guys among others, are sitting in the trenches with our shirt-tunics off – killing, funny as it sounds, lice. When the Germans charged onto the beachhead, they encountered a wall of massed artillery fire from the East bank. It was as though a black curtain had been put up. The earth rocked, all was smothered in smoke and clumps of blown-up dirt. One of our officers just went berserk; he was screaming something and trying to climb out of the trench. We had to hold him back, tie him up and call the medics – the man had plainly unraveled in this hell. Subsequently things unfolded as follows. That massive artillery fire from the Left Bank stopped the German offensive; their tanks were forced to retreat. At which point, while they were busy for some days trying to regroup, our units crossed the Dniepr in the other direction, leaving behind only barely camouflaged wooden simulation targets that had been delivered in advance, painted green and set up along our original beachhead positions. Our entire Third Tank Army under the command of General Pavel Semyonovich Rybalko returned to the Left Bank, made a two hundred kilometer quick march and, covertly crossing the Dnepr once again opposite Lyutezh and was advancing toward Kiev from the North. It clearly came as an unexpected blow for the Germans – they had left few reserves in the city and we were able to capture it without suffering heavy casualties. By the way – not to make too much out of it – but shortly before the Bukrin offensive Stalin signed an order indicating that the first two thousand soldiers and officers to cross the Dnieper would be made Heroes of the Soviet Union. And I *was* one of those men – we crossed on a ferry, me and my entire maintenance crew. Our new location was at the so-called *GPNC*, or MOCH – Main Observation and Communication Headquarters. Prior to the attack we positioned ourselves so as to be able to survey the battlefield with binoculars. We evacuated the damaged or malfunctioning tanks right under enemy fire, quickly patched them up and sent them back into battle. (All major, heavy-duty repairs were done at armor repair plants in the rear). As you can see, I still haven't made the Hero title; nor have many others. Instead, I was decorated with an Order of the Patriotic War Second class, of the first issue, still on plate mount... That's the way it went down..."

"But on another note: all through the war we were plagued mercilessly by lice. And not just we – so were the Germans; in fact, if you came close to one of the bodies, you could literally see lice stirring at the throat under the collar, crawling out of the corpse to look for a new victim. During the offensive we would always clean up our dead, but left the German bodies temporarily untouched so that the soldiers could look. Picture such a German sitting in the snow, already stiff but still wearing his knapsack with full kit: toothbrush, boot-polishing brush, deerskin padding that turned one side of the pack into a pillow. Whereas our soldiers carried field bags called 'Sidors' – holdalls with foot cloths, a hunk of bread, etc. Anyway, there they are, sitting in the snow, arm or leg sticking out. The most horrible thing was when the tanks ran over them and you heard that crunch of bones under the caterpillar belts. That is something I haven't been able to forget… In winter we used to bury them pell-mell: you dig pits for the officers but bury soldiers in shallow graves, or sometimes just cover the bodies with heaps of wood. There was an old man from the gravedigger crew who was always drunk. 'Son,' he used to say, 'if you don't drink, this job will soon drive you insane'… Once, I recall, the soldiers found a whole cistern of some swill. They tasted the contents: pure alcohol. So we took an empty oil-fuel barrel, washed it anyhow, and drank this foul-smelling alcohol at New Years' Eve. The next morning there was a heavy bombing raid. Someone cracked a joke: 'a hundred grams in the evening, a hundred kilograms the next morning'… Another find I remember is cans of condensed milk. We broke off the lids and scooped it all out with mess-tins. No can was used twice; the next guy in line would just open a new one. The whole cellar was flooded with that milk… Elsewhere still we stumbled upon a storage room with various packages: cookies, chocolate, quarter-liter bottles of Cuban rum. We simply cleaned out the place, snatching that rum and stuffing it anywhere we could. We had to toss out our maintenance kits and some other stuff. Yeah, all sorts of crazy things used to happen…"

Lyalya, who's been unusually quiet, suddenly chimes in:

"He came to Moscow carrying only a suitcase. He had a wool sweater, one of those things donated by the Americans. Well, believe it or not, there was a louse sitting in every mesh opening, the whole thing was crawling with it. I had to throw it in the stove."

"All true. There were indeed plenty of lice. Way too much if you ask me. Those parasites fed on everyone, soldiers and generals alike. And no wonder, with the unsanitary conditions we had. You were lucky if you got a few hours' stay at some settlement – at least you could get a splash of water, may be even a quick wash. I had this orderly who used to always go around scratching himself. 'Well, they had their lunch, now they are looking for dinner,' he'd muse philosophically. I don't remember his last name – I used to address him by his patronymic, Nikitich. He was an older man of that avuncular type. He always looked after me, even chided me at times if the maintenance guys brought something: 'Trust me, Isaac Abramovitch, you have no need for any of their trophy staff – cigarettes, cigarette cases, or anything else. Take lieutenant Bozhko. What's become of him? Got himself killed. And he was after trophies big time, always frisking them corpses.' The man was positively superstitious that way, constantly exhorting me: 'Remember, Isaac Abramovitch, no trophies!' The minute the guys brought something, he'd be at it: 'No, take it away, he won't accept it.' Or something along those lines. In fact, that was why I only brought a few guns with me when I got back: a Parabellum, a Walther and some such. Lyalya, do you remember this Shura woman we used to know back in Moscow? Well, I ended up giving my Walther to her boyfriend. She herself was the enterprising type. Always bragged about how she could turn anything into cash. The gal would say things like 'You ask a lamp post to give you a ruble, and it won't; I ask the same post – or any tree, anything – and they will'... I still had this one gun kicking around somewhere – or at least had it till 1949 or so, by which point I was already serving in Odessa. A Brevitata, an Italian brand. Quite a handsome job, too – nickel body, ivory handle, a real beauty. I have to thank my driver – it was he who stuffed it into my suitcase, together with the sweater and the rest..."

It was already lunch time, and Isaac knew that any moment now Lyalya would start nagging and rushing him, but it just felt so good to feel like a hero again.

"Just one more bit for the sake of entertainment. I had two drivers during the war. One was nicknamed Popout; another, Blowball. And they happened to share one trait: both somehow managed to nap while on the move. Each would be asleep at the wheel, Popout leaning his head to one side, Blowball to another. You come to a turn sign, and they pay zero notice, keep on heading straight and end up at the wrong locality. Then you have to look for them all over in order to get them back. There were actually lots of odd types about. One of my men was this fellow from Moscow – I eventually lost track of him, guess he got killed. So, we are hit with a heavy bombing raid, everyone's ducking for cover, and he is just standing still, out in the open. I yell: 'Come on, get down into the trench! What the hell are you standing there for?' And he says, 'What, you think I am chicken?' Go figure. I heard similar things about our First Commander: he too barely bothered to hide during raids – didn't want the soldiers to think he was afraid. Sometimes the guards had to almost wrestle him to the ground. But the general that came later, well, the minute the Junkers planes showed up in the distance, he'd strain his ears and dash for his dugout, or for the special trench. For generals they used to set up a really nice dugout, given time and opportunity; or else plank the trenches in wood, things like that. A general's a general, no matter how you cut it. So, you know, there were many things for both eye and ear... Or take the goings-on I witnessed during my spell as Signal Battalion Commander. At night the radio station crew goes to sleep on their plank beds – all save one sentry outside, armed with a rifle. Well, I'd often catch those sentries, especially girls, perched on some tree stump sleeping, rifle propped against the wall. Just where they'd been gallivanting all night is anyone's guess. Many of them had lovers in Corps Headquarters – colonels, lieutenant colonels. So, there again I'd just flip out, yelling and cursing and just short of kicking them – whatever it would take to make them get up and do their duty. Especially after that time the radio station went missing."

"Isaac, did you already take your diabetes medicine?" Lyalya finally interjects. She seems to be feeling better today – less volatile, less cranky. Isaac cracks a smile.

"Look at my little dove; she keeps plying me with all those medicines, which somehow taste different each time. Well, what are you going to do? Can't have the tail wagging the dog, right? I'd never touch any of that stuff if it were up to me."

Lyalya gives a wistful sigh.

"Well, what *I* would like right now is some boiled potatoes from the *Besarabsky* market, with some real Kiev tomatoes on the side..."

Meanwhile, we learn that Lyalya's developed yet another problem: there is a tiny skin crack on her good foot, right under the little toe, which makes it difficult to walk. Having gone through the drawers, Anyuta finds some ointment, but just as she is already wrapping the spot in bandages, Lyalya, far from reassured, demands an emergency appointment with the doctor.

"What have I done to deserve all this? Why am *I* the one to bear everything?"

"Now, now, Mommie. Try to be patient," Isaac coaxes.

"You don't understand. How can you possibly know the pain I am in? It's simply mind-shattering!"

Sensing the brewing storm, Isaac comes up with a diversionary maneuver.

"You know, when I got wounded the second time, they had to cut me alive. No anesthesia, no nothing. Yet I managed to bear it all regardless."

"How did it happen?" I rush to his aid.

"You mean how I got wounded? It was a shell. It left our electrician dead and several more men wounded. As for me, they lifted me up and felt for wounds and found none, but it turned out something was in fact there. I've seen it happen a lot: right after a profound shock a man cannot really grasp, let alone feel, the full extent of his injury. The soldiers still wanted to walk me to the nearest settlement. 'No need, I can manage myself,' I tell them. 'Just carry on, fellas.' It was only later, as I was wading through the snow with, you know, blood trailing behind me and squelching away in my boots – it was then that I began to feel it. I remember finally reaching the settlement and running into some signalers. "Where's the infirmary, fellas?" I ask. 'It's over there, on the other side of the village,' they point. Then I blacked out. Came to already on the operating table. Turned out I had a massive shrapnel wound in my back. The nurse gave me a glass of vodka, on which I nearly choked, whereupon the doctor began to pull out the fragments. All I could do was grit my teeth. I guess they were simply out of narcotics. The doctors were working in appalling conditions, often under fire; that infirmary was set up under a tent, a marquee of sorts. So, they did their best and then sent you to the evacuation hospital in the rear. I was officially out of commission for six months following discharge. They sent me to Moscow as a senior engineer at the Central Agency, in lieutenant colonel Zhupahin's department. This Zhupahin turned out to be a dead ringer for Hitler – same mustache, same parted hair. A really genuine guy though, at least as far as I am concerned. Always treated me like a son. Whenever we received vouchers for duds or what have you, he'd call me right over: 'here, veteran, give this to your wife, tell her to buy herself a nice blouse."

By now Lyalya is silent; resting with her head slumped listlessly against the back of a large armchair – a virtual broken doll. Must have nodded off, I guess. Taking advantage of the opportunity, Isaac jumps back in the saddle, and once again his poor limping Pegasus carries him along down the broken memory lane.

"At that time I pretty much bunked out at my department head's office. During the day I used to hide the mattress and bed sheets behind the safe; then, once everyone had left (we worked from ten AM to ten PM) I would put two desks together and either go to sleep or read some papers and things. Long story short, one of those nights, after everyone had gone home, I pulled up another desk, drew the lamp suspended from a ceiling closer with a rope, spread the sheets and lay down to read the papers. Suddenly the door opens, and in walks armored force marshal Fedorenko, Chief of Main Armored Tank Directorate. I recognized him right away – my eyes were good back then. So, here I am, lying around in my shirtsleeves and, pardon my French, underpants … I leap to my feet and begin to pull on my pants. He says, 'No need to get up, captain, I just wanted to talk to you. Were you there when general Kobtsev got killed? (This was our Corps Commander, Hero of the Soviet Union). Tell me everything in detail'… And Kobtsev was killed in that encirclement sooth-west of Kharkov, when we were being mowed down by aviation, artillery, what have you. We had only one tank left. The general, wounded in the leg – I saw him wade through the snow in his socks, trailing blood – was dragged into this tank by the security platoon. My commanding officer, colonel Vetrov, the deputy of Corps technical support, was also seriously wounded. We pushed him into a small, already half-destroyed van and hooked it up to the tank, but the towing line snapped the moment the tank tore off. Well, now what do we do? First, my maintenance men and I pull Vetrov out of the bus. Then, at gunpoint, we force some infantry men to give us a sleigh (a single-harness affair): 'Come on, we've got a heavily wounded colonel here!' We easy him down onto the sleigh and race along the caterpillar belt tracks. The fire around us is so intense, it's insane. We shoot back in all directions till we run out of ammo. Long story short, we soon lost the trail, but then spotted our nurse Tasya Bubnova lying wounded in the snow – with a shell fragment in her, ehm, posterior. She'd been riding on that tank with the security platoon and fell at some point. In a word, she told us that as they were helping the general down into the turret, she tried to hold up his head and saw it suddenly shake. 'That's when I realized,' she said, 'or at least suspected, that he may have had a bullet lodged in his head.' And probably that's in fact what happened. So, I tell all this to marshal Fedorenko, and he follows intently and then asks: 'So, this is where you sleep?' 'One's got to live *somewhere*,' I explain. 'And my turn won't come up soon, if ever – they have colonels and lieutenant colonels on the waiting list. Everyone here told me to just forget it, there's no point trying.' The marshal says, 'Well, I'll let you get back to sleep now. Good night, captain.' Thanks me and leaves. Then in the morning my superior calls me over: 'Whatever have you done? How come they want you at the headquarters? You better hurry, his adjutant has phoned already.' So, I get down there, Red Square, NKO[2], second building, and the marshal's adjutant, lieutenant colonel, is already waiting. 'Captain Chernyak, so-and-so? Here, take this letter to NKO, first building' – yes, I remember it like it was yesterday – 'and see general Polyakov, the chairman of Economic Board.'"

"Isaac!" Lyalya cuts in. "Help me up, I need to use the bathroom."

"Coming, Mommie… In a word," he concludes, "they gave us a room in the *Novo-Moskovskaya* hotel on the Balchug Island. That was where all the military families used to live at the time. So that was that… Coming, Mommie, coming…"

"What are you doing, you're carrying me like a log!" Lyalya protests. "Go from the side – take hold of my side and lift me up sideways! You'd think he'd learn by now."

Once she disappears behind the door, Isaac lets out a sigh:

"My wife is what they call the 'genius of mankind.' She finds so many flaws in me; I wonder how any single person can have them all. Especially in the kitchen: anything I cook gets criticized: too much of this, too little of that, and so on. Of course you can't compare my cooking to those things she used to make – each of her Napoleons was like a cake for all times and people! We could easily open up a business here. But the way she is now, well, that's just her illness. I always took care of her, you know. Back in Moscow, that winter she was pregnant I used to walk her to the Metro in the snow – was afraid she might fall. And when she was on her sixth month, I made her quit her job. We figured we should be able to manage without the maternity pay; I was already making enough at the point. Plus, there were those 'letter coupons' and all that jazz.

---

[2]   Acronym for *Narodnyj Komitet Oborony*, "People's Commissariat of Defense" (Translator's note)

"Is that what we called them?" Lyalya chimes in, siding awkwardly into a chair.

"Yeah, that's the term. And here's the funny part," Isaac continues. "The coupons were letter-coded according to rank: the generals got those marked with letter 'A,' so we called them 'letterAtors'; guys like me were 'letterBetors,' and those with no rank were 'ohCrappers.' Or something along those lines... And then we also received 'supplementaRations.' Remember those, Lyalya? Things like 'Humpback salmon in personal juice'?"

"In *own* source. Oh, and there were also 'ration-books' for groceries – they had coupons for flour, butter, meatballs, and sugar."

Isaac gives a roguish grin.

"Yeah, those were a riot too. There was this funny story going around: an officer walks into the *Voentorg*[3] and hands over his book. 'Sorry, comrade colonel, we've cut out your meat balls already.' 'But that impossible! My wife checked just this morning. They were still there.' 'Oh, I am sorry, here they are. They just got folded.' Another version went like this: they've run out of meatballs, so the saleswoman hollers to the cashier: 'Zina, do me a favor, just void comrade colonel's meat balls and punch in meat paste!'"

"Listen to this Odessa bum," Lyalya complains. "And that's not even the worst thing to have come out of his mouth."

Isaac is positively glowing: some support is better than none. He tries to keep the ball rolling:

"Sometime after the war, may be a year or so, they decided to get rid of coupons. Instead they introduced rank-based bonuses. Then they began to downsize. I was offered a transfer to the *MVD*, the Ministry of Internal Affairs. Everyone was warning me: man, you're making a mistake of the highest magnitude. But I couldn't resist the temptation: Odessa, the sun, the sea... Well, we've been knocking around the country since, from city to city: Khabarovsk, Baku, Yerevan – all of them, before finally settling down in Kiev. And now here we are in Savannah."

"And it's one fine mess, too," Lyalya mutters.

---

[3]   Acronym for "World Trade Organization" (Translator's note)

187

FEIGA

The room is spotlessly clean, with lots of photographs. The largest features the entire family: daughters, sons, grandchildren and grand-grandchildren.

"I have five children... There were six, actually... Belochka died during the war... I never laid a finger on any one of them... The older ones all took care of the younger ones. Five children, five characters. Someone wants something; another one wants the same thing. But where do you get things? The house my father left me had some furniture – five beds and a cupboard. All my children are nice, may they all live long and stay healthy. I'd cook a big meal in the morning and rush off for work. I'd come home late, and they'd be waiting: 'Mom, we left some soup for you, just reheat it.' My Senya used to tell the neighbors' children, when they came over: 'Don't touch that, we've left this for Mom'...And just as well, because they used to come over and eat everything. I kept a bottle of apple cider behind the cupboard. Well, Ganya, our neighbor's boy, a rather strapping fellow, found it. Before the holidays I went and reached for it and there was nothing there. I told him: 'My children are not your friends, and you are not in charge here. From now on don't you ever set your foot in my house! If you try, I'll pour boiling water over you.'"

Her eyes are lit up; she is going through the scene as if it were unfolding this moment.

"For thirty-two years I worked as a conductor. A forty-two ruble salary. Getting up at four in the morning, coming home at night. Everyone in the city knew me, same as in the village. A few times I had to work during Easter and collective farm workers gave me all kinds of things. All at once they'd bring eggs, Easter buns, cakes, milk in clay jars, cheese curds... I mean, what was I even supposed to do with all this? But they'd remind me: 'Fanyechka, we know you've got five kids. Just give it to them.' They were all really fond of me... Of course, back then I was cheerful, hard-working and far from fat. It's only here that I ballooned up to this size..."

"Do you play the violin?" she queries. "I love the violin. When we lived in Bobrujsk, there was a violin player there. Kapler by name. He married a prostitute, got the whole town buzzing with the news. She bore him two girls. I remember he had this long curly hair... There was also an Armenian shoemaker, Hachik. I once brought him a 'cut' for high boots (one of those leather samples) and he made them so rough and tight, I couldn't wear them at all. So I brought them back. He looked them over and said, 'I must have picked up this bad style from the locals. Leave them here; I'll make you a new pair free of charge."

Hastily, as if at random, she thumbs through the pages of her former life, trying to make us stay a bit longer. It is indeed easy to be affected by her slightly throaty voice, by the charm of her smile. But is it really possible that after this many years one could retain this sort of childlike spontaneity? Couldn't there be a touch of disingenuousness in this nice silver-haired old woman, so reminiscent of my bedridden for years – and now deceased – grandmother? She too would use those little tricks to draw your attention, to make you more attached.

"My mother had eight children – six sons and two daughters. I was the sixth. Mother was a good cook and loved to keep the house clean and orderly. The neighbors used to say to her, 'Mar'yasha, one day someone would kill you over that pitchfork!' It really shone like gold. Father was good at house-building, than worked as a butcher, carrying meat carcasses. They used to warn him: 'You'll give yourself a hernia; you've got to quit this job.' Well, he did end up with a hernia."

She lets out a sigh.

"I remember Mother making those delicious *kugelach* for *Peysakh*. She'd soak some *matzos* in water and add eggs, chicken fat with *schmaltz*, and salt. Then she kneaded the mix, put it into the *kugele* – she had those big special vessels with rods, each containing three cups – and put it into the oven. They'd come out all fluffy and tall. You could eat them like that or put it into broth. She also made stuffed chicken necks – flour with fat and schmaltz, a bit of potatoes as desired. All sewn together with thread. *Kailalah* it was called. The entire family would gather at the table. After the meal, the girls washed the dishes in a pan and the boys toweled them."

"I must say though, I did have a sharp tongue. If someone gave me a hard time, I didn't pull any punches. I was loved, but also feared. When Yudel, my first husband, decided to marry me, he came to my mother and said: 'If you don't give over your Faygeleh, I'll hang myself in your yard.' 'But she is still a child, she's only fifteen!' 'If I don't take her away,' he says, 'My friends will snatch her!' So we went to see Dr. Babushkin, who certified on sight that I was three years older. My first husband, Yudel, was a director of the printing press in Kobryn. I didn't really want to live there, away from my parents and their house, but eventually he won me over and it turned out to be a good life, sweet as clover. First Maya and Emma were born, and then Belochka – but she would die during the war, when she was just three years old. Then my husband left for the front and I went back to Bobruisk… I remember Mother weeding the garden even as the bombs were falling. 'Come on Mom, what are you doing!' I scream, 'It's time to cut away!' And she says, 'You can't run from the war, you've got to learn to get by'… That's how it was. We took very little with us – two blankets for the kids, house keys, register of tenants. Just as the last cart crossed the bridge, the bridge fell under the bombs. Through woods we got to Rogachev, traveling by foot. Then, a ride to Buguruslan, and from there we got shunted off somewhere to the north, don't remember where. It was very cold, the frosts had already come, and I had nothing but a dress on. It was there I got frostbite on my legs… We decided to go to Tashkent and got on the special train, but they took us off at Yangiyul. State farm #10, section #5. The chairman was an Uzbek. Everything was well organized. I got a job tying grapevines and picking apples and pears. Mother was working too. We received corn flour rations and learnt to bake flatbreads and make hominy, *mamalyga*. We were also getting milk for the children. But then trouble came. First, Mother developed pellagra and died. Then my fourteen-year-old brother, Dodik. Then my sister, who was seventeen. My daughter died of pellagra too, and soon father's hernia became strangulated."

A phone rings, interrupting her tale.

"Hello, precious. How are you feeling?.. Leaving for work?.. I feel like I've been beaten somehow… I took a shower in the morning and ate half a bag of bread twists and took my blood pressure pill. Now am about to have a half plate of oatmeal with my blood thinner…You could get me some watermelon…a half…That's all, I guess… Something else I meant to tell you…Keep forgetting things… Anyway, I'll call you later, sweetie."

She explains while turning back to us:

"This was Mila, my daughter. She always tells me, 'Mom, each time you are taking a shower, we get worried'… See, my children installed a hand shower, so I sit down in the tub, sponge myself with soap and then rinse with hand shower. I love to keep things nice and clean. I am the one in charge of cleaning the bathroom and the kitchen. Too bad I can't be removing dust… Do have some of this bun, dear. It's not sweet, hardly any sugar… Or may be you'd like some stewed fruit? I made it myself just this morning… Lykeh it? I'll give you the recipe. You just throw in some bay leaf in the end and let the mix simmer on low heat while you are watching TV."

Feiga's TV is always on. She keeps watching American oldies over and over, admiring her favorite characters whose pains and joys move her as deeply as if they were her children's. They are so much with her, it seems, as to be gradually replacing real-life interaction.

Lately she's often been ill, complaining of pains in her legs, and her sudden asthma attacks have made her too anxious to venture far from 'the machine' – her electric inhaler.

"Just how am I supposed to live like this?" She suddenly turns pale, begins to wheeze. Her hands shake as she fills the small cup with ready-made medicine and, placing the plastic mouthpiece in her mouth, she sinks anxiously into a chair.

Meanwhile it's already time to take Lyalya to the doctor, so we get up and excuse ourselves. Her lips still closed around the mouthpiece, Feiga throws a weak wave.

Our visits to her usually begin with sorting out the mail: piles of ads, bank statements, bills, donation requests.

"They keep sending all those reams of paper," Feiga complains. "Should I keep this one or can I throw it out?"

"Keep it if you want, it's really up to you."

"Eh. I've had it up to here with them. Into the trash it goes...It's like we live in a paper state...Yesterday," she recalls, "my children took me to a Chinese restaurant. I ordered some soup with dumplings, then some of, you know, their chicken on stick with broccoli and string beans. So my Emmochka says: 'Mom, we'll have a surprise for you when we get back.' Want to see? It's right over there – a new trash can, white, with lift-off lid, plus those soft fish pattern mats. The next morning she calls: 'So, how'd you like your surprise?' And I tell her, 'You really didn't have to, it's way too expensive. And why throw away my old bin? I got used to it after washing it for thirteen years.' She says, 'Mom, we aren't millionaires and are not about to make a bundle anyway, but you are all we have.' My children are so nice, may they always stay healthy, they've been always working hard. That's how I brought them up, too. They often went hungry but were always clean and neatly dressed, in sparkling clean shirt collars... In Bobruisk, after the war, I had practically nothing to my name. It was real tough, let me tell you. My first husband, he was a jewel of a man, but he perished during the war. The second, Lyova, fifteen years my senior, was a mechanic who fixed cars and bikes for a living. But he turned out to be bad news: stopped working and began drinking and being mean to the kids. What can I tell you? It was an endless nightmare… Finally I had enough and just kicked him out. He kept coming back asking for another chance, promising to stop drinking. I let him stay another four months, at which point I got pregnant again. I couldn't begin to tell you how it was – sometimes I felt barely alive. Once I came back from work and sat down by the kitchen table to help Milochka sort out some beans. Suddenly she screams: 'Mom! Behind you!' I turn around and there is my Lyovka, drunk, going at me with an axe. I quickly grabbed a pitchfork and chased him for three blocks, from Oktyabrskaya street to Sovetskaya to Pushkinskaya. The neighbors saw us and began to ask: 'Fanya! Fanyechka! What happened?' After that I told him: 'Don't you ever set your foot here unless you want to end up on a scaffold.' So he went to the head of our Depot and said, 'You've got a conductor here named Feiga Litvina, who steals things.' Our director was a retired serviceman, Bunyak, a very good man, I have nothing but kind words for him. 'And who are you?' he asks.

'I am her ex-husband.'

'You help to support the children?'

'She can make do on her own.'

'They are your children, you creep!' He gets up from his desk – and he is a big guy you know – and shows my ex the door. – 'I'll show you 'making do'!' So Lyova got thrown out and just rolled down the stairs…

There was also this controller, Sashka, a former sailor and kind of mean. He caught me once when there were two fare dodgers on the bus – I was lost in my thoughts and had missed the warning signal from the driver, who always turned on interior lights when he saw controllers coming. So Sashka writes a report and they call me in to the superiors' office. Well. Zhenya, his secretary, says this must be it: my head's on the block and I am getting fired. I enter the office and see there is a briefing going on and Sashka and other controllers are there too.

'Morning, Ivan Trofimovich.'

'So what's your story, Litvina?'

And I give it to him straight:

'You know me, Ivan Trofimovich – I am not a proud woman but I am a mother with five children and a forty two ruble salary. Even if I did take something to get my kids a bread bun, it's not like the state would grow poor. At least that's the way I see it.'

He gets up and turns to the controllers.

'Just look at her, all of you! You got nothing better to do than foul up this woman's inspection sheet?! She survived this hellish war and managed to keep her children alive and family together. Now leave her alone, you hear me? If only to make sop for the children.' Then he pulls the inspection sheet from Sashka's hands and tears it up. – 'Go, Litvina,' he says, 'just don't abuse my trust.'

"After this I never had to sign Sashka's sheet again. He'd get on and I'd go: you heard Ivan Trofimovich, didn't you? Just do me a favor and get off at the next stop... Eventually he left off doing it... As for the drivers, they all loved me and guarded me with their life. And I treated them well also. They even used to fight over me with the dispatchers: 'Give me Fanya!' 'No, me!' 'Listen fellows, may as well pull your Fanya apart!..' My dispatchers, Zhenya Margolina and Bela Galynskaya, gave me all the best routes so I could make more extra money. For the two of them I don't have a word of reproach..."

"As for Lyova, he would die later in Mogilev. I said to Milochka, 'Your father's dead. You go up there and I'll stay here with Grishen'ka – there's a 5.30 am bus to Orsha via Mogilev.' At ten minutes to five I come to remind her that it's time to go. And she says, 'Please Mom, just go to bed. What has he ever done for us? Has he even once bought anything for me? Like shoes or socks or sneakers? We managed without him just fine'... So she never went... Well, may be you'd like some tea?" She begins to fuss. – "Here's some cake – it's from my granddaughter, Svetochka. I can no longer bake anything myself, I got too much pain in my arms. In the old days I used to make a really nice Strudel – *Mandala* in Hebrew, with tart plum jam. And here at this place, I was baking bread in moulds. One roll for the manager, one for the driver. They'd see me and holler, Feiga, you baking more bread soon?"

Suddenly, a note of childlike pique enters her voice:

"I must really pull you up on something though. Why did you have to call me from Lyalya's? Particularly asking how I was feeling. I mean, with that bad eye of hers!.. You know, she once ran into Klara and said, 'You really look great, dear, and such a lovely outfit.' And later that day Klara falls right on the porch. Her entire face was black and blue. So, what did you think you were doing asking me how I am feeling? And that Isaac of hers – why, he's such an awful boor! He once insulted me to the core. He can barely put two English words together and yet has the nerve to make fun of me: 'Bus is BROKEN, bus is BROKEN!' What happened was, everyone was downstairs waiting for the bus. And I just came over and asked how come it wasn't there yet, may be it broke down or something. And he starts mocking me: 'Bus is BROKEN, bus is BROKEN!' Made me look like a total fool… He and his Lyalya, they are just two mealy-mouthed know-it-alls – always giving themselves airs and snubbing the Americans."

Now old grudges come bubbling up to the surface.

"And what about that Sima? Or her sister, Basya? Let me tell you something about those two. They keep saying to me, 'You, Feiga, lack knowledge and education, you have no clue about anything. But we, we are so well-rounded and all: we don't just argue, we discuss literature. You don't read much literature, do you? You being a housewife?'… Now take this Sima. So her daughter-in-law is Russian – so big deal, why hate her for it? My children married Russians and I still love them, now they are my children too. I was the one who brought them here in the first place. I told them, children, we should all go to America. But this Masha from *Dzhuika*, the Jewish Community Center, wouldn't let my Mayechka in. So I called HIAS and said: I SPEAK ONLY RUSSIAN. CAN I SPEAK? Mayechka is my daughter and is living with me. So her husband is Russian, so what? I am old and sick and I need her with me… I was bawling them out – really gave them a piece of my mind… And this Sima can't get along with her only son because his wife is Russian. Because she is, you know, so very sophisticated, so self-involved! She always did as she pleased, always came and went, not wanting any children, then, bang, she has a son… Whereas I created a real family and raised five children. My Emma worked as a house painter in the Soviet Union for thirty two years; Milochka has been always carrying the can; Maya, Senya, Petya – they are all working too… That's how I brought them up. Now my family is like the International. I even have a black grand-granddaughter who can speak some Russian… See, I always keep the Bible on my desk, it says everything about this life, now that's literature for you. I read a couple pages before bed, say Amen, and go to sleep. Once you God in my life, whatever he does is good. We are all in his hands. My father, may he rest in peace, was a *kohen*, Rabbi's right hand. He used to wear special straps on his hands, a gold plate over his forehead, and that handsome shawl, a *tallith*… Too bad I can't go to synagogue these days because of my asthma. See, here's my breathing machine, with those black and white little bottles. I shake them and pour the medicine here and breathe it in. I am really stuck with this machine now...You should eat some more though – please finish this cake or I'll get offended."

Her cheeks turn pale; the pink ovals of the eyelids seem more pronounced. The fit is coming on, but she's holding up – she clearly needs to get something off her chest.

"Listen – and let's keep it between us – my Mila recently started to go to Church, or to some new sort of synagogue, I don't know. And she's been telling me: 'Mom, you must accept Christ as your personal savior – he is our only savior on this earth. 'When I,' she tells me – 'when I was in a hospital and already on my deathbed, I prayed to him and he saved me'...Well, what can I tell you? I have plenty of respect for Jesus, as we all should – he was born of a Jewish mother and cared for us all and suffered for our sins. But does she really have to talk about this thing with her clients? You know, they come to her for their manicure-pedicure, plus many of them are Jewish and each with their own head on her shoulders and their own views. So why push it on them? They'll just stop coming in if she keeps this up..."

This isn't the first time their big family ship has sprung a leak. But if previously she's always maintained her grip on the helm, now *she* seems unsure which way to turn and is reaching out for some advice or support... She herself admitted at some point: "These days I am only fit to run my kitchen and my bathroom, pardon me for saying."

"So you drove Lyalya to the doctor again? You know, this sort of thing could just drive you bunkers. Every week she's got to have her APPOINTMENT! Never mind we are all sick here. I also need to see a doctor. Last night I hardly slept at all, my legs hurt so much I was practically climbing up the wall! Wish I could get me some painkiller or poison."

Her anger doesn't last though. She returns from the kitchen looking much calmer.

"I am going to have a bowl of cereal with honey and then take my pill. See, this one I take in the morning, and here are my heart pill and my blood thinner and my pill for cramps... Have you had your breakfast yet? I am not supposed to have any beef, only turkey and chicken. Every morning I make myself some oatmeal. No fried stuff. No pork. No fat. There are plenty of things I'd like to eat, but I also want to live some more... My Emmochka had her birthday party yesterday.

She cooked – made some cold dishes, fried fish, and cucumber salad. The whole family came. Svetochka brought a cake. So I just couldn't help myself – all that fruit with whipped cream. Svetochka's been concerned about gaining weight – even though when she was thin as a nail everyone was asking, 'is your husband not treating you right?' Me, I was never fat in the Soviet Union, it's only here that I began to put on the pounds... Anyway, we celebrated for a while. Then Yurik said: 'Grandma, I don't lykeh the way you look. You keep coughing. You should go to the doctor.' So Svetochka drove me home, and then around eleven Mila and Vitalik came over with my medicine from the pharmacy and some tablets, coated black. She rubbed this ointment into my chest and wrapped it with a shawl, and I felt better. And while she was doing all this, this husband of hers just sat there doing nothing. Eventually he fell asleep. That's all he does mind you, eat and sleep... The way he sees it, why should he work? Why get a real job?.. And then he has the nerve to ask Milochka, 'Honey, are you done yet?' Then I ask her, why did you take him with you in the first place? Don't you know the kind of person he is? Whatever for?! Did he not get enough sleep at home? Was he plugging away at work, nine to five? My daughter is here specially to treat me, and all he wants is go to sleep! So it's eleven o'clock, big deal! You don't lykeh it, you go home! Otherwise just sit there and don't say one word to either her, or me, or the entire family! Be quiet as a mouse! You freeloader, you've been living with her thirty five years, and what have you given her?"

Feiga gets so worked up, she jumps up and pounds the table with her little fist.

"I literally can't stomach him. Mila's been grinding away at work while he, you see, is an *artiste*: summer's too hot, winter's too cold, so he stays in all day clicking away at his computer reading up on who said what and who's sleeping with whom. Last night I really gave him an earful: know your place, I said, just sit there and keep your trap shut."

She really can't seem to calm down.

"It's such a sore subject for us. Even Andryusha, his son, tells him: 'So that's your job, staying home? Don't you see the rest of us slaving away? If you want to paint, fine, I'll be your buyer. I'll give you $200 for each painting.' And he lives in Florida, so he drives down in a month: 'So Dad, do you have a painting for me?' 'I wasn't in the right mood.' 'Fine, I've had enough of this. I am taking your car and taking Mom with me and you are on your own.' Good grief! He's always given

Milochka so much trouble. Even before he came here she told him, 'Once you cross the ocean, you can go wherever you damn well please.' But he wouldn't let her go or give her custody of the kids."

The phone rings again.

"That was Senya. Back in the Soviet Union," she muses, "– back there he had such a life; I couldn't begin to tell you. His wife was a bona fide prostitute, pardon me for saying, so the marriage was one twelve-year ordeal. They had a son, Vovochka, who had to often stay with me since the mother was always drunk. They lived near the marketplace in Bobruisk, Port-Artur. It was first a military town, but then the houses were leased out and they got into one of those. The place had only one room, a kitchen and a tiny hallway. I used to drop by and check up on my grandchild on my way to the marketplace. Then I began to bring him to my place after the kindergarten, to wash and iron his clothes. After a while someone put her wise: 'Lena, you won't be having more children, you only have Vovochka. If it goes on like this, they could declare you an unfit mother and give him to his grandma.' So she started picking him up at the kindergarten and I had to ask the manager not to give her the child. I just said, 'He lives in such atmosphere, I wouldn't wish it on anyone.' Meanwhile Sen'ka would leave for work every morning without any breakfast. He'd come to me during his break: 'Mom, could you give me something to eat?' While he ate I would tell him: 'Why is now she picking up Vovochka at the kindergarten? So he'd pick up your ways? How long are you going to let this go on? What are you even getting out of the whole thing? You come home, there are always bottles on the table – vodka and whine or what have you – but it's not like she'll be making you dinner anytime soon. How long, I ask you?'... 'Mom, I need to think.' Finally he tells her, 'I am going away for awhile.' He was a driver and often went on business trips, and that's when she was bringing in the boyfriends. So, he said, 'I am going on a business trip for three days, may be four, don't know for sure.' Well. He makes sure she sees him putting in some shirts, t-shirts and pairs of socks into his bag, steps out and heads straight for my place. Stays with me overnight and leaves for work. At night goes back to his house, comes in and looks…"

The memory seems so fresh, Feiga reaches for a tissue to wipe off some tears.

'You know, it's really the story of my life – something out a tale of one thousand and one nights. My son sees Vovochka… who must have been eight or seven at the time – no, even younger, he wasn't in school yet. The boy is sitting in the kitchen sleeping with his head on the table, like this. Senya opens the bedroom door and sees his wife sacking out in bed with her steady. Wine, vodka, snacks are all over the place. He said nothing, just packed his clothes together with Vovochka's things and showed up at my door at three am. 'What happened?' I ask. 'Mother, I've just had enough. I come home, the child is asleep at the table and she's with her boyfriend, drunk as a skunk. I am not setting my foot in there again and Vovochka's going to stay with you for awhile.' The kindergarten was two blocks from me, opposite the Young Pioneers' House. I dropped him off and reminded the manager: 'If his mother shows up, don't you give her the child – he shouldn't be in that sordid atmosphere witnessing her goings-on'... In a while Senya divorced his wife and married this Ira."

Meanwhile it's already time for us to move on to another floor. We need to stop by Lyalya's, read her the mail, arrange her medicines. Then check if Tamara's taken her morning pills. But Feiga is not about to let us go:

'Shall we play some Rums*? Let's have you deal – my hand's killing me. I must have gout already. See, my finger is getting all crooked. I already had multiple surgeries on another finger, and now this one's getting crooked too... What have we got in 'buying'?.. Ah!.. Ok, I'll exchange it...Oh, MY GOD! I've exchanged air for eggs! Look what I threw away – the Red Jack..."

We always enter this fading life's still harbor feeling completely at home. Floors Four, five, eight – Lyalya, Isaac, Feiga, Tamara. By now we are almost family. Feiga thinks we should make it official:

"Why not move in for good? It wouldn't hurt you to live for yourself, for once. What else do you need? We've got everything here and it's really convenient. Remember how I told you my light went out? I just came downstairs, saw the super and told him my BULL wasn't working."

"Your what?.."

"You know, BULL, English for *Lampochka*,' Feiga explains.

"You mean BULB!" I laugh.

"Whatever, he understood me just fine and sent in Jerry. I told him, NO BULL, NO WORK. OK, I'll try to remember: bulb, bulb." She laughs too. "Point is, I've got a working bulb now."

Feiga's family has as many members as leaves on a tree. Like birds in a tight-knit flock, they gather on all occasions to laugh, cry, or lament the good old days. Children, grandchildren, grand-grandchildren. In a large, handsomely framed photo she hovers, like a white dandelion, in the middle.

"Here I already look ill. Really frail. I used to never miss a single family occasion. Now I just don't have the strength. Trouble with my heart, trouble walking. The children call me every day. They just brought some *Belochka* candies from a Russian store – my mouth always feels bitter from all the medicines... Just recently we had some staff come over and cut our nails. You know how you have to first soak them in hot water, but those folks didn't bother, they just kept tearing them instead. So, I looked at what they were doing and said to myself: 'Feiga, go home. Your Milochka will come over and do your nails. I had, as you know, frostbite on my feet during the war... If you could only see my toe nails then!..."

"My Emma's husband, Syoma, has his birthday coming soon," she perks up. "He's turning seventy. Everyone's coming – family from Brooklyn, from Israel, from Philadelphia. They've already made the menu. Senya's wife is making aspic... Olyechka, Emma's daughter-in-law, is cooking fish...Svetochka is bringing cake and some amazing chops – no pork, strictly beef and turkey. She adds some potatoes, grated carrots, lots of onion, and raw cream of wheat for greater effect... The chops come out all fluffy and delicious. Everyone in our family can cook. It's just that...I feel so sorry for Syoma. He's such a good man... But now, when you enter the room and see him lying down on a sofa, it's almost like seeing a child – if you didn't know you would never think there was a grown man there... Yesterday he was feeling better and asked for some sour food, so Emmochka grated some beets and made borsht... But he only had two spoonfuls... I know this means death is coming... Such things hardly bode well... Dear merciful Lord, we always do as you will, but please, help him."

She begins to weep.

"There is this one doctor down in Atlanta. We all chipped in and sent Syoma up there, and he went and stayed a whole week in a hotel. She said someone cast a spell on him, and tried to ward off the harm. By then he already couldn't swallow his food because of the chemo... Poor Emmochka was totally worn out. She'd rush off to work in the morning and then spend all night in an armchair by his bed. Every minute he'd need something: 'Emma, I am thirsty; Emma, turn me over; Emma, are you there?' I couldn't begin to tell you. I don't know how she endured all this. Just think, he used to be such a healthy, cheerful, good-looking man – never sick once. Back in the Soviet Union he was a parquet floor layer, but then trained to be a butcher. And how he could sing and dance *lezghinka*! And how generous, always! No matter who visited him, he'd never let them leave empty-handed lest anyone be offended. He was a living dynamo, and now... Now you wouldn't recognize him, he just lies there on a sofa, as helpless as a child. The doctors say: 'We've never seen anyone with his diagnosis suffer for this many years.'"

In two weeks she tells us, her voice choked with grief:

"We've just been to the cemetery. They put up a tablet with his first and last name and date of death. We had a good cry, Emmocka and I. I said I hoped he prayed for all of us when he came before the Lord. The children brought some pebble and made a heartlet pattern on the ground... Now Emmochka went back to work... Oh, well. Where was I? Yes, in the morning I had two spoonfuls of oatmeal, took my two pills, and left some of my gowns in the sink for a soak. I've got this deep sink that is really good for washing your clothes. As for the *londra*, I don't go there anymore. I recently saw the blind man from the ninth floor bring down a dog mat for a wash – it was all shaggy with hair. So I haven't gone there since."

"Well, you've got some junk here... More junk..." Anyuta is sorting out the mail. "You don't need a computer, do you? Because they are offering."

"I sure don't."

"But why not? You are a modern woman, aren't you?"

"Thank you, but I've had enough trouble with this stuff as it is. What with my artist son-in-law sitting all day at his computer so their line is always busy."

"But you can talk to anyone over the Internet!"

"Ah, but it's not the same! Besides, I really don't see the point... For instance, I just called my Petya in New York. Yesterday was his Ira's birthday. I was calling and calling to no avail... Then I called him at work, at the airport, and they tell me, 'Try his *celaphone**...yes, *celaphone*. So I dial the number and he picks up right away. 'Where are you?! Where is everyone?!' I ask. 'What do you mean, where? Ira's at work, Lenochka must be out with her girl friends, and I came back from work late at night and went to sleep.' 'Well, I just wanted to say happy birthday to Ira,' I explain. I give him the latest about Emma and everything and ask for everyone's telephone-cell phone number. They all have those *celaphones*. I tell Petya I miss them since I am all alone here. So he starts coaxing: 'Come visit us, it's a two hour flight, I'll pick you up at the airport and you could stay for a few weeks.' 'But Petya, what do you mean come visit?! You know I can't live without my machine: what if my breath failed in mid-air?.. Not to mention that all of you'd be away – you two at work and Lenochka at school. What would be the point of me sitting around by myself? Or am I wrong?' 'You are right as always, Mom,' he concedes, 'It's just that I haven't seen you for so long. Maybe I could come down to Savannah for a week, now that our business seems to be settling back into shape.' 'Well, now you are talking. Feel free to come any time – and don't forget to bring some pictures of your house!' I've heard tons about their beautiful house from Milochka and Senya, you see… Anyway, I am not sure but I think there is some inflammation in my left eye and something wrong with the right one as well. Hope it's not the same infection that was going around when Syoma got ill, touch wood. He was so dear to all of us, Lord bless his soul... I already had cataract surgery on both eyes, but it went badly. Now one eye is nearly blind. You know how those doctors are – always fixing one thing and breaking another. I finally lost all hope in them and said, look, just get me the eye glasses for reading the large letters – the small ones are a blur anyway. So I manage somehow. But look at all those glasses I've got!"

"But how do you read the Bible then?" I ask. "Isn't it all in superfine print?"

"Oh, but it's the Bible!" she retorts, not unreasonably, then suddenly remembers: "By the way, Anyechka, we're supposed to make an appointment with Dr. Raygone." She fumbles for the number, "Wait, I've got them all right here."

She proceeds to thumb through the business cards.

"Here's the heart doctor. Here's Dr. Urinegone, the kidney specialist. And here's Mr. Gofman, the jeweler. I was the first one here to meet him, by the way. He is really very nice, if you need your gold sized down or anything… Oh, here's another heart doctor – this one's supposed to be the best. But you know, I remember walking into his office, and he just sits there with his legs crossed and asks: 'So, are you feeling any better?'

I mean, what kind of question is that? If I was feeling better, I wouldn't be coming in to see you, would I?"

She picks up the phone.

"What is it with them, they just keep calling and calling... Hi, Borya... There you go again, asking me how I am feeling. Lord be my witness, one day I am better, the next I am a mess... You always keep forgetting my age. Anyways, how is Shura doing?.. What?! Oh, my Goodness! Lyova?! But he was as fit as a fiddle! I don't even know what to say... Poor Shura, she must be feeling all alone now. Do the children visit at least?.. I know what it's like to lose a loved one. But it's just horrible, the way things have been going, people have been dropping like flies... At least let's hope our children stay healthy – we've been ill enough so they don't have to be... By the way, do you keep in touch with our Bobruisk crowd? Really, everyone?.. No, I've been forgetting things – I either get their phone numbers mixed up or spend hours trying to recall the Yiddish for 'ceiling' ...Well, it is what it is. Only the Lord knows how many years we got left."

TAMARA

Our first meeting with her is not what you'd call pleasant. Her hair is a mess of dark, graying locks, her lips are constantly moving as if she was sucking round a cherry pit in her mouth. She speaks too fast and so low, you have to come up right next to her to make out anything: "Oh, what have I done? I've just killed us all. Everyone. We'll all perish. I have nothing, nothing. I am naked, I have nothing to wear. That's it. No money left. Can't pay my rent. We won't last till evening. Not Katie, not the puppy..." From under the shaggy eyebrows, the small, watery eyes peer with fear and resignation.

"Tamara, would you like me to visit you sometime?"

A trace of human curiosity enters her eyes. Straining her chords, she asks:

"But how would we understand each other? Don't we speak different languages?'

And again:

"Nothing left. Nothing to wear... I've just killed us all. Everyone."

"How about a stroll down the hall," I offer cautiously.

"But how can I? We won't be able to get back. Won't be able to open the door. There are no keys. No money for rent. This is it. This is the end."

I take her by the hand and lead her to the door. With some mild resistance, she minces after me, still muttering what now sounds like total gibberish. The hall is about thirty meters there and back, with two elevators in the middle. Each time we walk past them, she starts at the voices inside and tries to bolt for safety around the corner. I try to distract her:

"Here, let's try an exercise. Raise your hands. Arms sideways. Try to touch the walls with the tips of your fingers." She obediently follows my movements. "We are hunting. Raise your knees – we are wading through the swamp. Raise them higher, higher. We are trying to be quiet – there's a duck straight ahead."

"That's a dog," she corrects me, pointing to the end of the hallway.

"So it's not that hopeless," I reflect, keeping up the game. Back in her room, I fish out a wide rubber band from under the table.

"Well," I say, "Now we'll be exercising every day and training for the Olympics. Who knows, you could be the next band-stretching champion."

"We won't live till then. We'll all perish."

"At least we'd all perish at once."

"But will you come again?"

So things aren't going bad at all. Still, she continues to whisper:

"What have I done? Killed. All killed. Katie, the puppy, Sasha – all gone. Nothing left..."

"Tamara," I call, gently.

She is lying on the bed, pillow flung to the floor, already dressed and with her hair recently washed. On the table there are some dirty dishes, plastic pillboxes with morning and evening pills, and some crumpled paper towels.

"Ta-ma-ra..."

She twists her mouth wryly, her hand covering her face.

"I am not here. Not here. I have nothing to wear. I am naked. I've ruined everything. Oh, what have I done?! Where to go? I don't see anything. There is water over there – you can't pass through. I'll fall."

"Tamara, look. I brought a Domino set. Shall we play?"

"How could I? There's no table. No anything."

"Well, I can come back tomorrow if you don't feel up to it."

"You won't live till tomorrow. We'll all perish."

She gets up and, catching a glimpse of herself in the mirror, begins to comb her hair.

"What have I done? I've ruined everything."

Suddenly she smiles, just with her lips, and peers at me timidly from under her overgrown, unkempt eyebrows, as if to check if I am still there. And again she is moving her lips in that darting motion reminiscent of a chewing rabbit's.

The TV is on, some American show. It's the girl who comes in the morning; she always turns it on so she doesn't get bored while Tamara's taking a shower. Then she calls out somewhere, grabs something from the fridge and dumps it on the table, pours a cup of water and – "Bye-Bye" – she's done with her shift.

Soon Tamara is all wrapped up in the game, no longer chewing and only occasionally dropping dice onto the oil-stained carpet. She is even refusing her one dollar lunch, so I put it away into the fridge.

"You can take it out later and put it in a microwave for one minute."

"But how am I going to get into the fridge?" It isn't fully clear whether she is being facetious.

"Don't you know where your fridge is?"

"Sure I do. It's outside, down in the alley."

"That's right. The kitchen's down in the alley, and we are here on some filthy square…"

"And there's nowhere to hide," she chimes in.

"Hide from whom?"

Suddenly:

"From myself."

This is the first time I've seen her laugh.

Tamara and I are taking a stroll through our little park, along the new trails paved with cement. The benches, woven out of smooth metal, are cool to the touch. In the center, there are some canopied tables, also cased in black, and four grills. The park trails are lined on each side with tall stacks of clumpy, still unlaid, turf. It's early March: first real spring days, with the tweeting of birds and the tumult of green shoots bursting through the flesh of the earth.

"Look how beautiful it is. I suppose that's what they call Life's feast."

Tamara looks around timorously, her every step measured in hesitation. Then she stops, her cold rough palm squeezing my fingers tighter.

"Oh, what have I done? We won't pass through. We'll perish there. Katie, the puppy, everyone."

The tree that fell after the night's rain hasn't been taken away yet. Chunks of broken-off bark have laid bare the rotted core, but one thin branch barring our way is alive, its young leaves still unfurling.

"This is the end," Tamara says, halting in bewilderment. "We won't be able to get back. I've ruined everyone. Nothing left. No keys. No money. Can't pay rent. Nothing to wear. This is it… Over… The end…

"So how's Tamara doing?" Feiga inquires.

"So far we've been slapping' bones. When she plays, she forgets her fears."

"Let me tell you something. When her husband was still alive, may he rest in peace, he'd often take her to play Bingo at *Dzhuika*. He'd buy three cards for her and four for himself. But t his daughter, Katie, she would take away all his money. He'd beg, 'please, just leave us two dollars for Bingo.' Well, it's easier to lift a twelve-storey building than get money out of her… I loved to play too. I used to go with Marta, this American woman from the eleventh floor. Later, when I couldn't breathe without my machine, we began to play here. I really got into this Bingo thing. We'd get together twice a week and buy those quarter dollar cards. Someone would bring the sweets and the soda. I still don't see what the big deal was. The manager wouldn't let us play for money. You can play for dolls if you like, he said. So my children bought me loads of dolls, but that's hardly fun, is it?"

Dolls, dolls. The word gets lodged in my mind. *Hardly fun, is it*? What if I tried to make Tamara go back to her childhood impressions, to reawaken in her memory something buried deep, possibly still intact? That is, to go back to square one, gradually restoring all the broken links.

Excited, I rush upstairs, grab a paper towel strip and write the first thing that pops into my head:

Mary had a little _____
Whose fleece was _____ *as snow,*
And everywhere that Mary _____
\-

She fills in the blanks in a broken, childlike hand, mixing Cyrillic and Latin characters.

"Good job!" I compliment her. "Now why don't we try to remember some story from your own childhood, just an episode a few lines long. In fact, that's what we are going to call it," I write on top of a blank sheet: 'An Interesting Incident in My Life.'"

"I can't… Nothing will come out of it." She grows instantly anxious.

"We don't have to do it right now," I reassure. "You can write it tomorrow or the day after."

"I won't live till then. We'll all perish."

"Well, it's fine either way. I was just curious…"

For a few days the sheet remains on the table. I try to make sure it's in front of her at all times, giving the seed I planted in her troubled mind a chance to mature. Finally, I find myself looking at a few quavering lines that keep slipping awkwardly into the corner of the page.

AN INTERESTING INCIDENT IN MY LIFE # 1

I was eight years old at the time. I was supposed to start school in September. One day during the summer I saw some older kids not far from our building – I thought they were taking each other's photographs. One girl was holding a long stick, and another was calculating something on some device and listing some numbers. I came up to them and asked if they could take my picture. The girls laughed.

'So, stand over there, arms on your hips. One, two, three, done. The picture will be ready tomorrow, just be here, same time.'

I told nobody, came, waited and waited, than went home and cried. Papa explained later that they must have been geologists, and promised to take me to a photographer when he got a free moment. My sister Zina went to pick up the picture. When I visited Tashkent, I found this picture and remembered being "photographed" by the geologists. I was just a little girl.

Tamara S. (Sukhova)

"You've earned a prize," I produce a Snickers bar from my bag, where it had been languishing for days. I keep my fingers crossed, hoping she doesn't get scared off…

In her second story she is already a schoolgirl and is on duty that day. After the lectures the students stick around waiting for the milk delivery. She comes down to the first floor and picks up all of forty packets. She has trouble carrying them but keeps a stiff upper lip and volunteers for duty the next day as well. She comes to school very early, but the girl who was supposed to be on duty, Olya, wouldn't yield her turn, so it nearly comes to blows. When the teacher appears just in time, she tries to explain that she just wanted to help Olya since the milk tray was too heavy to carry. Well, Nina Vladimirovna lifts the tray and, realizing it is indeed heavy, says: 'Enough! From now on only the boys will be picking up the milk.'"

It does look like we are moving in the right direction. Each time her handwriting is more firm, more even. Neatly dressed and with her hair already combed, she now waits for my arrival herself, eager to read to me, hear my opinion, receive praise. It is as though we were piecing together an elaborate vessel of her broken life, the way back in childhood one made colorful patterns out of bits of broken glass found in the garbage.

"I was terrified," she recounts. "Felt as if something had just snapped inside. The airship had floated away, and there in the cockpit were my skirt, the equipment, the candies they used to hand out to us before each flight... Fortunately, they were able to bring it down by shooting through its envelope..."

Back then she was studying to be a pilot at the Institute of Lighter-Than-Air Engineering, and on her fifth solo flight, while performing an emergency landing, she forgot to release the guide rope. The cabin hit the ground, she was thrown out, and after a few minutes in shock, saw the aerostat drifting away... After a heated debrief, she had to withdraw from the Institute. She entered a navigator-radio operator training program and graduated in two years.

In 1938 they were sent to Novosibirsk. Worked on the ground, in the airport. The eatery was in the city. Potatoes. Herring. Tea. If you wanted bread, you had to stand in line from early morning. They all received fur-lined overalls and felt boots with galoshes. One of her galoshes got lost somewhere in no time.

In 1939 they got transferred to Moscow. The quarters were in some former duchess's castle. Beautiful Park, sculptures. She particularly remembers Torvaldsen's 'The Three Graces.' They studied Morse code and math and were given physical training. It was a troubled time, full of rumors of the coming war.

"The pilot I got had only four years of school, and was kind of coarse, too. 'A woman on board means there's trouble ahead,' he used to repeat. In 1941 Grizodubova, who was then in charge of international flights to Vnukovo-2, assembled a regiment manned by civil aviator recruits, and I was flying in the Second Squadron, carrying people from Moscow to Central Asia. Around the same time Raskova, upon Stalin's proposal, put together a women's regiment. We would bring her girls in their tenth grade of High school for training. During the war some of them – those who couldn't manage, whether for lack of time or aptitude, to qualify as radiowomen, mechanics or navigators – were parachuted into the enemy's rear with a special assignment. Of course, some of those missions ended tragically. I remember how, as we were approaching Kiev, one of the girls, Efrosin'ya, whose turn it was to jump, wrested herself free and dashed toward the cockpit to throw herself at the flight commander. 'Darling, sweetheart," she cried, 'I beg you, take my maidenhood! I don't want it to be a German!' I tried to stand up for her, but the parachute jump instructor was yelling that, rest assured now she had no say in her life anyway. The other girls were jumping just fine, joking around and laughing; I actually thought they must have all had a few."

Once, she recalls, their radio burned out in mid-flight, and the pilot, now relying solely on the direction finder, wandered off course – the line hadn't been checked in a while. They had to land somewhere in a rye field, with some damage to the plane. The peasants who gathered round to look said they were not that far from Bugulma. They consulted the map and decided to fly blind to Omsk, the closest airport.

"We did reach it, but were still unable to contact the tower for the landing clearance. As a result we collided with one of the local planes. The pilot died in the crash. The rest of us were arrested; authorities in Sverdlovsk were notified. Vasily Stalin flew down and cursed in the choicest language. We got a five-month suspension from flying status... Still, we were in the middle of a war. Even the invalids were flying planes. So they found something for me too.

Once again memory brings her back to her girlhood. During our next meeting she hands over with a shy smile a few carefully written pages:

A TRUE STORY

*When I was studying at the Institute of Lighter-Than-Air Engineering,
the following happened. A dirigible bound for Khabarovsk crashed
into a mountain while approaching Irkutsk. The balloon went down,
enveloping the gondola; the impact caused a hydrogen explosion.
All of the twelve crew members died. The pilots were buried at the
Novodevichy cemetery. We, the students and flying cadets, were part
of the funeral procession. They had erected a memorial, a grey marble
tombstone with special enclosures for urns where all the names, ranks,
and dates of birth and death were inscribed. I was holding the urn
with the remains of Metlitsky, the radioman. A twelve-salvo salute was
performed.*

*After the ceremony the caretaker offered to show us the memorial
of Alliluyeva, Stalin's wife, and related the story of her tragic death.
Stalin had a fairly heavy temper. He was often mean towards his family
members and the domestics. The wife endured all the wrongs, but
sometimes felt the need to confide in a friend, Stalin's relative, a young
Georgian man. Once she told Enukidze that she wanted to end her life,
and asked him to bring her a gun. Enukidze really tried to talk her out
of it, arguing that life was beautiful, that she had to try to find something
to enjoy, especially since she had children. She was not convinced.
'If you don't bring me a gun, I'll have to hang myself, which is far
more gruesome.' Finally Enukidze gave in. They said good bye to one
another. Later the same day Alliluyeva came to her husband and said
she'd rather die than continue to suffer his insults. 'Then go to your
Enukidze and complain to him!' 'Fine, I'll do that.' She left, pulled out a
gun and shot herself. Stalin was in shock. He asked for Enukidze. Closed
the door to the room with his wife's body. Enukidze came. 'Did you give
her the gun?' 'Yes, I did.' Stalin called the guards and ordered: 'Take
him to Lubyanka and grill him. Bring me the interrogation report when
you're done.' In five hours they handed in the transcript. Stalin signed
it without looking. 'To be shot!'*

*The memorial was beautiful. A white marble stone. A small
sculpture of Alliluyeva's head on top. Some lilies-of-the-valley below.
The inscription: Alliluyeva-Stalina, dates of birth and death.*

The head of Kremlin Hospital refused to sign the obituary notice, suspecting foul play. She was fired immediately and dispatched to Lubyanka.

Tamara S.

What really made me happy is that she now had fewer and few relapses into her former morbid state. Her stories, too, were coming out more refined and coherent, almost in a manner of memoir notes. I found her latest particularly compelling in this regard.

YEAR 1945

We are now officially the Tenth Guards Division. I just made Lieutenant of the Guards. My crew just got a flying assignment to Tashkent. Right upon landing the airport manager asked if we felt up to a particularly challenging mission to Aral sea, where some fishermen were caught in distress. We said yes. They issued some warm kits and ordered to maintain communication with the weather station and the lighthouse at all times. We were only supposed to use the local aerodrome as a last resort. For the fishermen they gave us tarpaulin and some rations – water, tuna cans and bread. The weather was good. We soon spotted a group of men on a block of ice. There were too many of them, you couldn't take them all in one trip. The moment we landed and taxied up to a halt, all hell broke lose: the fishermen made a dash for the plane, pushing and cursing one another, each trying to get there first. The flight commander shouted at them, asking to keep calm. 'We'll take 25 men. The rest on another trip. The weather is fine, so there is plenty of time.' One of the fishermen, apparently the foreman, shot back: 'We don't believe you. You either take everyone or no one.' The commander closed the door and turned to us: 'There's got to be something we could do to gain their trust. We've got to leave one crew member here. There are only four of us. It'll be tough without the radioman, but we have no choice. Now straight up, Tamara, can you stay?'

I was scared. What if they don't come back? But there is no refusing either. The pilot announced to the fishermen: 'We're leaving one crew member with you. She's our navigator-radio-operator. But I must warn you, if I find out you've mistreated her in any way, she gets on the plane without you.' The fishermen said, 'No worries, commander, we ain't no animals.' Still, I was full of misgivings. In aviation, anything could happen.

In a few hours the plane came back. The men got worried again – there were still thirty one of us in total. I had to reassure them, 'We're taking everyone now.'

After we landed in Tashkent, the pilot spoke of my 'act of courage' in his report. The port manager officially thanked us all and sent a telegram to the regiment commander that also mentioned my 'courage.' After all, staying on a block of ice did involve considerable risk. Then the regiment's wall newspaper ran a piece on our mission. They asked me for details, but I got too embarrassed, thought it'd be immodest. So, our pilot spoke instead. I received some applause. They also gave us a monetary award. I got 1000 rubles. It was big money then.

Tamara S.

Now that was something, coming from Tamara!

"May be now you could write about your plane accident?" I press on. "You must still remember the crash and what happened after."

The old fear creeps back into her eyes.

"Nothing happened." She is visibly embarrassed.

For some time following the conversation she writes nothing, says little, behaves in a somewhat erratic manner. Could I have gotten carried away, have unwittingly rushed things?

Over the next few days she remains agitated, complaining of headaches, of being unable to sleep at night. But by now I am so impatient, so eager to find out what really happened, that I keep on pushing her to revisit that tragic moment in her mind.

First thing after the weekend, I come up to the eighth floor as usual. The door, usually left open a crack, is latched shut. I knock: "Tamara!.." Not a stir inside. Bewildered, I go back downstairs and call her from there. She is not picking up. I come up again, start pounding on her door.

Finally the lock clicks open. She stands there barefoot, nearly naked. The eyes under her disheveled mop radiate futility and fear.

"I am not here...I've perished... Only one elevator is working... Oh, what have I done!.. I've just killed them...Both my Katie and the puppy...It's the end."

On her desk, a page with a newly-begun entry:

THE STORY OF MY DEMISE
...When boiling crayfish, put them in cold water first. That way they slowly go to sleep without having to suffer...

LIFE GOES ON

As I read Tamara's densely-filled pages, or listen to Feiga's disarmingly childlike reminiscences, or follow Isaac's wartime tales with their relish of broad humor, I keep thinking of the passing generation. A generation born into a life almost entirely stripped of joy.

And yet it was still a life, a life with all its deeply-inscribed hues, smells, desires, follies...Now, however, the survivors find themselves slipping listlessly down its final slope – all frail and half-blind and ridden by illnesses, gradually losing their familiar links with the past, losing memories as such – yet still clinging desperately to their earthly existence, struggling to keep hold of time that is ebbing mercilessly away...

Tamara is somewhat better. Still, I am hesitant to resume our literary experiments. Maybe it would make more sense to try something else – something milder, less obvious.

Lyalya has been in the hospital for four days, going on five. They suspected another stroke because of her dizziness, general weakness and slurred, incoherent speech. A CT scan yielded no clear picture; she's been scheduled for another. Isaac is there all the time trying to be useful, pestering the nurses with his 'Help me, help me' and constantly calling Anya to clarify this or that, to make sure he hasn't missed or forgotten anything.

By the time we come into her room, she has somewhat recovered, but still has difficulty speaking and keeps trying to get up.

"I need to go to the bathroom. Help me to get to the bathroom."

Isaac tries to hold her down.

"Lyalya, you are not supposed to get up, the doctor said it's forbidden. Look, you've got wires all over you."

"I want to go outside. I can't breathe in here..."

"Lyalya, be patient. You know, when I had a penetrating wound in my left eye with injury to ocular fundus..."

"Get this blockhead away from me," Lyalya snaps in frustration. "I can't bear the sight of him!"

Anna tries to reason with her.

"See, you're hooked to this IV and the catheter. The nurse is going to give you a bed-pan, just hang on one minute."

"I can't use a bed-pan. I need to get to the bathroom."

"Why not go into the bed, just to show them."

Startlingly, my gag draws a perfectly appropriate response:

"I'll do it here, and then behind the door, too. Better yet, everywhere. A little something for each and everyone." She smiles. "Just get this Isaac away from me."

After we promise to drive him home, she calms down and even lets us cover her up...

She would pull through this time, too. Isaac, all cheered up, will continue to toil away in the kitchen, breaking now and then to listen to his radio or coax me into raking over his past together.

We also get invited to Mama Feiga's birthday party. The birthday girl, sporting a fresh haircut, manicure and bright lipstick – your regular hand-painted Matryoshka doll wrapped in a down-hair shawl – has already used her machine and is now sitting at the head of the two-room-long makeshift table overflowing with all sorts of dishes – everything is either home-made or comes from a Russian store. Someone is still running late; they call to say we should start without them.

"Mama, first toast is yours."

Her eyes are moist, glistening.

"Thank you, dear God, for gathering all of us here. When thirteen years ago they told me I had to pay five hundred dollars for my children, I said to them: 'Feiga will eat only bread and drink only water if she has to, but all her children will be living in America!' They asked, 'But how could you afford to pay fifty dollars a month if you only receive ninety one?' Those imbeciles! They really thought it would make me fall part... Well, I've lived through a terrible war and raised five children by myself. They are all hard-working and responsible and they don't drink. America and the whole Savannah can be proud by my family. None of you ever asked for handouts or stayed on Welfare for a single day, and I've seen from you nothing save joy and happiness. May you all stay blessed and healthy and may I continue to take joy in my family."

"No worries Mama, no worries!"

"We all love you! Many happy returns!"

"To our one and only!"

The wineglasses clink, the knives and forks clatter and sparkle as they plunge into the holiday table's fragrant belly, a veritable cornucopia of flavors and smells. Where do you even start? There's more here than your eyes can take in.

"Could you serve me some of that salad, dear? And the other one, with the drissling*, Feiga asks. "One is Emmochka's, the other is Maya's work. Try this *Challah* – Seryozhka bakes it Soviet-style, just as in the good old days. Do you laikeh it? It's our way, everyone brings something homemade... Did I tell you my former co-workers just rang me up with the spiel? How's our Heroine Mother, Many Happy Returns and all that. Gave so many wishes, I'd live to a hundred and twenty if they all came true. Anyway, they are all in Brooklyn now. Lyova Fishman, Dina Kutzer, Ella's Grisha, Shura, Zhenya, Sonya Gonchyar, Ida, Bella... whatever her last name is... It's on the tip of my tongue... The drivers used to love me; they would fight over me with the dispatchers. Give me Fanya, give me Fanya... Hey, you may as well tear Fanya apart... I could have gone on working, all things considered. But what happened was, Maya went to the bus terminal and told them, 'I came here all the way from Grodnyi, and I want you to fire my mother, she is already retired, she's worked herself to exhaustion, she raised us all by herself and now it's our turn to take care of her'... And the thing about Maya is, she tears up as easily as me, so she stands there crying and I am crying with her. She says, 'Would you please just fire her.' 'But how can we fire someone like your mother? She never shirks any tasks, never refuses anything to anyone. Why, Litvina is the pillar of our community.' And I was, too: they need a conductor, I'd be the conductor; they need someone by the cash register selling bus tickets, I'd be the first one they called. 'So you see, we have lots of love and respect for her. Let her stay on some more.' But Maya sticks to her guns. 'I specially came all the way here'... Well, they were quite accommodating in the end – even threw in a bonus before letting me go. Not to mention all those letters of commendation – and my goodness, I left scores of them behind, too!" She pauses, scanning the table for another treat. "I have this stomach condition, you know? Gastritis. What do you call it in English? I keep denying myself everything... But never mind, I'll just brew myself some medicine in the morning, one cup before breakfast... Now my Maya, she is always dying for some potatoes. She could live just on potatoes. May be a bit of herring or mackerel on the side, but that's it..."

The clatter of plates dies down. One by one the guests, finally full, begin to drift away from the table. Senya picks up the guitar.

"Oh, *Faygeleh*, my darling *Faygeleh*, my *tayerinke**... Mom, do you remember how you used to give us twenty kopecks so we could buy ourselves some ice cream for Chanukah?"

Yes, she remembers everything.

"I'd come home from work and they'd start wheedling: mama, I want *haneke gelt**, please, *haneke gelt*... Where could they have even learned this?"

Someone turns on the music. Senya kisses each of her pink cheeks, gently picks her up, and leads her away from the table.

"What on earth are you carrying me around for? You forget I am no longer eighteen."

"Let's dance, Mother, let's dance. This is your party – our party."

Ah, how sweet it is, this whirl of the gently swaying *Freilach*. How strange, the way it makes you want to forget your age. And you almost do, with all those dear, familiar faces swimming round. It's just that somehow it's becoming difficult to breathe. The sounds grow louder and faster, and suddenly it feels as if she were coasting downhill and falling into a snow bank that is spilling apart in many fiery arrows.

"Take it easy, Mama. Just breathe."

"Mama, do you hear me? Stay with us, Mama!"

Someone is already calling an ambulance, someone applying a damp towel to her chest.

"Oh, why are you ruining my children's party, Lord?"

"Stay with us, Mama!"

Kiev – Savannah, Georgia.

THE ARTIST: PARABLE

They lived in the valley, along each bank of the river. The vine growers and winemakers, on the rocky right bank; the plowmen and bread-makers, on the left. They all built their houses by the water: the vine growers, with stone; the bread-makers, with clay. The soil gave enough bread to survive, enough wine to make merry. Twice a year they would all gather on one of the banks. First, during harvest; then, when the wine ripened. Having eaten their fill and grown heavy with drink, the men would spin by the river in a sleepy roundelay, leisurely choosing their mates. Next morning the brides would dress up in lace and come down to the river for water, their timid butterfly flutter crowning the seasons' feast. Afterward the dresses were put away into wooden chests, where they would gather dust for years.

To keep his parish pious and obedient, the Lord made a list of "good and wicked deeds", which decreed once and for all that "the range of carnal enjoyment be dictated solely by the procreative need, while any deviation from this balance is disharmonious and sinful". Lest some yield to the temptation of exceeding the proscribed limit, parish elders were assigned to them. The better to revere those elders, the valley's inhabitants were told to build a House of Prayer on the high bank, where plowmen and winemakers alike could convey their gratitude through prayers and earthly gifts. The elders were strict in enforcing the ritual. Investing themselves with supreme authority, they even forgave some minor offenses to the particularly zealous worshipers. In the upper realm they turned a blind eye on this, saying: "Let them, as long as the pillars of the Temple are safe."

Apparently though, while the Creator was kneading his clay, he failed to notice the Tempter steal behind his back and toss some embers into the pan, their heat provoking a secret desire to cross the forbidden line and see what lies beyond.

It fell to one plowman's daughter to breach the custom. All of a sudden she felt the urge to dress up, to make herself feel desirable. Her husband, returning from the field and seeing his wife in front of their hut dressed in white lace, grew afraid that someone could've witnessed her folly. He thought of nipping all this extravagance – this whimsical mood of hers – in the bud, but said nothing, taken in by her charms. That night he was unusually affectionate with her. Afterwards she drew him into similar mischief more than once, fearfully awaiting heavenly retribution for her transgression and trying to conceal it from everyone. But how do you keep such things hidden? Fatefully, she confessed everything to the Almighty in her prayer.

Hearing this, the Lord grew angry: "It's the Devil's work! He is up to his old tricks again!" And, although one woman's lapse threatened neither earthly peace nor heavenly harmony, he told his Archangel: "As she's been wanton, let her bear children in pain! This will teach the others!"

In the hierarchy of heavenly servants, the Archangel Michael occupied the post of a specialist in Earthly affairs. He was already old; his wings all tattered by the centuries of wandering between Heaven and Earth. Sometimes, disguising himself as a ferryman, winemaker, or plowman and feeling compelled by all human hardship, he took so much to his part as to forget the actual purpose of his arrival. There was a tiny cave in an out-of-the-way corner of the bank where he kept a wine mug and a set of layman clothing. He'd change there and leave his wings and cloak, always afraid someone might discover and steal them – it would surely cause all sorts of trouble!

That particular time, he arrived a bit late and was already quite tipsy by the time he found the plowman's hovel. Witnessing the ordeal of the young mother delivering the fruit of her love, the Archangel was driven to tears. He chased away the clouds and splashed a ray of spring sunshine into the narrow window. An intricate pattern of color, as if in a kaleidoscope, quavered on a clay wall just as the baby's cry filled the narrow hovel. The mother couldn't hear it – the poor thing was already gone…

The baby grew into a cheerful and lively boy. At five years old, he surprised his father by painting the walls inside their hut. Returning from the field to find his son atop the table, wielding a stick of charcoal to drag a whole heard of small black donkeys onto the ceiling, he simply scraped off the images without scolding the child. Assuming that their black coloring was not to his father's liking, the boy used green and orange for his next surprise greeting. Now the donkeys were frolicking along the walls and ceiling, while flowers and tufts of grass appeared all over the floor. The little artist was standing on the table, looking questioningly at the father. The latter thought for a moment and said:

"Alright, let them frolic."

One hot summer night the door of the hovel was left open and the donkeys ran off into the neighboring yards. Everyone started playing with them, festooning them with wreaths and flower garlands. When the little herdsman came to collect them, other children followed him to his hovel. It was the day of the harvest feast, and the adults were baking bread for the guests from across the river. The holiday was already coming to a close when the children's rowdy gang burst in on the roundelay, confusing its solemn ranks. Their faces hidden behind masks, both frightened and thrilled by their own daring, they jigged their heels to spur the green-and-orange donkeys that, miraculously, looked completely alive. Before long, tumult gave way to merriment. The parents began to recognize the children. Some were trying on their masks. Others offered hunks of bread to the donkeys...

Years passed, and the plowman's son grew into a handsome youth. Lively and hardworking, he was everyone's favorite. He was good at learning and soon surpassed everyone in various crafts. What he liked the most, though, was painting on walls of old houses, cloaking them in color. "You'll be bringing beauty into our lives," people decided. "You won't have to move rocks or follow the plow. From now on you are an Artist; paintbrush is your tool."

Annual feasts gradually turned into gay carnivals that wouldn't subside for days. Even the preceding weeks seemed less dull, bearing as they did a poignant promise of mirth. The maids on each bank would be sewing fancy outfits to catch the dreamy young man's attention, and even some of the brides, it must be admitted, also harbored hopes of bestowing secret caresses on him during the feast. But when the bonfires were lit on the bank and the smell of fresh-baked bread and young wine filled the air, he would mingle with the crowd and watch the revels, glad to see his friends so trim and limber in their latest dance, with its whirl of elaborate costumes and its hot tangle of bodies and glances.

Yet there is no stopping the boiling passions. Spilling over the brim, they fill the nocturnal riverbanks with the enchantment of lovers' voices and muted laughter. The Archangel sent in to ensure that merriment's peak wouldn't violate the proscribed "balance" and "harmony," shall be sleeping peacefully upon a heap of hay under some tree after a mug of good wine...

Once, as he was climbing the rocky trail leading up from the river, the plowman's son saw a very young girl, daughter of a winemaker who lived on the very edge of the settlement. Skittish as a doe, she ran off to her hut without a word. Afterwards he often chose that trail hoping to see the lovely stranger once more. When he finally did, her eyes shone with joyous anticipation.

Winter frosts were coming, and the earth, shedding its multicolored cloak, sank into a dull torpor. Once, passing by his darling's hut, he touched up the stone wall with his brush, gracing it with a decumbent crown of wine leaves. Their vibrant green livening up the stones, they seemed indistinguishable from the real ones. Everyone who passed by was compelled to stop and run their hand against the leaves. Neither roadside dust nor freezing winter winds could damage the wondrous image. And when the first spring rays warmed the earth, a miracle happened: a live vine burst forth from the stone wall, soon shooting over the entire hut. The trees were just beginning to put on new leaves, yet the winemaker was able to reap an ample harvest. The vale inhabitants, hearing the news, began to want the same marvelous vines for their own walls. The Artist spent days painting on stone and clay walls on each side of the river. When asked how come the vine wasn't coming alive, he didn't know what to say.

The Archangel, in his plowman's guise, decided to come to his aid. "Tell them they haven't yet earned God's grace," he whispered into the Artist's ear. But the young man didn't seem to hear him, venturing upon some thought:

"It is probably because of my other blessing, my love for my darling. I am only a man; I can't divide this love among all of you. Each of us follows his own path, makes his own choices."

"But haven't we earned it?" protested the plowmen. "Have we not been laboring hard in the field?"

"Have we not been picking our vineyards clean of rocks?" the winemakers echoed.

"Have we not given enough food to the hungry? Enough drink for the thirsty?"

"You've led us astray and confounded our thinking. Where is that path each of us should follow? Just give us the same thing you have."

Someone suggested:

"Let's call the elder and let him decide."

The ancient's words were unexpectedly stern:

"The shores of our life are eroding under the tides of unbridled desire. Already many of you've strayed from the fold – scorning all piety and contrition and withholding your prayers and gifts from the Prayer house. This is an offense to God. As for you, young man, you aren't a boy any longer and should realize you've chosen a dangerous path. Leave us and go your own way!

"Just submit and repent," whispered the Archangel. "They'll let you stay."

But the young man hadn't yet learned to forget and forgive. That very night, gathering his brushes and some painting essentials, he left the village and headed up river toward the source high up in the mountains. Exhausted by the journey, he fell asleep by the brook. Upon awakening he saw the same plowman who'd been admonishing him the previous night, perched on a flat rock by the stream and looking very old in the morning sun. A pair of casually folded wings stuck out from behind the man's hunched back, and his blue eyes betrayed a hint of a genuinely earthly sadness.

"Surprised?" the plowman inquired gently. "It's me – Michael, the Archangel. I've been following you since the time you were born."

"I think I remember you from the other day…"

"You are still so young," the Archangel sighed. "You don't yet know how to get around obstacles. I told you to submit, but you didn't seem to hear me. Now I am here to get you back. They need you. They've already changed, you see; I am afraid they'll no longer put up with all the prohibitions and restraints. But they don't know how to live without them either. That fire you've sparked in their hearts could turn into a fatal conflagration. I saw their outcry and their anger: after you left, they began to tear down the stone wall, pulling out the vine and trampling on its fruit… Here on Earth, one must watch one's every step." The

Archangel got up, unfolded his wings. "Just swallow your pride and go back!"

"But I don't know how to help them. I can't give them what they want."

"I'll give you more time. You can stay here and think. It's nice here." He cast a look around. "There is spring water, and the air is as fresh as ether. But don't forget my advice. The grape harvest feast isn't far off; I could reconcile you with the village. You belong there."

He flapped lightly with one wing, dropping a short cutting of grape to the ground.

"That's all I could salvage yesterday."

It took a while for the Artist to get over those harsh words. When the twitter of birds and the murmur of the brook finally reentered his mind, he came to a decision. "For now I'll stay here. And then... time will tell."

The whole day he was turning over rocks to build shelter and gathering heaps of brushwood for the hearth. By nightfall sadness gripped him again. So as not to be left alone with it, he picked up his brushes and, as if from secret recesses of the soul, his darling's features poured onto the canvas. The eyes, full of meekness and curiosity. The delicately curved neck framed by the cascade of shiny hair. He lit a lamp before the easel so that night shadows would leave no trace on the canvas, and fell into a reverie...

After ten dawns, the glade was unrecognizable. In the middle, a fire burnt in a tall stone base topped tightly with fir tree branches. Nearby there was a wicker sleeping ledge; a bit further aside, an easel with the portrait. The entrance was adorned with a curtain of wooden beads, a vine full of new leaves twining on each side. During the afternoon the Artist kept busy – drawing, cutting wood, carving. When he sat down to rest by the spring, mountain goats would come out of the wood to drink from the brook, a kind he never saw back in the valley. Captivated, he'd pick up his chisel, and before you knew it he would be holding a lifelike wooden toy in his hands – a gift for children. So the days were going by.

Down in the valley they were threshing grain in preparation for the yearly feast. On elders' orders, the masquerade, dancing and decorations were all cancelled. Even to mention those things was forbidden. Only the roundelay, that tried-and-true custom, was still tolerated. All the same, many were secretly hoping that one day the young man would be back.

At last the hot fragrance of all the bread being baked in the valley reached the mountain glade, and the Artist began to prepare for his journey. He extinguished the hearth, packed into his knapsack the wooden toys and the gems found by the brook, and was about to set off when he was suddenly felt dizzy and strangely feverish inside. Panting, he came back inside the hut and fell down unconscious. When he came to, it was already morning. The sun was out, the birds were singing. The Archangel was sitting at the same spot as last time.

"Don't be rash," he said. "The Almighty doesn't think this is the best time for your return. You still haven't reached perfection as an artist. It was he who's sent you this illness… We aren't supposed to contradict him but, as we are friends, I may as well tell you that these days I hardly understand him myself. May be he is getting old and can no longer see far, or else he's grown weary of earthly chores and, overlooking many things, is quietly pushing people toward an abyss."

"But the feast is still in full swing, there should be enough time for me to get away with my darling."

"Cool your heals. They've already taken her. Your pals were fighting over her like savages ready to kill each other. I don't know how to help you without angering God. Well, here is some canvas and paints he wanted me to give you. You are going to be here for a while now…"

The Artist was disturbed and discouraged by the news.

"I see that you are as powerless before God as we all are. I've been dreaming, living on the hope of seeing her again. But since fate has decreed otherwise, I am ready to appear before his judgment."

"Don't be in such a rush to get there. All in good time. When your turn is up, he'll call you. Besides, in all my years here I've seen enough human joy and sorrow to know: on Earth both are sweeter, more intense… So get back to your work. Get busy with your brush. Try to pour your thwarted love onto the canvas and, believe me, you will get your due."

The inhabitants of the mountain glade have long grown used to the peculiar stranger and became quite fond of him. Early in the morning he'd come out of his hut and go over to the brook to bathe. Birds would be singing, twittering, chattering away in different keys. The fish, instead of swimming downstream, would rush toward him, gracefully swaying their sparkling purple fins, and mill by his feet, spraying his face playfully with water. Squirrels, by now completely tame, frisked around in the grass like children, playing hide-and-seek.

After quenching his morning thirst with spring water, the Artist would return to his easel and wait until memory came to imprint onto yet-untouched canvas some faces from the past. Lots of finished portraits already hung on the stone wall. The old plowman with a wooden staff in his hands, with his dim gaze and a wry crease of the mouth. A ruddy-faced winemaker with his roguish grin. A young bride in white, beaming with naive delight. Some giggly children playing with a cat. Portraits of nanny-goats and she-donkeys, their almond-shaped eyes cast with palpably human sadness. There were also portraits of Dance, Laughter, and Surprise.

One particular piece just wouldn't come together – a woman with an infant in her arms. He already had the title: "The Mother of All Living." Although he couldn't have had any memories of his own mother, he thought of her often, imagining her in various guises. Once she came to him in his sleep. Upon awakening, he rushed toward the easel to capture her features. He was able to recall the delicately oval face, the hint of smile in her lips, the halo around her head. Only the eyes were empty, as if someone had taken out and carried off her soul.

Days flew, months went by, and whole years passed – yet he still hesitated to leave the glade and go down to the valley and his people. It now took effort to recall those he once held dear. The faces on his portraits, gradually stripped of concreteness, were growing spare, more austere. And he himself no longer greeted mornings with a smile. He looked older, his face grown with thick stubble. Only the Archangel, who continued to visit him regularly, was rubbing his hands in delight. "Soon you should reach perfection, and then the Almighty might call you to paint his Heavenly Temple."

One day the Artist asked:

"How are things down in the valley? Or are you no longer concerned about the locals' fate? I recently had a dream where I was climbing the rocky trail leading from the river. Everything around me was so still, I could hear the humming of blood in my temples. Exhausted, I tried calling for help, but no sound returned."

The Archangel took his time responding. Eventually he sighed wistfully:

"It's as if you did visit. By now even I can't sort out this mess. Everyone's fallen into all-out wickedness, raiding each others' homes like barbarians to repay old scores. The wine in the cellars is mixed with blood. They are pillaging and burning down the fields, all in the Lord's name. Dragging him too into their feuds. On the left bank they've built another House of Prayer, with many domes, and, supposing themselves chosen by God, are poised to slaughter all the infidels. I feel sorry for them, having known them for so long."

He flung down his wings. Outwardly, the two of them could easily pass for brothers: both with grey beards and wizened faces.

"Pour me some wine," the Archangel requested. "I want to forget about my duties for a while... Here with you, I feel at ease. How fragrant is the grass and the water from the brook, how delicious the juice from your vine! I remember how you brought it to life with your brush – there, back in the valley. Is your spirit still as strong, now that you've perfected your craft? Has your heart retained its compassion for your kinsmen?.. Perhaps you should come down to the valley and try to get them back to their senses? Here, take my wings, they are still in good shape. There'll be a cave on the riverbank: hide them there, deep inside. Without them you won't make it back, not to mention I'd be in a world of trouble. I'll be praying for you."

Having hidden the wings, the Artist was heavily climbing the familiar rocky trail. He recalled things lightheartedly and without grief: "This is where she spilled some water from her jug. In a sweet streamlet it trickled down into the hollow between her narrow shoulders. I followed her nearly to the front of her house and then suddenly hollered a greeting. Dropping her jug, she sprang away like a chamois over the rocks... Life's gone by, yet I remember everything still. Remember her every movement."

In place of the hut, some dust-covered rocks were scattered. On some of them, here and there, traces of his old mural were still visible. He turned and looked around. Not a single winemaker's house in sight. Among the ruins, under the looming grey sky, chimney stokes rose up like ghosts. The entire left bank was smothered in smoke.

"I am all alone here... Last man on Earth," it occurred to him suddenly. For the first time, after all his years of reclusion, he experienced the fear of solitude. Just as in his recent dream, he wanted to call for help, but was unable to. Overcome by a mortal exhaustion, he fell to his knees. His brush grazed a blackened wine leaf, turning it into a white bird. And instantly a miracle occurred: the bird flapped its wings and, bursting out of stone, soared upwards. The Artist picked up the fallen brush and with a practiced gesture painted a new bird, then another, and more... Summoning remaining strength, he stumbled back down to the valley. Among the remnants of winemakers' and plowmen's old houses he was able to make out the outlines of his paintings, half-erased by time. He began to retouch these originals, his magic brush turning them into lovely birds. And all of them, coming alive, soared up to gather in a huge flock hovering over the river.

Then, crawling out of their burrows and stone caves, people began to gather around him, the way beasts in a forest are drawn to the firelight. Hollow-eyed and covered in rags, they trailed after him in silence, watching the birds, barely born under his hand, fly up into the sky. They followed the creatures with their eyes, reaching up with their arms as if to touch this precious marvel with their blackened palms if only for a brief instant, and the Artist saw their eyes come alive and their faces brighten. He wished that their hearts and souls could once again grow open to the long-forgotten feelings of love and compassion for each other. It was then he heard the familiar voice:

"Rest now. You've finally fulfilled you destiny."

Savannah, Georgia.

NOTES

* StoryCorps – an American project, which includes recording of the stories of different people's private life, mostly in the form of dialogue, in order to reproduce portraits of the current generation. The records are stored permanently in the Library of Congress
* "The Yellow Kings" ("Taxi from Hell") - one of the most popular novels of the 80-90s about the life of New York taxi drivers - immigrants from the Soviet Union
* Amphipod – a miniature river shrimp that lives in colonies of fine limestone, serves as bait
* Fishing paste – a fish bait in the form of pea porridge mixed with semolina (flour) and vegetable oil
* Communalka - a communal apartment typically shared by several families. Each family had its own room, which often served as a living room, dining room, and bedroom for the entire family. All the residents of the entire apartment shared the use of the hallways, kitchen (commonly known as the "communal kitchen"), bathroom and telephone (if any)
* Generation One – one of the charitable organizations in Savannah for adults 55 and older
* Rums – a card game
* Cellular phone (broken English)
* Dressing (broken English)
* Tayerinke – darling (garbled Yiddish and English)
* Hanukkah gelt – money traditionally given to children for Chanukah (Yiddish)

Printed in the United States
By Bookmasters